MW01595083

DESIGNED TO FAIL

Virginia DeMarce

Designed to Fail Copyright © 2020 by Virginia DeMarce. All Rights Reserved.

All rights reserved. No part of this book may be reproduced in any form or by any electronic or mechanical means including information storage and retrieval systems, without permission in writing from the author. The only exception is by a reviewer, who may quote short excerpts in a review.

1632, Inc. & Eric Flint's Ring of Fire Press handle Digital Rights Management simply: we trust the *honor* of our readers.

Cover designed by Laura Givens

This book is a work of fiction. Names, characters, places, and incidents either are products of the author's imagination or are used fictitiously. Any resemblance to actual persons, living or dead, events, or locales is entirely coincidental.

Virginia DeMarce
Visit my PoFP page at https://ringoffirepress.com/authors/demarce-virginia/

Printed in the United States of America

First Printing: Aug 2020
1632, Inc.

eBook ISBN-13 978-1-953034-39-7
Trade Paperback ISBN-13 978-1-953034-40-3

CONTENTS

Dedication

*To the sixteenth and seventeenth century inventors and
practitioners of the episodic picaresque novel,
especially*

*Hans Jakob Christoffel von Grimmelshausen (1621-1676)
author of*

*The Adventurous Simplicius Simplicissimus:
The account of the life of an odd vagrant named
Melchior Sternfels von Fuchshaim:
namely where and in what manner he came into this
world, what he saw, learned,
experienced, and endured therein; also why he again left
it of his own free will.*

ACKNOWLEDGMENTS

The major acknowledgment, of course, is to Eric Flint for writing 1632, which spawned this fictional universe, and for inviting me to be a part of it.

Thanks to the numerous denizens of the 1632 Tech forum on Baen's Bar who, during the spring of 2019, participated in lively discussions concerning the status of the city of Bremen and the economic problems that would face the Province of Westphalia.

Thanks to Eric Flint for giving me permission to use the material in the Prologue, which saved a lot of explanation later on.

The proverb says that the making of laws and sausages should not be observed. The same is true of books. Thanks to my late husband's cousin, who is also my genealogical friend Gail Von Bargen, for the use of her surname; to my cousin Mark Thames for an apt sentence; to Tim Walsh, the vicar at Grace Lutheran Church this year, for a discussion of imprecatory psalms; to my son Karl for a bit of New Testament Greek and some notes on Luke 16:1-13 from his isagogics course, to Laura Runkle and Michael Miller for a timely reminder in regard to Doctor Strangelove, and to Jim DeMarce himself, to whom I was happily married for forty-seven years, for the use of one of his favorite aphorisms, slightly modified.

In May 2020, during the Covid-19 shut-down, a young bear decided to wander the streets of Falls Church, Virginia. I owe a subplot to his efforts to stake out a territory.

As always, I am profoundly grateful to all the historians and researchers who spend time in early modern European archives and publish their results. Please see the Afterword for a discussion of some of their products.

For this book specifically, I am grateful to all the world's music teachers at all levels who enable children to sing and play instruments well and with joy. My five now-adult grandchildren would like to thank Twila Anderson, Lori Fulk, Eric Martins, Kevin Carr, Levi Nagel, Leigh Redfield, Kari Hurley, Linda Moeller, James Kieselhorst, Naomi Fritz, "and a whole stack from college, too." They also have kind words for the teachers at Fox's Music in Falls Church, -Virginia, and the Levine School of Music in Arlington, Virginia.

From Baen's Bar, for assistance with the Battle of Bornhöved, Anette Pedersen for a useful article and especially for the maps of the 1813 Napoleonic Era conflict, Bjorn Hasseler, Robert E. Waters, and George Haberberger.

Many thanks to Walt Boyes, the editor in chief of the Ring of Fire Press, for struggling with my manuscripts, and to Gorg Huff for turning them into something that is e-book friendly.

Virginia DeMarce

PROLOGUE

June 1634
Copenhagen, Denmark

"Into the new USE province of Westphalia," Axel Oxenstierna droned on, "we propose to include the following: Münster, Osnabrück, Schaumburg, Verden, Lippe, Lingen, Bremen, Hoya, Diepholz, and—"

He paused for a moment, here, and Mike Stearns was sure the Swedish chancellor had to force himself not to give King Christian a sharp glance.

"—Holstein."

But, except for a scowl that seemed more ritualistic than heartfelt, Christian IV made no objection. Seated almost across the huge table from Oxenstierna and right next to Gustav Adolf, he simply consoled himself with a royal quaff from his goblet of wine. Which, for its part, was royal-sized.

A bit hurriedly, Oxenstierna went on. "Said province, as we have already agreed, to be administered on behalf of Emperor Gustav II Adolf by Prince Frederik of Denmark."

Here he gave Christian's second oldest son in the line of succession a very friendly smile. The twenty-five-year old prince smiled back, in a semi-friendly manner.

That didn't surprise Mike, however. He was pretty sure that Prince Frederik was still smarting at having been passed over in favor of his younger brother for the plum position, which was being the quite-likely eventual co-ruler of both the USE and the Union of Kalmar—and Sweden, for that matter, if it turned out that he and Kristina got along well enough. Instead, he was being offered the consolation prize of a newly formed USE province to administer. Yes, yes, it would be a big province, and unless Frederik was hopelessly stupid he'd easily be able to see to it that he was chosen as the permanent ruler once Westphalia was ready for full provincial status instead of being an administered territory. Still, it was very much a consolation prize, and very obviously so.

Eric Flint, *1634: The Baltic War* (Baen Books: 2007), Chapter 68, p. 696.

DESIGNED TO FAIL

SECTION I

The Gate of Heaven
July 1634-September 1635

CHAPTER 1

Bremen, July 1634

Frederik, son of King Christian IV of Denmark, duke of Holstein, and still archbishop if no longer prince-archbishop of Bremen, drew up his horse as he approached the bridge that crossed the moat. His small retinue—extraordinarily small for a provincial governor appointed by the emperor of the United States of Europe—paused behind him.

He looked toward the *Ansgarii Tor*. By the standards of a medieval Hanseatic city, Bremen was not heavily fortified. Not by the standards of a world in which a city's walls were perceived as defining its honor. But, certainly, it was heavily enough fortified to present a significant obstacle if the city fathers decided not to let him in; those walls had kept quite a few armies out during the past fifteen years.

He had been appointed governor of the new Province of Westphalia by Gustav Adolf less than a month ago.

He had been the designated successor to the prince-archbishop of Bremen, thanks to the political maneuvering of his father, for considerably longer. Prince-archbishop of the *Erzstift* Bremen, by virtue of which he would have had a seat in the *Reichstag* of the Holy Roman Empire—if that entity still existed. Which it might or might not. The Habsburgs were unlikely to give up without a further fight, if one gave any thought to the tenacity with which they had been waging war since 1618.

The city of Bremen was *de facto* not under the authority of the prince-archbishop. Things had been that way for a while—for about 450 years, if a person wanted to be picky about it. This meant that local politics were often more than a little bit touchy, since *de jure* it still was.

Instead of smiling, he drew his rather thick lips inward, pinching them between his teeth. He had watched at the Congress of Copenhagen rather than talking. One of his conclusions was that the complexities and nuances of contemporary politics made Michael Stearns, the up-time leader so precipitously catapulted into the position of prime minister of the newly organized USE, restless. Restless, impatient, and more than a little contemptuous. He did not appear to be a man who would live with a legally ambivalent situation for four and a half centuries. Probably not for four and a half years. Quite possibly not for four and a half days.

Still, whether Bremen was under the jurisdiction of the prince-archbishop or not, it was most certainly, by fiat of Gustav Adolf, king of Sweden, high king of the Union of Kalmar, emperor of the United States of Europe, and commander of the largest army around, under the jurisdiction of the governor of the Province of Westphalia.

As such, he intended to enter through the Ansgar Quarter gate. St. Ansgarius, who had lived and died not too far short of a thousand years ago—well, probably nearer to eight hundred years ago—had been the first archbishop of Bremen. And—Frederik quirked one eyebrow slightly—of Hamburg.

His horse shifted under him, restless.

The slight creaks of leather and metal behind him, the occasional raising and clopping of a hoof on cobblestones, might mean that his retinue was restless. Or uneasy. If the city fathers of Bremen chose to refuse him admission at this first juncture of his new calling...

But the gate opened. He proceeded slowly toward the market square, through crooked streets and between tall brick houses that were probably, given the small windows, drearily dark inside; past the new guildhall of the cloth merchants, doing everything decently and in order, giving the people lining the streets a chance to see him. Wishing that Gustav Adolf had seen fit to delegate a somewhat larger company of the largest army around to escort him.

"Nobody's ever going to call him handsome," a watching woman commented.

"Impressive nose, though," her friend Jutta answered. "What would Herr Jensen say? The old man at the bookstore who loves to use such long words? A prominent proboscis."

"That lump in the middle could mean that he's broken it at some time." Trinke stood on tiptoe and craned her neck. "Good seat on a horse. He's not fat, but he shouldn't be developing jowls yet, as young as he is."

"I thought Scandinavians were supposed to be blonds. His hair's dark brown. And so curly."

"There's a lot of it though, not thin or stringy, so he's not likely to go bald. He's probably one of those children who were born blond, but their hair gets dark when they grow up. I sort of like that feather in his hat."

"I like the hat. It looks like crushed velvet. I wouldn't mind having one like it myself. He'd be better off without the mustache and little goatee."

The gubernatorial procession was moving on toward the city hall.

"It's hard to tell from here, but it looks like his lips are sort of full and puffy. Maybe he's trying to hide that."

"Overall, though, there are a lot of worse-looking men in the world."

Jutta laughed. "A lot of better-looking ones, too."

He entered by the side of the ancient guildhall, the *Schütting*. On the opposite, northeastern, side of the square, the four *Bürgermeister*, one from each quarter of the city, were waiting for him, lined up in front of the arches that were the main feature of the remodeled Flemish Renaissance facade of the originally Gothic city hall, flanked by the twenty members of the city council, the *Hochedler Hochweiser Rath*, five from each quarter of the city: *Liebfrauen, Ansgarii, Martini und Stephani*.

They were arrayed below the statues of the Holy Roman Emperor and the empire's seven electors that proclaimed Bremen's centuries-long ambition to become a free imperial city, independent of the prince-archbishops, owing allegiance only to the emperor, and with its own vote in the *Reichstag*. An ambition that had never become fact.

He rode past the eighteen-foot-high Roland statue that symbolized the council's right to supreme criminal jurisdiction as well as the medieval Hansa's commitment to free commerce and trade, hoping that upon this occasion, the highly noble, highly wise, councillors would be more noble and wise than was customarily the case when it came to their dealings with the prince-archbishops.

He dismounted.

The protocol was stiff.

As governor, he officially broke the news to the city council of Bremen—the *Calvinist* city council of the *Calvinist* city of Bremen— about the guarantee of religious toleration in the constitution of the United States of Europe.

He glanced to the side of the square at the ancient cathedral of St. Peter, so old that the lower portions of the mixed stone and brick construction were Romanesque in style, and the archbishop's palace. Then, leaving his official retinue under Captain von Bargen with the city councillors, he mounted up and rode out by himself through the gate by which he had entered and part way around the wall. He dismounted and walked in through the narrow Bishop's Needle gate that the council had imposed on the archbishops during those parlous

450 years: a gate too low to admit a mounted, armored rider. This time, he was followed by a line of Lutheran diocesan officials, pastors, and school teachers, headed by those among the noble canons of the cathedral's collegiate chapter whom he had been able to rouse from their normal lethargy. The majority of them did not qualify as theologians, having gained their seats through family connections.

Arriving back at the city hall, he announced the establishment of regularly scheduled Lutheran services at the cathedral, the *Dom*, St. Petri. The impending church services were his own innovation. The cathedral had been the church of the canons, used for special religious celebrations and special events of the archdiocese. But since the parish churches of the city were Calvinist, had been for forty years, and at this point it did not seem prudent to stress relations with the city council further by demanding them back, it would become a parish. Given how long St. Peter's had been essentially abandoned, there would be a lot of cleaning to do in its Gothic interior.

He would have liked to accompany this by a ceremonial opening of the cathedral doors. However, after nearly a half-century of being closed, they were probably stuck, and it would take a great deal of huffing and puffing on the part of construction workers to get the hinges loose. That would have been neither impressive nor edifying. Not to mention that the south tower looked so shaky that it might fall down any day if vibrations disturbed its perilous equilibrium.

Now wasn't that going to be an expensive construction project? Reconstruction project—one for which he would have to find funds, if he didn't want to risk having it come down on the worshippers now that the building would be back in use. He made a mental note to recommend that Bremen's Lutherans should use the entrance near the sacristan's house on the north side for the time being and concentrate their activities at the rear of the building.

They could. There weren't a lot of Lutherans left in Bremen. He wiped off these mental cobwebs and announced that, additionally, he was establishing a Lutheran Latin School at St. Peter's. Mental note—*again, for the time being, put the school in the adjoining archbishop's palace, currently unused for any other purpose. Eventually construct a modern building in the Domshof on the north side. And a public library. With an equestrian statue of Gustav II Adolf looking heroic in the middle of the square.*

Bowing slightly to the gathering of Lutheran clerics, he turned himself into the provincial governor again, informing the mayors and council that if they proved to be reasonably cooperative in the future, he would negotiate with that same Gustav II Adolf, who was now their emperor, for an imperial charter that would turn their Calvinist *Gymnasium Illustre* into a degree-granting university. This was accompanied by a few terse words about his intentions to support the expansion of educational institutions in general within the new province.

Getting such an imperial charter would be a trick if he could manage it, given that the future Lutheran imperial reluctance to license Calvinist establishments would most likely be as strong as the past Catholic imperial reluctance to license them (all having to do with the fact that Calvinism had not been comprised within the Peace of Augsburg of 1555). Given the short timing of managing this day, though, the prospect was something he could dangle in front of their noses as an enticement that might get the mule-stubborn patricians of this place to modify their natural tendency toward recalcitrance. For now.

* * *

Having gotten entree into Bremen as his first accomplishment, an easier one than he had expected, Frederik duly partook of the ceremonial meal hosted by the council and then led his party once more out of the *Ansgarii Tor* and across to the west bank of the here shallow Weser River, where he had set up temporary quarters in the *Neustadt* where the city's population was currently spilling over its official boundaries—spilling to the point that there was now an *Alte Neustadt* and, since the end of hostilities, a sprawling *Neue Neustadt* in which everything appeared to be lively, messy, and disorganized.

The *Alte Neustadt*, the *Neestedt* in the local *Plattdeutsch* vernacular, as large as the medieval city on the other side of the river, had been established as a planned expansion for the defense of Bremen a decade earlier, furnished with modern fortifications, walls with eight bastions, according to the plans of the Dutch engineer Johan van Valckenburgh. Its resentful residents by and large considered themselves to be the shortchanged stepchildren of the privileged city on the east bank.

The *Neue Neustadt* didn't have fortifications. Or any other normal amenities. It was noisy and muddy. Not to mention smelly; the swine market was flourishing. From Frederik's perspective, it had one major advantage as a place to stay. However much the city fathers on the east bank aspired to acquire a large hinterland and place it under their jurisdiction, thus far they had not managed to do so. His overnight headquarters were in the *Stift* lands.

He set out to take stock of his new responsibilities—being completely sober and still awake, while his officers and staff had mostly succumbed to the effect of too much beer and wine at the banquet.

Frederik opened his field kit, rooted around for a bit, and hung a blank sheet of paper, one of the big ones that ordinarily got folded eight times to make books, on his easel. He had set the easel up the day before. It traveled with him.

He drew a stylized crown. At least his appointment as governor had somewhat mollified his father in regard to Holstein. Or lubricated him. Along with a goodly quantity of wine, of course. Christian IV's personal habits were one of the reasons that his second son was so abstemious.

Another dot. His older brother Christian had been married to Magdalene Sybille of Saxony for six months now. The up-time encyclopedias said that he did not have children; nothing had happened to challenge that assumption, no matter how many other things were not working out according to the patterns in those books from another world. The happy couple had retired to their own palace and were busy being patrons of the arts. Or possibly, he thought sardonically, being patronizing to artists. Based on the observations he had made of his father's endeavors as a builder and collector, the two frequently went hand in hand, and nothing he knew about John George of Saxony would lead him to believe that the man's daughter might take a different approach to the people who had designed and decorated the buildings of Dresden or composed and performed the music that was played for the elector, whether at public events or private social gatherings.

A third dot. He considered once more his position vis-a-vis his brother Ulrik and reflected that it was no fun being second-string. And after his first superficial survey of his new province, likely to remain so.

He drew a line. Then, beneath it, a little sword.

The governor of the Province of Westphalia did not, *per se*, coming out of the Congress of Copenhagen, have any military forces assigned to him in his administrative capacity other than the one company that was with him today.

That wasn't "any significant military forces." It was "any" military forces as far his role as governor went. He didn't have a militia. He didn't even have a regiment. His situation was unlike that of the president of the State of Thuringia-Franconia, which had created a "national guard" when it was the independent New United States and kept it when it joined the USE; unlike Brunswick or Hesse, each of which had at least a nucleus from the central hereditary principality around which the new province had been formed; unlike the Main or Swabia, which had some remnants of the Swedish army of conquest available to the imperial appointee and General Horn with several regiments in the background.

How large would the military force that he didn't have need to be? To cover the extent of the province, nearly three hundred miles from far northeast to far southwest? Looking rather like a large-headed serpent, the head in Holstein, that had swallowed a goose egg before its short tail petered out in the southwest at Bochold squeezed between the borders of the Low Countries and Essen. He would be surprised if the neck, the land bridge they had given him, was as much as forty miles wide.

The new Brunswick, from Harburg opposite Hamburg in the north to Göttingen in the south would be more like a hundred seventy-five miles. Only Thuringia-Franconia, from north to south, came close, and that jurisdiction would soon have a railroad through much of the distance; some had already been completed.

He pulled the paper off the easel and attached a fresh sheet.

At the top, he placed a random list of numbers.

Nobody knew how many people lived in the Province of Westphalia. Almost certainly fewer than resided in the State of Thuringia-Franconia.

He had the best idea in regard to Holstein, of course—Holstein as a whole, regardless of its various internal divisions among the branches of the House of Oldenburg. His father's agents had tax registers; the pastors kept church registers. The war of the past fifteen years had not caused too much devastation. There might be 230,000 people there.

On the left margin, the drew a round dot; the name of the region; the possible number of people. On the right margin, he drew a Luther rose as a symbol for Lutherans.

The *Stifte* of Bremen and Verden, together, he thought, would have less than half that, but not much less than half that. Here again, he had access to tax and church registers. Two more dots. More Lutherans.

Another dot. By contrast with those numbers, the city of Bremen's population should be comparatively insignificant. Before the war, it had counted just under 23,000 residents; even though its numbers had swelled, crowding the residences and spilling outside the walls, the *Altstadt* still could not have much over 35,000. And growing fast, of course. But in their ability to wield political and economic influence, the cities were always far stronger than their sheer number of people would lead an observer to believe.

He snorted. Consider the case of Hamburg, that inconveniently independent imperial city forming an enclave in the middle of Westphalia. A prosperous city which, by the logic of the up-timers who wanted to "simplify the borders," should have been, along with its substantial revenues, allotted to Westphalia, but had managed to claw the status of an imperial city with a vote for its mayor in the USE House of Lords. Still, the city of Hamburg could not have over fifty thousand people within its walls, though it had managed to pirate from Gustav Adolf a significant hinterland that, by rights, should also have been allotted to Westphalia. And as people kept coming, as Hamburg kept growing, it would represent a constantly increasing threat to the success of Westphalia.

Ignoring the nuisance that Hamburg would undoubtedly become to all his endeavors, he drew a new symbol in the right margin next to the city of Bremen. Calvinists. A book, symbolizing the *Institutes of the Christian Religion*.

There weren't many people in the little land bridge territories that Oxenstierna's minions had thrown into the province to connect Bremen to Osnabrück and Münster. All of the Lippe counties combined, with the addition of Hoya and Diepholz (whose records were jealously guarded by the Brunswick-appointed officials who had been administering them for a half-century), would not amount to fifty thousand.

Probably.

That amounted to no more than "my best guess." He drew a circle around them. And gave them both the Lutheran and Calvinist symbols. A mix.

In the southwest? Most of the church registers were kept by Catholics; he had no access to them. It was astonishing how many of the tax records seemed to have mysteriously disappeared.

Osnabrück—the *Stift* as a whole, not the town, which at present was down to about 6,000 inhabitants—had ... probably more people than Holstein. Before the war, both *Stift* and town would have had quite a lot more, but the campaigns of the past 15 years had not been kind. A new symbol, a papal tiara. Catholics, but mixed with Lutherans.

As for Minden, the city was perhaps the same size as Osnabrück, but the *Stift*, tucked as it was between Hoya and Lippe, was considerably smaller. And should logically have been put in Brunswick, given that the Lutheran bishop was the older brother of Georg, Duke of Brunswick at Calenberg and ally of Gustav Adolf. He drew an auxiliary circle linking Minden to Hoya and Diepholz.

Tecklenburg—the Province of Westphalia had this little island of Calvinists by default, because it was tucked in between Lingen and Münster and had to be somewhere. Oxenstierna hadn't even bothered to mention it, any more than he had mentioned Minden. Or Steinfurt, another little Calvinist island, with its non-university-degree-granting *Hohe Schule* full of Dutch students. A Calvinist island with Mennonites.

Everybody deserved a few Mennonites. If they were in Altona and Wandbek in the north, next door to Hamburg, then why not in Steinfurt in the south? The city fathers of Bochold had never been zealous about expelling them, no matter how often Archbishop Ferdinand of Cologne ordered it. Moreover, when they were expelled, they usually walked across the border into the Low Countries, a matter of a couple of miles, and stayed there until things calmed down. He added a symbol for Mennonites: a fully grown adult trying to cram himself into a baptismal font.

And Altona had a Jewish settlement.

He could use a better map than the one he had. For which he could use a survey team. Which he did not have and could not afford to pay if he could find one.

Münster itself? Before the war, the town had some ten thousand people, not counting at least another fifteen hundred non-citizen residents, including clerics and students. The town had been down to eight thousand at the time of the Ring of Fire, but was filling up again, according to reports. He thought that there were probably ten to twelve thousand by now, with more coming.

The *Hochstift*, the prince-bishopric as a whole, *Oberstift* and *Niederstift* combined, had to be the single most populous subdivision of the province, even after invasions and epidemics. Well, the *Niederstift* not so much; the three Ämter of Meppen, Vechta, and Cloppenburg were large in extent, but thinly settled. Perhaps another fifty thousand people, quasi-Lutheran in the previous century; only half-heartedly re-Catholicized over the past twenty-five years in spite of the strenuous efforts of the Jesuits. The *Oberstift* might be more populous than Holstein and was officially Catholic; in practice, a mix of Catholics, Lutherans, and Calvinists. A minimum of two hundred fifty thousand inhabitants. Maximum? He had no idea; it could be a third more. Or twice that many, if you included those working as migrant laborers across the border in the Low Countries. He would count it as at least nominally Catholic. Another tiara.

Overall? As a total? The new province contained fewer than a million people, he thought. Around nine hundred thousand. Fewer than Thuringia-Franconia, but it might well be the second-largest. Of those, perhaps a hundred thousand at most, probably fewer, lived in cities and chartered towns—granting that Lemgo, Rinteln, and their like, each with five thousand or so, should be classed as cities and settlements of a thousand as towns as long as they had a charter. Which they should. They functioned as cities and towns, trade centers. Nienburg would fit with those smaller ones, except that it was in Hoya, which in spite of anything that the Congress of Copenhagen might have said, would effectively have to remain in Brunswick in the interest of brotherly harmony with Duke Georg.

Kiel in Holstein and Stade in *Erzstift* Bremen each had about eight thousand. Those numbers were firm, which was more than he could say about most of the ones he had been doodling on the pad in front of him.

Before he could establish a provincial militia, he needed a census, to figure out what the real personnel resources were and how they were distributed.

Before he could take a census, he needed some kind of central administration to conduct a census and execute other necessary measures.

Before he could staff and pay a central administration, he needed some kind of Estates or other legislative authority to grant taxes over this disparate body of hitherto unrelated entities so the province would have revenue coming in.

But, other than saying "elect one," the USE constitution provided no guidance whatsoever on the subject of how one constituted a body of provincial Estates *ex nihilo* or even *ex* two dozen or more tattered remnants of medieval institutions whose existing members had no desire to cooperate with him or one another.

One had only to look at the cathedral Osnabrück. Of the 24 canons, the *Domstift* featured a small Catholic majority; the remainder were Lutheran—a division which reflected the confessional divisions in the region. Harmony was scarcely an expectable or expected achievement.

Before he could conduct an election ... he needed a census and some kind of central administration.

He concluded his doodle with a flourishing circle and tacked the sheet of paper to the wall. Sat down and glared at it, harboring suspicious thoughts about Oxenstierna and Swedish intentions within the Union of Kalmar. Was Westphalia a province designed to fail?

Designed to fail on his watch? Designed to humiliate Denmark—more specifically designed to humiliate his father—with his failure?

As he prepared for bed, one minor consolation occurred to him. At least most of the area spoke *Plattdeutsch*, close to Dutch and Frisian, rather than the *Hochdeutsch* of Thuringia, which might be an obstacle to any of the interfering up-timers who took an interest in what he might do in and for his new area of responsibility. The up-timers. Those. *Diejenigen.*

Unless, of course, they were shrewd enough to send a properly educated, Latin-speaking, down-timer as an observer.

As to who the Swedes might send … for they would send someone …

He picked up his evening devotional reading, by means of which he was managing to combine the proper pursuit of piety with the prudent project of improving his English, given that God according to His gracious will had caused the arrival of Stearns, Cantrell, and their ilk into his own world, by each day completing a chapter of the recent translation that his Aunt Anne's late husband had commissioned and the appointed committee had so successfully carried out.

Deliver me from mine enemies, O my God; defend me from them that rise up against me. Deliver me from the workers of iniquity, and save me from the bloody men.

Psalm 59. An *imprecatory* psalm, as his professors had called it.

Thou therefore O Lord God of hosts, the God of Israel, awake to visit all the heathen: be not merciful to any wicked transgressors. Selah.

Selah indeed. The proper translation of the word was unclear, according to scholars of the Hebrew language. The *Septuagint* put it into Greek as an interlude or intermission. A pause to think about what one has prayed, perhaps? Or possibly, he thought quizzically, God had simply included a message to the choir director about how the passage was to be sung.

Even if they return at evening; even if they make noise like dogs; scatter them; consume them in wrath ... Consume them, that they may not be: and let them know that God ruleth in Jacob unto the ends of the earth. Selah.

And at evening let them return; and let them make noise like a dog, and go round about the city. Let them wander up and down for meat, and grudge if they be not satisfied.

Yes, David had an outstanding grasp of how things worked. Frederik looked back, a few lines above where his finger marked his place. "Slay them not, lest my people forget: scatter them by thy power; and bring them down, O Lord our shield." A slain enemy could be turned into a martyr by his followers. An embarrassingly humiliated enemy, on the other hand ... might be angry but frequently saw his support dwindling. May justice be done!

He recited Luther's evening prayer from memory and went to sleep.

Virginia DeMarce

CHAPTER 2

Quedlinburg
July 1634

The abbess of Quedlinburg, bones groaning, descended from her carriage. The roads from Copenhagen to southern Brunswick had not been in good condition. The roads from Lübeck to Quedlinburg, to be more precise; she had naturally covered the first half of the trip by taking a ship, as anyone with common sense would do. And broken the land journey twice, once in Hamburg to see what the city, physically and politically, was looking like since the end of the war. Then again in Calenberg for a week to see darling Anna Eleanora and play with her children. Still, nearly 225 miles of sitting on a carriage bench left a person stiff and sore.

She moved her shoulders to loosen them up. A person who, if not yet old, was no longer as young as she used to be.

If she was stiff, the *Stift*'s prioress, her second-in-command, was standing even more stiffly. Radiating stiffness.

"Yes?"

"While you were gone, the foreign woman arrived."

"Which foreign woman?" That was not an unreasonable question. Quedlinburg received international guests with some frequency.

"The one you have brought here as a teacher. The one who is one of those up-timers. Who are not noble, whatever their flatterers and fawners may say about them."

The abbess looked down her prominent, pointed, nose and nodded. "I will see her."

Then she considered her groaning bones. "After I have had a hot bath."

That turned into, after the bath, a bowl of soup and a nap as well. And fresh clothing. The sedate dark colors she considered appropriate to her quasi-religious status as a canoness of the *Stift* accumulated road dust visibly.

"Oh, I didn't mind waiting," Iona Nelson said cheerfully. "I've been busy unpacking crates and getting my classroom organized ever since I got here. I brought a whole wagon load of stuff. I have so many ideas about what I can do with the girls."

The abbess thought that breezy up-time good cheer was probably part of what so irritated the prioress. The idea that someone of lower status might possibly have a right to *mind* waiting to be received by someone of higher status would be hard for her to grasp. *Mind* waiting to be received by a born duchess of Saxe-Altenburg? *Mind* waiting to be received by a half-sister of the current duke, a cousin of the dukes of Saxe-Weimar, the holder (until the recent series of unfortunate events, as the prioress undoubtedly thought of them) of a voting seat in the Imperial Diet?

Personally, she did not consider the events since the Ring of Fire so unfortunate, even if she would not have a vote anymore. The Congress of Copenhagen had subordinated Quedlinburg to the duke of Brunswick: darling Anna Eleanora's husband, in fact. There were a lot of worse possible superiors if one must be mediatized. She had assumed office in 1618; her entire tenure had been marked by the war.

She reflected a moment on the shape of the new provinces of the United States of Europe as depicted on the rather generalized map that

Chancellor Oxenstierna had distributed. Her copy was tucked away in her luggage, safe from road hazards; the maid would unpack it and bring the papers to her office tomorrow. Her memory of it was clear, though. Somebody had done some fancy juggling with the borders to get Quedlinburg tucked in where it would be safe, into comfortably Lutheran Brunswick rather than uncomfortably radical Magdeburg. Or Saxony. While Saxony was Lutheran, of course, her relationship with John George and his officials over the years had often been uncomfortable. Because. Because John George thought everyone else should always agree with him, whereas she frequently did not, and said so. He was of the Albertine line of the Wettins, of course, which did not help. She, as a Saxe-Altenburg, was Ernestine.

She hadn't hinted about the desirability of Brunswick as a placement, of course. Not exactly. Perish the very thought. But who could even guess what kind of map-making mayhem one of Oxenstierna's Swedish subordinates might have achieved if not given some gentle guidance, given how rapidly and, in the final analysis, haphazardly, everything had been thrown together.

Michael Stearns, however fine a man the up-timer might be, simply did not understand the nuances. Didn't want to, she suspected. Rebecca Abrabanel, on the other hand, did. She chose Rebecca as her segue into conversation with Mrs. Nelson. "Melissa Mailey, I'm sure you know her, has Rebecca reading an author named Hannah Arendt. At one point, at the Congress, she laid a quotation from her on the table, reminding us that 'those who choose the lesser evil forget very quickly that they chose evil.' It was not particularly well received."

"I've met Melissa, of course, but didn't know her well. She was at the high school, not the middle school. And we didn't have much in common. She was intense, I always thought. Not my kind of teacher. I've always been more of the type to coax the kids that I teach into realizing the point I'm trying to make rather than to drive them into it. Or it into them. Let them have a peek at the future rather than throw it right into their faces. My kids were younger, of course, at the middle school."

"Well I am glad, for the sake of the future of the students at this particular school, that you decided to come." The abbess set her cup down on the table. "So sorry for the circumstances that led up to that decision."

They observed a moment of silence in memory of the late Billy Nelson.

"He's in a better place, of course. Just no longer here with us." Then Iona laughed a little. "Archie Clinter, the principal, doesn't think I'll stick it out; almost the last thing he said when I left was that he'd make it clear to my replacement that it will be a one-year appointment, in case I decide to come back to Grantville. No matter how much I tried to explain to him why I think the things you are doing are so important, when you come right down to it, Archie thinks that Grantville is more important than anywhere else."

She placed her hands flat against one another, resting her chin against the thumbs, slowly opening and closing her fingers. "He's not the only one who thinks that way. It's a kind of arrogance. It could come to be a problem for us—the up-timers—in the long run."

"Arrogance," the abbess replied, "is not something that you from Grantville, you from the future, are uniquely privileged to possess. In fact, it may be one of the reasons that so many of us have assumed that all of your people are nobles."

"And how," Iona continued more briskly, could I resist coming to the *Stift* when the new college that you are adding on top of the existing school is going to be named for Katharina von Bora?" She looked out the window. "But please, can you tell me *exactly* what happened in Copenhagen. As much as you can, that is, if some has to be kept confidential. It might help me … deal with … some of the opinions … cope … um, attitudes …" Her voice trailed off.

"That would take more than one conversation. Likely more than ten or a dozen. It might be better if I present it to all of the canonesses in a series of talks. But if you are being confronted by opinions and attitudes serious enough that you think you need to 'deal with' them, I can give you a preview, at least. Since the *Stift* here is Lutheran and has lost its political independence, that's what most of the canonesses will be concerned with?" She raised her eyebrows.

Iona nodded.

"I'm not surprised. Nor that they blame it on the up-timers and are taking umbrage. The students, when they arrive for the new term, should be less inclined to do so. But not entirely uninclined to be resentful, so let's start with what has happened to the various Lutheran ecclesiastical principalities, not just Quedlinburg. I suspect that not a single one of our canonesses will be distressed that the independent Catholic principalities have also lost their political independence. If anything, they will regard that development with a certain amount of glee." She started in on a summary.

"And then there's the appointment of Frederik of Denmark as governor of the Province of Westphalia. His position is tricky. He's wearing a lot of hats. It's not just the problem of dealing with the city of Bremen, but, for example, even more confusingly, not only does the religious authority of the archdiocese extend far beyond the secular territory of the *Erzstift*, but also parts of the secular territory of the prince-archbishopric are under the religious authority of the diocese of Verden. In fact, they're about ten percent of Verden's parishes. It will help some that Frederik is prince-bishop of Verden as well as prince-archbishop of Bremen—he has been since 1623, subject to the vicissitudes of war as to whether he was actually in possession or not—but probably not a lot. Human beings are naturally as territorial as, well, some animal that is territorial. The administrative staff of the two jurisdictions will constantly snap and nip at one another.

"Since 1623? He was how old?"

The abbess frowned. "Ah. Fourteen, I believe."

"That's just sick! When I was instructed as a Lutheran, when I was getting ready to be confirmed, one of the things that they taught me was that part of the reason that the Reformation happened, besides *sola fide, sola gratia, sola scriptura*, was to get rid of that sort of thing. Pluralism. Children being put into positions of church leadership because of politics and money. That sort of thing."

"Martin Luther undoubtedly had good intentions," the abbess conceded. "They did not, however, survive the reality of royal and *Hochadel* politics in northern Germany and Scandinavia. Christian Wilhelm of Brandenburg was two years old when he was elected as the Lutheran archbishop of Magdeburg. He's still alive, although the cathedral chapter deposed him in 1628. Nor, at lower but still exalted levels, were the local nobles willing to give up the advantages that came with being able to drop a younger son or unmarriageable daughter into a clerical slot—a cathedral canonry or a foundation. If you want to understand the reality of how government bureaucracies function, even if they are church bureaucracies, it's always a good idea to keep a firm grasp on the doctrine of original sin."

"If the same man usually held them both, Bremen and Verden, since they became Lutheran, why didn't they combine them?" Iona asked.

"To maintain the two separate votes in the *Reichstag*, of course," the abbess answered. The Catholics did the same thing with Münster and Osnabrück, for example. In theory, they weren't supposed to any more after the Council of Trent; in real life, the practice persisted with little change. I believe that the younger son of the late Ferdinand II is technically the bishop of four or five dioceses. Gustav Adolf is doing it now, in the secular world, with his own votes in the USE House of Lords as duke of Pomerania and duke of Mecklenburg.

"The two votes are why Christian IV maneuvered so hard and so long to get one of his sons installed in both dioceses. And young Ulrik as prince-bishop of Schwerin, of course, though nobody quite knows what's going to come of that now that the Union of Kalmar has been reestablished and he's betrothed to Princess Kristina. He'll hardly have time to worry about Schwerin. Frederik's two separate votes in the Imperial Diet are votes that are gone, now, of course. Along with Schwerin's. And mine. Bremen and Verden have been subsumed into the Province of Westphalia; Quedlinburg into the Province of Brunswick. At least Frederik has the consolation that he'll still be voting in the USE House of Lords, which I will not."

She leaned back and smiled ruefully. "It probably shows too much vanity and worldly ambition that I regret the loss quite a bit." Then reached for her wine glass. "The city of Verden is going to be snappish for the same reason, the same regret, since it, unlike Bremen, managed to become an imperial city in the fifteenth century and has now lost that status.

"Additionally, we have absolutely no idea what the emperor—Gustav Adolf, I mean, not young Ferdinand III over in Austria—plans to do about the Imperial Circles. They've been the main way the various principalities in the Holy Roman Empire have managed to work cooperatively—on the comparatively rare occasions that they have ever managed to work cooperatively—for well over a century. The prince-archdiocese of Bremen, like Holstein, belongs to the Lower Saxon Circle—*Niedersächsischer Kreis*. The Prince-Bishopric of Verden, on the other hand, belonged to the old Westphalian Circle—*Niederrheinisch-Westfälischer Kreis*, as did Münster and Osnabrück, also Minden, which are now in the new Province of Westphalia. The circle also included quite a few territories that were in the Holy Roman Empire but aren't in the USE. We can blame it all on Charlemagne, I suppose, if we go back far enough, even though the circles the way they exist today—or existed until a couple of years ago—weren't introduced until 1500. Does Gustav Adolf plan to abolish the circles? Somehow remodel the circles to match the new provinces? Ignore the circles? Nobody knows."

She shook her head. "I read that book about the *Thirty Years War* by Frau Wedgwood."

Iona smiled ruefully. "A lot of us have read it since May of 1631. Many who never expected to read it. Or even knew that it existed. Including me. It was one of the early reprints that came out of Jena."

The abbess nodded. "I do not understand at all why she classified the intervention of Christian IV as a 'Danish phase.' He didn't intervene as king of Denmark. He intervened because as duke of Holstein, he was a member of the *Niedersächsischer Kreis* and effectively its head. That he was also king of Denmark at the same time was entirely an accident. Except, of course, that the tolls for shipping through the Sound as the king of Denmark meant that he could afford to mount armies."

The silence dragged on for a few moments. "It might be interesting for both of you if I introduce you to Frederik some time."

"I don't think it's likely that our paths will ever cross," Iona said. "I'm sure it's the ambition of every important young nobleman to meet a middle school music teacher who is closer to sixty than to fifty."

The abbess looked at her consideringly. "I'm not so sure. It could be important, to use your word, for him to acquire a better understanding of you; of the up-timers generally, I mean. There are two kinds of politicians, in my experience. Those who subscribe to 'those who are not with me are against me' as their general principle of operations; the other more likely to assume that 'the enemy of my enemy is my friend.' Or, if not a friend, at least a potential temporary ally with whom one can reach a potential temporary consensus until the next turn of fate's wheel.

"I don't know precisely where Frederik will fall; I am not sure that he does, either. He's still young. His Aunt Hedwig is one of my best friends. I visit her whenever I can; often enough that one of the rooms in her dower residence, *Schloß* Lichtenberg, is referred to as 'the abbess' room'." She laughed. "I hope that I don't show up so often that I make a nuisance of myself. In any case, she maintains that he is clever. Not brilliant, but shrewd. If he ever comes to understand, as I have, that the up-timers might, sometimes, be … not comrades, precisely, but persons with whom he could forge some precarious areas, limited areas, of common interest …"

Since Iona had never heard of Aunt Hedwig, whoever she might be, she let this last flow lightly over the surface of her mind and kept a hold on *fate's wheel*. "Do you know what a kaleidoscope is? Or a carousel? There was a song I loved: Joni Mitchell's 'Circle Game.'[1] We're being spun around in time. I'm to the point that when I go to bed in the evening, I wonder what turn the next morning will bring. Much less the next week. Or month. Or year."

---

[1]https://jonimitchell.com/music/song.cfm?id=39

Virginia DeMarce

CHAPTER 3

July 1634
Bremervörde

Before he did anything else, Frederik had a funeral to attend. His predecessor as prince-archbishop of Bremen, Johann Friedrich of Holstein-Gottorp, had died in April. What with the war and all, his body had been embalmed and put in storage rather than interred with appropriate pomp and ceremony.

Before he could attend the funeral, he would have to organize it. Have it organized; the administrative staff of the *Erzstift* would do the detailed work, of course, but he had to decide how he wanted them to handle it. While he might not yet have acquired a staff when he was wearing his hat as governor of Westphalia, he did at least have one to administer the secular jurisdiction of the *Erzstift*.

In theory. If he could take control of it. The canons of the Bremen cathedral had been, at best, apathetic in regard to the innovations in the city; most of the administrative staff reported to them individually. The middle managers were displaying minimal enthusiasm for episcopal initiatives that might require them to give up their comfortable lives as country gentlemen and actually exert themselves.

As the duly elected coadjutor, Frederik had succeeded his great-uncle in Bremen quite independently of having been appointed governor of the province of Westphalia by Gustav Adolf two months later. The prince-archbishopric's lands, those under its civil administration, consisted of only about a third of the ecclesiastical archdiocesan territory. Most of them lay in the area to the north of the city, between the Weser and Elbe rivers.

He was, he presumed, still responsible for the spiritual welfare of all Lutherans within the larger limits. Nobody had told him anything to the contrary. That had little in common with running the *Erzstift*. He would have district superintendents and consistories to deal with, pastoral appointments to approve, trial sermons delivered by candidates for those parish appointments to listen to—all the familiar routines of a bishop for which he had been educated.

In addition to his new political duties as governor of Westphalia, which were almost overwhelmingly more extensive than those of a prince-archbishop of Bremen and prince-bishop of Verden would have been.

He had a funeral to attend and some Augean Stables to sluice out. He would combine the funeral for his predecessor with the matter of dealing with "his own" cathedral canons in *Erzstift* Bremen. Who most certainly needed to be dealt with. *First things first. I think that I'd better clean my own house before I start trying to sluice out everyone else's, no matter how extensive the problems of the rest of Gustav Adolf's new province are.*

✳   ✳   ✳

This time, he was setting up his easel in *Schloß* Bremervörde. Also called Vörde Castle, in the town of Bremervörde, about forty miles northeast of Bremen in the direction of Stade, it was the largest fortification in the region as well as having been the effective capital city of the *Erzstift* since the thirteenth century.

It would be a nice place to live, if all he needed was a nice place to live. Damp, of course, but no more so than anywhere else in northern

Germany or Denmark. The castle was located on a fortified island in the Oste River. Those fortifications protected the residence itself, a house with several wings, designed to impress, built in the modern Renaissance style, with both formal gardens and more practical vegetable gardens.

It would not do for his permanent residence as governor of Westphalia, being too far north. He would need to choose a place where neither Bremen nor Hamburg could so easily isolate him from the remainder of the province if, for some reason, they decided it was expedient to cut him off. Which meant that he was going to have to appoint an administrator for Bremen. It might no longer have a vote in the Imperial Diet, but somebody had to run the local government. It wouldn't run itself.

He made a note to leave Captain von Bargen here when he went south, along with half of the company that he had brought from Copenhagen. Appoint him *Statthalter.* Charge him with responsibility to poke and prod the canons to keep things moving. Promote Lieutenant Meyer.

But that was tangential to the moment.

It was going to be more than a trifle touchy to put together a satisfactory guest list for the funeral. The mothers of both Gustav Adolf, now emperor of the USE and his own superior when he was being the governor of Westphalia, and Count Ulrich II of Ostfriesland had been duchesses of Holstein-Gottorp, sisters of old Johann Friedrich. By virtue of that, both men, the deceased's nephews and one another's first cousins, certainly should be invited.

Ideally, neither of them would come.

Frederik pulled his lips inward, chewing on them. He could not brush over the numerous implications of the successful petition of Ulrich II of Ostfriesland to join the United Provinces—he'd done that already before the Congress of Copenhagen. Gustav Adolf certainly would not be inclined to overlook it. By adding Ostfriesland—and

Bentheim, but that was smaller and not of significance for this particular funeral—the United Provinces had become larger. The two counts had set an effective limit on imperial Swedish ambitions in that particular direction unless Gustav was willing to spend more on the conquest than would be practical.

Because the United Provinces were part of Don Fernando's "Low Countries." There were times when Frederik hoped that it bothered Oxenstierna, when he was trying to go to sleep at night, that the new Province of Westphalia that he had constituted also had a low-lying coast. Nobody yet had a reliable gauge of how ambitious the former *Cardinal-Infante* of Spain might be.

And there was still Oldenburg to consider. He would have to invite Count Anton Günther, who was his own cousin. Not to mention a cousin of Emelie, who was now married to Count Ludwig Guenther of Schwarzburg-Rudolstadt, who was prominently associated with the up-timers. The count and Emelie had both been at the Congress of Copenhagen; ideally, it was to be hoped, they would deem it too far to return north so soon for a funeral.

He turned his attention back to the prospective guest list.

In the end, it didn't suit anybody, but almost everybody, both those who attended in person and those who did not, was about equally dissatisfied. That was probably the best he could have hoped for.

*　*　*

He convened the meeting of the canons in the chancery building. Like most of the construction in the region, the amply large L-shaped structure was brick. It had been damaged in the siege, back in 1627, but since repaired and refitted. Each of the canons had an elaborate, comfortable, chair. The support staff, a goodly number of permanent bureaucrats, stood or leaned against the walls.

Frederik cleared his throat.

"It has been brought to my attention that the ex-mistress of my predecessor, a woman named Anna Dobbel, is living on a diocesan-supplied retirement estate at Beverstedtermühlen."

It was possible, even, that his predecessor had entered into a morganatic marriage with the woman, but that was a topic better avoided. If it had occurred, then his predecessor had violated the oath he had taken at the time of his election, to the effect that he would remain unmarried. In any case, he had managed to get the Holy Roman Emperor, Ferdinand II, to legitimate and ennoble their two children in 1621.

Since everyone in the room already knew about Anna Dobbel, none of them responded.

"We need to have a serious discussion about the requirement you have established that the prince-bishop may not marry and its results. It is inconsistent with the Lutheran view of marriage and Luther's repudiation of the Catholic doctrine of clerical celibacy. In what way is your requirement different from what Luther complained about among the noble high clergy of the Catholic church in his day, such as the notorious archbishop of Mainz, who treated their positions as sinecures and kept mistresses?"

Since it wasn't any different, and had been introduced for essentially the same practical reason, namely a concern on the part of the canons that married bishops with legitimate children might convert elective ecclesiastical territories into hereditary secular ones, such as had happened in Prussia the century before, none of them had an immediate answer.

"It has also led to significant legal expenses."

Frederik referenced the complex lawsuit in the *Reichskammergericht* involving the late Johann Friedrich's unsuccessful attempted betrothal in 1600 to a sister of Count Anton Günther of Oldenburg. The canons had sued to prevent it; after several years, Johann Friedrich had sued to break it off unilaterally, and Count Anton Günther had sued to enforce it.

This, too, was quite true. Lawyers cost money and those suits had dragged on for a dozen years.

The canons appeared to be, on the whole, remarkably unstirred by his exhortations. When it came to sowing seed, his admonitions appeared to be falling on extraordinarily stony ground, well-supplied with thorns and nettles.

He turned around and motioned to the guard standing at the door, who left.

A few moments of silence ensued.

The guard returned, accompanied by a slightly scruffy middle-aged man wearing a well-worn Geneva gown with a clerical collar.

Frederik smiled at the gathered canons. "May I introduce you to your new chaplain."

Hermann Hütter, the pastor of the parish of Lunsen, who had had the guts to publicly call out Frederik's great-uncle and predecessor for fornication and adultery, stepped up on the podium, approached the lectern, and delivered few trenchant words based on a reading of Jeremiah 26:8-15, with special focus on verse 13: *Now reform your ways and your actions and obey the Lord your God. Then the Lord will relent and not bring the disaster he has pronounced against you.*

Frederik let Hütter's proclamation echo around the room for a while.

"Since the *Erzstift* is no longer an independent secular principality, but only a subordinate administrative unit of the Province of Westphalia, you, if you wish to retain your status as canons of St. Peter, will henceforth serve the spiritual needs of its Lutheran residents. Alternatively, each of you may choose to become simply an administrator for one or another business matter of the territory for the length of your own life, after which your canonry will no longer offer a sinecure for the local nobility. Instead, the stipend will rather go to an ordained pastor with theological training who is willing to assume the spiritual responsibilities that the members of this chapter, you who are canons of the cathedral, have so blithely neglected up to this day."

The canons might have minimal interest in religion, but few of them were stupid. Focusing on the aspect of this speech that conceded that each of them now in place could, in fact, keep his income for the remainder of his own natural life, they adapted. After all, who was to say that Gustav Adolf's new regime would last and that all of this would not be revoked in due time.

Frederik was conferring with von Bargen and Meyer about last minute details when one of the bureaucrats who had been standing at the back of the room during his confrontation with the canons—the confrontation that Meyer, who had rather familiarly associated with Eddie Cantrell and several other up-timers during the months that Cantrell was in Copenhagen, persisted in flippantly describing as a "come-to-Jesus meeting"—knocked rather timidly at the door.

"Your Grace?"

"Yes?"

"I do have one more slight complication that I would like to bring to your attention. How will the new USE policies on religious toleration affect the way we as the administrative staff of the *Erzstift* handle the two functioning Catholic convents that have survived the Reformation?" When he received no immediate reply, he added helpfully, "Buxtehude *Altkloster* and Buxtehude *Neukloster*, over near Hamburg."

Frederik stood a minute, pulling his lips inward and chewing on them. Then he pushed them out. "I, ah, interpret the new policies to mean that we do not have to *handle* them at all anymore. Or, at least, no more than we will *handle* a guild or a municipal hospital by ensuring that they obey the laws of the land. Draft a letter advising the Catholic ladies that they are now the pope's problem." He paused. "Not mine."

CHAPTER 4

August 1634
Himmelpforten

I f only he could have dispensed with Lutheran ladies so
expeditiously.

This particular lady was named Gerdruth von Campe. From
what he could decipher from her spate of words, since at least
1629, the same year that Ferdinand II, egged on by his ambitious
confessor Lamormaini, had issued the Edict of Restitution to reclaim
formerly Catholic church properties in Germany that had been taken
over by Protestants since the 1555 Peace of Augsburg contrary to the
provisions of that treaty, she had been prioress of a little *Damenstift*
named *Himmelpforten*, so she could not be young.

Neither was she elderly or frail. From her extensive correspondence,
she had seemed to be energetic and possessed by a spirit of
determination in regard to the urgency of the matters she was bringing
to his attention. In person … in New Testament times, the spirits that
possessed people had often been demonic in nature.

Not that the lady was demonic. Just unyielding. One of those people
who knew her rights and had every intention of standing on them.

Porta Coeli. The Gate of Heaven. *Klooster Hemelpoorten*, as it was called
by the local people. It had been founded in the thirteenth century as a

convent of Cistercian nuns. When *Erzstift* Bremen became Lutheran, the lower nobility of the region, having no wish to give up an institution so useful for their sisters and daughters, simply converted it into a Lutheran *Damenstift*.

A tiny, local, uninfluential, mini-Quedlinburg, he thought with some amusement.

The members elected a male provost as their legal warden and their representative at meetings of the Estates of the *Erzstift*.

They chose a *Vogt* to manage the farms, the watermill that the inhabitants of ten or so neighboring villages were obliged to use, the sheep folds, and to collect the rents due from the endowed lands that they leased out. Each of the leased farms contained less land than a family needed to support itself; that was how the convent assured itself of a supply of hired men and maids.

The *Vogt* also arranged whatever military protection it might need in the normal course of events and exercised police functions in the abbey's jurisdiction. This amounted to preventing hunters from poaching, farmers from pasturing livestock where they shouldn't, lumber pirates from cutting trees, and fuel pirates from digging peat, as well as pursuing culprits who were observed doing such things. Once the *Vogt* caught the miscreant, the provost judged him.

While the provost and *Vogt* did their jobs (or shirked them, as the prioress was now vociferously complaining), each of the twenty or so conventual ladies, each a daughter of the local lower nobility that had emerged from medieval *ministeriales*, had a home of her own, with her personal maid, in which she lived a comfortable, reasonably pious, unmarried life. The *Stift* also sponsored a village school, which usually employed an educated schoolmaster with a Latin School background and produced a reasonable number of graduates who met a higher standard than the products of most village schools managed to do and went off to Latin Schools in their turn.

Porta Coeli's provost was usually one of the canons of Bremen cathedral—not coincidentally because the canons had to confirm the *Stift*'s election of any candidate for the provostship.

Before the Edict of Restitution, the provost had been Franz Marschalck von Bachtenbrock, who was ... considerably older than the prioress, having held the post since 1591, been evicted during the Restitution, and since restored to it. And considerably less energetic than the prioress. Nor, the prioress had written repeatedly in the letters that led to the arranging of this in-person meeting, was he displaying the initiative and steadfastness, perseverance and tenacity, that would be necessary if the *Damenstift* were to recover from the damage it had experienced in the war.

Frederik had observed in his dealings with the canons at Bremervörde that Marshalck evinced no evidence of being one of the chapter's more alert and active members. He fell more on the somnolent end of the spectrum, having slept through most of the meetings. That was unfortunate, since the archdeaconry for which he was theoretically responsible was huge. He did not appear competent to exercise either his spiritual obligations or the secular administrative tasks that Frederik had offered as an option. Perhaps he could appoint a deputy ...

"When the Leaguists overran the entire *Erzstift* in 1628," Gerdruth von Campe was saying with a furious shake of her fist. "In September 1629, the Imperial Commission of Restitution ordered *Himmelpforten* to hand in a complete register of all its possessions and revenues," she continued. "In short, Marschalk complied. In person. The farms had already been plundered by the Leaguist soldiers.

"Everything in the abbey church. Everything we had in storage in Stade. All the furnishings. Altars; religious paintings; vestments, communion sets—everything needed to perform the liturgical services. Ferdinand's men took them all and handed them over to a Jesuit named Mathias Kalkhoven who usurped the position of provost. The

Jesuits started collecting the tithes from the parishioners; they told the peasants that the Society of Jesus was their new lord. The restitution commission evicted us, since not one of us was willing to convert to Catholicism and take a pension from the Antichrist in Rome. And when the Jesuits fled from the wrath of Gustav Adolf's armies two years later, all of those things disappeared with them! What do we have left? One chalice! And a lot of desolation.

"Which," she declared, "the late Prince-Archbishop Johann Friedrich did not help by returning from exile so indebted that he persuaded the Estates of the *Erzstift* to grant him the revenues from all its monastic institutions for his lifetime."

She expected Frederik to fix things. Sooner rather than later.

If he had time, he could listen to versions of this story twenty times more.

Open the gate of heaven.

This was one little institution. There were so many more, each one with a similar story.

He wrote to his father.

He needed an allowance.

If the king would be so gracious.

Westphalia had no core with an existing province-wide bureaucracy such as Amalie Elisabeth could rely on in the new version of Hesse-Kassel, much less with Duke Georg's comparatively intact and only modestly enlarged Brunswick, he pointed out.

Westphalia, as an entity, as a whole, had no revenue. As yet, he had neither the time nor the staff to arrange that some portion of the revenues accruing in each individual section should be diverted for support of a central provincial administration.

Once he could construct one.

* * *

Christian IV looked at his trusted private secretary for German matters and shrugged. "I did realize that Westphalia was going to be on its own. That Oxenstierna was not going to let the little victory that this appointment constituted come cheap to me."

The secretary nodded. "It has not escaped my notice that since Torstensson's victory, nobody in Gustav Adolf's administration has even glanced that direction. It's been pretty hard to miss, given that Ahrensbök is in Holstein, and those armies who were marching around inside what was your jurisdiction and is now, under the USE, your son's jurisdiction, have gone off to other campaigns. The Swedish king focuses intently upon his interest of the moment."

"Throw a little money at it. That will help for the time being."

"So, what is he going to do if outside problems come up while Gustav Adolf is focused elsewhere? With the Low Countries? With Oldenburg, even?"

The king smiled a little bitterly. "Pray, perhaps. I sent him to my new military academy at Sorø, but his entire practical military experience has been with the Danish forces besieging Lübeck last spring? Where his major contribution was to help lead the retreat. After Sorø, I had him educated to become a Lutheran prince-bishop. In the long run, that's going to be useful for the administrative end of things. For matters of offense and defense, not so much, but at least, thanks to Torstensson, nobody is actively attacking the Province of Westphalia at the moment. Nor is this son of mine likely to attack anyone unprovoked.

"Send money."

Christian IV stood up. "While I think of some way to tweak Gustav Adolf's tail."

*　*　*

"I simply *cannot* stay here in the north smothering every smoldering peat fire that breaks out," Frederik proclaimed to Lieutenant Meyer. "We're heading over to Verden on Wednesday, but I'm not staying there more than a week. Get preparations under way for me to process through the land bridge and down to Münster. I have every intention of getting there within the month and setting up my headquarters for the winter."

CHAPTER 5

September 1634
Verden

Frederik's days were punctuated by the arrival of mail bags from Magdeburg.

He didn't have a secretary he could rely upon to sort and annotate the contents.

He didn't even have a secretary he could rely upon to open the letters.

He didn't have a secretary yet.

The bags contained letters that he generally sorted into three categories.

Things that someone in the USE Department of the Interior wanted him to do before breakfast.

Things that someone in the USE Department of State urged him to accomplish before lunch.

Things that someone in the USE Department of Transportation thought it was urgent for him to accomplish before dinner.

All of which were accompanied by memoranda. Procedural memoranda. Legal memoranda. Memoranda about the proper style in which to write memoranda.

He was, all things considered, glad that no one had yet furnished him with a radio.

Yet.

Things kept coming at him quite fast enough.

The mail bags from Denmark didn't arrive quite as frequently as the ones from Magdeburg, but they did arrive. This one contained money. Or, to be more accurate, vouchers and letters of credit upon which he could draw funds. Funds that should be ample, if he was careful.

❋   ❋   ❋

Verden was a former episcopal principality of which he was still the bishop, if not the prince-bishop. The Catholic Franz Wilhelm of Wartenburg who had been installed in his place by Ferdinand II after the Edict of Restitution had done a lot of damage during his 1630-1631 tenure of the office. The cathedral's canons were unhappy. No more obstreperous than those of Bremen, but no more cooperative, either.

After all, in the days of the *Stift* they had been able to elect their bishop and ... shall we not use the word extort? ... perhaps not demand? ... obtain concessions from the successful candidate in return for their vote. Whereas, even if Frederik of Denmark was the same man wearing a different hat, the governor of the Province of Westphalia had been imposed upon them by Gustav Adolf without so much as a 'may I' or a 'by your leave,' much less a substantial concession.

Within the former principality of Verden lay the city of the same name. Unlike Bremen, Verden had succeeded in obtaining the status of a free imperial city some two hundred years earlier. A status which it now had lost. The city fathers were ... profoundly dissatisfied ... that the new governor imposed upon them by the USE, the same USE that had taken away their *Reichstag* vote, was also, if when wearing a different hat, the successor of the prince bishops from whose jurisdiction they had managed to free themselves.

The prince-bishops who had continued to hold the cathedral and pertaining premises in town as an immunity district, which had not pleased and still did not please the municipal government.

Frederik's full lips quirked—a municipal government whose members were at least, for the moment, unlike in Bremen, Lutheran. Having expelled the Catholic members imposed upon them during the Edict of Restitution.

He would have to tell them about the USE policy of religious toleration. Which would be ironic, coming from a Lutheran bishop.

As with Bremen, the spiritual jurisdiction of the bishops of Verden covered a larger territory than the secular jurisdiction of the now-extinct *Stift* had done. Much larger: the *Stift* lands amounted to only a quarter or so of the diocese. There were places where its jurisdictions overlapped with Bremen. And vice versa.

Frederik thought it was inevitable that a day would come when the archbishop of Bremen and the bishop of Verden were not the same person, with ensuing problems.

He devoted the week to sorting things out. There were some advantages to being both bishop and governor. He abolished the immunity and placed the towering Cathedral of Saints Mary and Cecelia, along with its surrounding precincts in the old town, on the east side of the Aller River, under the normal the city laws. That was not sufficient to appease the hurt feelings of the city fathers, but might be a first step toward achieving their eventual cooperation with measures that he would necessarily, as governor, have to impose.

But he did have to repeat to them several times what the emperor's new regulations in regard to religious toleration meant, effectively. The message was taking some time to sink in.

If some Catholic former Catholic city councillor who had been forced on them by Franz Wilhelm von Wartenburg wanted, for inexplicable reasons, to come back to the city, buy a house, and once more participate in Verden's municipal politics, they would have to let him.

If some Catholic cleric who had served in the city under Franz Wilhelm von Wartenburg came back to the city and set out to establish a Catholic parish, they would have to let him.

If enough Catholics moved into the city to populate a parish, the city fathers would have to let them be.

"No," Frederik admitted to the mayor in a moment of unusual openness," I don't like the idea, either. I don't recommend, though, that you risk openly defying the edict. In the city of Bremen, after all, it is working to the advantage of Lutheranism."

The thought that the Calvinists of Bremen now had to endure the presence of a functioning Lutheran church within their walls did, finally, ameliorate Verden's grievances in a small way. The politics of *Schadenfreude* succeeded for the time being.

September 1634
Bremen

The perfume from the swine market in the *Neue Neustadt* was something that walls and bastions could not keep out. It wafted over them into the streets and taverns of the *Alte Neustadt*, combining with the indigenous fragrances resulting from bad drainage and crowded living conditions. The area inside the walls was overfilled since the end of the Baltic War, mostly with people who felt grumpily disadvantaged compared to the privileged, if equally overcrowded, residents of Bremen proper on the east bank.

"If we're going to elect delegates to the USE parliament," Gerrit Bemmeler said, "I don't see why we shouldn't be electing the members of the *Rath* too." He glared in the general direction of the market square. "Overturn the patriciate's grip on the *Hochedler Hochweiser Rath* and open the *Bürgermeister* positions to general election by the citizens of the city as a whole." He had been reading Spartacus.

"Who is this 'we' that you speak of? For that idea to do us any good," his older sister Agnes argued. Cynical and pragmatic, she considered him a dreamer. "First," she commented, "they'd have to admit us, over on this side, as citizens of the city. Saying 'elect the councillors' instead of letting them basically choose their own successors when one of them retires. Or dies, which is the main way the *Rath* loses its members, sounds good. As propaganda. But the way things are now, electing them would only benefit the people over there." She pointed in the general direction behind her shoulder to over there.

Over there, the *Altstadt*, where, in a tavern, "Oh the freedoms of Bremen, the wonderful freedoms of Bremen about which our divinely appointed superiors prate so endlessly," Peter Schorfmann proclaimed over his beer. "Freedom for whom? For the star-appointed mortals, fortunately descended from a long line of successful ancestors, surrounded by a constellation of successful brothers, uncles, and cousins, plucked from private life to dwell in the hallowed halls of the *Rathaus* … where all the other councillors, even those who bear other family names, are also their cousins, because of the way the patrician families intermarry. The councilmen are not, mind you, elected by the people. Not even by that select group known as adult male citizens, much less by us who are nothing but workers! What are we allowed to do? Permitted to do by their conciliar excellencies? Petition for redress of our grievances. It's their choice whether or not they bother to read the petitions. As a member of the Committees of Correspondence … "

Schorfmann had been to Hamburg, where he had joined a local CoC and promised his recruiter to spread the good word in the other metropolis of the Elbe-Weser triangle.

"Peter," Bernd Rosenkötter, "you're drunk. *Besoffen*. Shut your mouth."

"I am not," Scorfmann said with pained dignity, "*that* drunk. *Nicht sturzbesoffen*. I could still walk. If I could stand up. Just think. Our esteemed authorities take such pride in arrogating to themselves, as followers of John Calvin, the name of *Reformed*. If you ask me, what this city needs is another kind of reformation."

"Nobody asked you. Anyway, it's no different in any other city."

"It's different in Magdeburg."

"Magdeburg got razed to the ground by Tilly and most of the people killed. Is that what you want for us? They only have different laws now because everything they had before is gone. And, even so, Mayor Guericke there is one of the old patricians, even if he is introducing a lot of the reforms that the up-timers want."

Out in the street beyond the open tavern door, there was a clatter of dangerously high wooden shoe pattens on the flagstones. Then a lantern with two candles, carried by a maid, preceded the passage of several cloaked and bonneted ladies who had, presumably, spent the earlier part of the evening at a party, laughing, gossiping, discussing current events as reported by the newspapers, arguing over the merits of their favorite romance novels, singing, and even dancing with one another until their fathers and brothers came to fetch them home. A party where the current events discussion touched, if briefly and only in passing, on the political structure of the new USE. One of the young men accompanying them turned aside into the tavern, saying, "Ho, Schorfmann, I haven't seen you for a while. What have you been up to?"

At an otherwise unremarkable evening party the same evening in the *Liebfrauen* quarter of the *Altstadt*, hosted by the wife of one of the city council members, her cousin's gangly son, newly returned from school in Leiden and quite bored, listened to the same complaints that he had heard all his life about Bremen's never having achieved the status of an imperial city.

It was absurd for the old men and women to keep nattering on about it. Gustav Adolf had abolished the *Reichstag*, so now it never would.

Except, of course, that the new parliament also had some imperial cities. With the head of the city (one mayor, not four, of course) having a vote in the House of Lords.

Like Hamburg.

A young man who could map out a new route to imperial city status in the new polity for his *Heimatstadt* might well expect to be appropriately rewarded in the way of municipal status and honors.

Gustav Adolf, it was widely known, had no particular fondness for Calvinists.

The new people, though … the up-timers and the Fourth of July Party … they proclaimed their belief in religious tolerance loud and long. Tönnies Breiting kept his face blank and examined his fingernails.

In the disorganized mess that was the *Neue Neustadt* … they kept slaughtering pigs.

Frederik opened a letter from Alverich Knaub, one of the household stewards who had accompanied him during his years of study in France and the Netherlands. Knaub was pompous; Knaub was bombastic, in many ways self-righteous, and usually overly pleased with himself. He was, however, also efficient—not once had Frederik ever run into budgetary difficulties—and available. Frederik was in direly short supply of available resources, so he had persuaded Knaub to "retire" and take his wife and children to settle down in the city of Bremen, where he had been born and was some sort of cousin to a family of shipping magnates who had fallen on hard times, in order to provide him with a pair of ears inside the city.

Knaub reported, complained about, the ubiquitous presence of rebels and revolting revolutionaries, up-time propaganda and growing membership in the Committees of Correspondence, all over Bremen. He called upon the governor to intervene and squash it.

Squashing it was also Frederik's first impulse. But with what? He didn't have the resources to squash it, either in the way of political support in the new province as a whole or in the way of *force majeur*.

His second impulse was to let them fight it out, on the "sufficient unto the day is the evil thereof" principle, because at least while the Bremer were brangling with one another, they wouldn't have the time or energy to focus on actively opposing his efforts to organize the province as a whole.

Plus, from what he knew of the up-timers, they probably wouldn't have much interest in Bremen. Not that he knew much about them. When the early hires passed through his father's court, in 1632 and 1633, he had still been away at the university. Then he was with the Danish army during the League of Ostend episode. From Oct. 1633 up to Anne Cathrine's marriage in June 1634, his assignments from his father kept him away from the court, so he didn't get to know Eddie Cantrell; his meetings with up-timers at his sister's wedding were brief and superficial. His only real experience was observing at the Congress of Copenhagen.

Plus, he *had* to spend this winter doing something about the situation in Münster and Osnabrück.

He had people in and around Bremen now. A couple of the canons had turned out to be reasonably useful. Captain von Bargen could keep an eye on things from Bremervörde. There was even, heaven help him, Knaub. They would keep him apprised. For the time being, Bremen could wait.

September 1634
Magdeburg

Ben Leek shook his head. "Westphalia? It's going to be 'West-failure' if you ask me, and a big one. No real industry. The rivers aren't going to do that Danish kid much good. The best one is the Elbe and Hamburg's sitting right squat on it. That's right. The independent, and mostly hostile, imperial city of Hamburg is sitting on the Elbe. The strongly-wishing-it-were-independent, and mostly hostile, city of Bremen is sitting on the Weser. The Ems, whatever could be made of it in the way of navigability, goes through Ostfriesland before it reaches the sea at Leer. Ostfriesland has joined the United Netherlands, so nothing is going to go out or come in without the permission of Fernando and Fredrik Hendrik. A lot of it, especially in the north, is going to be a bitch for building railroads: peat, swamp, and a high water table. Let me tell you: as a prudent investor, I wouldn't sink a wooden nickle into that province."

Pete Rush shook his head.

Ben scowled. His son Tom tended to share almost every opinion that his old man expressed, which he found to be a highly satisfactory state of affairs; his son-in-law was more inclined to be argumentative. Ben attributed it to an insufficient sense of practical business and an overabundant amount of time in R&D for Greg Ferrara.

Before he could rouse himself to trample on whatever idea that Pete might have this evening, though, Phil Hart, who was serving as special liaison from USE Treasury Department to the Federal Reserve Bank of Grantville, interrupted. Or tried to. Saying something about heavy levels of existing indebtedness.

"From everything I've heard at Transportation," Edgar Frost said, "Ben's entirely right about the railroad problem."

Jere Haywood, whose B.S. in Civil Engineering carried some weight in these matters, said that he had to agree with Edgar, adding that the only decent potential deep-water harbor up in that direction was in Oldenburg, which wasn't even part of the USE.

"I'm with Ben." That was Bill Roberts from Magdeburg Concrete. "If the Province of Westphalia wants anything from us, they're going to have to put cash on the barrelhead in advance. If you ask me, it would be too dicy a prospect to carry them on credit, the way things are set up over there."

Bill was married to Ben's cousin Debbie.

Phil opened his mouth again. As a bureaucrat, though, he didn't have much hope of making headway against a table full of businessmen in full spate. Fortunately, he thought, they weren't the only people in the USE who had money to invest.

Not that, as far as he knew, anyone from the administration of the Province of Westphalia had even approached them. Or anyone else. Yet.

September 1634
Rinteln

Frederik was pleased that had been able to keep on Lieutenant Meyer's schedule when it came to his formal procession toward the southwest of the new province. Hoya and Diepholz had each required only a polite meeting with the existing Brunswick-appointed administrative staffs to assure them that if everything proceeded as normal, he had no intention to interfere, followed by a banquet.

Everything one did in life was followed by a banquet. He ate as little as possible, since indigestion was unpleasant. He drank a little as possible because ... inebriation could lead to disastrous results. Think of Noah. Think of Lot. Think of Ephesians 5:18. Galatians 5:21. Think of St. Paul's admonition to Timothy concerning candidates for the office of deacon, which should, logically, apply all the more to bishops, even secular ones.

He admonished himself not to avoid the issue. Think of his own father.

His generous and beloved father, who drank far more than was good for him.

He shook his head and set up his easel.

Minden was likely to cause trouble, even though it presented itself as docile for the moment. He should give both the municipal officials in the town and episcopal administrators in the former principality the news that the up-timers had extraordinarily strong opinions regarding some down-time customs, so they would do well to follow the course of prudence and mend their ways.

Lippe, with three branches of the family of counts.

Schaumburg.

Several days later, he left Schaumburg feeling rather pleased with his idea of hiring the unemployed faculty of the currently non-functional university at Rinteln to staff the chancery of which he was in desperate need. Founded the year after hostilities broke out in 1618, with classes not starting until 1621, it had never attracted much over a hundred students and had not survived the 1629 Edict of Restitution's confiscation of the building in which it was housed. He had put the medical school professors to dealing with the plague issue on the border with the Low Countries and sent Gisenius with most of the theologians north to assist Pastor Hütter's efforts to knock some more sense into the recalcitrant cathedral chapters in Bremen and Verden.

He sent a couple of the theologians to Minden with copies of a book that Rinteln's university press had published anonymously in 1631, the *Cautio Criminalis*. He pinched his lips in with distaste. The author was now known to be the Paderborn theologian Friedrich Spee von Langenfeld, who was not only Catholic but also a Jesuit. The up-timers seemed quite impressed with his argumentation, though. At least, they caused a great many memoranda on the undesirability of prosecuting witchcraft to arrive by way of the mail sacks from Magdeburg.

Logic would have told Frederik to pick his staff from Bremen and Verden. Logic didn't work—not in this instance. He didn't trust a one of them. Well, maybe one or two from the *Erzstift*, but he needed them to stay where they were. As for the city, all the aspiring bureaucrats and attorneys who sprang from the loins of the entrenched generation of Bremen's patricians were Calvinists. Calvinists might well be tempted to look with undue favor on the grasping Rhenish ambitions of the landgrave of Hesse-Kassel.

Or logic might have told him to recruit his staff from Holstein. But that presented difficulties, owing to his father's also being duke of Holstein as well as king of Denmark. Diplomatic niceties, in and out of the Union of Kalmar. His father's German chancery was mostly staffed by nobility from Holstein. Consequently, he had some prudent concerns that anyone he chose from Holstein would intrigue with cousins in Copenhagen, Glückstadt, and points in between.

As a provincial organization, Swabia was no better off than Westphalia; possibly worse, but Georg Friedrich had his own personal income from Baden and sons to stay there and administer his own lands for him—much as Albrecht was doing for the rest of the Ernestine Wettins. And Georg Friedrich was one of Gustaf Adolf's officers; he had additional income from that. And a regiment.

One of the realities was the local estates were stingy when it came to granting tax revenues for maintaining armies. Archbishop Ferdinand, at a maximum, had never had more than two or three thousand men authorized and funded. Those were long gone, and probably good riddance.

Frederik would make do with what he could find.

He kept Rinteln's lawyers and liberal arts professors for his own use. Once he got the university running again, he supposed he would have to give them back, but in the interval, they were happy enough to be receiving salaries.

Virginia DeMarce

CHAPTER 6

October 1634
Münster

There was an aphorism to the effect that in Münster, either it was raining or the church bells were ringing. If both were happening at the same time, it was Sunday.

It wasn't Sunday; it *was* raining. The rain was dripping off Frederik's hat, onto his shoulders, as he drew up his horse in the main square.

He should have sent a company of soldiers accompanied by financial and legal staff well ahead of him to do reconnaissance and make arrangements since, practically, there was not going to be any way for him to avoid putting his major administrative center in this city, even though it was about as far away from Denmark's areas of primary interest as he could get and still be within the borders of Westphalia.

Whatever troubles might develop in the northeast portions of the new province, those of the southwest, getting it to accept the regime of a Swedish emperor after the depredations that had been committed on its people by Swedish armies, were, he thought, necessarily going to be more intransigent. And the *Oberstift* bordered on the Spanish Netherlands section of the new kingdom of the Low Countries where the new king, Don Fernando, the former *Cardinal-Infante*, was still an unknown quantity and unquestionably a brother of Philip IV of Spain; not the probably more rational, and certainly more Protestant, United Provinces, where he would be dealing with Fredrik Hendrik.

Anyone who had studied how the spillover of the Dutch wars of a half-century ago had ravaged this part of Westphalia would not question his decision to locate the new province's permanent capital in the south.

He hoped.

Rain ran down the back of his neck and under his cloak, a chilly streak against his skin.

Any minute now, some officious official was likely to emerge from one of the buildings on the square to greet him. When they came through the gate, one of the guards had taken off running in the direction of the center of the town.

It would be interesting to see who showed up.

The *Erbmänner*—the patricians chosen into the city council by a convoluted, four-stage, process? Mostly Catholics, but some Protestants; those mostly Calvinist, but a few Lutherans; almost all of them would-be gentlemen of leisure, feeling severely put-upon and burdened by the requirement that if they wanted to reside in the city, they had to assume some of the burdens of maintaining civic life.

An alderman? There were two on the city council, advocating for the interests of the 34 masters who represented the 17 guilds in the *Gesamtgilde*?

Someone from the increasingly vociferous *Gemeinheit*, noisy enough by themselves but now spurred on by the external influence of the Committees of Correspondence, that was demanding a larger place in the city administration for ordinary workers and artisans?

Or a functionary? A jurist or a notary, to demonstrate how little significance the council proposed to ascribe to the arrival of the new provincial governor?

The suffragan bishop, Claessens, who was still here and exercising Catholic episcopal functions in the name of Ferdinand of Bavaria, the pluralist archbishop of Cologne who also held this see? Even if he didn't show up today, a meeting with him would be on Frederik's agenda, and soon. Topic: the meaning of religious tolerance as proclaimed by the USE. Get rid of Archbishop Ferdinand's requirement that only Catholics could obtain citizenship in the city. Abolish the law that the sale of heretical books was prohibited. Make it clear that the requirement that parents could only send their children to Catholic schools was void.

Most of which would be welcomed well enough by the majority of the people, who were far from wholehearted supporters of the Tridentine Counter-Reformation's strictness in spite of a generation's effort by the Jesuits. There were people still alive here who could remember fondly the halcyon days of confessional haziness in the late sixteenth century when communion in both kinds was occasionally celebrated at Catholic masses, accompanied by the singing of Lutheran songs; far more who remembered the prevalence of a married Catholic clergy, whether the reformers of Trent classified the women as "concubines" or not. Their memories did not have to be long; as recently as twenty years ago, the episcopal visitation had estimated that the proportion of the Catholic clergy in the diocese who lived in some type of quasi-marital relationship amounted to ninety-five percent.

A representative of the cathedral chapter, all of whom were members of the Westphalian nobility with networks of kinship and patronage extending far beyond the city? Few of them voluntarily gave up the noble lifestyle of hunting and drinking. Perhaps even one of the archdeacons?

The Jesuit *collegium* was huge. Before the war, it had counted over a thousand students. Frederik seriously doubted that it would send anyone to greet him. Nor would any of the other convents and monasteries, of which there must be at least a dozen, all told, running the gamut from wealthy cloisters accepting only nobles of the region outside the city to small tertiary orders largely drawing from the city's artisan families.

In the end, it was two of the magistrates from the council who emerged from the city hall, accompanied by a small entourage of flunkies. A Kerckerinck and a Schenckinck, perhaps. Or a Steveninck and a Nunninck. Perchance a Bischopinck and a Wesselinck or a Wermelinck and a Grevinck. There was a certain soothing rhythmic quality to many of the family names.

This evening, he would dine and sleep as a guest of one Ludolf Burmeister, Protestant and holder of various municipal offices over the decades.

That left open the question of where he would dine and sleep on subsequent evenings.

Where *would* he reside?

Where would he find working space for his staff?

His first impulse was to seize the existing *Domdechanai* of the Catholic cathedral chapter of the *Hochstift*; simply appropriate it. Unfortunately, that was not feasible because of the USE policies on religious toleration, any more than he could simply turn the cathedral Protestant. Or St. Lambert's. Or the *Apostelkirche*. Or the Church of Our Lady. Or St. Servatius. Or St. Ludger's. Or even St. Peter's, even though its recent date of construction, only 35 years earlier, for the may-they-be-confounded Jesuits made it tempting. Extraordinarily tempting. So tempting.

Was there anything that had become Protestant during the Reformation era and the Catholics had then grabbed back as a result of the Edict of Restitution? Unfortunately not; the wretched Bavarian archbishop of Cologne had taken everything into his grasping hand even before the war.

He would have to build a new, modern, Lutheran church. Preferably right in the face of the Jesuits. Attract enough Lutherans to the city to make the investment worthwhile. He made a note to have Johann Rist, his newly acquired private secretary, tell one of the lawyers he had brought from Rinteln get in touch with his appropriate counterpart in Münster. There was certainly an adequate supply of them.

He and Rist were beginning to develop a certain mutual respect.

Speculations regarding a possible future church did not solve the question of a residence. He looked out Burmeister's second floor window at the row of gabled houses on the west side of the square. Built of limestone in the local variation of Renaissance style, they mostly belonged to wealthy merchants. Would any of them be for sale? Or rent? Or were any of the owners in dire disgrace with the USE? He'd have Rist assign someone to look into it. One of those would do for the time being.

In addition to the new Lutheran church, he should construct, eventually, a new, modern gubernatorial residence on the other side of the Jesuits. Box them in. He made a note to tell Rist to have someone look into land ownership issues on the surrounding properties.

The residence would need a Protestant chapel, naturally. He was still a *summus episcopus*, if in a rather ambiguous way. A tradition from the first one that the elector of Saxony had constructed at *Schloß* Hartenfels in Torgau and Martin Luther had dedicated in 1544. The one at Schwerin. Or one such as his father had completed at Frederiksborg only the year before the Thirty Years' war broke out. A chapel which would lead the congregation to gather around the baptismal font, pulpit and altar-table, the focal points of preaching and communion. An altar at the eastern short end. Below the organ. Of course, he would need an organ. The governor's pew and oratorio on the west. The pulpit on a side wall, in the middle. Galleries for visitors.

That would be far in the future of the Province of Westphalia. His father's bounty was liberal, but certainly did not extend to construction projects, which probably, from the divine perspective, did lie in the same general realm as storing up goods in barns. There were more urgent necessities than buildings.

It dawned upon him that he needed a chaplain. His own chaplain. Now. Or, at least, sooner rather than later.

He probably shouldn't simply take over the city hall, either, although that would not come crosswise against the up-timers' views on religious toleration. It simply wouldn't be prudent. Carving out some space within it for his staff might be a workable option for now, though. For the meantime.

Eventually there would need to be a new chancery building. A barracks, once he built up a regiment. But first, get his newly acquired staff settled *somewhere* and put them to work.

But first … he sighed and went downstairs to face yet another ceremonial banquet.

November 1634
Bremen

Newspaper reports about the unrest in Bremen spread throughout the USE. In the city itself, the *Hochedler, Hochweiser Rath*, in hopes of regaining control, annexed the *Alte Neustadt*. In response, a movement fronted by those who identified themselves as members of the Fourth of July Party, unquestionably backed by the threat of the Committees of Correspondence, had forced through changing the name of the *Hochedler, Hochweiser Rath* to the more modern and republican *Senat*. That was only the most symbolic development. Behind that lay the restructuring of the local citizenship laws that accompanied preparations for the province to vote in the upcoming national election.

Alverich Knaub continued his regular reports. According to his observations, the internal strife was escalating. For the time being, the traditionally chosen four mayors and twenty councillors still held office, but there was swelling demand for a sweeping revision of the way in which the city was administered. The Committees of Correspondence were demanding that the incumbents be forced to stand for election, running against challengers from outside the patriciate.

Knaub's mood was increasingly testy. Money to maintain his household was a problem. The horrible storm that had spread destruction over Denmark and the duchies of Schleswig and Holstein had not entirely spared northwestern Germany. Extraordinary tides had risen far up the Weser and Elbe both, backing up the waters, flooding the river bottoms; even, in some places, changing the course of the channels. The small fleet that his family operated had taken damage. The investment dividends that supplemented his retainer from Duke Frederik were way down; his expenses were not.

And his daughters were running wild, being exposed to up-time influences, unsuitable clothing styles, radical ideas that were permeating the entire city. Knaub was appalled.

December 1634
Münster

"I have a lot to do here," Frederik said to Rist. "Not more urgent things, necessarily, but ultimately more significant things, I believe. Neither do I want to head back to Bremen in midwinter weather."

Rist was not yet to the point of giving his employer advice. He sat there, watching the governor draw dots and circles on the paper he had affixed to the ever-present easel.

"There have been demonstrations, but no riots.

"There have been caucuses and public meetings; oratory in the city hall and griping in the taverns; petitions submitted.

"Knaub insists that there is a constant underlying threat of violence, but so far, aside from ordinary fistfights and such that the constabulary can handle, no actual violence.

"There's nothing in my authority as governor to allow me to unilaterally intervene in the way a city chooses to administer itself. Not unless it undertakes to act in ways that are clearly contrary to the constitution and laws of the USE."

Frederik stopped talking out loud and stared at the easel.

Which isn't happening in Bremen, he thought, *as far as I can tell,* no matter how distressing Knaub finds it all. On the contrary, I suspect that the Stearns is hearing the news with delight, along with the rest of the FoJP. And Oxenstierna is likely hearing it with considerable *Schadenfreude,* for however little he may care for the reforms that the Bremer are throwing themselves into, he will be chuckling because they can only cause more trouble to me.

Rist saw no reason to interrupt the sudden silence.

Frederik strode over to his standing desk and grabbed a piece of used notepaper, striking out the lines that were already on one side of it and scribbling on the reverse.

"Here." He handed the note over. "Put this in proper form and send it out today. I'll do a longer memorandum tomorrow."

Rist looked at it. "Who is Emil Jauch? I don't have an address."

"I worked with him in Lübeck during the retreat last spring. I need someone in Bremen, since I can't go myself. I can't use anyone from the *Erzstift.* That would immediately get tangled up with the church problems. By now, that will include von Bargen. I need an emissary plenipotentiary to mediate and arbitrate the internal unrest in the city— someone not immediately identified with either the old *Rath* or its opponents. Send it in care of my half-brother, Christian Ulrik Gyldenløve. You have that address; he'll know where to find Jauch."

"Gyldenløve?" Rist said doubtfully.

"Goldenlion. Our father has given that surname to all of his acknowledged bastards. Christian Ulrik is my brother Ulrik's twin by another mother."

Rist raised his eyebrows.

"Kirsten Madsdatter gave birth to him one day after our mother gave birth to Ulrik." Frederik pulled his full lips in, chewing on them with disapproval. "Kirsten was one of the queen's maids of honor." Frederik pursed his lips, pushing them out. "Our royal father must have found her presence in my mother's chambers convenient when he was feeling horny.

"He's as smart as Ulrik. Studied at the University of Leiden; excelled in Latin and the classics; could well have become a professor if our father had permitted him such a path. After that, he received the same military training as Ulrik—exactly the same, both of them under von Arnim in Saxony. All he's lacking to be a wholly satisfactory royal scion is a female parent of *ebenbürtig* lineage with a marriage certificate." Frederik grimaced. "Even without those, he is, as far as our father is concerned, destined to become an officer, a courtier, and a diplomat. With a suitably prestigious marriage."

Rist had nothing to say.

✳ ✳ ✳

"My Lord Governor, were you expecting guests?"

The footman stood stiffly at attention this night, a date so shortly after mid-winter that the dark came miserably early.

The governor of the Province of Westphalia, already attired in a fur-lined evening robe and comfortable, equally fur-lined, slippers, a snug fur-lined cap on his head, stood up, placing the book he had been reading face down on the stand next to his chair.

His comfortable, leather-upholstered, reclining chair that his father had sent him for Christmas.

The stand that held a modern mantled lantern, the kind that threw so much more light than a candle, that his brother Ulrik had sent him for Christmas.

"Who is it?"

"They came to the gate; the guard called Lieutenant Meyer, who has accompanied them to the house himself."

Frederik abandoned the warm fire burning in the ceramic tile stove and made his way out into the cold hall.

"*Glædelig jul*," came a voice from the foot of the stairs. "I didn't have a present for you, so I brought myself."

Frederik rarely scurried, but this time he made an exception, folding the young man in an enthusiastic embrace. "What are you doing here? Come upstairs. Get warm." He looked at the other man. "Meyer, do go to the kitchens and get a mug of hot broth before you go back out in this weather. The cook's helpers will still be cleaning up." Then ... "Christian Ulrik, who is this?"

"I ... sort of need to explain things."

"It's the adorable Bente Luft, then, I presume. And a long story. But I keep a bachelor household. No housekeeper; no live-in maids. How long have you been riding in this wet snow? She looks to be half-frozen. I have no one to help her with a hot bath, no one from whom to borrow warmed clothing for her ... "

The footman, standing as stiffly as before, cleared his throat. "My Lord Governor, if I may speak?"

"Yes, Vendt?"

"My home is not so far distant. I can send one of the potboys for my wife and mother. Let them know what is needed."

"Good man; good idea. Let it be done." Frederik turned back. "Now come upstairs, both of you. I have a good fire burning."

"My Lord Governor, if I may speak?"

"Yes, Vendt?"

"It might not be unwise to remove as much of their soaking wet outer clothing as possible here in the hallway and send it to the kitchens to be dried, rather than have it drip all the way to the living quarters."

"Oh, yes." Christian Ulrik pulled the wet hooded cloak from the girl's shoulders and knelt down to remove her boots. "Are there at least some extra slippers around?"

The footman cleared his throat.

"Yes, Vendt."

"It might not be unsuitable to have one of the potboys fill some warming pans with embers and use them to ameliorate the damp that has likely crept into the bedding in the best guest chamber."

"Vendt," Frederik said with some exasperation. "Just let it be accomplished. All of it."

After Vendt's female relatives had arrived bearing sacks of supplies and borne Bente off for cossetting, Frederick sank back into his chair. He picked up the book, placed a bookmark, and closed it. There didn't seem to be any prospect of further reading this night.

"Please explain."

"I have ... fallen out of favor with His Majesty."

"How?"

"I want to marry Bente."

Frederik pulled his lips in. "Why now? She's been your sweetheart since the first time you laid eyes on her, which must be two or three years ago. She's followed you from one posting to another—easy ones and difficult ones—with perfectly good cheer, unless I've missed out on some gossip. I know that you've already made financial provisions for her; she'll be taken care of if anything happens to you."

If anything happens was always a concern for a young military officer.

Not to mention that she hadn't brought him a dowry. There was a perfectly practical proverb: *A fair wife without fortune is a fine house without furniture.* Not that fathers were generally inclined to provide dowries when no marriage was involved. He wasn't sure what old Luft's financial situation might be. Toll keepers in the Danish royal service had sufficient opportunities to make profits, both legitimate and somewhat less so. With prudent investments, if there came to be a marriage, there might be a dowry as well.

"His Majesty has his eye on an advantageous marriage for me. Into the Lykke family, as it happens." Christian Ulrik screwed up his mouth with distaste. "He tried to talk me into sending Bente to Norway. When I refused, he called in her brother and tried to influence him, gossip about dishonor to his sister and all that." This time, Christian Ulrik snorted. "As if there would be any more gossip now than there has been all along. From the first, I came to a complete understanding with old Luft at Helsingør, assured him that I would always treat her honorably, and see that she was always cared for."

Christian Ulrik turned so that his other side was to the stove's warmth. Frederik's pantaloons were long on him, and loose. Looser than they would have been two years before, when they last saw one another. *I am*, Frederik thought a little ruefully, beginning to put on weight. The curse of the sedentary.

"I promised. *Promised.* An oath that I could not keep if I were forced to dismiss her. Which I said to the king. Who then said that if I would not dismiss her, then he would dismiss her father from his position as toll-collector. A position in which he has served our royal father honorably for a long time. Then …"

Frederik only nodded. He did not need to hear what came next. Christian IV of Denmark had a legendary temper, particularly when someone thwarted his will. Particularly if he had been drinking when somebody thwarted his will.

"So I said that I would not only keep her, but marry her. Take her, her parents, her sisters and their husbands, and get a commission from Don Fernando in the Low Countries. I don't see why I shouldn't marry her. She's a commoner, but her family is perfectly respectable. I'm the one who's a bastard."

Christian Ulrik let the ensuing silence drag on for a couple of minutes. Then … "It's not as if I'm ever going to look at another woman with desire. I didn't whore around before I met her; I knew the minute I saw her that she was the only one I would ever want."

Frederik sorted through that mentally, pitying the wretched fate of the romantic man—of romantic men in general; consider the plight of Romeo in that play—and wishing that his easel were here in his private sitting room and not in the office downstairs. Everything was easier when he could *see* things laid out in front of him.

The easiest first. "What have you done with her father, sisters, and the rest of the human menagerie?"

"Left them in Hamburg, in a decent inn. No reason to drag them all down here when I wasn't sure what you would have to say. Or, if you turned me off, what Don Fernando would have to say. Possible diplomatic ramifications and all those things."

Christian Ulrik switched the side benefiting from the stove's warmth again. "She's expecting. I don't want to father a bastard. It's not the easiest thing in the world for a child to be."

"I'm fairly sure," Frederik answered, "that I can persuade some pastor to skip the banns if necessary."

"We can wait three weeks. Or three months, if need be. She's not that far along."

"Where are your funds deposited? Your working capital and what you settled on her?"

"Hers were invested in Lykstad-Glückstadt as the Germans call it. I switched them to Altona when we passed through, in case anybody got ideas about confiscating them. Mine are in Lübeck."

"Good enough." Frederik brought his hands together as if he were praying. "I think it would be prudent if I pass this across Gustav Adolf's desk before we proceed any farther."

Magdeburg
December 1634

The newspapers reported a rumor that Christian IV was petitioning Emperor Gustav Adolf to have his son Frederik awarded the title of Prince of Westphalia.

Ben Leek waved his copy at his son as they ate breakfast. ""Ridiculous!" he proclaimed. "How on earth would anyone figure that the Danish kid might deserve a promotion already. He's been in office for six months and hasn't accomplished a single thing."

Papers in the rest of the USE quickly picked up the story.

Grantville
December 1634

Hal Smith checked with his daughter-in-law Joanie, who had, after all, spent a year at the Danish court as governess to the batch of half-royal daughters.

"I don't know. It might be, I suppose. Royals and nobles are deeply into titles. But something about it bothers me. At the court, of course, they spent a lot of time doing protocol-ish things and ritual-ly things, like receiving ambassadors and holding parades. But they didn't spend all of their time dressed up in their best, like they were ready to pose for an official portrait. They joked around; they laughed." She stopped. "Do you remember that little rhyme from somewhere?"

> *Speak roughly to your little boy,*
> *And beat him when he sneezes.*
> *He only does it to annoy,*
> *Because he knows it teases.*

Hal admitted that he had heard it somewhere.

"What's worming around in my mind last now are the last two lines. Christian IV may be a king, but he has the sense of humor of your average eight-year-old boy. And his nose is bound to be a little out of joint about the Union of Kalmar. If he could figure out a way to prank the glorious Emperor and High King of this and that … I wouldn't put it past him. But don't quote me on that."

Hal didn't quote her. Not to anyone. He did keep the thought prudently in mind when examining the various clauses of the contracts for aircraft construction that he made with both the USE and Denmark.

Virginia DeMarce

CHAPTER 7

January 1635
Münster

Rist managed to catch a chaplain. Joachim Lütkemann, in his mid-20s, on his way home from studying at the University of Strassburg.

"Professor Gisenius heard from Professor Dannhauer that he was on his way to Rostock, looking for a position—he's from Mecklenburg, or maybe Pomerania—and headed him off."

"If he is the same age as I am," Frederik asked mildly, "is he likely to be any wiser or more well advised?"

"He's at least more likely to be able to keep up with you on a horse than someone three times his age." Rist, only a couple of years older than Frederik but much less athletic, had agonizing memories, more in his buttocks than his brain, of some bruising rides when his employer determined to be in a certain place at a certain time, no matter what. "Also, Dannhauer is noted for his focus on pastoral theology rather than esoteric academic stuff."

One obligation could not be ignored. Even without a census, the province would have to conduct an election.

Frederik had thought about it in August. He had started worrying about it in November, but at that point the question of how to do it was still up in the air. Election day was advancing upon him ominously, like an attacking *tercio*. Slow moving, day by day, but with a ghastly certainty of its arrival.

The various "how to do it" designs on his easel had thus far ruined eight large sheets of expensive paper. On both sides.

"We *will* have it organized in time for the election," one of the lawyers he brought from Rinteln assured him. "We're setting up a network of village notaries. The contracts for ballots have already been let to two printers in each district. Ideally, in each village, the voting would be monitored by both the bailiff and the headman, but in so many places a bailiff has responsibility for five or even ten villages. And the lordship is split in so many others. Nor do we want the lords supervising the way their serfs vote. You will be sending out a mandate authorizing the notaries to deputize official observers."

Serfs were voting? Frederik shrugged.

"I only wish we had more in the way of a militia to guard the polling places," he answered. "To assure the voters that they will be safe from reprisals, however they vote … reprisals from anyone from feudal lords and reactionaries to CoC fanatics and radicals … when they come to exercise their right. That day. And the day, the week, and the month after they drop their ballots in those boxes. I sometimes wonder if the up-timers realize how dangerous this might end up being for an ordinary peasant or a journeyman in a guild. We can't make the voting districts too large or it would be a heavy burden on people to go to the polls. But when they are small, even with a 'secret ballot,' it won't be that difficult for lords and masters to figure out how any person marked his paper. If there are fifteen voters in a village, the lord told them to vote for Herr X, but the returns show that four voted for Herr

Y ... We'll be putting out brush fires all over the province next summer."

February 1635
Münster

Thus far, nobody in Magdeburg had reacted to Christian Ulrik's proposed marriage one way or the other. Sometimes, Frederik wondered whether anyone even read his regular, conscientious, dispatches.

Still, when it came to maintaining his relationship with the federal government, he would be sure to dot all of his "i"s and cross all of his "t"s, watch every jot and tittle. Be punctilious, in both the literal and figurative sense of the word.

He smiled briefly at his own little joke. He enjoyed word plays.

February 1635
Osnabrück

If anything was likely to attract attention in Magdeburg, it was what came next. Before his own appointment became effective in June 1634, during the chaotic campaigns of 1631 and 1632, the Swedes had managed to install in Osnabrück the emperor's illegitimate son.

Also Gustav, but not Gustav Adolf. Gustav Gustafsson, born in Stockholm, now turning nineteen years old.

Install as Lutheran prince-bishop of the *Hochstift*—of which Franz Wilhelm von Wartenburg, the illegitimate son of one of the dukes of Bavaria (not of the currently troublesome Maximilian, but of one of his uncles, Frederik thought), was already the Catholic prince-bishop and had been for several years past. Franz Wilhelm had fled when the Swedes arrived; young Gustav was in possession of the episcopal residence at *Schloß* Iburg, the episcopal revenues, episcopal hunting lodge, episcopal everything. In theory, the Swedes had furnished him with older and wiser heads to advise him, but complaints were beginning to come in.

Yea, Osnabrück. It must be such a joy for anybody, much less a boy who wanted to get back to his career as a military officer, considering that his appointment had originally been as commandant of what was then a fortress in an active campaign field, to find himself still stuck there two years later, the campaigns having long since moved on. Nineteen years old, with no theological training, supposed to manage a former prince-bishopric in which there were twenty-eight parishes staffed by Catholic priests, eighteen staffed by Lutheran pastors, eight dually staffed with the two congregations using the church building at different times of day, and a currently non-functional Jesuit college that had, under Wartenburg, usurped the *Gymnasium Carolinum*, supposedly founded under Charlemagne and holding the proud distinction of being the oldest continuously functioning school in the Germanies. Until …

Besides which, there were two other competing Latin Schools, the *Domschule*, under cathedral sponsorship, and the *Ratsschule*, sponsored by the city council. There had been a tendency for centuries for bishops to try to close the municipal school and the council to try to close the cathedral school. Not that there was a clear confessional distinction. At one point in the previous century, not only had Lutheran students been admitted to the cathedral school, but its rector had been Lutheran as well. *Damenstifte* that were maybe Catholic again. This indolent biconfessionalism had actually functioned reasonably well until a dozen years earlier, when the new suffragan bishop had started to get energetic about Tridentine reforms.

Frederik shook his head. He wasn't supposed to be considering schools right now. He was supposed to be considering complaints about Gustafsson.

Gustafsson was supposed to be considering the logistics of it all. Not pestering the daughter of an important supporter of one of the rival mayors. Rival mayors being a separate issue: one had in a staunchly Lutheran way gone into exile rather then submit to the demands of Wartenburg; the second had in a staunchly Lutheran way stayed in the city to resist the demands of Wartenburg; the third had in a staunchly Catholic way stayed in the city and enthusiastically supported Wartenburg . Each, along with his partisans, considered that his way had been the only proper way to handle the situation during the era of the Edict of Restitution.

He'd have to do something. He'd … send Christian Ulrik to deal with it.

"Say something like, 'my mother was the daughter of the mayor of Copenhagen. Let me tell you something, buddy. It's not a good idea for a nobleman to mess with a girl of good *bourgeois* family unless she and her family are willing for her to be messed with.' "

✳ ✳ ✳

Gustafsson was dazzlingly good-looking.

Of course, Christian Ulrik thought, all the gossip maintained that his mother, a woman of Dutch merchant extraction named Margriet Slöts or Cabiljau, had been extraordinarily beautiful.

Then again, powerful men did tend to choose mistresses who were extraordinarily beautiful. Wives, not so much, with the result that Princess Kristina looked like she did. Or, for that matter, in his own family, there was no doubt that his father's gaggle of children by Kirsten Munk were far better looking than the three legitimate royal spawn.

He himself, bastard again, had some margin over those three in the looks department, by any impartial judgment rendered.

He looked at the boy again. *Handsome is as handsome does.*

Young Gustav had been fostered by Karl Karlsson Gyllenhielm, baron of Bergkvara, High Admiral of Sweden, his equally bastard paternal half-uncle. Off to the University of Wittenberg at age 14 for an almost purely ceremonial tour, during which he had been tutored privately and served a term as honorary rector. Then into the army, commissioned as colonel of a Livonian cavalry regiment, and then dropped into this spot as commandant of Osnabrück.

The boy was lively; according to those who knew him, honest and fearless; also mouthy and fearfully short-tempered.

And conceited. Which brought an observer back to *dazzlingly good-looking.*

Tell papa all about it.

The girl was named Margaretha. Seventeen to the boy's nineteen.

Indignant denial that he was pressuring her. "She likes me."

Well, yes, he had sneaked into her bedroom at night.

All right, yeah, he'd had sex with her.

And then he'd brought her out to Iburg, where she had stayed for a week.

"Iburg's pretty nice," he remarked inconsequentially, "now that I've gotten the damage from the last time someone occupied and plundered it fixed up. The rooms in a couple of the newer wings are even nicer. I don't see why she wouldn't want to live here. It's way too comfortable for some Catholic bishop like Wartenburg. I'm pretty sure they're supposed to wear sandals in the snow and flog themselves, aren't they?"

Christian Ulrik answered that those were hermits or ascetics or something, not bishops; then he managed to get Gustafsson back on track.

No, he had not "dishonored her and sent her home in shame." If it was up to him, she would still be at Iburg. Her father had insisted that he send her back home, threatening legal action if he didn't comply. Had actually served him with a warrant.

The week that Christian Ulrik had planned to stay in Osnabrück dragged out into two.

✻ ✻ ✻

Bente was afflicted with the temperamental miasma that often came upon expectant mothers. An up-timer would have said *pregnancy hormones*. Her future brother-in-law, who had never heard of hormones, resorted to the theory of imbalance of the four humors.

As the time dragged, she concluded that Frederik had sent her beloved away on a pretext in order to separate the two of them. Just as his father had wanted to have her exiled to Norway. This was accompanied by floods of hysterical tears that could not be stemmed by the ministrations of either Vendt's wife or mother.

Thinking, *that can't be good for the baby*, Frederik retreated to his office. Where he remained, dreading any more hassles that might result from having to deal with Lutheran ladies of various types.

He tried to calm himself with paperwork. He wasn't sure about much of what had come to the Germanies from up-time, but these boxes with their neat In, Respond Now, Respond Later, File with No Response, Trash, and Out labels were of considerable utility. Of course, the ones he had seen in Magdeburg had only been labeled In and Out, which was quite inadequate, but adding other categories had not been a challenge.

Lutheran ladies. Including the inevitable, eventual, wife he would someday take to his bosom. His mother had died when he was four; he had largely grown up under the supervision of male tutors, attended all-male schools, had little to do with his flock of younger half-sisters, and generally found himself at a loss when confronted with the female of the species. Which was, his father had trained him to think, generally predatory and out to sink claws into a promising young royal scion if he was not careful.

* * *

Meanwhile, in Osnabrück, Christian Ulrik was counseling that putting pressure on Margaretha's father would lead to lasting hostility and a lot of bad feeling. "Why don't you find a girl whose father is more agreeable? They're out there by the bushel, I guarantee you. Men who realize that a youthful affair with a man of high rank is a stroke of good luck for a girl, usually leading to a generous financial settlement, and concentrate on making sure that the contracts are as foolproof as possible. That's sure how my grandfather saw it; it was a stroke of bad luck for him that my mother died so young and the trust funds settled on me came along with a set of conscientious trustees who wouldn't let him waste my money."

Gustafsson protested that not only did he like Margaretha; she also liked him.

That was not unlikely. She was seventeen and he was dazzlingly good-looking.

Christian Ulrik handed over a letter from the governor that could be summarized as, "Thou shalt not seduce the daughter of a wealthy supporter of one of the mayors unless *both* the father and the daughter are willing and see advantages to it."

Gustaffson kicked a hassock, impatiently. "I've *already* seduced her. It's not the kind of thing that you can take back."

""Do you have a chaplain?"

"Dreary old stick!"

* * *

Unruly Osnabrücker somewhat soothed, Christian Ulrik returned to Münster, three weeks later than expected. He arrived back wet, half-frozen, and determined to marry Bente right now if not sooner.

Frederik's promised chaplain was, presumably, still on his way from Strassburg. At least, he had not yet shown up in Münster, which was no surprise considering the weather. The governor drafted a Lutheran pastor who had come into the city a couple of weeks earlier, traveling with a party of merchants which was, in turn, still stuck at the inn because of the same weather.

That, of course, caused a variety of jurisdictional questions to arise, all of which the lawyers from Rinteln pounced upon with glee. The ordination of the traveling cleric was not in question, as he was well known to his companions, but he had no call to a parish in the city. Nor was Lutheranism yet so well organized in the *Oberstift* that there was any Lutheran superintendent or consistory. It had been less than a year since Archbishop Ferdinand of Bavaria's vicar general had been energetically prohibiting Lutherans from living in the town at all.

Frederik swiped his hand through his unruly hair. Lutheranism wasn't organized at all, yet, anywhere in the *Oberstift*. Or *Niederstift*. Could he as governor appoint himself as *summus episcopus*, recruit a cadre of duly ordained clergymen, and set it on its way, more or less as he was managing his spiritual obligations in Bremen and Verden?

He made a note to ask the lawyers.

For the time being, the traveling pastor could make the entry in the church register of his own parish when he got back home.

The German pastor, who spoke no Danish, raised an eyebrow. "Bente?" he asked. "Is that a name?"

"It would be 'Benedicta' if the register were written in Latin," the bridegroom said.

The pastor recorded it as *Benedicta*. The groom's surname as *Guldenlöwe*. The permanent residence of both as the imperial city of Hamburg, since that was where they told him that Bente's father was currently residing. Christian Ulrik said that his mother was deceased, so his father went into the register as *Wittwer*—a widower. A father named Christian Guldenlöwe, residence Glückstadt.

When the weather broke, he returned to a small town near Freiburg im Breisgau, where, since the couple were not his parishioners, he copied the information into the few pages at the back of the parish ledger that he reserved for the baptisms, marriages, and funerals of "vagabonds." Nobody was ever able to locate a copy of the official marriage record on the various occasions that it was called for during the ensuing half-century.

Christian Guldenlöwe of Glückstadt, otherwise known as Christian IV, king of Denmark, was not pleased by the marriage and expressed that to Frederik in forceful terms. However, he was less displeased than he would have been if Christian Ulrik had carried out his threat become an officer for the Spaniard in the Low Countries.

On balance, Frederik thought, it was not a bad outcome.

Christian Ulrik took stock of the "couldn't locate any other pastor" situation and promptly arranged the installation of a primitive but usable radio connection for Frederik with the other major locations within the province, all the time thinking rather ruefully that when it came to technology, someone was going to have to haul his otherwise fairly admirable older half-brother, kicking, screaming, and dragging his heels, into the modern world.

CHAPTER 8

March 1635
Grantville

O n the fourth of the month, in the midst of an anti-Semitic riot
taking place in front of the miraculous town's synagogue, a re-
purposed building from the up-time, someone shot a man
named Henry Dreeson, the *Bürgermeister*, and another named
Enoch Wiley, a Calvinist minister. The assassin was presumed to be
one of the anti-Semites.

In Westphalia, Frederik read through the news reports with
considerable annoyance. This was almost guaranteed to make his life
more difficult.

Bremen

In Bremen *Altstadt*, the most widespread of the outrage was focused
on the appalling news that one of the victims was a Calvinist minister.
Among the city's Calvinist ministers, at any rate, but most members of
the old patriciate shared that perspective. The offence was featured in
at least a dozen sermons.

Schorfmann expressed admiration for Buster Beasley. "Like our
Roland, in the market square."

Bemmeler managed to work that into the CoC propaganda pamphlets, along with regular sidebars condemning anti-Semites. Tönnies Breiting moved from family gatherings to evening card games, music recitals to prayer meetings, dropping carefully calculated words into the ears of his prominent relatives.

Breiting's mother went to the bookstore every couple of weeks. She wasn't a great reader, but enjoyed the new romances and usually kept a devotional manual on her bedside stand for the edification of her husband. As *Frau* Breiting browsed the Harlequins, her maid Jutta loitered by the stand of cheap pamphlets, surreptitiously adding a few more radical ones that she pulled out of her pocket to the moderate titles that the store owner had agreed to stock.

As the unrest among the quarreling internal factions in the city of Bremen intensified, Emil Jauch arrived as the governor's emissary plenipotentiary.

Frederik admitted to himself that he had probably assumed emergency powers that he did not have in regard to the Bremen city government by making this appointment. He proposed to ignore that minor issue. If the mayors and council complained, Rist could send back a letter that featured the word "temporary" in several places.

Avoiding the word "expedient."

Knaub and Jauch both sent him reports. They did not bear much resemblance to one another.

Mainz

Gustav Adolf's appointed governor of the Province of the Main, the Swedish general and nobleman Nils Brahe, decided to get his younger sister Christina and her slightly younger-than-that new husband Erik Stenbock out of his hair by giving one of his colleagues a present. He would send them to Westphalia to work for Frederik.

It was not a long trip from Mainz to Münster. "Call me Kerstin." A young woman strode briskly into Frederik's office. "I don't care for the Latinized form of my name."

Frederik managed a practiced smile and produced it at intervals for the remainder of the day until he and his closest advisers finished up the welcoming dinner, Lütkemann said a blessing, and he ceremoniously saw them off to their hastily located and probably inadequate rental quarters. There was very little housing available these days.

After which he dropped the smile and retired thankfully up the stairs.

He had bought a second easel. He now had one in his office and another in his private sitting room.

A dot. Has Brahe sent them to keep an eye on his doings for the Swedes?

Another dot. Or for the USE? Is the emperor irritated because of young Gustafsson? Has the boy complained to his father?

A third dot. It is known that Brahe has become close to the up-timer from the State of Thuringia-Franconia, Colonel Utt. Does their assignment to Westphalia involve the up-timers? The FoJP?

That led to a fourth dot. Have they been sent to monitor the election process in the province?

A process that was in process, so to speak. His staff had put in a lot of work to get things set up throughout the province.

Quedlinburg

Iona Nelson moved around the band room, filing sheet music into the assigned cubbyholes on the wall. When she was feeling a little homesick for at least one aspect of Fluharty Middle School in Grantville over the Christmas break, she had persuaded one of the carpenters who worked for the *Stift* to construct a replica of its box wall.

She had nowhere near as much music as had been in the band room at Grantville, but she had an acquisitions budget. As pieces came off presses in Grantville, presses in Jena, presses in Dresden and Magdeburg, Frankfurt and Hamburg, she ordered what she needed. Then, if there was still money on the black side of the ledger, what she wanted.

She fingered two pieces of paper, stuck together. Probably a student who came in with a bit of jam from breakfast still on her fingers! There were some ways in which down-time students weren't noticeably different from up-time students.

The music sheets didn't separate as a result of the fingering. She walked over to her table and dropped them. Rather than risk tearing the paper, she'd bring back a damp cloth after lunch and carefully coax them apart. She finished filing the rest of the pile, looking over her shoulder toward the bottle-glass windows as the room suddenly darkened. The early morning had been nice, but if clouds were coming in, it would probably be raining again before she could go out for her evening walk.

On her way to lunch, she stopped half way down the second corridor to check the weather. The band room was in an older section of the building; this part had larger, modern, glass panes.

Lunch was *Salat*. Fresh vegetables drenched in a hot, vinegary, heavily herbed, sauce. She suspected that the other main ingredient of the sauce, besides vinegar, was melted bacon fat. It was not, for certain, olive oil. But such a treat after mid-winter's endless salted meat, salted fish, and pickles. Counting sauerkraut as a form of pickle, which in fact it was. She waited politely while the few other teachers who were not simultaneously *Stiftdamen* finished their meal in the small dining room assigned to them. The senior teacher started the common table prayer. She stood up, placed her napkin neatly at her place, asked the work-study girl (one of the innovations introduced by the abbess) who was waiting on them for a damp rag, and walked back.

Even if it rained this evening, she probably got in her mile-a-day transversing the halls of the building.

The sheet of paper stuck to the back of Elgar's "Pomp and Circumstance" wasn't another sheet of music. It was a sample Fourth of July Party ballot for Magdeburg Province.

Not one girl in band was old enough to vote.

She hardly knew what to do about voting. She wasn't a citizen of Quedlinburg, certainly, the way down-timers defined citizenship in a locality. She was a citizen of the USE, with the right to vote, but not of Brunswick and not of Quedlinburg.

She'd have to ask the abbess, once she got back from Magdeburg, where she was being political again.

She certainly was not going to ask that stuck-up prioress!

She folded the ballot and absentmindedly stuck it in her pocket. Ballots, Veleda Riddle, and the League of Women Voters. Some of the women standing right there when someone shot and killed poor Henry Dreeson and Enoch Wiley last months were her own good friends.

Poor Veronica. Poor little Annalise; the child's life had been filled with losses. Although the girl was not a child any more; she must be graduating from high school this spring.

It might be best to request an absentee ballot from Grantville. There was time.

She had her own stamps. Almost everyone else put their letters in a pile and the *Stift* franked them, but she wasn't about to ask so much as postage from that stuck-up prioress!

Who the next morning circulated an indignant memo that some intruding vandal had left FoJP sample ballots scattered in rooms throughout the building.

Magdeburg

Ben Leek looked at his granddaughter Bethany, who had just proclaimed her admiration for Buster Beasley. He hadn't expected her to start picking up liberal ideas, much less radical ones, when they decided to send her to high school at the DESSSFG (Duchess Elisabeth Sophie Secondary School for Girls, if you wanted to be technical), given that it was sponsored by the duke of Saxe-Altenburg, whose economic views were generally sound.

"Well I certainly don't approve of anti-Semitism. What do you think of me, Bethany, girl? But if those CoC people start rampaging around, initiating riots, I say that the emperor should step in with the army. If you ask me, 'when the looting starts, the shooting starts.' That's as good a remedy for urban unrest as I've ever heard."

"Grandpa," Bethany said. "They'll shoot back."

Bethany's mother, dedicated to organizing support and raising funds for the new Magdeburg Memorial Hospital sponsored by the Leek family in memory of little Jennifer Rush, who had died three years earlier of a childhood leukemia that was untreatable down-time, heaved a sigh and sent up a silent prayer of thanks that her daughter would go off to Quedlinburg in the fall and no longer be a daily irritant to her father-in-law.

Bremen

Tönnies Breiting pointed out that the FoJP was certain to win a majority of the vote in the city as a whole—not in the *Altstadt*, but when a person included the *Alte Neustadt*. Bremen was in the process of counting the vote more efficiently than most of the USE. Things had been lopsided for the FoJP in the *Alte Neustadt*. There were a lot of Bremen's patricians who now regretted the annexation. As things turned out, it would not enable them to exercise more control over the unruly inhabitants across the Weser.

"Close doesn't count," Peter Schorfmann countered. "Bremen is one district in Westphalia. Overall, it's pretty sure the province will vote majority Crown Loyalist."

"Minden will elect one of our men," Breiting protested.

"But a lot of the Crown Loyalists absolutely swear that as soon as Wettin takes office as prime minister, he's going to roll back this reform or that reform. If the expected transfer of power in June goes smoothly, then ... " Gerrit Bemmeler had turned into a planner; the closest thing to a strategist that the movement had in Bremen.

Knaub, nervous, had a long conversation with Jauch. Jauch, less nervous, had numerous conversations with the four *Bürgermeister* in regard to the changes in Bremen's city government that were likely to be adopted. The new city charter proposed by the reformers would pass, almost certainly. Narrowly, but it would pass, just as the annexation of the *Alte Neustadt* had passed in the local election.

Which meant that there would be city-wide special election in three months, as soon as the expected transfer of power at the national level was completed. The existing *Bürgermeister* and members of the *Rath* were going to have to run for office and contest for the popular vote.

Some of them against ... women!

For the Bremen patricians, there was little joy in Mudville, Agnes Bemmeler said. She had developed a strong interest in up-time popular culture.

And was going to run for the *Senat*.

Münster

On the last day of the month, the mail delivery from von Bargen in Bremervörde included a long letter—another long letter, be it said—from Gerdruth von Campe about the woes afflicting *Himmelpforten* and her general lack of success in retrieving those property items that had disappeared with Matthias Kalkhoven.

She was pondering the institution of a lawsuit, with the prince-archbishop's permission. The cathedral canons were proving reluctant to cooperate with her and Provost Marschalck was worse than useless in the matter, although it was his obligation …

Frau von Campe was a Lutheran lady. So was Christian Ulrik's Bente. So was Kirsten Brahe who might or might not be here as her brother's extra pair of eyes. So, for that matter was Gustafsson's nubile Margaretha. Even Kirsten Munk, with the near-demonic beauty that had caused his father to decide that he absolutely had to have her, even at the price of a morganatic marriage, with all the grief that followed, was a Lutheran lady.

Frederik took a deep breath.

Lutheran ladies were quite sufficient. He was profoundly glad that Catholic ladies were not in any way his problem.

CHAPTER 9

Münster
1 April 1635

There were advantages to the radio system, Frederik admitted to Christian Ulrik. On the same day that the vomit-splattered body was found beneath an open window, he received the news of the death of Duke Ferdinand of Bavaria, the pluralist archbishop of Cologne who also held the see of Münster.

For the time being, the old man's suffragan bishop would continue to do what vicars general did—within the parameters that his authority was now limited to Roman Catholic ecclesiastical matters. He had not stopped being a fanatical representative of what Frederik, in his own mind, classified as the most extreme measures of the Counter-Reformation; neither had Petrus Nicolartius, S.J., in Cologne, ceased to urge him on.

The parameters didn't mean that the vicar general stopped trying to interfere in the civil administration of the *Hochstift*, but they meant that Frederik could just say "no"

As for a likely successor … it would probably be some time before the canons and the pope could agree upon one.

He wrote a note for Rist to get in touch with Gisenius up in Bremervörde and tell him to recruit as many Lutheran clergy as possible for the *Hochstift*. He would deal later with the Calvinist nobility who were convinced that they had a perfect right to determine the religion of the residents of their own estates. While the cat was away, the Lutheran mice might as well have a high old time of it. Postscript: and someone who has experience in organizing consistories and superintendencies, because I don't have time to do it myself.

Frederik diagrammed various considerations of what the current tumult in the Catholic church might mean for Westphalia.

Factoring in that he would have to go to Magdeburg for some space of time; he was a voting member of the USE House of Lords.

Then news came in from Italy. No longer was it simply that the cathedral chapter and *the* pope would have to agree on a successor to Ferdinand of Bavaria. Now it would be the canons and *a* pope (any pope). Yes, it would probably be *quite* some time before a successor would be elected and installed over at Cologne. As for Münster, which the old archbishop had held in pluralism, it might be even longer.

He produced another set of diagrams illustrating the various considerations of what this might mean for the province of Westphalia. Locally, in regard to the Catholics in the city. More generally with the Catholics all through the former *Hochstift*, both *Ober* and *Nieder*.

Opportunities, opportunities. Possibly opportunities to frustrate the ambitions of that other Bavarian, Franz Wilhelm von Wartenburg.

Eckbert Bordemann, pot boy, aged ten, was an extraordinarily clever child. Notably more so than Jacob Stover, pot boy, also aged ten. That the cleverness most often expressed itself in mischief did not particularly distress Chaplain Lütkemann, as that was only to be expected when a man was dealing with boys. That Bordemann had a tendency to blame his exploits on Stover most likely fell under the immortal biblical question, "am I my brother's keeper?" and should be, within the limits of human possibility, corrected.

In any case, young Eckbert was about to complete the fourth year of required schooling. The cleverness should not be allowed to go to waste; it was clearly time to furnish him with a scholarship and enroll him in the Latin School.

Vendt, the footman, stood stiffly to attention when the chaplain brought this up. "It will be difficult."

"Difficult?"

"His family are among the serfs residing in the clerical immunities pertaining to the cathedral. The municipal *Polizeiordnung* prohibits such persons from taking up civic trades or entering the learned professions unless they are legally freed and sworn in as burghers. Which does happen, but not often. One might even say, rarely."

A few searching questions elicited the information that all of the servants attached to the household were serfs, Vendt and his family included. "*Stadtluft*," the free air of a chartered city that made a serf into a freeman after a year's residence, did not extend, in spite of the absence of any physical barriers, to the lands inside the city wall that belonged to the bishop and cathedral chapter. Legally, the immunities had different air.

That was why serfs brought into the city as servants were required to live in the immunities.

What would it take to free young Eckbert? Obtain his manumission?

Money, of course. Unless, for some reason, the lord to whom he was bound was feeling magnanimous. Which did happen, but not often. One might even say, rarely.

Lütkemann brought the issue before the governor.

Frederik shunted it over to the lawyers, who tracked the issues. Eckbert's parents were not bondsmen (*Wachszinsige*) of the cathedral chapter, although they lived within its precincts. Rather, they were bound to *Damenstift* Börstel, located on the northern edge of Osnabrück's diocesan territory, in the tradition of its medieval Cistercian founders, out in the middle of nowhere or as close to nowhere as was possible given the comparatively dense population of the region.

Cistercian—like *Himmelpforten.*

Frederik winced. The most recent communication received from the redoubtable Gerdruth von Campe …

Now there were even more Lutheran ladies to be dealt with.

Börstel's transformation from a convent into an institution of Lutheran secular canonesses had come gently, the lawyers assured him, almost a century ago, resulting in a peculiar combination of Lutheran doctrine, as expounded by the preachers it employed to deliver sermons three days per week, with maintenance of an abbreviated form of the traditional liturgical … …hours of medieval Catholicism, reduced to three rather than seven times per day. During the past fifteen years, unfortunately, it had been plundered repeatedly, suffered from quartering of troops by both contenders that exhausted its resources, and most recently the same unit of the Swedish army that had dropped young Gustafsson into the diocese of Osnabrück as commandant had…

To make a long story short, Börstel was flat broke. The abbess (one Gertrudt von Althauß), the prioress (one Elisabeth Kirstapell), and the cellarer (one Lucretia Wolbergh von Hären), speaking on behalf of the dozen or so surviving canonesses, averred that they would be willing to manumit any of the *Stift*'s serfs who might be living in Münster in return for a reasonable remuneration. As a token of good faith, they enclosed a copy of a manumission brief they had issued two years earlier for one of the maidservants in the city.

Not only would they be content (actually, they would be ecstatic, and would accept any offer someone made on the general principle that anything was better than nothing, but their attorney advised them not to say so) to free all others on the same terms, but were anxious to do so.

It wasn't any particular surprise that they were so willing. By definition, bound serfs living away in the city were bound serfs that were not needed on the farms or in the buildings of the abbey. The flat broke abbey.

Frederik advised his accountant to find the money to free the boy's family.

Chaplain Lütkemann cleared his throat and emitted the words "scholarship" and "tuition."

Frederik advised his accountant to find more money.

Vendt, standing stiffly, cast around in his mind for any child in his extended family who might be bright enough to catch the chaplain's eye. If Eckbert was going to Latin School next term, the gubernatorial household would need a new pot boy.

Not that the Vendts were bound to Börstel. He had no idea whether or not their own lord would be willing to manumit them, or on what terms.

And young Jacob Stover, not sufficiently bright, seemed destined to remain a serf.

*　*　*

Bente gave birth to a little girl. It all went easily and the child was healthy. Frederik stood godfather and chose to name her Ulrikke.

Virginia DeMarce

CHAPTER 10

June 1635
Magdeburg

The Crown Loyalists conducted a raucous celebration of Wilhelm Wettin's electoral victory. Make that most of the Crown Loyalists. Some of the more prudent, such as the landgrave of Hesse-Kassel and his wife, withdrew from the dancing and feasting and left town.

Frederik of Denmark had not even made it to town in the first place. He had sent a perfectly polite letter saying that something had come up, but he would try to make the parliamentary sessions later, once his vote was needed.

Everybody who knew Frederik was aware that he did not enjoy parties. Few people in Magdeburg knew him at all.

Gunther Achterhof and Gretchen Richter addressed the CoCs. Using the excuse that the assassination of Dreeson and Wiley had been done by anti-Semites, Mike Stearns and Francisco Nasi were orchestrating, with cold calculation, what they intended to be an irreversible and permanent change in the outlook of the Germanies. By removing the major obstacles to that change. *Krystalnacht* began.

Münster

Frederik stood at his easel, mulling his options.

Martin Luther's prescription for human behavior was that everything should be done decently and in order. That was clearly the preferable option. It was not always an attainable one.

Glückstadt should be safe enough from Stearns' radicals. A modern foundation, it was in royal Holstein. Even if Holstein was in the USE now, most of the people in the duchy who would be termed "reactionaries" by Stearns and his ilk knew that Schleswig was to their north and Denmark to the north of Schleswig. Where there was a king who was still the holder of these specific lands, his *Statthalter* administering them from Segeberg; a king who was also the father of the provincial governor. Serious written gubernatorial admonitions to behave themselves ought to suffice. There was no reason to assume that Glückstadt would be a major CoC target.

Or anything else in Holstein. Unless… he hadn't been to the duchy since he was appointed to office; not since the War of the League of Ostend.

It wasn't all royal, or even mostly under direct Danish jurisdiction; nothing like Schleswig. There was the Gottorp portion. Which was not a consolidated place on the map. Holstein-Gottorp had four major sections, three separate ones in northern Holstein, one on the west coast, one in the middle, and one on the east coast. With a fourth in the far southeast, toward Mecklenburg. Plus some scattered exclaves. Not to mention the parts that were jointly

administered by Gottorp and by Denmark.

If the nobility there or the patricians in Kiel did anything to draw CoC attention because they thought he himself was indifferent to what they were doing or might do … But admonitions would have to suffice for the time being. Some other day. He hoped that the CoCs of Magdeburg Province and Lübeck would have more immediate concerns in Mecklenburg.

As for Altona, the circumstances surrounding Count Ernest of Schaumburg-Holstein-Pinneberg's granting the first permanent residence permits to Ashkenazic Jews in 1611 made it unlikely that it contained any significant number of anti-Semites. When a ruling count invited court Jews into an old city—yes, there was often resentment about the competition in the field of finance. Altona had been a fishing village before its shrewd ruler realized that he could make more money by building it up. A Jewish community in what amounted to a new town might cause resentment, but those who resented it usually lived somewhere else.

In this instance, in Hamburg, where that FoJP nuisance Albert Bugenhagen was now mayor. He and his CoC cohorts would have to deal with consequences of having anti-Semites in their own playground. For Altona, an alert ought to be sufficient, with a warning to the surrounding area.

Bremen

"The instructions from Achterhof and Richter forbid us from touching ordinary reactionaries," Peter Schorfmann complained. "That doesn't leave us with much scope."

They were at Breiting's parents' comfortable house in the *Altstadt*. Breiting was much better placed to cover the expenses of their meetings than anyone else in the movement. He spoke up: "I'm sure there are some anti-Semites in the city. They're everywhere. But given that there haven't been any Jews here for three hundred years or so, they haven't had anything much to chew on."

Gerrit Bemmeler laughed. "Yeah. And a pope said that there were witches in Bremen, but that was a couple of hundred years ago. Before the Reformation. And he was probably talking about the *Erzstift*, not the city. Even then, the edict that old Prince-archbishop Johann Friedrich published—that has to be more than thirty years ago, now—

101

made it practically impossible to have a witchcraft trial. The evidentiary standards that he established as a prerequisite, proving actual harm and damages, were so high that a prosecutor could hardly hope get an indictment, much less a conviction. If there's still anyone around here who persecuted a witch, he has to be doddering toward his grave."

"So how do we handle it locally?" Bemmeler's sister Agnes asked.

She had become a fan of up-time drama. At this critical juncture, the Bremen revolutionaries were in danger of becoming rebels without a cause.

"There might have been a couple of witchcraft trials over in Verden," Breiting suggested hopefully. "I think."

Tönnies' sister Jisca motioned to the maid to bring in more beer.

"I am," she said, "so sick and tired of listening to you guys argue politics. I'm going over to Marieke's." Her mother's maid, Jutta, was too busy to accompany her through the streets; she made do with their chambermaid Trinke as a chaperone.

Alverius Knaub, who was incidentally to other things Marieke's father, listened to his older daughter and her friends chatter. Then he sent a report to Frederik, predicting that chaos and uncontrolled rioting in the streets were imminent.

Emil Jauch conducted his observations in a more systematic manner. After several conversations with the ex-mayors and ex-councilmen, after multiple meetings with the younger and more agitated of Bremen's patricians who had once had a reasonably entitled hope of ascending to mayoral and conciliar positions themselves if they did everything right, but now realized that they were almost certainly in a permanent minority in a city with a new FoJP majority; after consultations with the current FoJP municipal officers; following a few quiet evening consultations with both groups, lubricated by good food and better beer, he also sent a report to Frederik. Predicting that Bremen's reactionaries would remain quiescent unless something unexpected stirred them up.

Quedlinburg

"In the lands of *Damenstift* Quedlinburg," the abbess said in a measured tone of voice, "there have been witchcraft persecutions. In 1589, one hundred and thirty-three persons were executed on a single day. Nor was that the first occasion when witches were executed under the authority of my predecessors. As for Brunswick itself, both the core duchy and the newly incorporated jurisdictions, … I can only hope and pray that Duke Georg acts promptly."

"That was a half-century ago. Or more," the prioress protested.

"None of us are innocent."

Münster

Eric Stenbock introduced the up-time concept of Murphy's law into the conversation over dinner: whatever can go wrong, will.

"I prefer to think of it another way," Frederik responded. "Whatever contingency one provides for, what actually happens will be something that you didn't provide for."

"God warns of this, however," the chaplain Lütkemann interjected, "to prevent us from becoming arrogant and unduly prideful, that we may avoid the fault that the ancient Greeks called ὕβρις, if only we listen to His word. Or, as the Dutch devotional writer Thomas à Kempis put it, *homo proponit, sed Deus disponit.* Derived from Proverbs 16:9, I should think. Or possibly Proverbs 19:21."

"There is still nothing wrong with a man's providing for as many contingencies as possible," Frederik commented to Christian Ulrik after the dinner broke up.

The next morning, he called in his advisors. "Where are the greatest difficulties going to appear in Westphalia?" Frederik chewed on his lips.

It wasn't as if he was unfamiliar with witchcraft persecutions. They were endemic in Denmark, enthusiastically endorsed by its Lutheran bishops. In Denmark, saying Catholic prayers was categorized as an act of witchcraft by some of the clergy.

"In *Hochstift* Verden, the pastor at Wiedensahl, Heinrich Rimphoff, is a known fanatic and has been gathering supporters in recent years," Lütkemann said. "At Loccum Abbey, he's been a leader in the persecutions for close to ten years; there have been several executions. He's likely to put himself forth as a candidate for one of the cathedral canonries, but I have no way to predict what the upper bounds of his ambition may be."

Franz Gießenbier, the Rinteln lawyer whom Frederik had appointed as the province's chancellor, nodded. "I had Eichrodt"—that was Johann Eichrodt, another of the Rinteln law faculty now attached to the governor's office—"prepare an overview with documentation. You *are* directly responsible there, as bishop and not merely as governor. If you aren't seen as reining Rimphoff in ... "

"Find somebody who works fast. Get the *Cautio Criminalis* translated into German, get the manuscript to a printer, and flood the whole province with copies." Frederik slapped the table.

"The Lutheran clergy of Verden, or anywhere else, are not likely to be favorably influenced by a book written by a Jesuit," Lütkemann suggested.

Frederik stood up impatiently. "Then attribute the authorship to someone else. A Lutheran someone else."

"Copyright," one of the lawyers said hesitantly.

Frederik was not given to cursing. He normally avoided, as a matter of principle, not only blasphemy, but also obscenity and scatology. However ...

"Copyright be damned."

The meeting proceeded at a rapid pace.

"The county of Lippe and town of Lemgo are particularly problematic."

"Münster and Osnabrück, the *Stifte*, have had comparatively few witchcraft prosecutions. The town of Osnabrück, however ... "

"What shall we do over there?"

Frederik brought his hands together. "Tell young Gustafsson over there to get up off his nineteen-year-old duff and do something for a change; call on the exalted name of his father the emperor to keep the nobles and patricians quiet. Put leashes on the mayor and the council. Toss them into their own dungeons if that's what it takes to keep them from interfering with the CoC activities in the town as long as they stick to their targets. I'm informed that they have lists. Whether the lists include villages that burned two witches twenty years ago, I have no idea. I have no idea where the lists came from. Gustafsson's living in luxury on the revenues of the *Hochstift*, thanks to our gracious overlords the Swedes. Tell him to earn his keep."

"The situation is similar in Minden. Few prosecutions in the episcopal lands, but within the jurisdiction of the city council ... "

"So most of the problems will be urban."

"So are most of the CoCs," Lieutenant Meyer noted.

"Whom I am inclined to allow to march on Wiedensahl and *Kloster* Loccum without interference. Let them bear the onus of what is going to be done about Rimphoff."

"As Jesus said to Peter, as recorded by Matthew," Lütkemann chided gently the next time the governor came to confession, 'thou savourest not the things that be of God, but those that be of men.' Every fatality that will come out of this campaign, the death of even the most reprehensible man as well as casualties among innocent bystanders, will still be the killing of one of God's children."

"True," Frederik answered. "And in the same passage He asked, 'what shall a man give in exchange for his soul?' I doubt that any man knows until he has made the exchange."

Bremen

A CoC column pulled out of Bremen, headed for action in Verden. It met no government opposition on its path to Loccum, somewhat to the surprise of its leaders.

"If Master Tönnies gets himself killed," Trinke remarked to Jutta as she watched them go, "*Frau* Breiting is going to be unhappy. He's their only son."

"I hope they have sense enough to keep him on the sidelines," was the answer. "He's headed for law school, not a military career."

Bremervörde

Captain von Bargen threw down the transcribed radio notice that the *Tech* (what was a "Tech," he asked himself) had delivered, paced as far as the dimensions of his office in the episcopal chancery building would let him, opened the door with a jerk, slammed it behind him, and went out to pace the walkways of the formal garden. The flower beds were at their peak of bloom.

The Province of Westphalia wasn't only a job, for him. Not merely another army assignment. He had volunteered to serve the new governor, coming out of the Congress of Copenhagen. He was a son of *Niedersachsen*. He had a mother near Bremen; aunts, uncles, and cousins scattered from here to Stade. A brother with four cute children of his own who had married a girl from Kronenborg and settled there, near Himmelpforten. The Province of Westphalia was home.

He had an old schoolmate in Minden.

"I am very much afraid," Dietrich Blomberger wrote, "that based on newspaper reports about the occurrences in Mecklenburg, the known anti-Semites here, assuming that a cataclysmic armageddon and calamitous apocalypse will descend upon them even if they do nothing at all right now, in which they are probably correct, may decide that, instead of merely continue to rail impotently against the Jews in general, they might as well destroy the specific Jewish community in Minden before they are killed themselves by invading CoC columns."

It had taken von Bargen several minutes to wade through his friend's page-long single paragraph with its cluster of dependent clauses and subjunctive verbs. One thing he admired about the up-timers he encountered was how short, in general, their sentences were.

He rounded the end of a planting of pink tulips, which were past their peak, and stomped down the tree-lined *allée*, past the lilies, toward the terrace. Mounting the steps, he leaned against the balustrade, looking out over the symmetry of the whole.

There wouldn't be many indigenous members of the CoC in Minden at present; certainly fewer than there were members of the city militia. There weren't a lot to start with and most of those, according to the best intelligence he had received, with which Dietrich incidentally agreed, were off fighting in either the outright civil war in Mecklenburg or the quasi-civil war in the Province of the Main.

He descended the steps, heading back toward the entrance to the chancery building.

The governor was preoccupied.

There were occasions when it was easier to beg forgiveness than obtain permission.

He would take unilateral action.

He changed direction, hurrying toward the small barracks where his half-company was housed.

Minden

Minden's reactionaries had been displeased when a Fourth of July Party candidate won the city's seat in parliament.

They were going to have to turn the city government over to the usurpers too, now that the election results were certified. For today, they still controlled the militia.

There wasn't much overlap between the anti-Semites and the witchcraft persecutors in Minden. Hardly any, to tell the truth. The anti-Semites tended to be artisan class, egged on by members of the parish clergy. The city fathers were more preoccupied with burning witches than persecuting Jews, who were occasionally useful when it came to banking and lines of credit.

But the CoC campaign would be directed against both groups. And, as Pascal Wenke, the brickmaker, said persuasively, it was much easier to identify a Jew than a witch; identifying a witch involved prolonged legal procedures before a trial and conviction got to the burning at the stake stage. Witchcraft persecutions necessarily involved jurists, learned opinions filed by law faculties, formal trials. So they should all cooperate. At the minimum, the council should not have the militia *intervene* if he and his friends moved against the Jewish community.

The reactionaries listened to Wenke's presentation with more respect than they usually gave an ordinary working-class man. He left the meeting.

Some of his hearers thought that he had made his point effectively.

In a way.

"It may not be that easy to identify a witch to satisfactory legal standards," Nikolas Tissen said. "But it is quite easy to identify an up-and-coming member of the USE House of Commons. If we can point their little mob in the direction of Dirk Waßmann, with any luck he will happen to be a collateral casualty in an anti-Semitic riot. Then we should be able to appoint a more acceptable successor in office before the parliament meets."

Tielo Diederichs smiled. "Waßmann is an idealist. It shouldn't be much trouble to have someone tempt him to come out and stand up for those ideals, defending the oppressed in the face of an advancing mob. That should improve the odds that the casualty will be a fatality quite a bit."

"I'll take those odds," Jasper Wippermann said, "and raise you ten."

Oddly, ironically, Hinrich Botterbrodt, the captain of the city militia didn't see it quite that way. He, too, had been a schoolmate of Dietrich Blomberger. When von Bargen and his half-company arrived in Minden, they found a scene in which the Jewish community lay behind some rather effective improvised barricades, a mob mostly armed with *Morgensterne*, those long wooden posts with vicious spiked iron heads on the end, was moving to batter the barricades down, and in the middle the militia was trying to take the new Fourth of July Party member of the House of Commons into protective custody.

The members of the town militia generally had nothing against either expelling Jews or burning witches. However, they disliked working-class riots as a matter of principle. Additionally, most of them had sons in the city school and Waßmann was the school teacher. If the mob killed him, they'd have to go to all the trouble of finding a replacement.

The entire situation was complicated by the presence, a short way down the street, of

the mothers, wives, and daughters of Minden's absent CoC members, loudly if somewhat unmelodiously rendering Gerrit Bemmelman's *Plattdeutsch* translation of Woody Guthrie's "Union Maid," who had also turned out to protect the new parliament member.

Most of the militia put the women into the category of working-class rioters, right along with the anti-Semitic artisans.

Nobody ever knew who fired first. Sorting out the issue of who did what to whom in the four-way battle that broke out in Minden that day wasn't easy.

About twenty minutes into the melee, Captain von Bargen was hit by a bullet fired by a city militiaman who was aiming in the general direction of the anti-Semites. Probably. Probably aiming at the anti-Semites. That the bullet had been fired by a militiaman was unquestionable, because only they had rifles.

While it was hard to sort out the issue of who did what to whom, presenting von Bargen as a hero was easy. The CoC pamphlets made the most of him. A hero, bringing in the troops against the reactionaries, the anti-Semites, the witch-burners.

A hero for what reason was a little murkier, but they glossed that over.

Münster

"I barely got to know him," Frederik said to Rist. "What little I did get to know, I respected. Claus von Bargen. Claus Christian, I believe, was his full name. Prepare a letter of condolence to his mother, for my signature."

He paused. "Who's available to take over his duties as my regent in Bremervörde?"

"No one comes to mind immediately."

CHAPTER 11

July 1635
Magdeburg

Frederik begrudged every hour he spent in Magdeburg for the meeting of parliament. He was not a verbose man; he didn't have much patience with the verbose. He kept his mouth shut.

Charlotte Kienitz, one of the leaders of the Fourth of July Party from the Province of Mecklenburg, asked Ed Piazza where Helene Gundelfinger was. Helene, Ed's vice-president in the State of Thuringia-Franconia.

"She's in town. Just not in this room yet." Ed laughed. "She should be here later. Schools. That means sorting things out with the other ladies of the school committee, mostly the abbess of Quedlinburg, who is here visiting Mary Simpson. Plus, Veronica Richter is also visiting Mary Simpson. With Annalise in tow; she graduated this spring and Ronnie is in the process of dispatching her off to the preferred college. Preferred by Ronnie, in any case; I'm not so sure that Annalise shares her enthusiasm."

Melissa Mailey gave a laugh that was more pained that amused. "I swear, I've never seen anything that generates more wrangling over details than schools do. That's one thing the two worlds on either side of the Ring of Fire have in common."

Charlotte winced. "Last week, we had a woman in town from some 'boondocks place' as you would call it, Ed, off in the north of Westphalia Province; more boondocky than even Mecklenburg can manage. A kind of mini-abbess of Quedlinburg from some kind of mini-*Damenstift*. What was her name? Gerdruth von Campe. If you ever want to meet someone who can talk your head off, look her up."

"I'll pass," Ed said mildly.

Mary Simpson had encountered Gerdruth von Campe, too. As had the abbess. "She had letters of introduction from several of the administrators that Frederik of Denmark has put in place in the former Bremen *Erzstift*."

Helene Gundelfinger laughed. "The famous 'Prince of Westphalia' who has not yet been granted that desired distinction by the emperor."

"She seemed to be interested in the Normal Schools Project," Vanessa Clements said. "I'm the one who drew the lot of talking to her at length. Along with Lisa Dailey. Then we sicced her onto Tiny Washaw to discuss libraries." Vanessa laughed. "She seemed pretty pleased that we ladies are doing it ourselves, without having to have a man to be a provost and run legal interference for us or represent us in public. We may have opened whole new horizons for her. She seemed a little disappointed when I referred her to Heinrich Schlosser and David Elsisheimer at Countess Kate school in Grantville for more details and she realized that they were men."

Livvie Nielsen, Vanessa's amanuensis and general gofer, stuck up her hand. "Does anybody actually know what is going on in Westphalia? I've heard—a rumor mind you, but from a usually reliable source—that Christian IV is also pushing the emperor to make Frederik the hereditary ruler of Westphalia. You know, the way the dukes are in Brunswick and now in Tyrol, and the landgravine … her son, really, but you know what I mean … in Hesse."

That evening Mary Simpson wrote to her son Tom.

It doesn't seem reasonable to me. Well, maybe it's reasonable that Christian IV would want it, but it's unreasonable for anyone to think that Gustav Adolf might grant it. The way he has Ulrik and Kristina positioned, the last thing he would be interested in is undermining their control when Kristina succeeds him by having created a hereditary principality in the USE permanently headed by another branch of the Danish royal house. Not a cadet branch, exactly, since Frederik is older than Ulrik. But it would certainly fall in the category of having an 'overmighty subject.' Considering the struggle to control the nobility that the Vasas have had in Sweden ever since since the emperor's grandfather...

She finished the letter and encrypted it. A simple family encryption that Pete Rush had provided for them. Any intelligence officer in Europe could break the code, but it was enough to thwart the curiosity of the average curious postal clerk.

Tom shared the letter with Rita, who passed the rumor on to Rebecca Abrabanel without including her mother-in-law's cautionary words about its improbability.

Rebecca filed it somewhere in her preoccupied mind.

At the meeting of influential members of the Fourth of July Party, by now, it was assumed, simply taken to be a given. Westphalia, one of the "technically self-governing" provinces that nevertheless did not have an elected head of state, but rather one appointed by Emperor Gustav II Adolf, would always provide a majority vote for the Crown Loyalists. And Frederik of Denmark, the administrator appointed there, was not content to have the emperor's preferred title of "Governor." It had been all over the newspapers for a year. He wanted to be named "Prince of Westphalia." but the emperor had not agreed. So far, at least.

"Gustav Adolf will probably give in eventually, though," a backbencher muttered. "The fucking Danes are pushing for it hard enough, according to everything that a person reads."

"In the view of the moderate Crown Loyalists ... " the abbess of Quedlinburg said. The party of aristocratic ladies, most related to the Wettins or the princes of Anhalt's various subdivisions, was gathered in the parlor of the landgravine-regent of Hesse.

" ... that is to say, more or less, in our opinion ... "

The landgravine nodded.

" ... since with a few exceptions, the outstanding one being the State of Thuringia-Franconia, the important provinces are relatively homogenous in religious terms ... "

The landgravine nodded again, privately reserving the thought that even though Lutheran Hesse-Darmstadt had been assigned to the Province of the Main rather than incorporated with Calvinist Hesse-Kassel to make a new USE province, either way it had created an entity which was religously split, so that assumption of uniformity was a bit of an overstatement on the part of her fellow politicians of a Crown Loyalist bent.

" ... whereas an established church for the entire USE would lead to constant problems, it will be feasible enough, stable enough to require that each individual province settle on an established church. In the emperor's opinion, each of the eleven provinces should ... allowing the State of Thuringia-Franconia to opt for no establishment ... "

Grandma Richter announced to Gretchen that she and Annalise would be on their way; Mary Simpson was accompanying them on the trip to Quedlinburg.

Gretchen frowned. "But school won't be starting for two months."

Her grandmother beamed. "Yes. Delightful. Two months of quiet with not a squalling child to be found ... "

* * *

It had taken her a while to get to this point. A year or so earlier, back in Grantville, she had still been arguing it with Annalise, who had kept bringing up alternatives.

Prague: in Ronnie's view too far away, under *that man* Wallenstein's control, and without dormitories. Roths in Prague or no Roths in Prague.

Then Annalise resorted to Bamberg, which was not so far away and in the bounds not just of the USE but the SoTF. Saint Elisabeth's, the new women's university that Bernadette Adducci *from Grantville* was founding.

Still no dormitories, Ronnie had pointed out, and the tuition no cheaper than Quedlinburg. That it was a Catholic school, however much that might appeal to Annalise, was a matter of indifference to her grandmother, who had through the years been Lutheran, Catholic, Calvinist, and back again as the vagaries and idiosyncrasies of the principle of *cuius regio, eius religio* as interpreted and applied by the various rulers of the Upper Palatinate determined.

Ronnie had stood her ground. "Quedlinburg. If I can find the tuition, of course. It has supervised dormitories. Plus, Mrs. Nelson *from Grantville* is teaching there. You know her perfectly well, Annalise. She used to be at the middle school here."

The money had come from the investments that David Bartley had made on behalf of Jeff, Gretchen, and herself. Investments of which she had not been aware.

After the reality of the money sank in, she had quietly let the abbess know that she would reimburse the *Stift* for its expenditures on Annalise's scholarship and work-study wages. She didn't intend to let the girl know about their financial windfall: it was an item of nearly religious doctrine with her, more than anything contained in a recited creed of whatever denomination, that children appreciated things more if they had to work for them.

There was a proverb, after all: *An indulgent mother makes a slovenly daughter*. The same applied to grandmothers.

Bremen

"The Crown Loyalists have fucking got to be kidding," Peter Schorfmann exclaimed. "The way Westphalia is set up now, their party is a political majority. How have they managed to let it escape their attention that their own membership is split up religiously about on the same lines as the population as a whole. That means it's about forty percent Lutheran, mostly up here in the northwest and over in Holstein, but with scatters everywhere else. About forty percent Catholic, mostly down in the southwest, but more than scatters up here in the *Münster Niederstift*. Fifteen percent Calvinist, scattered everywhere. I suppose they aren't including the Jews and Mennonites and such, who are all pretty much FoJP."

Tönnies Breiting looked up from the memo he was writing. "Even here in Bremen itself, given how many Lutherans have moved in since the end of the Baltic War, and with the expansion of voting rights. Here in the city, it's not close to being uniformly Calvinist any more. Twenty percent of the population, maybe, are Lutheran? Maybe more, and it's only going to get higher since there aren't that many Calvinists out in the rest of the province who have any reason to come and settle in Bremen."

Gerrit Bemmeler agreed. "We're a little island in the middle of a large ocean, and likely to be swamped. What happens if we do get independent free city status, establish a Calvinist/Reformed church, and ten years from now Calvinists are in the minority? That's not unlikely, even in the *Altstadt*. If we—the FoJP, I mean—manage to persuade to emperor to grant us a decent-sized hinterland along with imperial city status and we bring in the *Alte Neustadt* and a chunk of unfortified land on both sides of the river, the Calvinists will become an instant minority."

Peter Schorfmann beamed beatifically. "If that happens, if we gain our vote in the House of Lords *and* control both sides of the river, think. We can choke the economic life out of the 'Prince of Westphalia' and the fucking Crown Loyalists who control his province."

Breiting shook his head. "Along with the economic life of the ordinary people who live there."

"Omelettes and eggs," Schorfmann retorted. "Omelettes and eggs, my boy."

Münster

"The 'important' provinces being 'relatively homogenous' in religious terms." Christina Brahe looked up from the recently arrived information sheet that the Crown Loyalist party was distributing to its adherents and probable adherents. "What are they thinking? Westphalia being counted as not 'important' in their opinion, I suppose. Or else it slipped their minds?" she complained to her husband. She had only been in the province for three months, but was already beginning to feel somewhat protective of it. Or, perhaps, possessive about it.

Magdeburg

"It's utterly ridiculous that the emperor is supposedly thinking about promoting that loser of a Danish prince from West-failure," Benjamin Leek proclaimed. "He's obviously accomplished nothing at all throughout *Krystalnacht*. Except for that one officer who was killed in some minor skirmish, nothing even happened there that rated more than three paragraphs on page four. Which is probably just as well; considering that he didn't even make a showing toward stopping that miniature massacre the CoCs carried out at Loccum, there's no way he could have coped with a major crisis.

"We're having a national crisis right now, right here, and he's already gone back to where he came from."

DESIGNED TO FAIL

Virginia DeMarce

SECTION II

He Who Fights and Runs Away
August-September 1635

CHAPTER 12

Schloß Lichtenburg, Prettin,
Electorate of Saxony
August 1635

The fourth daughter of the late King Frederick II of Denmark and the equally deceased Duchess Sophie of Mecklenburg-Güstrow stood looking out the window, reflecting briefly on Psalm 146. *Verlasset euch nicht auf Fürsten.* "Put not your trust in princes, in mortal men who cannot save you. He takes his last breath, he returns to the earth. On the same day, his plans perish." In the eyes of God, a ruler was as mortal as the poorest peasant.

In the eyes of rebels, also.

The up-timers who had landed so abruptly in this world, so drastically upending its equilibrium, had brought an English-language hymnal with them. She had bought a copy of the reprint, of course. One, written not so far from the "now" in which she was standing at a window, written less than a century from this "now," echoed the psalm:

Trust not in princes; they are but mortal;
Earthborn they are and soon decay.
Vain are their counsels at life's last portal,

When the dark grave engulfs its prey.
Since mortals can no help afford,
Place all your trust in Christ, our Lord.
Alleluia, alleluia!

Of the seven children in her family, she, one sister, and one brother survived to this day; he the current king of Denmark.

Bittersweet. Her childless marriage had lasted for nine years; she had been a widow nearly a quarter of a century.

She had never gotten along well with Christian's brother and successor, Elector John George of Saxony. Had not seen eye to eye with him in regard to her dower lands. Had maintained some limited freedom of action when it came to trade and commerce, ordering the canal dredged to improve transport, even when it competed with his exports; had tried to live as a faithful woman should. Founded churches. Aided the poor and built hospitals for the sick. Provided care for the disabled. Attempted to exemplify how one should display the fruits of faith. Somewhat ironically, elected into the *Tugendliche Gesellschaft* of like-minded Lutheran noblewomen.

"Virtuous" Society. The men of their families had arrogated to themselves the title of *Fruchtbringende Gesellschaft*, "Fruit-bearing" Society.

They'd given her the title *Die Grossthaetige* and the motto *Gott zu ehren.* "Mighty in deeds—To the honor of God."

Mighty in deeds? Because of her position—to some degree. Because of her influential connections—to some extent. Because she was, if not admired by the subjects in her *Witwensitz*, her "widow's seat," at least respected by them—more or less. Well-liked—not so much. She was hard on drunkards and a terror to gamblers whose paychecks went to cards and dice instead of the support of their families.

And when she said "jump," the only acceptable answer was "how high?" There *was* that. So: *well-liked*—not so much.

By a combination of those factors, though, she had managed to keep her territories from being attacked during the course of the war. Not by Leaguists, not by Swedes; not by Catholics, not by Protestants; not by Austrians, Danes, or uncontrolled bands of unemployed mercenaries. They were almost intact; nearly untouched.

Until now.

All in all, she would rather not see anyone die for John George's sins.

John George, who with his wife and youngest son Moritz had been killed by partisans in the Vogtland a few days ago.

She looked out the window again, at her little army drawn up against a different body of the rebel partisans.

Her reasonably well-trained and well-equipped little army, a squadron of mounted dragoons and a company of infantry; men who had served her well as they performed their duties, most of them for many years. Flanked by some of the militia from Prettin and a few from the villages—not many. Most of the men in the militia remained where they lived, to defend their families, friends, and neighbors against the expected plundering and looting.

Drawn up against a pressing crowd of far less well-equipped men. Less orderly men. Angry men.

Out of sight, hidden inside *Schloß* Lichtenburg, her foster-daughters, personal attendants, and domestic servants; some outside workers who could not be expected to defend the castle, elderly gardeners and young stableboys; townspeople and villagers who for some reason had been nearby this morning. Beyond her sight, the remainder of the residents of the *Ämter* of Annaburg, Schweinitz (which included *Schloß* Lichtenburg and the small town of Prettin), Seyda and Schlieben, all the villages within those districts, and all the people of those villages. Not a lot of people, a couple of thousand, but each one a subject to whom she owed the duty of protection. To the best of her ability.

It was a task for which the small army at her disposal would not suffice. It could not turn the partisans away; not drive them out. Not all of them. Those who remained would wreak damage.

She squared her shoulders and went down to negotiate.

Again.

This time with a man with whom she had no connections at all.

When Thomas Kleinitz looked at the liveried soldiers drawn up to oppose his men, he saw them overshadowed by the building behind them. It was large. Expensive. Modern, maybe fifty years old, not a fortress; even the towers had windows. Any architect who put big windows on the ground floor was a victim of idiotic overconfidence in the milk of human kindness.

The old monastery building, one that probably had the kind of towers, turrets, and slits that defenders could use to pour boiling oil down on people like him, had burned down, he'd heard.

The old building had been famous, sort of. Back in 1518, Martin Luther had gone there and met with Georg Spalatin, the private secretary of Elector Frederick the Wise, who had promised to back his rebellious monk. Which was neither here nor there. The electors had turned it into a royal palace after putting an end to monks and nuns; there had been enough battles in Saxony between then and now.

Maybe the boiling oil had caught on fire, which would have served someone right.

Behind him, there were men. Angry men.

Also, outsiders.

You didn't have to live very far away from a particular village for the people there to think you were an outsider. Ten miles would do it; fifteen miles was about a guarantee. Twenty miles? You might as well be from … well … Magdeburg. Or the legendary Grantville of the up-timers.

His men were Saxons, yes, for the most part, but not drawn from the old woman's villages, beyond a couple of dissatisfied wastrels who had been objects of her censoriousness. She'd kept this *Flecken* from being attacked by anyone's army, so far. The villages were ripe for the plucking. The men who lived in them, for the most part, didn't want to be plucked; didn't want their wives, sisters, and daughters plucked; didn't want their shops and farms plucked.

Not even by partisans of Gretchen Richter whose cause was righteous.

They were suspicious that *die Richterin's* righteous cause would draft their sons and brothers, drag them into her foreign campaigns as ruthlessly as any mercenary "recruiter" for Tilly or Holk might have forced them into his regiment.

They were, Andreas Amthor from over in Thuringia, whose brother Nicholas had been shot by the Croats in 1632, who had read more than one CoC pamphlet, told him the day before, "a pernicious nest of little self-satisfied *proto-bourgeois*."

Who were sadly lacking in major grievances. They had plenty of minor ones, everybody did, but …

The old lady hadn't done anything wrong, really, except be who she was: the sister-in-law of Elector John George of Saxony. The duty of the lord to subjects was *Schutz und Schirm*; she had given her subjects protection and defense against outside attacks. They weren't living like wolves on the heath. They didn't want to.

Consorting with the enemy, he supposed, would have to be the charge if she was on trial.

Not to mention that both the up-timers and the CoC were hellishly opposed to such classic activities as plundering and looting, which meant that if the men behind him got out of his control, he would be in deep shit. In a noose on a gallows was not impossible. Put there by enforcers from his own side of this uprising in Saxony.

The old lady's soldiers had rifles. Which were currently pointed at the ground.

His men had muskets, mostly. Which had fucking well better be pointed at the ground, but he didn't dare turn around to look.

He had enough supporters of the uprising with him, half-trained to three-quarters trained, to do a lot of damage to the soldiers he was confronting. But not without taking a lot of damage themselves.

He didn't have enough men to fight all the locals who didn't want to be plucked even now; he certainly wouldn't after they'd taken the damage those rifles could inflict. Their rate of fire compared to what he could manage … Would it be worth it?

Nobles. A man couldn't trust a word they said. God himself had spoken a warning in the psalms. *Verlasset euch nicht auf Fürsten.*

In front of him, the infantrymen were moving to either side, the mounted dragoons splitting their formation in the center and sidling their horses.

From behind the horses, a couple of footmen appeared and began to tug on the handles of the huge double doors.

CHAPTER 13

Westphalia
September 1635

Frederik was greatly relieved to be back from Magdeburg, even though he had returned to find that his staff had performed efficiently and there was a constitutional convention going on.

Or about to go on. Or a convention to draft a provincial charter going on. Or about to go on. Call it a charter convention. Province-wide, with delegates from each constituent territory and principality (which had been made feasible by the need to develop "election districts" for the nationwide elections).

Suffering from growing impatience (no Westphalian Estates to vote tax revenues equalled no tax revenues coming in), Frederik (or, to be technical, Rist in his name) issued a mandate unilaterally that every election district (not every polling place) was to send a delegate to a charter convention by a set date. Most did. Some of the delegates had actually been elected. Some of them essentially were appointed by the local lord. Some of them *were* the local lord.

Some things were non-negotiable. He put that forward in the mandate. Any draft the charter convention completed had to be in conformity with the USE constitution, or there would be no point in putting it to a vote. Among other things, that meant it would have to include provisions for religious toleration.

Some things were negotiable. Simple majority vote or two-thirds majority vote? Bicameral or unicameral provincial Estates? Or a "provincial legislature." Or a "provincial congress." Did it make any difference what it was called?

Well, of course it did. It would be a *Landtag*, as there had previously been a *Reichstag*. People knew what a Diet was and what delegates to one were supposed to accomplish. Why expect them all to start over?

But there had to be a province-wide *Landtag* representing the Estates. One clear truth lay before him. Frederik knew what Estates were and how Estates functioned, so unless the convention determined otherwise, they would remain "Estates" in his mind. Before he could staff and pay a central administration (given that the subsidy from his father was unlikely to continue *ad aeternitatem* and most certainly would not continue at all if at some future time the province had a governor who was not his father's son), Westphalia needed some kind of Estates, even redefined Estates that included serfs, and a *Landtag* to grant taxes over this disparate body of hitherto unrelated entities so the provincial administration would have revenue coming in.

Magdeburg had provided no instructions whatsoever pertaining to acceptable methods by which he was to achieve acceptable results in the form of a draft of a provincial charter. He did receive, by way of his father, who obtained it from a "consultant" he had hired in Grantville, a copy of *Robert's Rules of Order*. Since each individual territory that Gustav Adolf had tossed arbitrarily into the province had its own individual procedures, few of which were the same, Frederik announced equally arbitrarily that the delegates would either agree to use *Robert's* or the dissenters could pick up their marbles, go home, and have no say in the final product.

Frederik suspected, given the results of the negotiations for the admission of Tyrol to the USE and the *ad hoc* carving of Württemberg out of Swabia by its late duke, that Magdeburg had not worked out any set of accepted methods. He certainly hadn't seen any when he was there for the House of Lords.

So he appointed himself President *pro tem.*

Hardly anyone outside of the province even noticed the charter convention. That was fine with Frederik.

He might have even contributed to the obscurity of the event.

Various towns had wanted to host the delegates; others had utterly refused to host the delegates. He decided on his own discretion to hold it at Wildeshausen which was (a) about in the middle of the distance between Bochold in the southwest and the most distant reaches of northeastern Holstein, jutting out into the sea past Eutin; and (b) had come down in the world a lot since its medieval heyday, but still possessed a *Rathaus* adequate for holding the meetings. Moreover, its *Rat* hadn't expressed an opinion one way or the other. If the delegates weren't willing to pack themselves into the *Remter* (the chapter house of the former *Stift*) like salted fish in a keg, sleeping on cots, they could either rent space from the citizens (contracts would be inspected by lawyers) or live in tents. If enough of them ended up living in tents, that might spur them on to stop debating and adopt a draft.

Diepholz would have been more convenient for travelers, but that site would have introduced possible, and unnecessary, awkwardness with Brunswick.

The larger towns, even those that had not wanted to host the convention, were, naturally, indignant that the governor had designated someplace else. Someplace smaller and less distinguished. The sputterings of their mayors garnered a small amount of coverage in the news, but not much.

The newspaper reporters, who would have to hie themselves out into the middle of nowhere if they wanted first-hand stories, were by-and-large as indignant as the passed-over towns. Frederik did not regard their reluctance to go out in the field as a disadvantage.

Dismissing the journalists, present and absent, from his mind, Frederik started drawing bullet points.

He had to have a charter drafted. It had to be a charter that the USE officials in Magdeburg would accept. It also had to be a charter that the voters of Westphalia would adopt.

Non-negotiable. The final design contained in the Provincial Charter would have to provide for genuine provincial Estates. Province-wide Estates. A *Landtag*. Not some kind of compilation of existing local Estates. Non-negotiable because the existing local Estates that originated in the middle ages had been legendarily reluctant to grant taxes and other revenues to their ruling princes. Much less taxing authority; see for reference purposes the contemporary English, British, parliament which had caused his Aunt Anne's late husband, and now her son Charles, so much difficulty. Thus greatly limiting the ruler's scope of action quite sharply, in practice.

By the time the convention met, he had let it be known that his stance on this was adamant.

He didn't feel so strongly on some of the other issues, so he wasn't concentrating on them so closely. People in the rest of the province kept doing things whether he was presiding over this convention or not, and a fair number of those things ended up as memos in his In Box, flagged for his attention.

Seated at the podium, he looked out at the array of benches. Backless benches. Unpadded benches. Benches a little too low to be comfortable for the average man, a little too close together to allow easy passage between them. Along with the crowded rooming conditions, he had some hopes that they would contribute to a swift and efficient completion of this project.

When it came to allocation of seats in the new provincial Estates ... or legislature ... or congress ... or ... *Landtag*, yes, *Landtag* ... that were being sculpted (that sounded so much more elevated than "ground out like sausage"), the approach favored by most of the delegates who were themselves local lords, or who had been *de facto* appointed by local lords, or were already members of existing local Estates—that type of person—was to grant each of the territories that had been thrown into the province the same number of delegates, regardless of population.

"Somebody," Rist said direly at dinner that evening, "has been reading about the Senate of the United States of America."

"Or has been reading the *Britannica*," Christian Ulrik responded cheerily. "It has an informative article about 'pocket boroughs' as they exist, and for a long time kept on existing, in the British parliament's House of Commons."

Kerstin Brahe contributed that the American electoral college also offered certain charming possibilities to those who were deliberately setting out to throw sand in the grease that lubricated political wheels and axles. She wouldn't be surprised it some of these rural toads had come across a description of it.

At the next morning's session, Simon Gruber, delegate from Lingen, brought in a proposal for province-wide proportional representation which would set up an electoral system in which parties gained seats in proportion to the number of total votes cast for them, with local governments picking the people to hold each seat. That caused even more screeching than the parallels with the once-upon-a-time American Senate.

The popularly elected delegates to the convention regarded the proposals favoring non-popular representation with notably less favor than the local nobility of, say, Tecklenburg. Gerrit Bemmeler had been on a roll in his vociferous opposition and presentation of reasons why not. Primarily! Secondarily! Was there such a word as thirdarily? Tertially? He got lost in his own verbiage and the forcefulness of his oratory dribbled down to ineffectiveness.

"You should have stuck with 'firstly, secondly, thirdly,' Peter Schorfmann said that evening. "Good, straight, plain German is always better than fancifully Latinized German." Agnes Bemmeler, taking notes, nodded her head in agreement. "Let Tönnies do the talking tomorrow."

"Get to a radio," Tönnies said. "It's one thing to be a delegate. It's another to be a delegate who is the designated spokesman for the Bremen *Senat*. Draft up something on popular representation on which we can make a 'Here I stand.' Fast."

"What's the point of making such a fuss about how representation will work in the rest of the province?" Peter Schorfmann thought that was a reasonable enough question. "Why are we putting so much effort into participating in this convention? What Bremen wants to do is secede from Westphalia, not send delegates to its *Landtag*."

"Oh, perish the thought of the word *secede*," Bemmeler said. "Most of the up-timers, the ones we need to have our backs, the Fourth of July Party people, don't like it at all. They had a whole civil war about it somewhere in the future."

"But look at Württemberg. If what they've done under Eberhard's will doesn't amount to seceding from the Province of Swabia, I'm blind, deaf, and dumb. And the FoJP has backed them and turned his girlfriend Tata into a national CoC heroine." Schorfmann threw up both of his hands in exasperation.

"One of their proverbs," Bemmeler said, "runs, *consistency is the hobgoblin of small minds*."

Agnes frowned at her brother reproachfully. "No. It comes from a collection of essays by an author named Emerson. I bought a reprinted copy at Jensen's bookstore less than a month ago. 'A *foolish* consistency is the hobgoblin of little minds, adored by little statesmen and philosophers and divines.' The crucial word in understanding it is 'foolish.' *Dumm. Unklug. Töricht.* Whatever else the national FoJP leadership may or may not be, so far it has not shown itself to be foolish. Tata is of great utility for what we want to achieve."

Tönnies Breitung stood, leaning his back to the wall, thinking about little statesmen and philosophers and divines.

Most of the CoC in Bremen, most of the CoC members of the *Senat*, for that matter, were sailing along in cheerful confidence that Frau Abrabanel, wife of General Stearns, she was, that Ed Piazza, that the other FoJP national leaders would surely, surely back Bremen's wish to be a free imperial city. Surely, since Bremen would give their party one more sure vote in the USE House of Lords if it happened.

Another proverb ran, *the only sure things in life are death and taxes.*

If Bremen did not succeed in breaking free …

He stood up straight. "Bemmeler, forget that. Don't draft the memo to the *Senat* and take it to the radio right now. Give me an hour to get my thoughts in order; I'll draft it."

"But not send it without running it past the rest of us." Schorfmann's voice revealed his irritation. Breiting might be CoC, but … for Peter Schorfmann, he would also be a twig and sprig of the patriciate's family tree as well. Never entirely free of the suspicion that his commitment to the cause was … less complete than that of the rest of them.

But the memo was good. Persuasive. "Gerrit does the talking," Breiting said. "I'm not much of a public speaker."

So Bemmeler stood up again the next morning, speaking for the *Senat* of Bremen. Popular representation in the new provincial Estates was non-negotiable. The principle of 'one man, one vote … ' Err. 'One person, one vote.' "

Agnes had directed some input at the first draft of the radio message to the *Senat*.

Some groups on both (or multiple) sides of the issue took up "we shall not be moved" stances; one outright reactionary who had come across the phrase, used it to defend the point he was making in an impassioned speech, which was picked up by the newspapers and led to considerable hilarity among the up-timers who read about it in Magdeburg.

At least, the few who noticed the paragraph on page three; the reporter who sent the article in was a second-stringer. But Pete Rush spotted it. Even Ben Leek laughed. Phil Hart forwarded it along to Grantville and Bamberg.

Bemmeler's impassioned speech defending the principle of popular election seemed to be going well until Magnus Jurgens from Loccum Abbey, which had borne a certain grudge against Bremen since the events of *Krystalnacht*, arose from his seat, dashed into the floor space that separated the podium from the benches, skirted the tables where various scribes and scriveners were taking minutes, and punched him in the nose. Sigmund Romberg, jumping up from the front row, grabbed Jurgens' shoulders to pull him back; Jurgens' colleague from Verden shoved Romberg to the floor. The defenders of popular representation surged from their seats to defend Bemmeler; the defenders of proportional representation rose to drag them down, with every intention of silencing the speaker. Half the people in the room were crushed into the small space between the front row and the podium, jerking one another around: elbows in stomachs and knees in groins. The other half were standing on the benches for a better view of the entertainment.

Frederik banged his gavel on the lectern in an agreed-upon rhythm that sent one of the guards at the door running and brought the Wildeshausen city militia, whom once-Lieutenant, now Captain Reineke Meyer had briefed and conveniently stationed in the back corridor of the *Rathaus* for such all-too-likely emergencies.

Bemmeler finished his speech. The evening was uneasy; groups of delegates caucusing, muttering; avoiding one another. Some taverns held only those who favored one position; others the supporters of the opposition.

But the next morning's session opened calmly enough. They even managed a vote, by which popular representation, while not winning, squeaked through with a plurality.

The honorable delegate from Tecklenburg proposed a run-off between the two voting proposals with the greatest support. The honorable delegates from Bremen cried foul.

Then ... *Frau* Hanna Jacobi, from Friesoythe, heiress of a large peasant farm, larger than many a noble manor, one of the most conservative of the conservatives, arose and moved that if all adult individuals were to have the right to vote, it followed that they must be clearly identifiable, so each person in the province must adopt a fixed family name, not a patronymic, and fix it to the family line by heredity. No more Jan Classen who was son of Claus Janssen who was son of Jan Friessen. No surname; no vote.

Frederik sat, twirling the gavel, and thought. It had some merit, if it could be accomplished.

"What kind of a name is Jacobi?" Schorfmann could not resist contributing. Agnes dragged him back down into his seat and told him to shut his mouth. He popped up and yelled, "Patronymic."

"Borne by my family for four generations! My father's name is Hendrik!" *Frau* Hanna usually gave as good as she got.

"Nor farm names, either," someone shouted from the rear of the room. "No changing your name when you lease a different farm, anymore. No making a son-in-law adopt his wife's farm name if he wants to take over the lease."

"Out of order! Out of order!"

While Frederik was gathering his thoughts, Magnus Jurgens—who, obviously, bore one of the despised patronymics—stood up and said that if this was to be imposed on commoners by the aristocratic Crown Loyalists and their sycophants, then it should be imposed on nobles as well. If there were to be no more farm names, then also no more "von" this or that, using the names of landholdings. Either adopt a family name, like Wilhelm Wettin had done, or else pick one of the landholdings and make it a family name. If the vice-president of the SoTF could be a Gundelfinger permanently because she'd had some long-ago ancestor who came from Gundelfingen, then some arrogant "von Lenken" in this day and age could turn into a "Lenkener" and stick with it.

According to *Robert's Rules of Order*, none of this was properly on the table. Frederik banged his gavel and said so.

Over the rising din, Jurgens howled at the top of his lungs, "I so move." From his colleague from Verden, a powerful, "Second the motion" arose.

"Out of order," yelled the delegate from Tecklenburg. Jurgens charged forward again, this time followed by a dozen other men who were jumping from bench to bench to avoid the crowded aisles, mostly skirting those delegates who still remained seated—but not always. The scribes prudently grabbed their papers, ledgers, pens, and paraphernalia, disappearing under the tables with all of it. Romberg was holding his own; Friedrich Horst from Hoya had two fist-fighting delegates who came from, Frederik thought, somewhere around Quackenbrück, and had been arguing against one another since the first bang of the gavel, under control, each of his massive hands pinching a neck. It was starting to subside. It had remained one more simple brawl. Punching. Shoving. Slapping. Hair pulling. Kicking.

Some of those kicks had to be painful, but ... an ordinary brawl. Nothing that a group of schoolyard bullies wouldn't do when hazing new boys.

Until Gruber cracked Jurgens' head against a corner of the scribes' table and Horst, letting go of the two men he had previously grabbed, picked up a bench. After that it involved daggers, poniards, and a few short swords. Before Frederik could signal for the town militia with his gavel, Carstens from Meppen hoisted himself onto the podium and grabbed it out of his hand, throwing it at Horst as if it were a hammer before setting out to drag the governor off his chair and back towards the space between the podium and the wall.

Fortunately, the guard at the door had enough initiative to summon the militia without being signaled to do so. Which, technically, put him in violation of his orders, but Frederik wasn't going to make a point of it. Hiring the man himself might be the better option.

After order was restored … By the time the brawl was over … By the time the militia and the surgeons had completed their tasks …

He adjourned the session. Gave them a couple of days to cool off.

Smirked.

Personally commended all the ladies who were delegates for having, most of them, refrained from participating in the fights and praised them for exemplifying parliamentary decorum.

Leaked the commendation to the newspaper.

Several aggrieved delegates, when they had their chance, informed the newspapers that the governor had exercised intimidation and stifled freedom of speech. Which was another right guaranteed by the constitution of the USE.

When the meeting reconvened, the delegates from Bremen were able to present themselves as voices of sweet reason. And took the opportunity to present additional demands for points that Bremen thought would improve the charter as it would be presented to the people for a vote. Points that were not on the official agenda as it had been prepared by the governor in advance of the charter convention.

Frederik reacted to Bremen's new proposals with reasonably good grace as far as his public face was concerned, adding them to the agenda, permitting them to be considered by the rather chastened delegates and voted up or down. The convention adopted several. Proceeding decently and in order.

Privately, he resolved to revoke the relevant provisions the first time an opportunity arose.

Frederik did not enjoy making significant concessions. Concessions that he did not want to make.

Virginia DeMarce

CHAPTER 14

September 1635
Westphalia

"So Westphalia has a draft charter." Frederik propped his feet up on a hassock without bothering to remove his boots.

"That *was* the purpose of the convention." Erik Stenbock laughed and picked up his stein.

"It's far from ideal. Although … I am reluctant to admit it, but the one proposal from Bremen, that the charter itself shall be put to a popular vote rather than submitted to the Estates of the individual territories for ratification … isn't bad. It will at least be faster. The individual Estates could have dragged it out for years before we got a majority for ratification. We can put it to a vote in mid-winter, once the harvest is over and the peasants have a bit of free time to hear about it in the village tavern. Circulate some broadsides, I suppose. Presuming that it passes, hold the inaugural session in … when? … April, I suppose. In Münster. The draft charter doesn't set a date for it."

"It couldn't," Kerstin said pragmatically. "No way to predict when it would go into effect."

"But we gave away too much. Gave in too often. As the proverb goes: *Verkäuft der Fürst das Amt, so hält der Amtmann offenen Markt.*

Virginia DeMarce

Whenever a lord sells a manor, his steward sells everything on the open market. To paraphrase it somewhat. The FoJP will reap the benefits."

"What are you going to do about the second session, in the fall? The one the charter sets to be held in the north?"

"Bremervörde simply is not suitable. It will have to be in Bremen, I suppose."

"Or," Christian Ulrik grinned, "if the Bremer simply get too full of themselves between now and then, how about Glückstadt?"

"Ahhh! Wouldn't that inflict some *miseria et melancholia* upon your reluctant subjects."

"Tsk, tsk. Citizens, not subjects. Only Gustav Adolf gets to have subjects in the USE. All the rest of us are serving its citizens."

"Although, not its 'free citizens,' always and only."

"Please. Let's not revisit the controversy over voting rights for serfs. Not right now. In Westphalia, they voted in the last election. For the USE as a whole, it's a nightmare, and the legal conditions and practical burdens of serfdom are so different from region to region. Aside from what the USE constitution says, which isn't much … just that serfs are citizens, but without specifying exactly how or why."

"Other than that Mike Stearns insisted on the provision back in 1633."

"Which is true, but not in the constitution."

"And Carstens from Meppen is now asserting that he did not harbor the slightest intention of harming the governor, but was motivated by the purest of intentions and attempting to make sure that no one else hurt him by accident."

"Leave him alone," Frederik said a little wearily. "He is ambitious; I am undamaged."

Everyone except Joachim Lütkemann wandered off to bed. The governor didn't often want to talk. Occasionally, he did. Rarely The chaplain tried to give him the opportunity when it happened.

For twenty minutes, nothing happened. "*So hält der Amtmann offenen Markt*, Frederik said abruptly. What do you make of Luke 16:1-13?"

"The parable of the unjust steward? It's generally held to be one of the most difficult in the New Testament, when it comes to exegesis."

"How is it that hard? A steward who is about to be fired curries favor with his master's debtors by remitting some of their debts. A version of the proverbial servant who sells everything portable off in the open market once the lord is no longer in control. That's straightforward enough. At the end, the master commends him for being so clever. I've taken a look at Tyndale's exposition, the booklet called *The Parable of the Wicked Mammon*. It's difficult reading; the English language has changed much more in the past century than High German has since the days of Martin Luther. He manages to find a moral in the story. That 'we with righteousness should be as diligent to provide for our souls, as he with unrighteousness provided for his body.' Which I did not see any evidence of in the words of scripture."

"As I recall, Tyndale's exposition was based upon a sermon that Martin Luther delivered in 1522. Luther did not avoid tackling some of the more … shall we say problematic … parables. And for all our emphasis on the literal words of scripture, rather than the Catholic error of allegory, a parable is a parable. It's no more meant to be read literally than poetry is meant to be read as prose."

"Great," Frederik muttered, "What does this mean?"

"Those words are not only a heading in the catechism. Luther took them from Acts 2:12, the description of the descent of the Holy Spirit at Pentecost. 'And all were amazed and perplexed, saying to one another, *What does this mean?*' But first, to return to the parable, the steward mismanaged his master's goods. If he hadn't done that, he wouldn't have been dismissed."

Frederik twirled the wine glass he was holding.

Twirled it upside down, the chaplain noticed. It had been empty for two hours and only half filled at the start of dinner. When the innkeeper's wife had cleared away the table settings and put out a fresh decanter, the governor had kept his glass but not refilled it.

He took a deep breath. "So, the steward mismanaged his master's goods; when the master found out, he dismissed the steward. Notice that I have omitted the adjectives in this summation. Some translations, some commentaries, cause me unease in how they bring the adjectives out of the Greek ... as the one you quoted did, above. The 'unjust' servant; the 'unrighteous' servant. He was unrighteous; we are all unrighteous by nature. But for purposes of the parable, it is clearer, I believe, if it is read as if we read it as the 'steward' or, perhaps, 'servant' of the unrighteous Mammon.

"Then," Lütkemann shifted uneasily in his chair, "the steward adds cheating to mismanagement; writes off a lot of what he's been sent to collect as his last job for the master, in hopes the debtors who benefit from his cheating will take him in and let him live comfortably. He doesn't want to do menial labor or beg, so he does what he can to make sure he won't have to."

"And?" Frederik raised his eyebrows.

"The master admires the dipshit for being shrewd. Commends him. Where we meet the big problem."

"What do you define as the big problem?"

"A lot of commentators, preachers, books, essays, sermons—what you will—over the centuries then assume, given that it's Jesus who is telling the parable, that the master giving the commendation has to be Jesus himself, as the speaker. Or God the Father. Which they find fairly confusing."

"Who is speaking, then?"

"I think," Lütkemann answered, "within the limits that I am a young pastor, far from being one of the Church Fathers or even a modern university professor, that in that place in the parable Jesus was quoting what a master who *was* himself the 'unrighteous Mammon' would say; showing us what the world admires. Then ... "

Frederik interrupted. "And οἰκονόμος for the steward is the root of the word that the up-timers use for their science of 'economics,' I am told. They might term him a 'manager.' My father has sent me a reprint of an 'economics textbook' from Grantville. Their English language is far from comprehensible to one who has managed to master the Bible in King James' authorized version. Or even the plays of Shakespeare. I am struggling with the 'labor theory of value.' It is difficult to envision our footman, the good Vendt in Münster, as the ultimate foundation of all earthly wealth as he stands there polishing the brass knocker on the door."

Lütkemann sighed and tried to retrieve his train of thought. "Then, I think, Jesus changed the subject, and we, you and I and all the translating committees, don't live in the days of Jesus, don't live in the days of Luke, and our ears possibly may be as poorly tuned to the *koiné* of the New Testament as they are in hearing the subtleties of Tyndale's past English and Grantville's future English. We don't catch the change of subject when he turns it. When he switches over to saying, 'the world, Mammon, admires this kind of cleverness, because the steward has successfully garnered a comfortable financial future by being thoroughly sneaky, but ... '

"*Might* the remainder of the parable be validly interpreted to indicate that Jesus was nudging the hearers, urging the hearers, to ask themselves whether or not they were using their material wealth to advance and support eternal goals shrewdly as worldly people use theirs advance their worldly goals?"

Frederik raised his eyebrows. "As we, all sinful people, mismanage God's gifts to us. That's basic. Catechism level. You're saying that the tricky bit is what comes next."

Lütkemann wandered off into muttering additional considerations involving New Testament Greek. "Now in verse 9, one might translate thus, 'And [or 'but,' but 'and' seems to work better] I [I, even I] say to you, 'Make friends for yourselves, by means of unrighteous [dishonest] money' [from the Aramaic, we believe; μαμων?], in order that when it runs out [λείπω, fail utterly], they will welcome you ['that you may be received'; impersonal, better than 'that they may receive you'] into the eternal dwelling places ['tents; σκήνη implying an abode']."

He didn't have the Greek text before him. Thankfully, this was not a scholarly study or a class. He was musing, from memory. When he was diverted from his trip home, the luggage that he had shipped ahead of him had continued on its way to Rostock. Where, as one of God's good gifts, his expensive and treasured Greek New Testament was now reposing in safety with his parents.

Nor had Frederik been keeping up his Greek since completing his university studies.

"The steward is a man who thinks, 'phronimos,' not a man who is wise, 'sophos.' He plots, he plans, he designs. In a military sense, almost, he engages in maneuvers. He has determined a goal and is doing what he perceives as necessary to achieve it. But that is not the wisdom of God.

"After the change of topic, Jesus is pointing out that Christians should use the worldly blessings that God showers upon us, for all good gifts come from above, as we hear in James 1:17, 'Every good and perfect gift is from above, coming down from the Father of the heavenly lights, who does not change like shifting shadows,' to support the church. We should use our master's wealth to spread the Gospel so that the presence of others there will add to the joys of heaven."

"That must be a remarkably convenient conclusion for pastors," came Frederik's cynical reply.

"Look at the conclusion, in regard to serving the 'Mammon of wickedness' [from the Aramaic again, possibly with an emphatic ending? or a genitive?]. What is it that the unrighteous master respects? To use money to make friends for ourselves? We are by nature in no way worthy of God's respect, but because He has saved us, now we are His servants. Who should serve Him well."

Lütkemann tried harder to call up mental images of notes he had taken years before. Images that were mostly more than a little fuzzy around the edges, to say the least. In verse 10, consider: The one who is faithful [πιστός faithful, trustworthy] in a least thing [in a very small thing; μικρός, least] is also faithful in a great thing, and the one who is dishonest [unrighteous; ἄ-δικος unjust, dishonest] in a least thing [a very small thing] is also dishonest in a great thing.

"Remember the conclusion of this section," Lütkemann summed up, "verse 13, that no servant can be a faithful servant of two masters at the same time. 'No servant [literally 'nobody servant'] is able to serve. You cannot [you are not able to] serve God and mammon [money, wealth]. One cannot serve both god and Mammon.' The steward, I think, in the best translation, was not an 'unrighteous servant' but rather a servant of the unrighteous Mammon. And in that capacity, he did well."

He sought for a lighter note on which to end the evening.

"I do recall something of Luther's sermon on this parable: Luther stated that we should take this parable in a common-sense way. The Lord himself does not praise what the steward did as good, but points out that the world would say something on the order of *that was a clever ploy*. Luther added, 'Just as when a whore draws a string of men following after her and I say: *she is a clever whore, she knows her business*.' "

Frederik winced as he put his wine glass down. A clever whore had come close to bringing his father to ruin. For Kirsten Munk was a clever whore; or a whore with a clever mother. Noble-born, but still a whore who shrewdly bargained her body for money and position.

The words of the parable echoed in his mind as he prepared for bed. " … cannot serve two masters; for either he will hate the one and love the other, or he will be devoted to one and despise the other."

Who was his master? Or, perhaps, who were his masters?

Quedlinburg

Among the students at Quedlinburg, Annalise and Bethany were the ones most resorted-to as references and sources by the down-time girls. Annalise, considered "sort of up-time" even though she wasn't, among those on scholarships and in the work-study program; Bethany, actually up-time, by those of noble origins and others whose families paid their tuition in full. When it came to the newspaper articles featuring the phrase, "we shall not be moved," each of them tried her best to explain the civil rights movement of the 1960s to her friends.

Each from her own perspective, which was a bit skewed for each of them. For Annalise, what she knew about it came from her Grantville high school textbooks, but the social studies teachers weren't emphasizing up-time history any more, having enough of a challenge in getting their students up to speed on the here-and-now. Bethany didn't even know that much, since she had attended the DESSSFG in Magdeburg and her classes hadn't covered it at all. She recalled a few occasional comments at family dinners, the name of President John Kennedy; the name of Martin Luther King. The last of which introduced great confusion into the conversation.

"So anything you can send will help," she wrote to her mother. "Aside from that, things are going well. You can't imagine how excited the older ladies here were last summer when Mrs. Dreeson visited and they got to pass around her dentures and examine them. They're still talking about dentists and Grantville."

Iona read about in the newspapers too. The other teachers were more interested in her evaluation of the governor of Westphalia from the perspective of an up-timer.

"It's hard to know what to make of the man. I did look him up in the 1911 *Encyclopedia Britannica* reprint that they're buying for the abbey library. It's past the volume for 'D' now. I sure hope that Denmark's nobles are battening down their hatches now that they can see the tornado cloud coming. Or maybe mending their ways."

She had to explain tornadoes, saying, "We didn't have them much in West Virginia, any more than you do here; they came more out on the Great Plains than in mountains; can't build up steam in up and down hills. But they made impressive television. And the ground is flat up there on the north coast, like Kansas—I've seen some of the photos that Tina Marie Hollister has taken since she married Lucas Sartorius and moved up that way.

"As for what I've read about this Frederik, though … In old-fashioned westerns—you know what movies are?—the actors came with white hats and black hats; you knew who the good guys were and who the bad guys were; where you should cheer and where you should boo. I suppose, from what I've seen reported, this man, this guy in Westphalia, is more like the famous duke of York."

"What on earth do you mean by that? Which duke of York?"

"It's a nursery rhyme." She sang,

> *Oh, the famous duke of York,*
> *He had ten thousand men;*
> *He marched them up to the top of the hill,*
> *And he marched them down again.*
>
> *And when he was up, he was up;*
> *And when he was down, he was down.*
> *But when he was only half-way up,*
> *He was either up nor down.*

"This guy in Westphalia? From what I can tell by reading the papers, he's neither up nor down."

But her mind was already on other things. Kansas had brought up *The Wizard of Oz* and she was pretty sure she had a score somewhere in the music she had brought with her. Maybe an abbreviated version in the spring …

Virginia DeMarce

CHAPTER 15

September 1635
Saxony

Hedwig, dowager-electress of Saxony, suggested leaving by way of Torgau, by way of Mockrehna and Eilenburg, through Taucha and Schkeuditz, as a route for her departure, since the roads were better. Kleinitz discouraged the idea, citing the presence of units at Torgau whose officers he wasn't acquainted with and who might not honor his letter of safe conduct. Not to mention unrest generally, along the rest of that way. So even if the *Dübener Heide* might be harboring bands of rebels … undoubtedly *was* harboring bands of rebels, he thought but did not say … it would be better if her party used the northern paths and went as directly as possible to Halle.

Yes, even if that did involve a ferry. She would not have any wagons to be hefted on and off the flimsy rope-and-pulley raft that counted as a ferry.

That was the partisan leader's ultimatum. She and her people could go. Things, material possessions, beyond what they were wearing and the food they would need for the journey, they would leave behind. All the things in the Lichtenburg and its outbuildings; things he could use to induce his followers not to plunder the villages and villagers of which she seemed to be so solicitous.

All right, he granted, of her soldiers, she could take fifty riders. With their horses. The squadron of dragoons and mounting the infantry.

"With their weapons," she persisted.

Overall, fifty fewer trained soldiers in and around Prettin, even if they did take their horses and guns, wasn't a bad bargain. The old lady, if she took fifty men, would be leaving as many to fade in among the townsmen and villagers, stiffening the local militia, prepared to take offense at mistreatment of those they regarded as their charges.

Also enough horses, she argued, for those of the ladies and servants who could ride. Carrying the children, the old men, the feeble, double.

"Is the trouble of the extra horses worth it?" Kleinitz asked. "It's only three miles or so to the Elbe ferry at Dommitzsch."

She pointed out that it was a rare horse that was willing to get on a ferry if not trained to it. Her men would put as many of the horses on the ferry as they could persuade to get on the ferry. Possibly trading some of their military horses for civilian slugs in the process. They'd leave the rest behind; Kleinitz's men could retrieve them and add them to the count of *things*.

Things with which which she was ransoming her people.

"People," Kleinitz countered, "you are so arrogant as to think of as yours."

So she left.

Wondering what the partisans planned to do with the grand ceremonial clothing. What use did they have for a dress of foam green and sky blue silk, embroidered with gold and silver thread, ornamented with lace? Even she had only worn it once, to the wedding of John George and Magdalene Sybille. The dress of golden yellow silk; the one of salmon pink? Carefully preserved, but also hardly worn; a widow had no use for such sartorial gaiety.

What use did they have for the family portraits? The china figurines?

The weaponry, no matter how ornamental, she presumed that they could use.

Hopefully Kleinitz would persuade them to sell it rather than wantonly smash it in the storm of fury that sometimes followed conquests. Like a miniature sack of Magdeburg. She hadn't forced them to mount a siege.

What, even, would they do with the buildings? The upkeep was not cheap. The annual bill for roof repairs ...   What use would the notorious Gretchen Richter have for them? A hospital? A school? A prison? If Lichtenburg went up in flames ... she would regret the loss of a pleasant home.

But not as much as she would have regretted the loss of lives if she had not surrendered it. The men she had left behind to protect her dower villages, to protect the servants at the *Schloß* who were not accompanying her because they had family in the villages, would do what they could. *Not that it will do much good*, she thought sourly as the party straggled single-file along the walking path that led to Halle and sanctuary in the USE.

The walking path that Kleinitz had assured her would take her party two days, at most, to cover.

Two days at a brisk march by a healthy man, perhaps. It was close to fifty miles in a direct line; considerably more by the path. During which they were shadowed by partisans to make sure that they did not veer away. No detouring to nearby villages to replenish their supplies. After the first, horrible, night sleeping by the roadside, some relief at Düben, almost twenty miles along, where they were allowed to stay overnight, sleep indoors, and purchase more food. She had not been allowed to bring money; the captain of dragoons had some. She had no idea how he had managed it.

Düben, where four years earlier Gustav Adolf and John George had met to forge an alliance against Ferdinand II.

She had danced with Ferdinand once, before he became Holy Roman Emperor.

He was dead, as was John George.

A second night sleeping by the path, children crying and old men grumbling. Then another night indoors at Delitzsch. Where, probably, children cried and old men grumbled, but at least she had a closed door between herself and them. She wrote out a voucher to the innkeeper, a promise to pay him when she could.

She hoped, a little viciously, that the shadowing partisans were having another uncomfortable night outdoors, on hard ground, tree roots under their ribcages and insects in their hair!

Followed by a final exhausting stretch to Halle, fifteen miles between dawn and dusk, with bedraggled people. They arrived south of the city as dark was settling in.

Halle an der Saale

Sergeant Jim Allen looked up from the scribbled sheets of next week's railroad schedule, now in its fourth revision. "What the hell?" He didn't like his assignment. How did a member of the SoTF National Guard end up being detailed to work as a railway scheduler. He'd liked it better in the NUS Army the first two years after the Ring, when he got to do some fighting, at least. Then a year at Erfurt working in the supply depot on the railroad part of military procurement. That hadn't been too bad; Dennis Stull was one of the good guys. Plus, it had a whole Grantville community now—Meaghan was still there with the kids. No place to billet dependents at Halle, yet; not many up-timers here, even if he could find a place for them to stay. Bill Plotz, his half-brother, laughed at him and said it served him right for even starting to go to college: learn to use a spreadsheet and they'll make you do it. Even if you only had three semesters at a community college. "Retribution for getting above yourself, Jimmy my boy." Bill only had a high school diploma, but he was a captain in the TacRail unit now; had been at Ingolstadt, had been at Regensburg, was moving east with Stearns. Seeing some action.

If the noise outside was any indication, some action was happening right here at the depot office. Right now.

Men yelling, mix of the local German and Amideutsch. "Get those shitball horses off of the tracks!" Dung, excrement, "Crap, crap, crap!" What the German soldiers avoided in the way of using God's name in vain, they sure made up when it came to anything a human or animal ass could produce. Most of them were peasant boys, of course: they grew up with horse manure and cowpies. *Lousy Krauts.* Which he still thought in private, even if he wasn't allowed to say it. Poop, poop, poop! All the time, like they were three years old. There was one private who went around saying, "Pigeon droppings."

"Allen, get yourself out here!"

That was in English. Eric Hudson, old Willie Ray's grandson. Sprig of the Grantville upper class, if you could say that Grantville had one. He'd graduated from high school in that first class after the Ring of Fire, straight into the army, then Erfurt under Stull; married Gena Kroll, Stull's secretary, while they were there. Nothing like schmoozing up to the big boss. Now the kid was here as the other up-time scheduler.

They were supposed to be training a lot more schedulers. The railroads were expanding fast. Training down-timers; not enough up-timers to go around any more. He'd turned that part of it over to Eric, who got along with the Krauts better.

He got up and went out onto the platform. And weren't there Krauts here right now? It looked like a couple of hundred of them. Riding, walking, all on the railroad right-of-way, coming up from the south.

Liveried soldiers who were *not ours*! Raid! Halle was unnervingly close to Saxony.

Companies scrambling out of the barracks over on the other side, carrying weapons, the corporals trying to get their squads to form up.

But what were their camp followers doing all mixed up with them, in the middle, almost as if the soldiers were bodyguards?

An old woman, riding out of the middle of the gaggle on a damned fine horse, keeping a damned fine seat, toward him. With the guy who appeared to be the captain of those soldiers behind her. And two steps to the left.

"I am Hedwig, sister of King Christian of Denmark, who is an ally of Emperor Gustav Adolf."

"Sure, lady,'" Jim said, "And I'm the Shah of Iran!"

"She's not that old," Eric wrote to Gena after things had calmed down. "Probably around fifty, I'd guess. She just looks old, the way so many down-timers do, even the rich ones. Jim had more than a bit of trouble dealing with it all. She had a half-dozen very, very, upper class young ladies. The rest of the women were servants. Kids. Old people. And, let's not forget, fifty armed men who had that 'if you want to start trouble, be my guest' look about them.

"I think it was them that finally got Jim to take her seriously. Plus that the down-time officers were 'my-ladying' her, but the whole thing was a mess and we sure didn't have any place to tuck them in bed for the night."

Eric chewed on the tip of his pen thoughtfully. They'd telegraphed for instructions; radioed for someone, anyone, from the SoTF government who might possess something that resembled diplomatic credentials to deal with this. Got Mark Early, who was the SoTF consul in Magdeburg.

Yeah, yeah, back home, *when* in the twentieth century and *where* in West Virginia, states didn't have their own consulates in Washington, DC. But Grantvillers got in enough trouble in Magdeburg and environs, simply by being themselves, and considering themselves pretty independent, that Ed Piazza thought it was worthwhile to have someone available to talk them through the system. The consular services there had started when the SoTF had been the NUS and he'd left them to do their thing. Mark had been stationed in Germany for a couple of years, back up-time. His wife, she'd been Susan Reading before she got married, was on Stearns' personal staff when he was prime minister. Lost her job, now that Stearns was a general, but she'd land on her feet. Work for Becky Abrabanel, maybe. She'd find something.

And Mark figured it out.

Honest to God, no matter how soldiers griped about them, sometimes the civil servant types came in handy. He put his pen to the paper again.

"So we ended up arranging for the lady and the gaggle to be shipped up to Magdeburg on a special train. One of the lady's friends, who turned out to also know Mary Simpson, an abbess of somewhere or the other (though where a nun would get money, I have no idea) guaranteed the freight and Mark said she'd be good for it. It was the duke of Saxe-Altenburg who paid the invoice. I've got no idea, either, why he'd be paying a bill run up by a nun; I'm pretty sure that he's Lutheran. And that nuns are Catholic ladies.

"I sort of doubt that she left Saxony voluntarily—probably pushed out by the uprising. But if she was a refugee, she had it easy compared to the ones who came into Grantville the first year after the Ring of Fire."

Mark Early accompanied the train back to Magdeburg. *Frau* Hedwig's little army would follow with the horses, watched, of course, but no longer with serious apprehension, by companies of the National Guard.

Magdeburg

Mark Early collected a deeper understanding than Eric of the circumstances under which the dowager electress left Prettin. "I was reminded," he said to Susan, "of that movie Ms. Mailey used to quote from all the time. She was pretty fond of *Dr. Strangelove*. It must have come out about the time she was hitting her stride."

"Oh, yeah. 'or: How I Learned to Stop Worrying and Love the Bomb.' What quote were you thinking about?" Susan yawned.

" … to choose between two admittedly regrettable yet nevertheless distinguishable alternatives."

Dorothea Sophia, duchess of Saxe-Altenburg and abbess of Quedlinburg, was on the platform to meet the special train.

She didn't have a house in Magdeburg, not even a rented one. Now that she was no longer a member of the *Reichstag*, it was an expense she could not justify to herself, much less to the committee that supervised the budget of the *Stift*. When she came to the capital, she stayed with friends. At present, Mary Simpson. As soon as she had escorted Veronica and Annalise to Quedlinburg and settled the girl into the designated Katharina von Bora College wing of the building, she had returned. There were still details concerning other schools to wrangle about.

Thankfully, the news of the impending arrival of Electress-dowager Hedwig and gaggle had been welcomed by the imperial palace staff, who were a little bored because the emperor was in the east and Princess Kristina was out of town. They stashed her into a luxurious guest chamber, the ladies-in-waiting into slightly less luxurious chambers, and the gaggle into nooks and crannies here and there, dispatching her soldiers to be provided for at the barracks.

" … going to stay with Frederik, of course."

The abbess blinked.

"It's obvious," Hedwig cocked her head back and looked down her nose. "After all this time as governor there, he still does not have a hostess. He is completely ignoring that aspect of a regent's duty. Who better than I? Although, of course, what he needs is a wife."

"Who? Honestly, right now, there aren't that many young women of ducal rank in the *Hochadel* who are available and suitable. And if you go below ducal rank, because of the principle of equal birth, *Ebenbürtigkeit*, his children won't be eligible to succeed in Holstein, if it comes to that someday. Which it well may, if the Chosen Prince and his wife have no children." The abbess tapped a finger on the table. "It's not like we're as sloppy as the English."

"It's disgusting," Hedwig tapped her foot on the floor, echoing the rhythm. "An English king could marry a beggar maid and, under their laws, his child would still succeed to the throne. As if the lineage of the mother is not as important as that of the father!"

"And Lutheran. Or willing to convert."

No options in Saxony. All of the late John George's girls were married; Frederik's brother Christian, the Chosen Prince, had nabbed the last of them. Saxe-Altenburg had only the one, who was betrothed to Duke Ernst. Saxe-Weimar?

"That family doesn't even produce daughters. Not as a general rule." The abbess laughed.

"The Brunswick girls are all too young. Their maternal aunts, the Hesse-Darmstadt girls, are all married. The Baden-Durlach girls, Friedrich's daughters, are all too young. And of his unmarried sisters, the next to youngest withered into the grave a couple of years ago and the youngest is sickly."

As for Wuerttemberg, "Although the ages are right, Eberhard left that ridiculous will when he died last May and his sisters have committed themselves to lives of scholarly celibacy." The abbess laughed. "Not that I can fault them for making the choice."

"Ansbach?"

"Any Hohenzollern would be a last resort." Hedwig sighed. "Well, the least I can do is try. Sound out some of the Calvinists. But none of them are of ducal rank. Even Hesse-Kassel is only a *Landgraf*; the remainder *Grafen*, counts. Anhalt might do. When I was a young wife, newly married, I became a good friend of Dorothea Maria."

The abbess nodded. "Wilhelm Wettin's mother, Ernst's." She made a moue. "Bernhard's. "

"She spent some time explaining to me how … touchy … it was that the ducal family of Saxe-Weimar did not classify the counts of Schwarzburg as *ebenbürtig* in spite of the antiquity of their title. She was from Anhalt, of course. If one of the Anhalt girls would convert from Calvinism? Who is available?"

"Eleonore Dorothea married Wilhelm, of course, and accepted Lutheranism. There's Kunigunde, then Johanna. The youngest, Eva Katherine, would be best for Frederik in age, if she weren't so scarred."

The two of them kept a moment of silence memorializing the ravages of smallpox among even the highest of the nobility.

"*Ebenbürtigkeit* may be loosening as a requirement, though. Amalia, the wife of Fredrik Hendrik, the *Stadhouder* in the Netherlands, is merely a countess of Solms."

Hedwig sniffed. "The Netherlands can do as they may. That family may be 'princes' of Orange over there, but in Germany, they are merely counts of Nassau. Amalia is sufficiently *ebenbürtig* for him."

Brunswick

When Hedwig left Magdeburg, she had not only riders to escort her, but also a carriage and several wagons. An appeal to her brother had succeeded.

The tolls on traffic through the Sound were such a blessing in the matter of disposable income for the kings of Denmark. The nobles certainly were stingy in granting taxes from the land.

The procession headed, by way of Wolfenbüttel and Goslar, to Calenberg. Duke Georg of Brunswick had ambitious plans for a new capital of his enlarged province in the city of Hannover, but the war had interfered. His family and civilian staff were still cramped into inadequate quarters in the old castle. Most of them—some of the staff were in Hildesheim, eight miles or so to the east, and the three oldest boys were in school there with their tutors.

She had fostered Anna Eleanor of Hesse-Darmstadt for three years before the girl married Georg. Darmstadt was the Lutheran branch of the Hesse lineage, which was good. But still, like the Kassel branch, only landgraves by rank. No question that the girl had married up. What had been done about *Ebenbürtigkeit* in this instance? She hadn't seen the marriage contracts herself.

With the Brunswick custom by which only one brother took a wife of rank and the others made morganatic marriages, at least there wouldn't be competing claims when Anna Eleanor's sons came to inherit. It would have been worth investigating if she had an available sister, but she didn't: all were married or dead.

Nine children, four of them boys. The oldest girl had died as a toddler, so eight now. Four little girls to play with for a week.

Worth the carriage ride on bad roads, the wheels ploughing through sand and mud even though it had not rained recently, to an uncomfortable medieval structure, out in the middle of the country, originally built between two branches of the Leine river, converted from a water fortress to a *Schloß* over a century ago, but still damp from moats and badly damaged from the seven or eight years that Tilly's troops had occupied it.

Why Anna Eleanor didn't put her foot down and move to a decent-sized town like Neustadt … ? Calenberg might be Georg's fondly regarded ancestral home, but … There were limits! Calenberg didn't provide much more in the way of amenities around the *Schloß* than a mill and a gallows.

Quedlinburg

"I think everyone here was a little disappointed that she didn't visit Quedlinburg," Bethany Leek wrote to her mother, "even if all the excitement in the newspapers about her 'daring escape' is probably blown all out of proportion. But of course, it's the abbess who is her friend and they met up in Magdeburg, so it wouldn't have made sense."

CHAPTER 16

September 1635
Münster

At least, Frederik had known that his aunt was coming long enough to have his staff find appropriate quarters. Barely adequate quarters. Not in town; he had to put her in a manor house some distance from the center of the city. Several canons who belonged to the far-flung and multi-branched lineage of the counts of Merveldt had proved to be… intransigent and uncooperative. Not surprising when the current head of the Westerwinkel line had served as chamberlain to the wretched Bavarian nuisance who had been archbishop of Cologne. Was still chamberlain *in vacante* to the archdiocese of Cologne.

They claimed to be *Uradel*. They were a bunch of jumped-up *ministeriales* who had made a fortune from the defeat of the Anabaptists a century earlier; one of them had taken Jan van Leyden prisoner and been amply rewarded.

The family should consider itself fortunate not to receive more significant retribution than involuntarily hosting a dowager electress of Saxony at one of its nearby manors. From the *Drostenhof* in Wolbeck, she could incidentally keep an eye out on what the retainers of the late Catholic prince-bishop were doing at *Schloß* Wolbeck.

Which was measurably better than having her live with him, and a minor benefit of his own residential situation. He was still in a cramped townhouse rented from an absentee merchant, its only charm being its convenient location.

His staff was still cramped and crammed into inadequate quarters in the city hall. Quarters that he had arbitrarily requisitioned. *Beschlagnahmt.* The city council still wanted the space back, not that they had been pleasant about vacating it in the first place.

Within weeks, Frederik was dismayed to discover that while Aunt Hedwig was content to deposit her entourage in comparatively rural quasi-retirement for the time being, she had no intention of remaining there herself.

She returned to town. Rented a neighboring townhouse. On credit. Made her presence known.

In her opinion, Frederik was not making the kind of an impression that a ruler—well, even a governor—should. She'd visited Denmark the year before when the chosen prince, Christian, married one of John George's daughters, Magdalene Sybille. She'd been present for the all the displays and spectacles, processions and parades, fireworks and entertainments. She had enjoyed them.

Anything at Lichtenburg, of course, had been much smaller in scope. And more sedate, as became a widowed dowager. But she remembered other grand presentations from before she was widowed; from her own wedding. Outdoor performances and pageants; her groom had been obsessed by tournaments. Which had been forgivable in a boy of nineteen; less so when he got himself accidentally killed in one nine years later, by which time he should have grown up. He had been less enthusiastic about plays and ballets. She loved them. Theater. Music. Dancing. Masquerades. Banquets.

One of the surprises she had encountered in Magdeburg was the up-time woman, Mary Simpson, who in these matters was a true kindred spirit.

Frederik's digestion moaned with misery at the suggestion of more and longer, more elaborate and longer, more highly spiced and longer, banquets.

"What do you mean?" she asked. "How can you possibly be coping without a chef? Without a court designer? You haven't even established your own wine cellar! And do you want eels for dinner?"

Frederik had never wanted eels for dinner in his life. He consulted with Christoffer Gabel, the young accountant he had recently hired to track his personal budget (always insufficient to need), as distinct from whatever budget the Province of Westphalia might be in process of developing (equally insufficient to need).

That amounted, in practice to tracking the allowance that he was receiving from his father. Which, Gabel confirmed, was generous, but not sufficiently generous for the governor to afford Aunt Hedwig.

Then a young cousin of the footman Vendt caught her eyes as being clever, with deft hands. She decided it would be worthwhile to train the girl as a fine laundress, specializing in laces and embroidered linens. This resulted in her buying the girl out of serfdom—along with her parents and minor siblings, of course—which the lord in question (that nuisance von Raesfeld) had made a fairly expensive proposition.

And she brought up the question of finding him a wife.

Reiterated the question of finding him a wife.

Said that she would consult with his father about finding him a wife, given the childlessness of the chosen prince and the extreme youth of Princess Kristina. There was no telling what might happen.

Frederik had enough.

"There are two options. Only two. If you do not wish to return to Denmark, that is."

He thought that Denmark would be a lovely solution to his dilemma, but an unlikely one for Aunt Hedwig to choose.

She did not appear to welcome the news of limited options.

"The first is that you can retire to Thedinghausen."

That would solve another problem him. Thedinghausen *Schloß*, as it stood, had been built by Great-Uncle Johann Friedrich for his lover. Not the *bürgerlich* lover currently pensioned off in Bremervörde, mother of Johann Friedrich's two legitimated and ennobled children, who was still very much alive and playing the role of "grieving widow" to the hilt while collecting a generous pension from the archdiocese.

Rather, he had constructed Thedinghausen for a noblewoman, the widow of a former archiepiscopal adviser and steward Heinrich Corlehake Hermeling, now resting among the saints of the church triumphant for some two decades. After a sequence of rather … iffy … financial transactions with the equally late archbishop, one hand washing the other. Upon the occasion of an overnight visit to Hermeling's home by the late archbishop a couple of years before that, Johann Friedrich had found Hermeling's young wife Gertrud to be charming, utterly charming. After Hermeling's death, the archbishop and the widow had experienced a lovely, lustful, interlude, much to the outrage of the pastor at Lunsen, that continued for some years and included the building of a beautiful modern *Schloß,* until Gertrud's sudden (and in Frederik's opinion, fortunate) death in March 1620. Great-uncle had nonetheless completed the building the next year.

"Thedinghausen," Frederik said with all the persuasiveness he could command, "is not equivalent to *Schloß* Lichtenberg, certainly. It is not as large and has no attached villages, but attractive, comfortable, and the outbuildings have been kept in good repair.

"There may be some challenges to your occupation of the property, but I'm certain that you are capable of dealing with them."

Great-Uncle had given the new *Schloß* to his illegitimate son Friedrich von Holstein immediately after the charming Gertrud's demise.

Frederik, as successor, and in his role as defender of the assets and budget of *Stift* Verden, had retrieved it, pensioning off the young man and his sister Christine von Holstein, now married to a von Hagen from Mecklenburg. Also, Gertrud had a surviving, married, sister—the von Heimbruchs were from Brunswick—who was heiress to her properties. All of them were almost sure to make nuisances of themselves with lawsuits, but surely Aunt Hedwig would be capable of handling persistent appeals to the *Reichskammergericht*. It would be useful to have someone in residence who could handle them—one less thing for him to keep track of himself.

"It should prove to be an ample residence, where you can continue to live out your retirement in comfort."

At the expense of Verden *Hochstift*, he thought, rather than out of my own pocket. It's not like the *Stift* doesn't have to pay the upkeep even when it's empty.

"It's upriver from Bremen," he said coaxingly, "but only a couple of miles—close enough that you could conveniently visit the city for cultural events and shopping for a week, every now and then. Even take in a sermon at the cathedral, now that we have reinstated Lutheran services there."

And wouldn't it annoy the Calvinists of Bremen if she showed up, a numerous entourage in tow. He took some pleasure in the prospect.

"The interior is beautifully decorated."

Aunt Hedwig averred that she would think about it.

"The other option," Frederik said temptingly, "is that you could take on a major project."

Bremen

The FoJP administration in Bremen was far less concerned about Lutheran services in the cathedral than the Calvinist patricians of the *Hochedler, Hochweiser Rath* had been. Certainly less so than the city's Calvinist clergy. Being native Bremer, most of them, and *cuius regio, cuius religio* having been around for quite some time, most of them were nominally Calvinist by virtue of having been brought up as Calvinists.

If they had been reared as druids, they would probably be nominal druids.

The cathedral services hadn't been mentioned in their conversations for months.

"Frederik gave the concessions at the charter convention," one of the mayors commented. "How long do you think we can keep them? How far can we push them?"

"What if he decides to revoke them and shows up in person?"

"He's sticking to the script when it comes to religious toleration. He'll show up as governor if he shows up at all, so we won't get the fun of making him walk through the Bishop's Needle."

"Focus, focus. Our aim is to become a free imperial city with a vote in the USE House of Lords."

The CoCs concurred with that aim, but tended to indulge in more philosophical debates. At least, the more academic among them, students and such, tended to indulge in more philosophical debates.

"I have an up-time textbook on something called 'business management.' It's a reprint, with annotations in Amideutsch. Doesn't say who did the annotations. But Professor Grotius, the Dutchman who's at Jena now ... " Tönnies Breiting's family had dispatched him off to law school whether he wanted to go or not, so he only participated occasionally now. It says, "Keep your goals firmly in view, but be flexible as to your methods."

"I saw something like that," Agnes Bemmeler said, "but it was, 'Keep a firm grip on your goals.' Is that a significant distinction?"

"According to the annotations—I do suspect they were added by some researcher in the State Library in Grantville, because who else would have convenient access to so many different up-time books?—there are several versions of both parts of the maxim. 'You must be stubborn with your goals,' or 'You should stay flexible in the approach and the methods.' I think.... "

Hans Schwarzkopf, another Marburg law student who had come up with Breiting for a chance to see what was happening in Bremen, asked, "Are you trying to justify a flexible method of making ethical decisions? Some form of raison *d'état?*"

Peter Schorfmann frowned at him. "Is that a version of Machiavelli's 'the end justifies the means'? Whatever the means end up being? Spartacus writes about that in some of his pamphlets. If that's what it's all about, we don't need to borrow it from the up-timers. We have it ourselves and have had it available to us for a century, at least."

Neither Knaub nor Jauch knew anything about these conversations, so they reported nothing to Frederik.

Hamburg

Daniel Bartoll, happily employed by the FoJP administration of the imperial city of Hamburg, as supervisor of the cattle market, looked out upon what he had created and found it good.

The immediate purpose of the Hamburg FoJP was to aid the Bremen FoJP by putting pressure on the Province of Westphalia.

If they choked Westphalian farmers' access to the cattle market and loading docks … No *when* they choked Westphalian farmers' access to the cattle market and loading docks … Frederik would have to give up his opposition to Bremen's independence.

Oxenstierna's stinking Province of Westphalia, full of cows and reactionaries, but without much else in the way of economic resources to support Gustav Adolf's personally appointed, hand-picked, *Hochadel,* reactionary, Crown Loyalist, Danish governor. "Prince of Westphalia. Pfaaah!" He cleared his throat and spat.

The requirement had been there for centuries. Three days. Before cattle or swine from the north, Jutland, Schleswig, Holstein, may be ferried across the Elbe and exported to the south, they must … must mind you … be available for sale to Hamburg merchants for three full days. Three entire days.

Three entire days *at the price that Hamburg sets.* Is that too much to ask? It's the responsibility of the government of the free imperial city of Hamburg to ensure that its citizens are provided for. Not to mention the obligation to provide for the USE troops here.

It's our *ferry*, too. We run it.

Which brought up the matter of ferry costs. It's only reasonable that *we* regulate them—certainly not Westphalia!

Now as for grain, how about mandatory warehousing in Hamburg-owned facilities as a prerequisite for loading dock use? With appropriate fees, of course.

When he was outlining his plan, somebody had asked if this was fair and just.

"All's fair in love and war," he answered.

"We're not at war. Westphalia's part of the USE too."

"We're at war with the reactionaries, and Westphalia's a hotbed of them."

"What if the up-timers object? They've forced the abolition of all the noble toll stations. Called them obstacles to trade. That's why we can't stop the Westphalians if they get hold of barges, load them upstream, and float them past us."

"Don't worry. I've gotten one of their business management textbooks. It makes pretty clear what techniques we can use and still be well within the boundaries they impose. Welcome to the wonderful world of usage fees, my friends. No petty noble will extort anything from the ignorant peasants as they bring their animals to the port for shipment." He smiled blissfully. "We'll get it all at the end."

As Albert Bugenhagen, the Fourth of July Party mayor of Hamburg, commented during his consultation with his stalwart supporters, there was no one in Magdeburg who had any vested interest in seeing Frederik succeed in administering Westphalia. Certainly not the FoJP, but not the emperor, either; there was no way he had truly wanted a son of the Danish king in office over here. He'd been pressured into it—probably something to do with the Union of Kalmar. That was obvious. Anyone who looked at the way the Province of Westphalia had been designed at the Council of Copenhagen could see that the Swede had designed it to fail. Neither Gustav Adolf nor Oxenstierna could cherish any desire to see the second son of Christian IV of Denmark in an important position inside the USE.

"Hold back," Bugenhagen imagined Oxenstierna –recommending. "Let him suffer an embarrassing failure, and then we can move in and demonstrate how it should be done."

Only the FoJP would move in; not Oxenstierna.

Virginia DeMarce

CHAPTER 17

Münster
September 1635

F rederik contemplated the imminent departure of his aunt, along with her accompanying train of Lutheran ladies, with considerable relief. It would also be a relief to have another competent regent for the *Erzstift* installed at Bremervörde. She probably would not regret refusing the offer of Thedinghausen. He hoped. It would be regrettable if she changed her mind. Bremervörde also had a comfortable modern residence, the Renaissance-style *Schloß*, and, of course, and the gardens.

Let her deal with Gerdruth von Campe and *Himmelpforten*, the woman's growing aspirations to turn it from a small regional *Damenstift* serving the local *Niederadel* into a major *Damenstift* of national reputation with an associated school and women's college on the model of Quedlinburg. Let her also cope with the remainder of the *Frauenstifte* plus the *Männerstifte* in Westphalia. May she swab up the aftermath of the CoC's intervention at *Kloster* Loccum. If that didn't keep her busy enough to forget matchmaking, nothing would.

But she did have a level of efficiency that might, possibly, let her do all those things and still cast about among the nobility of northern Germany to find him a wife.

He should put her administrative abilities to maximum use.

Draft a memo for Rist to put into proper form.

The regent at Bremervörde shall:

First dot:

Gather information on all the aftermath effects of the Edict of Restitution time period that are still having adverse effects on the Lutheran religious institutions of the *Erzstift*.

Hmmn. Why not? Subordinate dot. Of the entire archdiocese, for that matter.

He spared a passing thought in regard to his hearty dislike of Jesuits—specifically, at the moment, those who had ever dared to interfere with *Himmelpforten*, thereby turning a contented rural abbess into a mighty force of nature, a storm that bade well to drive everything before it, fueled by righteous indignation and pugnacious wrath. If somebody, somewhere, did not manage to locate the items taken from the abbey church … he would end up having to find the money to buy equivalent replacements. Which would not come cheap.

Second dot.

Find out what happened to the Jews in Stade.

How? Subordinate dot. There were Jews in Altona. There were Jews in Minden; the latter settlement should be grateful to the administration after what von Bargen did for them. Let the regent check with the Jews in Minden to find out where the ones from Stade had gone and tell them to come back. Well, perhaps it would be more diplomatic to ask them to come back. Request that they resume their business endeavors in Stade to the overall economic benefit of the Province of Westphalia.

Third dot.

Re-organize the customs station near Stade and furnish it with a reliable staff—consult Bente Luft's relatives, please; her father knows everybody who is anybody in customs and tolls, and he's still in Hamburg.

If an up-timer had been present, he would quickly have identified Frederik's smile as "grinch-like." The customs station was actually located in Brunshausen at the mouth of the Schwinge. It had played special role in trading on the River Elbe for a long time. Not the Weser: the Elbe. The Elbe upon which that thorn in his flesh, the Imperial City of Hamburg was located. If Hamburg was willing to effectively block the *Ochsenweg*, the old route that ran from Viborg through Flensburg, from Schleswig through Holstein, the *Viehstraße* that brought cattle to market ... to stifle the access of Westphalian farmers on the east side of the Elbe to the cattle market ... two could play that game. Gustav Adolf wouldn't allow him to stifle trade along the Elbe much. But he could ensure that there were annoyances, one of them being a functioning toll station on the western bank, downstream from the city.

Fourth dot. The grinchy smile got a little larger. Establish an enlarged cattle market and a cattle ferry over the Elbe somewhere near Altona. Wedel, a little place in *Grafschaft* Pinneberg, should be usable; it already has a small one. It may take some dredging to erect a decent set of loading docks, but that should pay for itself in almost no time. If Hamburg makes trouble ... see me for further instructions.

He saw Aunt Hedwig and her entourage off in spectacular style. She and her senior ladies-in-waiting in carriages, flanked by riders flying banners, followed by wagons full of servants and even more wagons full of luggage, boxes, crates, and kegs. She had accomplished quite a bit of shopping during her stay in the new capital of the Province of Westphalia. Only absolute necessities, of course.

All prudently preceded, at an interval of two days, by a road repair crew. The expedition should make it to its destination easily before the weather got bad.

"Does that maneuver count as cowardice in the face of the enemy?" Christian Ulrik asked slyly at dinner that evening.

"I'm not running away; shipping her off isn't quite the same, even if the principle of the thing is. She'd have had a matrimonial noose firmly around my neck within six months. I have no shame for having ducked."

"Nils had a book in Mainz," Kerstin Brahe said. "A collection of pithy up-time sayings. There was one by a poet named Goldsmith, about 'he who fights and runs away.' That he is merely conserving his resources. Are you conserving yours, or is your aunt conserving hers? She may return to the field. 'Live to fight another day' as the verse says."

"That's not up-time," Rist protested. "Demosthenes said something similar in a speech."

Which turned the conversation in another direction. Chaplain Lütkemann referenced a parallel in Tacitus. Christian Ulrik protested that marriage was not all bad—it could be very good. He was delighted to be married to Bente. He decided that he wanted her the first time he saw her.

"You and our father!" Frederik rather sourly. "One look at a pretty girl and you're sunk."

"I've only gone under once."

"When the time comes, I will make a sensible, well-planned, marriage. I don't want Aunt Hedwig trying to push me into it before the proper time has come." That was all he was going to say on the matter.

Lütkemann commented that women should not interfere in matters of state, referencing the passage 1 Peter 3:7 that described the sex as "the weaker vessel." Then he modified this slightly, recalling the role of Deborah in ancient Israel. Nonetheless … in principle …

For which he earned a slight stink-eye from Kerstin Brahe, who pointed out that in practice it was the women of royal and noble families who made most of the marriage arrangements—and that she had, for all practical purposes, arranged her own. So if the honorable Pastor Lütkemann was trying to say …

Rist managed to turn the conversation again.

As Frederik prepared for bed, he contemplated the Lutheran ladies he had encountered thus far since his appointment as governor and admitted to himself that he had certain doubts about the wisdom—or practicality—of reading that particular passage of the Bible literally. One should take the Word of God at its plain meaning, according to the *sola scriptura* doctrine, but he hadn't seen much sign of weakness in them. Obstreperousness, yes; recalcitrance, yes; pig-headedness, yes. Weakness? Not so much. Any resemblance borne by the ladies themselves to the delicate, fine porcelain that was now being manufactured for the decoration of their parlors and tables was, at best, minimal.

Other than that both were expensive to obtain and maintain.

Aunt Hedwig had left him with an invoice for her proposed refurbishing and refurnishing of the nice little Renaissance-style *Schloß* at Bremervörde. And she would almost surely want to modernize the interior of the church after she saw it.

He recited Martin Luther's evening prayer from memory and went to sleep.

SECTION III

Will Live to Fight Another Day
October 1635-November 1635

CHAPTER 18

Münster
October 1635

One thing could produce more wrangling over details than schools did. Churches.

Frederik was Lutheran. Denmark was Lutheran. That had been a beautifully uncomplicated state of affairs. He had grown up with the situation; absorbed it through his skin, consumed it with his cured ham.

Northern Germany had been somewhat more complex, but still comprehensible. While the principle of *cuius regio, eius religio* had not worked infallibly (see for reference the messy church history of the Upper Palatinate), nonetheless under the terms of the Peace of Augsburg, if a principality was blessed by God with a sequence of reliably Lutheran rulers, one could anticipate that it would develop a reliably Lutheran population. A state church with the ruler as *summus episcopus*.

Now correspondence informed him reliably that the Crown Loyalist majority in parliament and the emperor of the USE were expecting each province of the polity to establish a single state church.

After the same emperor—who was now off fighting in the east, his attention focused on other matters, leaving an increasingly impotent

Wilhelm Wettin as prime minister to try to ride herd on the bucket of eels that had voted him into office—yes, after that same emperor, little more than a year earlier, had arbitrarily created a province that …

Frederik counted on his fingers.

Nearly half Lutheran, but not half Lutheran. Not fifty-one percent, not likely to make up even a simple majority in the new legislature, even if all Lutherans could be expected to agree with one another and vote the same way. Which they could not be expected to do.

Nearly half Catholic. Which, fortunately from his perspective, would never add up to a simple majority either, even if their priests drove them all to vote the same way.

Calvinists were at least Protestant; one could think that it would be reasonable to expect that they would cooperate with Lutherans. But one would be sadly wrong. Consider Bremen. Too pigheaded to make reliable alliances; too few of them to be able to grasp important positions in the new legislature without alliances. But if he could manipulate them to keep a balance, some of them, sometimes, agreeing with the Lutherans on some things, the *Landtag* might at least get as far as electing a speaker.

And a tiny scattering of other ecclesiastical minorities, of which the Mennonites refused to take an active part in civil government at all and the majority of the Jews were still too cautious to try.

None of whom, thus far, had massacred any significant number of the others.

Krystalnacht had marked a slight deviation from that state of affairs, but one could make a reasonable argument that the events of June had not been generated by internal controversies but rather imported from outside. Carried out by Westphalians at Loccum and Minden, but after those Westphalians had been exposed to foreign, alien, ideas.

Rist took time off; went home to get married; stated that the betrothal was of considerable standing and it was time to convert it to a marriage. He would be gone for six weeks, which was annoying.

Rist's assistant, Gerhard Schepler, came in with another folder.

Orange. Churches again.

Thanks to the power of nepotism, Rist, whose sister was married to Schepler's cousin, had managed to find a competent assistant. Schepler had turned twenty and ought to still be in law school, but Rist had persuaded the young man from the county of Hoya to take a couple of years off from his academic wanderings. Since he showed every sign of becoming a perpetual student, his father had made no objection to his, praises be!, getting a job.

At heart, Frederik was still dubious about most up-time innovations, but beyond the In Box and Out Box array, he had taken the color-coded expanding pocket folder to his bosom. The shelves of the temporary archives he had established next to his office looked like a rainbow; they brightened even the gloomiest day. Which this day was. If it wasn't raining in Münster ... But today, as usual, it was raining.

It was unreasonable that he was inclined to seize upon an initiative of the Fourth of July Party. However. It was insisting that if each of the provinces was allowed to "decide for itself" what the established church should be, then one of the options must be "none of the above."

They wanted that for the SoTF and the Upper Palatinate, of course. Perhaps they would not know how to react when Westphalia petitioned to be included within that option.

"Piggybacking," Kerstin Brahe said. That was what it was called when you let someone else bear the burden of carrying the water for a policy or other boon that you wanted. If that was not a mixed metaphor. He idly doodled a pig walking on its hind legs with a yoke supporting wooden pails laid across its neck.

Not because he believed in religious tolerance. He didn't. He would far rather be a Lutheran ruler of Lutheran people. As things stood in Westphalia, however, out of sheer pragmatism, if he did not want a return to the chaos of the years following the Edict of Restitution in reverse …

He had consulted with his father. In fact, he had written in "just because you're paranoid, it doesn't mean that they aren't out to get you" mode, heavily encrypted, along the lines of, "This would ruin everything I've managed to hold together so far; Oxenstierna is out to cause Westphalia to fail and then will claim that it was my fault, which means that it was your fault, and under his leadership, Sweden will annex Scania now and all of Denmark eventually. Remember what the encyclopedias say they tried in 1658!"

To his father who, if he had religious preferences unconstrained by political realities, would probably have converted to Calvinism.

He was factoring in the strength of the CoCs in Westphalia, particularly in the larger cities. CoCs that had remained thankfully quiescent since *Krystalnacht*. Probably because they were consolidating their position and recruiting new members, to emerge even stronger at the next crisis.

Nonetheless.

At the moment.

They would support his position that Westphalia should opt out of having an established church. However much it might pain them to do so.

The CoC leaders in Bremen were mostly Calvinist: a majority in the city, but a minority in the province.

Frederik pulled in his lips, chewing on them.

The CoCs had no serious option.

Kerstin Brahe talked a lot, which was annoying. Not as annoying as the prospect of the arrival of another Lutheran lady within Frederik's inner circle, however, once Rist returned from his honeymoon. Not an unmarried one, though. Unmarried Lutheran ladies were the truly perilous ones. Particularly those of the *Hochadel* who had been Aunt Hedwig's protegees. So he should count his blessings.

From the up-time hymnal, a not-quite-down-time hymn verse flitted across his mind. Thomas Ken had not written the words yet, but would, within this century. Or would have, within this century. If it was the same century, even, in this altered world.

All praise to thee, my God this night,
For all the blessings of the light.
Keep me, o keep me, King of Kings,
Beneath Thine own almighty wings.

Preserve me from unmarried Lutheran ladies, O Lord. You have provided me with enough problems. He recited Luther's evening prayer and went to sleep.

Magdeburg
October 1635

The news of the emperor's injury at Lake Bledno, with his following illness and disability, reached the USE capital almost as soon as it happened. Thanks to radios.

It not only reached political movers and shakers; it reached the newspapers.

From the capital, it reached Münster almost as quickly. Münster and every other place on the Province of Westphalia administration's radio relay.

Berlin
November 1635

Dr. James Nichols was unable to determine when Gustav Adolf might recover from the not-exactly-a-coma state, he told Mike Stearns. The emperor was awake, but with serious difficulty in expressing himself. Even if he did recover to some extent, there would probably be brain damage. Oxenstierna ordered Princess Kristina to join her father.

Bremen
November 1635

There might be a national crisis in progress, but that didn't prevent local outbreaks of ordinary life. In Bremen, there were spats between Calvinist women and Lutheran women over allotment of stall locations in the weekly market; then additional spats when both parties found themselves dealing with Catholics who wanted to sell their goods—not a lot of Catholics but a steady trickle—moving in from the *Niederstift*, Cloppenburg mostly, but also Vechta.

It was unfortunate that Jutta had found herself in the path of a flying rotten cabbage.

It was even more unfortunate that Trinke had retaliated by grabbing several nice, firm, beets from the nearest stand and launching them in the general direction from which the cabbage had come with a powerful overhand throw.

Trinke had five brothers, two of whom had become fans of the new game called baseball.

It would have remained a normal spat among women if Trinke had not been a maid in the household of the mother of one of Bremen's most important CoC spokesmen.

Matters escalated all the way up to the city council. The beet vendor, who was of the Lutheran party, was demanding restitution. From someone. Whether it be the Calvinist beet thief or the Catholic who instigated the fray with the cabbage.

Tönnies Breiting felt obliged to speak out.

Knaub, in his report to the governor, viewed the situation with the utmost alarm.

Jauch insisted that everything had been blown out of proportion.

Frederik expected to hear from Aunt Hedwig, at length, any minute now, demanding justice for Lutheran beet vendors. Female ones.

None of which could be allowed to overwhelm the information that the city council of Bremen was using one Daniel Bartoll of Hamburg as a consultant in economic matters.

Osnabrück
November 1635

In the matter of whether, when it came to wrangling, schools or churches took the prize, there was naturally a third option. Sometimes one found the two combined, with results that were not merely arithmetic, but exponential.

In Osnabrück, there was an ongoing squabble between the ancient *Gymnasium Carolinum* and the Jesuits. That was a touchy one. The *Gymnasium Carolinum*, supposedly founded during the reign of Charlemagne, claimed to be the oldest continuously existing school in Germany. It had been "upgraded" by the archbishop of Cologne to a Jesuit university in 1632, but the city was taken by Swedish troops almost at once and restored to Protestant control. The charter had never gone into effect. Now the Jesuits were suing for possession.

They had brought suit in the *Reichskammergericht*, which Gustav Adolf had taken over, pretty much in its entirety, from the Holy Roman Empire and installed at Wetzlar.

That would have been straightforward, if a knotty problem for the lawyers, if it had remained a lawsuit. But the bad feeling aroused by the suit split the Lutheran and Catholic canons into bitterly contending groups. Then the two Lutheran factions supporting the two rival mayors, Modemann and Pelzer, took sides. The boards governing the *Domschule* and the *Ratsschule* got involved.

And Margaretha Timmerscheidt, now aged 18, said to her boyfriend, now aged 20, "why don't you issue an order saying that if they can't settle it peacefully, you'll turn the *Carolinum* into one of these new colleges for women."

Her boyfriend who was both the illegitimate son of the comatose emperor of the USE and the commandant of Osnabrück. His authority as commandant, which predated the appointment of the imperial governor of the Province of Westphalia, had … murky limits, undefined boundaries, and imprecise parameters.

Frederik sent Christian Ulrik, Erik, and Kerstin to Osnabrück to deal with it. If they couldn't squelch it there, they'd be off to Wetzlar.

Magdeburg
November 1635

In a meeting of the Fourth of July Party, Rebecca Abrabanel confirmed that Oxenstierna had ordered Princess Kristina to join her father in Berlin. That would give him control over both the disabled emperor and the heiress while he dismantled the constitution of the USE.

When one of the FoJP backbenchers from Westphalia rather timidly pointed out that Oxenstierna, as chancellor of Sweden, had no proper authority in the USE, all he got was a snort from Constantin Ableidinger in return.

At that meeting.

Münster
November 1635

But Dirk Waßmann from Minden was not alone in his opinion. As it happened, the governor of Westphalia, if sharing not one other political opinion with "those radicals," fully subscribed to the view that Oxenstierna had no legitimate independent political authority within the USE. He was merely one Gustav Adolf's Swedish employees. Essentially, Oxenstierna's status was no different from his own; less, if anything, for Oxenstierna had no vote in the House of Lords.

If anyone should be taking charge in the USE during the imperial incompetency, Frederik thought, it should be ... his brother Ulrik as *Statthalter* for Princess Kristina.

Leaving their father's status in the Union of Kalmar out of it for the time being. Their father, whose concerns about the structure of the reinstituted Union of Kalmar would make him inclined to exercise restraint *vis-a-vis* the USE's Crown Loyalists.

Stade
November 1635

When Aunt Hedwig did write, she mentioned beet vendors only in passing. Rather, after having been in residence for a while, she said, she had concluded that Bremervörde was the wrong place for what had become effectively the Province of Westphalia's northern capital: it was inextricably tied to the *Erzstift* and its ecclesiastical concerns. Frederik should leave it as a regional administrative center.

As for the second capital, which he certainly would need, given the extent of the province, nearly 270 miles from far southeast to far northwest, he should rather put it in Stade As a former Hanseatic city, Stade had sufficient prestige. As a location on the Elbe rather than the Weser ... it had significant potential.

Additionally, she had a proposal. While dealing with *Himmelpforten* (which had quite a lot of local support amidst all its tribulations; she thoroughly endorsed what Gerdruth von Campe was planning), she had made it a personal project to adopt the rather orphaned *Stift Neuenwalde* and had called in the abbess of Quedlinburg as a consultant in the matter of reviving and rehabilitating it. See the attached memorandum.

Frederik winced.

Damenstift Neuenwalde, a local foundation, poorly supported by its founders as far as finances went, accepted as canonesses not only girls from the local nobility, the *Ritterschaft*, of *Erzstift* Bremen, but also from the patriciates of Hamburg and Bremen and even daughters of well-to-do peasants if they could come up with a sufficient contribution to the endowment. It was in parlous condition. The buildings had burned in 1629, it was down to six canonesses, and hadn't had a prioress in place for a generation.

Aunt Hedwig proposed … At length.

Frederik put a note on the memo for Rist to take a look at it and went back to her letter.

Moreover, she said, Friedrich von Holstein, who had gotten a law degree from the University of Tübingen and been respectably employed in the bureaucracy of the Duchy of Württemberg until the recent unrest caused by Duke Eberhard's will, had lost his job. Consequently, he was back in the *Erzstift* and conspiring with his brother-in-law Gottlieb von Hagen, to institute a lawsuit in the *Reichskammergericht* for possession of Thedinghausen. The Mecklenburger to whom Johann Friedrich had married off Christine had sense enough to flee with his immediate household before *Krystalnacht* came down on him, but of course he'd effectively lost everything, so was nosing around for money. Since their other source of money might well be their father's family, it was possible that the Gottorps might make mischief in the *Erzstift* rather than having to provide for them in Holstein. Moreover, Gertrud von Heimbruch's sister, married to a Pomeranian, was thinking of getting involved, and *her* brother was a not unimportant official for Duke Georg of Brunswick, which could introduce complications all around.

She urged him to come north before winter set in heavily to inspect and put his stamp of approval on her initiatives. She wrote reproachfully that he had been neglecting the northern portions of the new province.

He looked at that suggestion with suspicion and wondered which prospective bride she wanted to suggest to him *this* time. And why there were so many Lutheran ladies. Although, in the nature of things, ever since Adam and Eve, the human race had been more or less equally divided between male and female.

Magdeburg
November 1635

"Nils is going to hold the Province of the Main out of it," Kerstin reported. "If any of the nobility go to Berlin to back Oxenstierna, it will be without his blessing; in fact, with his full disapprobation. He does not want to see the Union of Kalmar disrupted, and ... "

She looked at Frederik.

" ... if Oxenstierna launches an all-out civil war here in the USE between the reactionaries and the SoTF and its supporters in the other provinces, he'll create ... "

He looked back.

She continued.

" ... an unhappy king of Denmark. Who might possibly argue that as second in the Union of Kalmar, with the emperor incapable, he is the rightful regent for Princess Kristina. Not just in the USE. In Sweden. With lawyers."

"More probably," Frederik said rather mildly, "for Ulrik as regent in the USE and himself in Sweden. It would be an easier legal argument."

Chancellor Gießenbier nodded agreement.

If the administration of the Province of Westphalia should refrain from cooperating with Oxenstierna, what would be the position of the CoCs?

"They won't give you any open support," Erik Stenbock said frankly. "After all, you're the many-headed demon who is trying to get himself appointed as a hereditary 'Prince of Westphalia' as they see it. I expect that most of them would rather die than say a good word about anything you do as governor. They've become fairly sophisticated in political matters, though, especially the cohort in the city of Bremen. I don't think they'll sabotage you, either."

"As for Hamburg....." Gießenbier started to say. Then he thought better of it. "Albert Bugenhagen ... " Then he thought better of that, too.

His law clerk, a young man from Minden, listened to all these discussions with fascination. David Pestel never said so, though. He simply sat behind his mentor and took notes for him, using the "shorthand" he had learned from a manual brought by the up-timers and reprinted in Erfurt.

After Frederik received a letter from his loving Papa, expressing certain considerations in regard to the northern region of Westphalia, and another from Aunt Hedwig, he concluded that it was time for him to make another processional through the diverse bits and pieces that comprised the province, seeing and letting himself be seen, ending up by evaluating what might be achieved at Stade.

Christoffel Gabel protested that winter was not the season to make an extended processional; Frederik retorted that it was if he said it was.

He had more in common with his Aunt Hedwig than he was ready to admit. When he said jump ...

Kerstin Brahe and Erik Stenbock sent a letter to Nils Brahe in Mainz summarizing their critical evaluation of the status quo. "This may be the last time you hear from us for a while," she concluded. "We have to go to Wetzlar. With lawyers. Lots of lawyers. One set for the problems in Osnabrück. Another set for a lawsuit that's being brought simultaneously against Frederik as the governor, Frederik as the erstwhile prince-bishop, and Frederik as a person, all to do with property rights in the *Hochstift*. Should be fun!"

"Why," Johann Rist moaned to Joachim Lütkemann, "is this province still relying on horses and rivers for its transportation needs? Why aren't we at least looking into railroads? Making inquiries? Even Don Fernando over in the Low Countries is getting a start on railroads and the difficulties with water tables and such that his engineers are having to deal with must be at least as bad as they'd face here in Westphalia. Maybe worse."

"Get someone to look into it. Schepler, maybe."

Magdeburg
November 1635

As president of IBM, Ben Leek had a tendency to look at Gustav Adolf's coma and Oxenstierna's assumption of power in his name from the perspective their impact on the stock market. That would be, their unfavorable impact on the stock market. " ... stupid of the Crown Loyalists to expel Phil Hart from the Treasury Department. They're not going to find anyone preferable and it's not as if he's a political type!"

Pete Rush shook his head. "Being an up-timer makes you a 'political type' all by itself these days."

Tom Leek had a headache. The conversation around the table pounded on his temples.

"The Federal Reserve Bank in the SoTF ... ."

"David Bartley, they say, will … ."

"Impact on construction … " That was probably Bill Roberts.

"Now that Edgar Frost has left the Department of Transportation for Imperial Tech … "

"How long will it be before the Crown Loyalists start cleaning house there, too? The impact on R&D … "

"Is Jere Haywood going to stay here at Imperial Tech or head back to Granville?"

"I heard rumors that the landgravine of Hesse is trying to hire him. But … "

"I'm with Ben." That was Bill Roberts again. Bill was married to Ben's cousin Debbie."

Tom Leek stood up. "I'm heading home. This is affecting fundraising for Magdeburg Memorial Hospital, too; Amanda's all tensed up. David's getting repercussions from the down-timers at the Latin School, too. He says the political tensions among the parents of girls at the DESSSFG are even worse, given its close connection to the Wettins. I'm glad that Bethany is well out of it and tucked away safely at Quedlinburg."

CHAPTER 19

Magdeburg
December 1635

While ordinary people in most of the country read about the national crisis in the newspapers and otherwise got on with their own lives, the politicians in Magdeburg were preoccupied with it. Sometimes with more assumptions than facts. At one FoJP meeting, Albert Bugenhagen, the mayor of Hamburg, proclaimed, "At least half the stinking noblemen—

and just about all the *Hochadel*—from Brunswick and Westphalia are in Berlin right now, plotting with Oxenstierna." Anselm Keller, from the Province of the Main, chimed in that this was also true as one looked out from Mainz on his region.

Dirk Waßmann, the wimpy little backbencher from Westphalia, stuck up his hand and pointed out that, technically speaking, there weren't any *Hochadel* in either Brunswick or Westphalia. There were some *former*, now mediatized, high nobility who *formerly* ruled the various principalities that were thrown into Westphalia, but Brunswick didn't even have that. Except for the abbess of Quedlinburg, of course, who most certainly was not in Berlin plotting with Oxenstierna. As for a fair number of Westphalian and Brunswick *Niederadel*, he was willing to grant that they were in Berlin—but not with the approval of the governors of their respective provinces.

And not, he was willing to bet, any of them from *Erzstift* Bremen or *Hochstift* Verden. Not if they knew what was good for them. The dowager-electress took the position …

He was firmly told not to raise minor technicalities; subsided with a mutter about people not being free to create their own facts just because they liked them.

He'd been elected on a platform of shutting down the witchcraft persecutions that had plagued the city during the previous thirty years, which had appealed to the CoC. His main platform plank, "you never can tell when someone with a grudge will accuse your own mother or sister," might not have been strict party line, but had proven effective. His major qualification in the eyes of the rest of his constituents was that he had been thrown into prison for several months by the Catholic imperial forces during the years they occupied the town before the Ring of Fire and subsequent events.

He had no claim to fame other than having been present during the skirmish at Minden that led to the death of von Bargen. Which counted for nothing in this room, von Bargen having been representing the province's legitimately appointed governor rather than some heroic dissenter.

The count of Lippe-Brake is a manuscript collector, he thought rebelliously, unlikely to conspire with anyone; the count of Lippe-Schaumburg is young and inexperienced, old Count Hermann of Shaumburg having died only this year without heirs, and has ambitions to marry into the Hesse-Kassel family to shore up his position, so he won't do anything contrary to the wishes of the landgravine. The count of Lippe-Detmold *might* be in Berlin, but if so, I haven't heard about it. His Aunt Magdalena is certainly home in Herford doing her job as abbess, as *ordinaria loci* or, in the minds of those who objected to women in positions of ecclesiastical power, *monstrum Westphaliae*.

Perhaps one of Lippe-Detmold's younger brothers? There are three of them, all dissatisfied with a younger son's share.

There's definitely no *Hochadel* there from Diepholz, because the comital line is extinct and it's been mostly incorporated into Brunswick since 1585, which only goes to show that the emperor should have assigned it to Brunswick rather than Westphalia in the first place. And the same is true of Hoya, except that part of it went to Hesse-Kassel when the comital line died out in 1582 instead of all to Brunswick.

Aloud, once he managed to get a word in, he only said, "The least you people could do is familarize yourselves with local history, since it's perfectly clear that Chancellor Oxenstierna didn't bother when he cobbled the Province of Westphalia together. We—not 'we the FoJP supporters' but 'we the people who have to live there—are only lucky that both Frederik of Denmark and Duke Georg have been reasonable about it."

"Waßmann," Anselm Keller shouted, "stop being such a prig of a school teacher."

"There's nothing wrong with being a school teacher," came Constantine Ableidinger's counter-shout. "In any event, we shouldn't be worrying about petty noblemen. We'd better be asking ourselves what Gustav's Crown Loyalist provincial governors are going to do. Brunswick. Hesse. The so-called 'Prince of Westphalia' and his ilk."

Even Ableidinger had no idea where the story that circulated so widely had originated. By this time, it just was. So when Anselm Keller sullenly said, "They never made that Danish bastard a prince," Ableidinger retorted, "*Who* didn't? They didn't make him a prince because Gustav Adolf put his foot down. But what do you think are the odds that *Oxenstierna* won't hand him the title, if Frederik gets pissed at us and makes friendly noises toward Berlin?"

Dirk Waßmann thought about pointing out that Frederik was not actually one of the Danish bastards but rather a legitimate son of the king, but decided it was fruitless. Moreover, he currently held an imperial appointment from the USE that entitled him to a vote in the House of Lords under the new constitution, and that was that. If Frederik lost his job, he lost his vote. No different from the way that he himself, or Thomas Krage one district over, would lose the right to vote in the House of Commons if he lost the next election.

The title of *Fürst* that had once been held by the archbishops of Bremen and bishops of Verden had been … He glanced around at his fellow party members. It had been extinguished by *them*, right along with the old *Reichstag*. And they didn't even seem to realize what they had done.

Berlin
December 1635

Jürg Behr, more formally known, if he was speaking High German, as Georg Behr, had been a military officer for the Holy Roman Empire; then, after a rapid and prudent change of heart, a military officer for Gustav Adolf as king of Sweden after he intervened in the German wars and appeared to be on the winning side; then a military officer for Gustav Adolf as emperor of the United States of Europe. After all, a man had to earn a living somehow. His father, unfortunately, had lived far beyond his means trying to keep up with the lifestyle at the court of the dukes of Mecklenburg, and left his children burdened with debts.

But he remained a proud nobleman: not "von Behr," but Behr, with multiple branches of his lineage annexing the names of their various possessions to the family name. Born in Mecklenburg, fostered in Pomerania, with hereditary, fairly extensive, and, by the standards of the region, reasonably profitable, estates. Newenhofe, Düwelsdorff (known to the rude as —Teufelsdorf; spelled by the careless as Deifelstorff), Nustrow in Mecklenburg. But by changing sides, he still had not avoided some of the worst results of the coming of the

Swedes. The forced contributions in 1630 and subsequent years had been punitive, ruinous.

Der Schwed' ist gekommen,

Hat alles genommen

Hat die Fenster eingeschlagen,

Das Blei fortgetragen,

Hat Kugel draus gegossen,

Und alle Todt geschossen.

The Swede had indeed come and taken everything, even if he hadn't managed to shoot quite everyone dead with the balls poured from the lead taken from the windows he smashed. Currently, almost no Mecklenburg and few Pomeranian nobles had remunerative estates left. He wasn't one of the lucky few. Nustrow, where he himself had been born, unless things could be changed back, was probably gone for good: divided up among the serfs who had worked the land by the thrice-cursed Committees of Correspondence after *Krystalnacht.* There had been a nice little *Schloß,* decent moat, only about a century old: they had burned it to the ground. So much for the effectiveness of switching sides in a timely manner!

Which meant that Axel Oxenstierna, Swede or not, was currently his best hope, which was why he was in Berlin this winter.

If that didn't work … he had been married since 1621 to Hedwig von Heimbruch, from Brunswick. Who, as heiress of her sister Gertrud, had a possibly viable claim to the nice little estate called Thedinghausen in *Erzstift* Verden where they had celebrated their marriage. Not very viable, given that the previous prince-bishop's legitimated children had also filed a suit. But potentially, particularly if he could get Oxenstierna to see that a legitimate noble married to a legitimate noblewoman had a legitimate *hereditary* claim that should clearly take precedence over that of a couple of bastards and most certainly over that of the successor who currently held the see. Whose father, the king of Denmark, was bound to be a thorn in Oxenstierna's flesh.

Stade
December 1635

"There's another CoC pamphlet," Rist said, throwing it on the table. "Alleging that your father and you are agitating to have Chancellor Oxenstierna name you as 'Prince of Westphalia.' Are you going to respond? This time? Finally?"

Frederik, son of King Christian IV of Denmark, turned from the window through which he had been observing the ancient Hanseatic city he had now officially designated as the northern capital of the region he administered, his hands clasped behind his back, and looked down his prominent nose. "No."

Johann Rist waited, eventually resigning himself to the obvious fact that the governor of the USE's Province of Westphalia had no intention of elaborating on that statement. The man was not in the least given to sharing the "why's" and "wherefore's" of the decisions that he made.

"Do we have a response from Duke Georg yet?"

"Yes." Rist placed a folder of correspondence on the table considerably more sedately than he had thrown the pamphlet.

"Thank you. I'll call when I've decided on a reply."

Rist bowed himself out.

Frederik picked up the CoC pamphlet and placed it neatly in his "File with No Response" box.

"Prince of Westphalia." How convenient of the radicals to spend their time worrying about wild improbabilities when they could be creating real difficulties.

What had ever given Stearns' people the idea that he was petitioning to have his title changed to "Prince of Westphalia?" Why would he agitate for any such thing? He was neither a *Printz* in Denmark, where there was only one and that was his older brother Christian, the Chosen Prince, the elected heir to the throne, nor a *Fürst* in any German principality, which the English language oddly translated with the word *prince*. Nor had any member of the House of Oldenburg ever been a *Fürst* by birth or inheritance.

In an odd way, he was still the episcopal administrator, if no longer a ruling bishop, in Bremen and Verden, but an elective office as *Fürstbischoff* did not make one personally a prince. Aside from the anomaly of Anhalt, it was a status. It had signified that one headed an ecclesiastical institution that had a seat in the *Reichstag*. As his current status as *governor* gave him a seat in the House of Lords of Gustav Adolf's new parliament.

Certainly a prince-abbot such as the late Schweinsberg at Fulda had not been a prince. He had been personally a member of the lower nobility; a *Fürstabt* by virtue of the office he held. Frederik's mind twisted a little. If, by some freakish combination of ability and cunning, a commoner had ever managed to be elected as abbot of Fulda—or archbishop of Bremen—that man would have held such a title and have sat in the *Reichstag* by virtue of the office he held.

It might even have been possible—remotely possible—without the Ring of Fire. More and more cathedral chapters over the past century had gone to accepting canons who held university doctoral degrees in law or theology as equivalent in rank to those born to the nobility.

Governor of the Province of Westphalia—that title was, by its very nature, coming from Gustav Adolf, a temporary thing. To quote Job, "Naked came I out of my mother's womb, and naked shall I return thither: the Lord gave, and the Lord hath taken away; blessed be the name of the Lord."

But, so be it. Stearns and his Fourth of July Party had gotten the *Prince* idea from somewhere—probably from some unfounded speculation published in a newspaper—and the CoC radicals, including those in the city of Bremen, had run with it for the past year. Bless their black little hearts. It was a useful distraction.

CHAPTER 20

Quedlinburg
December 1635

The chairs in the room that was being used as an auditorium at the Abbey of Quedlinburg were straight. Wood. Hard. Veronica Dreeson re-settled her bony rear end in search of a more comfortable angle.

"Having Annalise here has made such a difference." Iona Nelson wanted to hug Ronnie, but didn't think that she would take it right. Not hug her because the chairs were hard—they were, but Iona contributed considerably more natural padding than the other woman—but because life itself wasn't easy. "I wouldn't have wished any harm for Henry, no not for the world, believe me that, please, Ronnie. But if it hadn't all happened, then she would have stayed in Grantville, helping you manage the St. Veronica's there, and things would have kind of kept rocking along."

"You," Veronica said, "understand more than most."

The two of them kept an unacknowledged moment of silence in memory of Billy Nelson and Henry Dreeson, both of them, in different ways, sacrifices to the changed world caused by the Ring of Fire.

"She'd have had to go to college somewhere," Ronnie said abruptly, "and she's not scientifically inclined, so she didn't want to go to the new technical college right there and spend the rest of her life in a lab coat working for Phillip Gribbleflotz in Jena doing something that bored her if she didn't absolutely have to. The way things are for us now, she didn't. If it wasn't here, it would have been Amberg, or maybe Bamberg. But she wouldn't have been home and I didn't want to stay in Henry's big house."

"Rattling around by yourself," Iona nodded. "I know the feeling."

"Do you know? Even when I complained loudest, I never thought that Gretchen and Jeff would take the children to Magdeburg. Well, Martha and Baldy stayed in Grantville, of course; he's more than half way through his apprenticeship now and she's in her second year at the technical college. I rather expected that all of them would be with Henry and me until they grew up and gradually each went their normal ways. But after the assassination … Jeff and Gretchen did take the four younger ones. Thea and Nicholas moved into their own place. When Annalise went, it would have been so empty."

There was a sudden, ominous, different kind of rattle behind the curtains hung in front of the large dais. Iona yelped, "Excuse me a minute," and dashed off.

"Children!" Ronnie muttered to herself. At least the rattle had not concluded with a crash.

Iona's head poked through the opening. "You might as well go back to my rooms and find a more comfortable chair for a while. We've sort of got an emergency here. If you can come back in a half hour, maybe, we'll probably be ready to go into the dress rehearsal."

By the time Iona got the drums (yes, the drums were the culprits for the rattle) reorganized, Ronnie was back. Iona signaled to Annalise and headed out to the chairs again. From backstage, you could never get a perfect idea of how it would all look from the front.

"I'd planned to do a program like this the first year I came," she whispered. "When I was traveling up from Grantville, my head was stuffed full of plans. I had no idea how much of a challenge it would be, adapting to an entirely different school setting and system. I didn't have the contacts, either with the rest of the faculty or with the community, to do one last Christmas. Or enough time with the children. And I hadn't had time to think what songs I would put in it."

There had been a lot of discussion, here and there, since the Ring of Fire, about what up-time music the down-timers would or would not "accept."

Iona was inclined to think that a lot of it was off the mark. She was willing to grant that she was just a middle-school music teacher rather than a great composer or performer, but, still ... Why didn't they stop to think? Outside of concert pieces, it wasn't like music was carved in stone. Outside of the realm of people with a lot of professional training, or sophisticated patrons of the arts, would it come down to a matter of "accept" or not? Or would it be more a matter of "if I like it, even a little bit, I'll just modify it until I like it even more"? If people liked a song—the melody and lyrics—but thought the harmonies were odd, they could just change the harmonies.

After all, most people didn't feel any real obligation to perform a song exactly as the way it was originally written, even up-time. She herself had turned SATB into SSA on occasion, if SSA was what she needed. Music got rearranged, and changed. If it wasn't, you'd never have had anything as different as Ella Fitzgerald singing *Mood Indigo*[2]— that magnificent 1957 recording—from some of the atrocious pop versions. *So there.*

Which had led to the rehearsal today.

Thank heavens for Annalise Richter. The girl wasn't a particularly good singer, but she had a talent for organizing small children, and that's where the program would lead off, gradually progressing in

---

[2] https://www.youtube.com/watch?v=jaq9Gx9GT5E Ella Fitzgerald - Mood Indigo (Verve Records 1957)

complexity as the performers aged, ending up with the young women of the new college. Junior college. The abbess had visions of a full four-year college, but there were staffing issues.

The curtain opened. The youngest children, already positioned, started to march around the stage to Tom Paxton's *The Marvelous Toy.*[3] The girls with the drum set made bop sounds, chug sounds, and other sound effects with supreme glee.

Iona nodded. That would work well. The littlest ones were almost all day students from the town of Quedlinburg itself. Down-time parents didn't usually send young children to a boarding school, barring some kind of domestic disaster that made it impossible for them to remain at home. Now that the abbey school was open to commoners, quite a lot of the more prosperous burghers had chosen it over the four-year girls' school that the city council had been running for close to a century. So she could count on almost all the interested parents of pupils at this level coming and, she hoped, liking it, if only because they admired their own special little performer.

Space for bows and, she profoundly hoped, applause.

Then the audience would stand and sing *Ein' feste Burg*[4] in the original uneven time signature. Well, in what for this audience was the standard time signature; the only one they knew. She couldn't see why so many up-timers thought that irregular time signatures would be a problem in the seventeenth century. A lot of the hymns she sang growing up had them, so, pouf on them! The *new* for this was the piano accompaniment, on a new down-time-built piano.

---

[3]https://www.youtube.com/watch?v=ahWcocGtEyA   The Marvelous Toy - Tom Paxton (with Sean Silvia) at Mason District Park in Annandale, VA

[4]https://www.youtube.com/watch?v=nDdHtOSHIXE   The Wartburg Choir: Ein feste Burg ist unser Gott, arr. W. B. Olds

Space for the audience to sit down and get settled.

The next oldest children, aged ten to twelve enter; yes, yay, all lined up in the correct order; Sabina Lechner comes to the front and announces, "The music of our day was not lost in the up-time world." *What Child Is This*,[5] set to the melody "Greensleeves."

She couldn't lose the visual interest, so the next was a standard seventeenth century line dance, familiar steps and therefore easily learned, but set to the up-time music of *Once in Love with Amy*,[6] alternating sung verses with instrumental interludes. Bethany Leek brought her up-time flute to this. She played it well. When it came to singing, she had reminded Mrs. Nelson, it was a good idea for her to stand in the back of any chorus or choir and hum softly. Iona remembered.

First real challenge. Annalise to the front, explaining that a particular kind of song beloved of the up-timers had been called "western," and they would now present three of these, moving from the simple kind taught to young children to the complex requiring a highly skilled performer.

Home on the Range.[7] The littlest to the front of the stage again, looking sweet. A sheet, with a painting on it, rolled down to the left side of the front curtains, showing a West Texas landscape. Or maybe the Dakotas? With bison, anyway, according to the legend. Or buffalo?

---

[5]https://www.youtube.com/watch?v=j3XTbTUBXos   2011-12-16 The Elm City Girls Choir - What Child is This

[6]https://www.youtube.com/watch?v=oqiNkkTwSn4 Frank Loesser - Once In Love With Amy

[7]https://www.youtube.com/watch?v=18IrXMjhb0w Home on the Range - Milwaukee Children's Choir

She had asked to borrow something from the high school library in Grantville, and this was what they sent.

Annalise again, with a little introduction, explaining that the tune for the next song was from this era, although it possibly, even probably, had not been composed quite yet, an Irish melody that would be called *The Bard of Armagh*. The middle school girls started *Streets of Laredo*.[8]

Iona hoped the audience would like it, because the next was going to be a lot dicier. Even the college-age girls had a terrible time getting the rhythm; she only hoped the pianist would keep them focused. *El Paso*.[88] She shivered with delight at the memory of Marty Robbins' haunting voice and hoped that the audience wouldn't shudder with distaste; not that the girls' version offered any significant competition to Marty.

Intermission

In case El Paso had been a bit too much, even for people who were paying out good money for the specific purpose of having an up-time woman teach their children up-time music, she was starting with a slight re-group after the intermission. Sabina came out again, reminding the audience of the survival of music of their own day into the future: a short medley of Quem Pastores[888] In Dulci Jubilo[18888] *and Puer Nobis*

---

[8]https://www.youtube.com/watch?v=EpFBT_NUECg Burl Ives - Cowboy's Lament (I couldn't find as a children's chorus, but remember that we sang it in grade school.)

[88]https://www.youtube.com/watch?v=R-y3DB0wLh4 EL PASO by MARTY ROBBINS: BEST VERSION ON YOU TUBE.

[888]https://www.youtube.com/watch?v=dG_oJICD-Dw The Choir of Canterbury Cathedral sing "Quem Pastores."

Nascitur,[18] with up-time lyrics, ending with what would be to the audience an extraordinarily contemporary, because not exactly written quite yet, hymn by Paul Gerhardt "whom many of you may have met at St. Jacob's in Magdeburg" and Johann Crueger: *O Lord, How Shall I Meet You*.[18]

Now, ages thirteen-sixteen. Osanna Merkur, a student from Suhl so no parents in the audience, which was a pity. Osanna was a miner's daughter, here on a UMWA scholarship. She spoke well in public, so had the task of explaining that there were other sources of up-time religious music than the European continent and distinguishing between folk "spirituals" and deliberately composed music in the same tradition.

Go, Tell It on the Mountain[18] (Osanna on solo, with the younger children joining in the choruses; Osanna wouldn't grow up to be Maria

---

[8888]https://www.youtube.com/watch?v=sOyEbmZUSHQ In dulci jubilo by R.L Pearsall/John Rutter performed by Piedmont East Bay Children's Choir's Ancora on December 2, 2017 in Berkeley, CA.

[82]https://www.youtube.com/watch?v=HbbYld6w6U4 O Splendor of God's Glory Bright (Puer nobis nascitur).

[83]https://www.youtube.com/watch?v=lc-3wB7Ol_g O Lord, How Shall I Meet Thee - Christmas Carols Lyrics & Music.

[84]https://www.youtube.com/watch?v=IU3Nu_0ufdI "Go! Tell It on the Mountain!" - UCC Children's Choir.

Callas, but she might equal Dolly Parton: Iona was waiting for her voice to mature before trying *Farther Along*[18]).

Shall We Gather at the River?[18]

Those two should go over well, but then she was taking a chance on Thomas Dorsey's *Precious Lord, Take My Hand*,[18] which she thought was much more impressive when rendered by an adult male bass voice, but on the other hand was so distinctive … There weren't a lot of girls at the college level yet, but they had worked hard on it, and the pianist, for a 55-year-old organist from one of the city's churches, had taken to gospel music as if he were born to it.

Let the sound die off.

To the left, over the sheet, there rolled down a large wall map of the United States of America with, clearly marked and a spotlight directed at it, the tiny portion of it that was Grantville.

This Land is Your Land,[18] with her hand-maneuvered, jury-rigged spotlight tracing from place to place as the song mentioned each of them.

---

[85] https://www.youtube.com/watch?v=igrBCBlsovU Dolly Parton, Linda Ronstadt, Emmylou Harris - Farther Along from the 1987 vinyl LP "'"Trio."'

[86] https://www.youtube.com/watch?v=hHO8GWllwz8 Provided to YouTube by The Orchard Enterprises
Shall We Gather at the River? · The Christian Children's Choir.

[87] https://www.youtube.com/watch?v=4Y1SZKJPrKc Children's Chorus of Washington -- Precious Lord Take My Hand.

[88] https://www.youtube.com/watch?v=FwgvM9yc5xU This Land is Your Land. Fairfield County Childrens' Choir.

Then she would come out. Thank them for their attendance. Invite them to come back next year to hear more about up-time music, all the time wondering if there was to be a next year.

And an encore, if the applause this evening justified an encore.

Randy Sparks' *Today*,[18] in unison by all the girls.

"It was a success," Ronnie said at breakfast.

"It wasn't bad," Iona admitted. "Without Annalise's assistance, it could have been a catastrophe. I'm so glad she chose to come to Quedlinburg."

"I chose it for her. She didn't have a strong preference. When Mary Simpson and the abbess offered her this chance … As a college for women, it's new, too, as new as the normal school in Amberg or Bernadette's experiment in Bamberg, but as a school, it's been established for centuries. And even if Annalise is Catholic and this is Lutheran, she's not the kind of girl ever to be obnoxious about religion. She's not upset by having to attend chapel with the others. It's not even as if I had anything resembling a lifelong religious commitment, given the way the rulers of the Upper Palatinate jerked us from one to another under *cuius regio*. Nor Gretchen, heaven help us!"

Iona nodded. "Plus, the girls she's meeting here are from influential families. Not that Annalise even appears to care about that. She's so sunny. Truly, all the time, she's mostly happy, and at her worst, she only gets mildly upset. Gretchen must have worked miracles, sheltering her from the horrors of those years you were with the mercenaries. Or else—what did they used to say about Reagan?—she's Teflon."

Ronnie beamed. She might be a down-timer, but she had met Teflon and she had loved it. She thought anyone who had ever scoured a cast-iron pot would love it. Among the few things she had taken from

---

[89] https://www.youtube.com/watch?v=teHe-JIj7EY   Today-Randy Sparks(original).

Henry's house when she joined Jeff and Gretchen in Magdeburg, Teflon had been a high priority.

CHAPTER 21

Berlin, Province of Brandenburg
January 1636

Oxenstierna ordered the arrest and imprisonment of Wilhelm Wettin, Crown Loyalist prime minister of the USE, formerly one of the dukes of Saxe-Weimar and consequently a citizen of the State of Thuringia-Franconia.

That last bit had sort of slipped the mind of Oxenstierna and his more fanatical supporters.

Jürg Behr agreed heartily with the action and took the opportunity of dropping a few chosen words about Thedinghausen and the less than energetic, enthusiastic, support that the governor of Westphalia was bringing to the cause of Restoring Things to the Way They Should Be.

He had concluded that "restoration" was a lovely word. He liked "restitution," too, for that matter, given its financial implications, but it had been unfortunately rather polluted for use in northern Germany by Ferdinand II's unfortunate edict of 1629.

Magdeburg
January 1636

Mathias Strigel, governor of Magdeburg Province and one of the prominent leaders of the Fourth of July Party, agreed with Rebecca Abrabanel that by arresting Wettin, Oxenstierna had lost the principle of being the legally legitimate government—handed the FoJP a belated Christmas present, a propaganda banquet on a porcelain plate. "He'll lose the support of most of the provincial governors. Hesse, for sure; Brunswick, too."

"Westphalia?"

Helene Gundelfinger from the SoTF was counting on her fingers. "Yes, Westphalia."

"But ... "

"Westphalia has a Danish prince as its administrator, governor, official head of state, even if he's not yet 'Prince of Westphalia.' His brother is betrothed to Princess Kristina, in line to succeed Gustav Adolf, as things stand. Even if Frederik doesn't like Ulrik much—and we don't *know* that he doesn't like Ulrik, though he's pretty much bound to resent him a bit—it is not probable that he would do something as much to the disadvantage of his own family as support this coup."

Rebecca returned to her original thought. "It's a bad mistake, a major blunder. Oxenstierna has given up the main thing that historically, counterrevolutions had working for them. He's given up the principle of legitimacy."

"Back home," Helene was counting backwards on her fingers, "there are a lot of people, up-timers and down-timers both, who are spitting mad about the way he's treating Wilhelm Wettin. Who's a hometown boy, in a way. It's not going to make him popular with the rest of the high nobility anywhere else in Germany, either."

"Why the hell not?"

"If he can do it to a duke of Saxe-Weimar and get away with it, and they do still see Wilhelm as a duke of Saxe-Weimar even if he renounced his title—his wife didn't renounce hers, remember—then he can do it to them."

Hesse came out neutral, as predicted. Amalie Elisabeth influenced Brunswick in the same direction, which was not a surprise.

The administration of the Province of Westphalia maintained a stony silence. Frederik fully agreed with the landgravine as to the lack of legitimacy of Oxenstierna's actions. Not that it took much to get him to view Oxenstierna from the angle described as *schief*.

Frederik did not interfere in any way when the province's city officials, newspaper editorials, or private individuals expressed their opinions out loud.

Lütkemann, the chaplain, found the admiration for Matthew 10:16 that Frederik expressed in the course of deciding upon his course of action mildly perturbing. The governor's personal exegesis and application of it was … not the orthodox theological interpretation. As phrased by the compilers of the recent translation into English, the verse read, "Behold, I send you forth as sheep in the midst of wolves: be ye therefore wise as serpents, and harmless as doves." Generally speaking, commentators did not see this as divine approbation for going forth as a wolf disguised in sheep's clothing. Luther's usage of *ohne Falsch*, "without deception," was in his opinion unquestionably preferable to "harmless." A wolf in sheep's clothing was engaging in deception. Not to mention that the biblical imagery pertaining to serpents had been more than a little problematical since the third chapter of Genesis.

The CoC-supported, FoJP-majority, government of Bremen found itself in the distasteful position of having to back Frederik's lack of action. This did not prevent the *Senat* from ongoing, if behind-the-scenes, consideration of the plans presented by Daniel Bartoll.

Quedlinburg
January 1636

"Grandpa," Bethany Leek wrote from Quedlinburg, "you may think that the Danish prince Frederik in Westphalia will come in to support Oxenstierna, but that's *not* what the *Stiftdamen* here are saying. They gossip while they're supervising our afternoon tea ... well, not tea, but you know what I mean ... refreshments ... and watch us embroider and do other down-time, lady-like, things, accomplishments that we're still supposed to master in addition to the more modern classes that the abbess has introduced for the junior college.

"We're all really excited about the cranked ice cream freezer that you sent, the old fashioned one made of wood staves, like a barrel. They're calculating when the abbey's year will reach a point when there will still be plenty of ice in the ice house for freezing and the dairy cows will start to calve so there will be fresh milk to get the cream from. The cooks are already saving sugar. Most of the food here is pretty soft, boiled to death, because so many of the older ladies don't have teeth. They're excited about a dessert that will literally melt in their mouths. So if it's a big hit, you can pass on to Chad Jenkins that he can expect a lot of orders for these freezers he's developed as a sideline, because the old ladies here are related to everybody."

She underlined "everybody" three times.

"Everybody who is anybody. And they say ... "

Basically, they said ... if you boiled down what Bethany required four pages to cover ... that the governor of Westphalia had undoubtedly read about himself in the *Encyclopedia Britannica* and found out about all the stuff that happened in the up-time world when he had to negotiate with the Danish Estates to be confirmed as Christian IV's successor after his older brother died without kids. That he was smart enough to learn something from what he read.

"That, most likely, the way he'd look at it, the moral of the story would be *noble reactionaries are not your friends*. Not if what you want in life is to be an absolute monarch. Most of the ladies, their fathers and brothers being nobles and pretty much reactionaries, I suspect, don't like the idea of absolute monarchs at all. No more than they like republics or democracies. Which seems a bit weird, but that's the way the ball bounces, Grandpa."

Ben snorted that the girl was nuts.

Ben's son Tom, Bethany's father, got a nervous feeling that Bethany was not tucked as safely away from all the political tension by being at Quedlinburg as he had hoped. He took the letter to Pete Rush, who showed it to his wife (who was also Tom Leek's sister, so that was no breach of confidentiality), who casually mentioned some of the ideas in it to Livvie Davidson, who worked with Mary Simpson—for Mary, really—on school reform.

Mary made a few comments about it in her next letter to her own son Tom.

Virginia DeMarce

SECTION IV

Begin as You Mean to Go On
January 1636-July 1636

CHAPTER 22

Holstein
January-February 1636

It was too early in the season, in the midst of these cold, unforgiving, winters, for serious work on the Duke of Holstein-Gottorp's new canal. Nobody was trying to dig through the ice.

The duke's canal. That was what most people called it. The official name was the Eider Canal. The funding came from a large consortium organized by a broker at the money exchange in Kiel, the institution that provided credit for almost anyone in Holstein who needed credit, be they merchants, shippers, millers, manufacturers, or nobles who so overspent their incomes on modern luxuries that they were willing to mortgage their land.

This canal was the largest project the broker had ever undertaken to finance. It would either make him a spectacular fortune or bankrupt everyone involved.

Jochen Giese was willing to take the risk. There was a known reason why Kiel, the largest town in the Duchy of Holstein, even if not precisely a major urban center at 8,000 or so residents, had no longer been a member of the old Hanseatic League when its remnants disbanded a few years earlier under the stresses of the current war. Kiel had been expelled in 1518 for harboring pirates. The brokers of the

Kiel exchange, many of them at least, had an instinctive understanding of the joy of piracy, even if not precisely on the high seas. Shipping and the annual *Umschlag*, the free market, meant that they had resources out of all proportion to the expectations most people had of such a modest little municipality, which could be advantageous. It wasn't every market that attracted not only buyers and sellers, entertainers and con-men, prostitutes and pickpockets, but also investors and lawyers. Even Hamburgers and Lübeckers found it advantageous, at times, to make a deal in Kiel. He, Jochen Giese, and Marcus Langemach, between them, would make this deal and make their lineages wealthy beyond anyone's dreams.

If it worked out.

He stood, looking over the route proposed for one of the cuts that would reduce the transit time significantly, as compared to letting the canal builders simply dredge the circuitous bends and twists of the Eider, and nodded. "Now," he said, "as to the lock placement, what are the comparative costs if ... " He and Duke Friedrich's agent fastened their hats down and pulled their cloaks tighter against the wind coming off the North Sea as they walked in a generally westward direction. He paid no attention to the occasional small groups of laborers who clustered around foremen who were directing their activities.

Giese had no particular interest in technology. He was a money man.

Hans Dubbels anchored one of the small groups of laborers. He was a big young man; a strong young man.

Also a smart young man. Twenty-two years old. Born in the year of 1614, according to his mother. Born a serf, because his parents were *hörig*. Belongings, if one thought of the basic meaning of the word. *Es gehört mir*. It belongs to me. Confirmed in the harshest form of that serfdom in the year same year he was born, when the ruling nobles adopted new legislation.

Serfdom was not only accepted by the rulers and nobles of Holstein. It was the foundation of the rural economy on the great manorial estates. "Bound to the land" wasn't the right way to describe it, except if that meant they weren't allowed to leave. Most serfs were workers. *Insten*. Only a few peasants were permitted to rent farmland for their own use in return for their services on the lord's demesne. Even those peasants' children were *Gesinde*, bound, from the age of six years onwards, to forced labor for the lord. Starting as goose-boys or dairy-girls and continuing until they could, maybe, eventually, marry and rent land on terms as burdensome as those of their fathers.

Or with even more burdens than their fathers. If the lord had not decided to cancel the tenure and draw even more land into his demesne, making them into *Insten* themselves.

If the lord gave them permission to marry, which he could refuse.

If the lord didn't conscript them and send them into some army to be killed.

No right to learn a trade without the lord's consent.

Mostly, no schools, even though once the pastor had let slip that in most of the Germanies, all children were taught to read and write.

"Bound to the land." Say rather, 'in bondage to the land's lord.' "

He wasn't a person, in the eyes of Lord Ahlefeldt. He was a tool, like the hammer in his hands was a tool.

Holstein was not all that large a duchy. Even a peasant boy could learn that there wasn't much serfdom in the western part. If a man could get there and stay there. Of course, the law passed the year he was born provided that escaped serfs must be returned to their owner.

The foreman called out an order and he gave another swing of his sledgehammer against the thick layer of ice frozen over the door to the storage shed.

Canal work didn't pay much, but something was better than nothing.

When Jürgen Rickerts heard the blow that told him how hard Dubbels was swinging that hammer, he frowned. The boy was too reckless, was likely to break something, would draw the attention of one of the duke's agents to their work group, and someone would identify them.

Jürgen wasn't intending to work on the canal permanently. He did hold a full farm on one of the Ahlefeldt estates and had left his wife and children there to run it during these coldest months. With care, they could keep the overseer from noticing that he wasn't present himself. They needed the money he could make.

Every year, it seemed, the lord shifted more of the costs to his tenants and demanded more services from them. If he was to fatten as many steers each winter as the lord was demanding, with so many harvests failing because of the cold, he would need one of the new silos. A silo might pay for itself in the long run, but in the short run, the farmer had to pay for it to be built.

Lord Ahlefeldt certainly wasn't going to make any capital investments on the tenant farms. He lived for excuses to abolish the peasant tenures and incorporate the land into the demesne he cultivated with slave labor. What amounted to slave labor. It was hard to tell the difference between the status of the *Insten* and the slaves of ancient Rome that the pastor talked about when he preached from the *Book of Philemon*. The pastor preached from *Philemon* to teach obedience and subordination. What Jürgen had gotten from the lesson was that he didn't want to see his children decline into *Insten*.

Dubbels swung the hammer again.

"Take it easy," Jürgen said, looking up anxiously as the duke's local agent walked past them with an unknown, but suspiciously well-dressed, man by his side.

Lammert Cordes and Cai Reimers just stood there. Reimers was barely sixteen and not the most effective boy on the Ahlefeldt estate. If you told him what to do and showed him how, he would do it. If it was something within his ability. Many things were not. He would keep doing it until you remembered and told him to stop. You had to remind him to eat his noon meal. You had to remind him to stop when it got dark, and in winter it got dark early. You had to remind him to go to the fire and warm up when his fingers started turning blue.

They might have been better off without young Cai, but it seemed like every year, the overseer treated the boy worse. He couldn't help being the way he was, and his mother worried about him so much.

He didn't have the strength to hammer this ice off.

Lammert was lazy. And a drunk, when he could get hold of liquor. He didn't have enough skill to hammer this ice off.

Then there was Tönnies. Tönnies Dirkes. Not one of them. Not from the Ahlefeldt estate. His father did carting services out of Eckernförde, up north in Schleswig. Armies, both the king of Denmark's and Tilly's, had come, not quite ten years ago, but getting close to it, now. Plague had followed them. By the time it was done with Eckernförde, 500 men had become 50 men. Who could tell where the people who lived in the town now had come from? Some scribe or clerk, perhaps, had a record. Tönnies had come slinking around the estate, tempting people with word of money to be made on canal work. A recruiter, he called himself. A trouble-maker.

"Tönnies, take a turn with that hammer," Jürgen said abruptly. "The rest of you go on over to the fire barrel."

Magdalene von Brockdorff's voice was shrill.

It had already been shrill the first time her husband, Otto von Buchwald, proud if less-than-prosperous lord of the estate of Muggesfelde, met her. Muggesfelde, which did not bring in enough money to support his Mecklenburg wife in the style to which she wanted to be accustomed, so he had to work as a provost for Duke Friedrich at Itzehoe.

She was five years older than he was, also. But she had managed to give him three children, then two more children when she was in her early forties, so the marriage had not proved to be a total loss, even though he would have to write off all the installments still owing on her dowry. The *Krystalnacht* in Mecklenburg last year had seen to that.

She refused to live out in the countryside in winter, of course. She and the children were staying in the family's *Freihof*, untaxed townhouse, in Kiel. The purpose of the *Freihof* was to give them a base from which to do the estate's necessary trading. Holstein's nobility lived off agricultural exports. These last few years, the yields had been abysmal. Income was down. That didn't prevent Magdalene from spending money like water, trying to turn a neat little red brick townhouse into a mansion. Interior, exterior, and furnishings.

She was fifteen years older than the other two women in the salon. Clarelia Reventlow, from Rixdorf estate, was married to his own friend and contemporary, Godske von Ahlefeldt, whose estate, Stubbe, was in Schleswig, up by Eckernförde. Beate Rantzau was Clarelia's friend and her husband, Bendix von Ahlefeldt, a multiple-cousin of Godske, was younger, too. He couldn't be much, if any, over thirty-five. His *Gut* was Haseldorf.

"Godske is going to do it." The volume of Clarelia's piercing soprano overwhelmed even Magdalene's voice. "I told him that he isn't going to let that carter's son get away with recruiting serfs off our estate to work on Duke Friedrich's canal. He's planning to go get them back."

Otto stopped, pulled his gloves off, and went back into the salon. "What carter's son? Tönnies Dirkes?"

"Yes, that one."

Otto frowned. Young Dirkes had been sniffing around Muggesfelde, too, in the fall, for no sufficient reason. He'd have to check with the overseer as to whether anyone was missing.

Clarelia's older, unmarried, sister Mette opened her mouth. "He's been on the Pogwisch manors, too. That Dirkes man has, I mean. Emerentia said so. Henning told her."

Emerentia. His widowed half-sister and the world's busiest busybody. Henning Pogwisch, Holstein's hottest hothead.

He pulled his gloves back on. "I'll go talk to Godske before I head out for Gottorp."

It took several weeks for the lords to ascertain who was gone, given that they had to check the presence or absence of thousands of men and boys. Even then, the information was far from complete.

Some men had possibly gone to work on the canal, but had come back for the spring planting.

Otto von Buchwald recommended to Duke Friedrich that he should have his local agents check the status of the canal workmen and send away any who could be identified as serfs. "Otherwise," he warned, "this is going to cause a lot of trouble for all of us."

An occasional man been absent during the cold season but had spent it with a woman on a neighboring estate with whom he had been living in a status of not-married for a decade's worth of winters and retorted with considerable indignation that nobody had ever complained about it before.

Otto von Buchwald was inclined to recommend that the most prudent course would be to quietly spread the word that if the men came back to where they belonged, then Nothing More Would Be Said.

Godske might have gone along with that, left to himself, but his wife was prodding him to Do Something.

Bendix, egged on by Beate, and Henning, who was courting Mette, put together a posse to retrieve the Haseldorf escapees, managed to find a couple, dragged them back, and had them flogged, after which Beate and Mette preened themselves all over the remainder of the small group of noble wives that constituted "high society," such as it might be, in Kiel.

Clarelia was a Reventlow. Magdalene's mother had been a Reventlow.

The Reventlows were not to be outdone by the Rantzaus.

Godske put together a posse of retainers, consisting of overseers, stable hands, and the like, from Stubbe, with Otto's reluctant assistance providing a similar contingent from Muggesfelde. Bendix and Henning joined in with enthusiasm; they had been rather enjoying their hour in the sun as heroes of the counter-revolution.

The criminals were not hard to identify. Many of the men in the posse had worked with them for years.

Hans Dubbels

Lammert Cordes

Cai Reimers

Tönnies Dirkes

There wasn't any resistance among the other canal workers. Most of them faded away as inconspicuously as possible.

Tönnies Dirkes, in exchange for being released into his father's custody and agreeing to leave Holstein, readily identified Jürgen Rickerts from Godske von Ahlefeldt's estate, who had already gone back home, as having been their foreman over the winter.

That involved the entire extended family of Ahlefeldts. Not limited to the immediate family of Godske but also cousins and in-laws (most of whom were also Ahlefeldts), all the way out to and up to the more distant connections serving Christian IV in Denmark.

Otto concluded that his old friend had gone mad. Or that the entire Ahlefeldt lineage had gone mad, with its Rantzau and Reventlow connections gone madder.

Godske not only dragged Dubbles, Cordes, and Reimer back to Muggesfelde and had Rickerts arrested at Stubbe, but not content with ordinary punishment, as Bendix and Henning had been, he put them on trial.

There was no such thing as public administration in eastern Holstein. Western Holstein, yes; the duke had his officials. Eastern Holstein, no.

Serfs in eastern Holstein had no right of appeal to higher authority, such as an imperial court or ducal court. No right to sue. No rights.

Godske accused the four serfs of treason. Not treason against the USE. Not treason against the Province of Westphalia. Not treason against Duke Friedrich of Holstein-Gottorp. He accused them of treason against himself, as their rightful lord. Acting, as under the grant of 1524 he had the right to do, as the accuser, the prosecutor, and the judge (there being no jury). He didn't carry out all of those roles, plus that of executioner, personally—just that of judge—but the men who fulfilled them were his employees.

Otto, over the impassioned protests of his wife Magdalene that if, for any reason, serfs escaped strict discipline for resistance, it would be the beginning of the end for not only their own family but for every feudal lord in Holstein, the same way that the nobility of Mecklenburg had been destroyed, intervened with a remonstration that the boy Cai Reimers was known to be simple and should therefore not be held responsible for his actions, but rather, on the basis of all existing precedent, remanded to the custody of his mother.

Godske ignored him.

The court found the four men guilty of treason and ordered them hanged.

It turned out that Godske's wife had arranged in advance for one of her connections in Westphalia to hire a man from a well-known *Henkerfamilie* and send him to Holstein. So there was an executioner available.

There weren't any newspapers in Holstein yet, outside of Kiel. The weekly in Kiel was extraordinarily discreet. Those in Hamburg and Lübeck had minimal interest in the back country of Holstein.

Of the canal workers who had faded away, a few returned and followed the posse all the way to Muggesfelde, up to Stubbe, and back. Three of them were about twenty years old.

Gode Meijer from Lütjenburg, not far from Plön, up northwest of Segeberg, followed because his mind told him, "There but for the grace of God go I."

Barent Jansen, from Dithmarschen in the far west, had been brought up on stories and legends of medieval peasant freedom fighters in the marshes by his grandfather.

Hinrich Bothmann was the scapegrace, black sheep, son of a Lutheran pastor from Ribe in Denmark proper, hired on by the canal company to do mathematical calculations.

And a Dutch hydraulics engineer. Cornelis Duyts. That might well not have exactly been his name; it signified "Dutch." He was about forty, good at his work, but his personality had never permitted him to get along well with bosses.

They made it to Lübeck, found a newspaper office, told the story of what they had seen and heard concerning these things to the publisher. Only what they had themselves seen and heard; they didn't know anything about the background. Cornelis and Hinrich agreed with one another that it was properly the governor's problem. Gode and Barent went along with them, although neither had a strong opinion. So they asked the publisher for permission to send it all by radio to Münster. Where Chancellor Gießenbier was a busy, preoccupied, man. It came to his clerk.

As it happened, the governor was in Stade. Radio being radio, that didn't delay the delivery of the message to him by more than a couple of hours. But he was a busy, preoccupied, man and told Rist to have Gießenbier deal with it.

To the immense astonishment of Cornelis and Hinrich, the governor's office radioed back, requesting that they come to Bremen or Stade if they were willing, authorizing travel expenses, and recommending that they get out of Lübeck into some place where they would be more anonymous whether they came to Bremen or not.

David Pestel was proud of himself.

Three weeks later, they arrived in Bremen, rented a room in the *Neue Neustadt*, mailed a notice to the address in Münster that they had been given, and picked up jobs as day laborers. There was no telling how long they might have to make the governor's money last.

Virginia DeMarce

CHAPTER 23

Münster
February 1636

I t was not the most convenient time for the problems associated
with Hesse's continued, illegal, occupation of the town of Dorsten
on the Lippe River to surface. But they did, which was the main
reason why Chancellor Gießenbier had little time to think about
Holstein.

The landgravine had no desire at all to give up what she and her
husband had grabbed during their campaign against Essen the previous
year. It was a matter of access to riverine transport, which she
regarded—accurately regarded—as crucial for the future of Hesse's
economy.

Dorsten proper was incontrovertibly in Essen, since the old town
lay on the south side of the river. Westphalia was involved as a
secondary party because the old town, like so many, was expanding
across the river as its economy grew. The portion across the river was
indubitably in Westphalia. The whole thing could get more unpleasant
than Bremen *Altstadt* and Bremen *Neustadt*, because both sections of
Bremen were, at least for the time being, in the same province.

Frederik sent negotiators to Kassel.

Johann Rist had obtained a reprint of the famous up-time history of the Thirty Years War at considerable expense and been bitterly disappointed in how little attention it paid to the Münsterland. After he had hired four experienced researchers in the great Grantville library, who went through the encyclopedias town by town and from one footnote to another, he armed the negotiators with a precis of exactly what Hesse-Kassel would have done to southern and western Westphalia, the *Oberstift*, from 1633 to 1634, if the Ring of Fire had not intervened, all the way until they reluctantly abandoned the last occupied territory two years after the Peace of Westphalia had been signed, with references to an eighteen-year-long occupation. They were to make it clear—very clear—that the landgravine had neither a moral nor a legal leg to stand on, given what she would have done.

Admittedly, in this world, she hadn't done it. Still, who was to say that if she was given a chance, she wouldn't. As an afterthought, he distributed the precis to every town council. They might not like having a Danish Lutheran governor; it might shake them up to realize that a Hessian Calvinist one would have been far worse.

Frederik would have also sent troops to garrison Dorsten *Neustadt* if he had them available, but he didn't.

Magdeburg
February 1636

The emperor, accompanied by his cousin Erik Haakansson Hand, arrived in the capital five days after Oxenstierna's death in a tavern on the outskirts of Berlin.

Münster
March 1636

Frederik picked up the folder from Georg. The duke of Brunswick-Lüneburg-Calenberg was a reasonable man. So was Loring Schultz, the commoner—a trained jurist, but still a commoner—he had appointed to run the Province of Brunswick while the duke himself fought for Gustav Adolf in the east. Of course, Georg's sons were too young, and his brothers were incompetent, which gave Schultz considerable freedom of action in the matter. Georg's wife was busy and it wasn't as if he would have appointed a potential rival from one of the other principalities that the Congress of Copenhagen had folded into his bailiwick. The duke of Brunswick was a reasonable man and that would have been well beyond the realm of rational.

They were all in consensus that the Province of Brunswick should continue to manage not only the secular administration but also the needs of the Lutheran churches of the former counties of Hoya and Diepholz. Those properly belonged to Brunswick and had since the line of the counts of Hoya went extinct over a half-century earlier. He saw no reason to switch the churches into Westphalia. They saw no reason to switch them out of the Brunswick Superintendency. Done. They were now somebody else's problem.

He took a piece of note paper, wrote, "Agreed; have Bucholtz add necessary verbiage," and clipped it to the folder, which he deposited in the "Out" box.

Andreas Heinrich Bucholtz was one of the twin sons of the late Joachim, who had been a Lutheran Superintendent in Brandenburg before his untimely death when the boys were in their teens. He'd studied in Magdeburg; had been at the university in Wittenberg, where he obtained his master's in philosophy in 1630, studying theology, when the Ring of Fire hit. Rather than going back to relatives in Brandenburg and finding a position as a tutor, as he had been vaguely thinking about because his mother was running out of money, Andreas spent the next two years in Grantville, and environs. Towed to the Congress of Copenhagen in the wake of Count Ludwig Guenther of Schwarzburg-Rudolstadt, he had made friends with other masters of the art of shorthand who sat around the table behind their employers. Thus his current, rather amorphously described, job in the Westphalian chancery. He was twenty-seven. He was an all-purpose writer. An adder of verbiage.

Next week, the governor would turn twenty-seven years.

That was the difference in your career prospects if you were born the son of a king rather than the son of a Lutheran district superintendent. He didn't begrudge it. Much. He did occasionally talk to his friends over beer about the Meaning of It All. Pestel pointed out that it made even more difference to your career prospects if you were born the son of a tailor. Or a serf.

Christoph Joachim Bucholtz, Andreas' brother, had finished up his degree at Wittenberg and come to Herford to clerk in the chancery of the Princess-Abbess Magdalena, born a countess of Lippe. Taken a doctorate in law at Duke Georg of Brunswick's beloved university in Helmstedt, and headed back to Herford for a better job. Christoph had political ambitions. Once the abbey no longer had a vote in the *Reichstag* because the *Reichstag* was no more, he got in touch with the brother who so fortuitously had been hired by the governor of Westphalia. Now he was one of the chancellor's squad of auxiliary lawyers. The chancellor had dropped the Holstein communications on his desk for review.

"The governor is a duke of Holstein." That was Christoph Bucholtz' first line of argument when the three men looked at the folder, over and over and over. "By lineage, he is one hundred percent German. As is his father. As is his brother 'Prince' Ulrik, for that matter. You have to go back nearly half a millennium to find actual Danes in the Oldenburg family tree."

"Not that much, surely!" David Pestel protested.

"Christian IV is king of Denmark, but he's German. The governor's mother was from Brandenburg. His grandparents, with the same 'king of Denmark' exception; seven of the governor's eight great-grandparents bore German *Hochadel* titles and the eighth, the 'princess of Denmark' in that line, was a woman whose German Oldenburg grandfather grasped the throne of Denmark a century and a half ago."

All three of them agreed. This thing in Holstein couldn't get lost, buried in the piles of paper on the chancellor's desk. They needed to tug it out; get it in front of the governor's eyes now that he was back in the capital. Pestel became rather insistent that the governor pay attention to a folder concerning actions by the nobility of Holstein. He nagged Chancellor Gießenbier. He haunted Rist's outer office.

In the inner office, Frederik tugged a memo pad from the shelf under the surface of his desk and penned a memo. "To Andreas Bucholtz—find Eichrodt and get him to prepare a *Gutachten* on the legal status of former ecclesiastical princes and abbots within the USE in general. When he's done, turn into pamphlet for publication." He put it into the Out box.

Rist stuck his head through the door. "Pestel is here. Again. You gave him appointment."

Frederik nodded."Send him in." And listened.

Now he stood at a desk in Münster, where in another world, in another dozen years, part of the signing of the peace that ended that war had occurred, would occur. Not only that war, but also the Eighty Years War in the Netherlands. The Dutch War of Independence, now so oddly resolved by an understanding between Fernando and Fredrik Hendrik.

Osnabrück, the other location where that treaty was signed, also lay within his area of administration.

He had gone to the trouble of standing in the rooms where both signings took place. Or would take place. Or would have taken place.

He turned back to the window.

St. Lambert's church. He had ordered the three iron baskets in which the bodies of the leaders of the Anabaptist rebellion of a century ago had been displayed removed from the bell tower. Stored. Filed without a response, if anyone should ask.

He once again picked up the original radioed report from Lübeck that Christoph Bucholtz had flagged for his special attention.

He was a son of the king of Denmark, who held extensive properties in Holstein even if he was no longer the sovereign. The king of Denmark, who was still sovereign in Schleswig and therefore must be notified because of the events at Eckernförde.

He was a duke of Holstein.

He was Gustav Adolf's administrator, governor if one would, of the Province of Westphalia, which included Holstein.

Any way a person considered it, Holstein was his problem.

As of this morning, a large and looming problem.

But not the only problem.

It would be so convenient if problems came one at a time.

Dorsten
March 1636

Frederik ended up having to go to Dorsten himself. The landgravine's agents there, his negotiators reported, had unearthed incontrovertible evidence that several of the important noble families in the region of the town had been involved with Oxenstierna's coup; that the family heads, while themselves remaining conspicuously visible on their Westphalian properties, or even, a few of them, deciding that it was a great time to make a visit to the Low Countries and departing for Deventer, had in no way interfered when younger brothers, nephews, cousins, even an occasional younger son, had gone to Berlin.

Von Twickelo. Von der Recke. The Hackfurt line of the Westerholdts. The Merveldts at Westerwinkel. Even some distant connections of the von Galen and von Velen. Not just minor, local, *Niederadel*. Not imperial *Freiherren*, owing allegiance only to the emperor, either; they had been mediatized to the prince-bishop of Münster; they were now subjects of the province of Westphalia. But they called themselves *freie Herren*. Not quite the same thing, but he had no doubt that each one of them harbored the ambition to become free and independent of any overlord, of any governmental authority. Catholics, many of them; Calvinists, some of them.

He wondered briefly if Claessens, the suffragan bishop of the still vacant archdiocese, had spurred them on. Unfortunately, the prospect that a fanatical Catholic might have been in collusion with Oxenstierna went beyond any realistic scenario he could envision. Reluctantly, he dropped the idea. There were conspiracy theories, but then there were also sheer conspiracy delusions. This was normal power-grabbing.

He might not have troops, but he had lawyers and notaries who delighted in following paper trails.

By the time Frederik was finished with the traitors (banished, most of them; permanently exiled on threat of execution), he had property. True, the lawyers had confiscated most of it for the benefit of the province and henceforth the dedicated revenues from those would go to cover certain specific administrative expenses. Such as the construction and maintenance of a suitable official residence for the province's governor (whoever he might be or become). Such as a decently sized chancery building. For the first time in his life, though, he had three comfortable, extensive, manor properties of his own, one with a nice little *Schloß*.

The landgravine not only wasn't surprised; she didn't disapprove. One of the strengths of the landgraves of Hesse-Kassel, before the enlargement to provincial status, was that about sixty percent of Kassel was direct domanial land, from which they collected not only the taxes, but also the rents and dues, to the immense benefit of the ruling family when it came to dealing with the noble estates. Acquisition of property was how things were done. If anything, she was a bit surprised at how modestly Frederik enriched himself. Under the circumstances.

Quedlinburg
March 1636

"The old ladies say," Bethany Leek wrote to her mother, "that the governor in Westphalia came down pretty hard on the conspirators but left the branches of the families that he couldn't prove sent anyone to Berlin alone. Sort of the same pattern that the emperor followed with the ones who actually were in Berlin. Most of the ladies don't have a lot of sympathy for the reactionaries in the Münsterland. They're of the opinion that they're an uppity bunch. Not to mention Catholic or Calvinist, most of them. But, anyway, they figure that either the rest of the Westphalian nobility, no matter what church they belong to, has either gotten the message by now or the governor will stomp on them later.

"Of course, the ladies are Lutheran and he's Lutheran, so that may tint their perspective. Or tilt it. Something like that."

CHAPTER 24

Bremen
March 1636

There was a lot of construction going on in the *Neue Neustadt*. Hinrich Bothmann had no trouble finding a job helping the foremen, doing routine but time-consuming calculations. That sort of thing wasn't much restricted by guilds. It was vaguely semi-learned, almost a profession rather than a trade.

Duyts was as dour as usual, but bilingual—not that there was much difference between Dutch and *Plattdeutsch*—and a hydraulics engineer. He got work with the new dredging company. For decades, no seagoing ship had made it up the Weser as far as the city; they had to stop downriver and offload to shallow barges for the final leg. There were up-timers with money interested in dredging projects.

Gode Meijer hired on at the slaughterhouse. Barent Jansen thought about it, gagged, and found a large-scale teamster who needed someone in the stables. That he could do. It wasn't the smell at the slaughterhouse that got to him. It was the blood.

And they waited.

Quite of a bit of the waiting was in taverns in the *Neue Neustadt*, since that was where they had taken their one small room, which was barely furnished with four straw-stuffed mattress ticks on the floor and one wobbly stand for a ceramic oil lamp.

"You'll have to buy the lamp yourselves, if you want one," the indifferent landlady had informed them. "We don't run to luxuries here."

In the taverns, Gode and Barent listened to the CoC members, quite a few of whom were now parroting Daniel Bartoll's ideas about how to play the political game. One evening, Meijer protested, "but the farmers." It was made clear that his input was unwelcome.

On the other side of the river, Knaub and Jauch both reported to Frederik about Bartoll once more, expressing concern about his growing influence and the wider welcome of his approach among the politically interested in the city.

Münster
March 1636

Frederik never entirely understood why so many other people appeared to be impelled to do things that created problems that landed on his desk.

Right now, he was glad that he had ignored the logic that would have advised him to draw his staff from Holstein. He surrounded himself, predominantly, with men who originated from locations as far away from Holstein as a person could get and still be in the Province of Westphalia.

Why had his great-great-grandfather, King Frederik I of Denmark (albeit in his alternate incarnation as duke of Holstein-Gottorp) granted feudal rights of high justice over their serfs to the nobles in eastern Holstein? That had already been obsolete when he granted them in 1524.

Of course, he'd been having other problems that year—he had only managed to grasp the Danish crown the year before. Peasant revolts.

Religious dissidents. Blame it on expedience. He'd been doing something to mollify the local nobles. Probably he'd thought he could retrieve it all later, which was the kind of imprudent thinking that led to all sorts of persistent problems.

Why had Gustav Adolf been stupid enough to get himself seriously injured the previous October? Aside, that is, from his being essentially who and what he was. Namely, a Swede. Sort of. The part that wasn't German.

Why had Oxenstierna done what he did between the emperor's injury and his effective recovery? Aside, that is, from his being essentially who and what he was. Namely, a Swede. Entirely.

Thank God, very sincerely, for Erik Haakonson Hand. Even if he was a Swede.

Thank God, very sincerely, that his father had held steady during those months.

Thank God, even, if a little reluctantly, for his little brother Ulrik, in spite of the fact that he, rather than Frederik, was betrothed to Princess Kristina and designated as the next high king of the Union of Kalmar.

There had been four months the previous winter during which those termed "reactionaries" by Stearns and his followers had hoped to reverse all that had been done since the Ring of Fire.

Which gave the nobles of eastern Holstein the idea that they could get away with … murder.

Call it *high justice*. Call it what you wanted.

It wasn't as if escaping serfs were anything new. Frederik wondered how many serfs from southeastern Holstein were working at the USE shipyards in Lübeck. But even the lords in Holstein had been marginally prudent enough not to pursue them into that jurisdiction when either Gustav Adolf or the up-time admiral was in place to drive the pursuers out.

Why had someone decided to dig an Eider Canal? Well, the answer to that was fairly obvious, as was the potential profit from having a way to transport cargo from the Baltic to the North Sea during the months when the Sound was impassable.

Why had the nobles of Holstein reacted so ... extremely ... when some of their serfs decamped to work on that canal?

Why?

Things had been disrupted at the time of the battle of Ahrensbök, of course, but that had not lasted long—nowhere nearly as long as many of the campaigns of the current war. There had been no enduring occupation of the region.

Many of them were closely related to the now-mostly-exiled nobility of Mecklenburg, of course, which had been sharply jerked to attention by the events of the *Krystalnacht* and then jerked again as a result of its attempted counter-revolution during the Saxon uprising. Largely, though, that had not spilled over into Holstein.

Why?

Escaping serfs were like the biblical poor. You would always have them with you. Or, to be more technically accurate, no longer with you. Looking backward, a few serfs, even a few dozen serfs, simply were not important enough to trigger what had happened.

Rist's assistant, Conrad Schepler, found the governor in the private study he had created behind the public office in which he received officials and petitioners.

Schepler looked around.

The table was laden with paper.

The boxes on the table were stuffed.

The governor, draped in a linen smock, was standing at an easel, painting the portrait of a local worthy who sat stiffly on a three-legged stool. Schepler looked at the canvas critically. The governor's technique was old-fashioned, in the stiff, brightly colored style of a century ago.

Within that limitation, it was a competent enough job. The worthy, himself old-fashioned enough to be wearing a ruff, would probably be pleased.

Particularly for its purpose. There was currently no Roman Catholic bishop of Münster. In the other world, Ferdinand of Bavaria had lived another fifteen years. His then-successor, Christoph Bernhard von Galen, was, in this world, only thirty years old and an unlikely choice on the part of the *Domkapitel*, particularly with Bernhard von Mallinckrodt, his own uncle, fighting him tooth and nail for the position. The *Stiftsadel* would not be inclined to accept another pluralist Bavarian, either. Hopefully not a Fürstenberg, either. Let the *Erbmänner* of the city keep fighting the local nobility and the cathedral chapter through every court in the empire and keep the office vacant as long as possible, which was why the governor was doing Heinrich von Droste-Hülshoff, the forty-year-old son of the city's late *Bürgermeister*, the honor of painting his portrait.

Schepler admired the portrait again. A man used whatever tools came to hand.

Having Franz Wilhelm von Wartenburg, another irritating Bavarian, alive, well, energetic, and legally installed effectively in partially Lutheran Osnabrück and officially in almost completely Lutheran Minden under the up-timers' freakish devotion to religious tolerance, restoring and maintaining a Jesuit university right under the gubernatorial nose, so to speak, was bad enough. The Province of Westphalia didn't need a second Catholic bishop in place. One was altogether too many.

"The lawyers are here," Schepler said.

The lawyers had a lot to say. "If someone had deliberately set out to design a system that would be unanimously loathed by the up-timers, he couldn't have done better than the one which has developed in Holstein," Franz Gießenbier summed up.

Frederik nodded. If anyone in Germany knew real estate law, it was his chancellor.

In Holstein, at least eastern and southeastern Holstein, real estate law and administrative law were, in essence, the same thing. Real estate law and commercial law were essentially the same thing. Real estate law and criminal law were essentially the same thing. The *Gutsherr*, the lord of a domain, held essentially absolute authority over the serfs, who were not only bound to the land, but also bound to personal service. If there were those who protested that it was not the same thing as the chattel slavery of ancient Greece and Rome ... it bore an extraordinarily close resemblance but was less favorable to the slaves. The unmarried children of a peasant in servile tenure were required to work on the lord's demesne or in his quasi-industrial, quasi-agricultural enterprises—Holstein exported cheese by the millions of pounds every year. The peasants were required to fatten steers at their own expense but forbidden to sell them at market: the export trade in cattle was reserved to the nobles.

"The up-time word," David Pestel said, "I think, is *authoritarian*. Or the historians in England have referred to such nobles as *overmighty subjects*, those whose powers rival those of the king himself."

The thought of overmighty subjects was not something that Frederik found appealing. The names "Corfitz Ulfeldt'" and "Hannibal Sehested" passed through his mind. Like everyone else, he had been reading the up-time encyclopedias. The limiting conditions that the *Rigsraad*, the Danish Council of Nobles, had placed upon him in 1648 before they agreed to elect him as king were undesirable. If he were a man prone to nightmares, he would have them about that *haandfæstning*.

Fortunately, he wasn't prone to anything of the sort.

He turned to his secretary. "Rist, check the linguistics of something for me. See if the Danish word *haandfæstning* is related to the up-timer term *handcuffs*."

He turned back to the lawyers. "So Buchwald's party claims that they did have legal right under the 1524 grant by the duke of Holstein, whereas we assert that they did not have legal right under the constitution of the United States of Europe."

Gießenbier looked back over his shoulder at the note-taking law clerk, who nodded.

"That's basically it," Pestel said, flipping rapidly through the last couple of pages.

Gießenbier employed a lot more vocabulary but reached the same conclusion.

Frederik asked himself, *Why me?*

He had planned to create something in the way of a provincial militia, separate from those of individual towns; had assigned Christian Ulrik to the project, but he had not had time. Other things kept coming up.

He had been thinking about it ever since he was appointed. He had been working on it. Christian Ulrik had been working on it. They hadn't gotten it done in time.

Frederik requested assistance from the USE army detachment stationed in Hamburg. The major who had been left in charge when the rest of Fey's regiment was withdrawn rejected the request quite properly, on the constitutional ground that federal forces were constituted to defend the realm against foreign threats rather than to be used to quell domestic disturbances, and he had received no orders from his chain of command to make an exception in this instance.

The Hamburg council, in its role as head of a USE imperial city, also rejected his request to borrow some of their forces. Not only, traditionally, was a militia required to serve only in defense against external attack, which the council's lawyers cited *in extenso* in their brief, but there were also practical political grounds. Those, of course, the lawyers did not cite. Frederik knew better than to bother asking anyone in Lübeck for assistance. The USE Navy went its own way and the mayor, Dieterich Matthesen, was even more strongly CoC-supported than Bugenhagen in Hamburg.

The city of Bremen would not cooperate because the city fathers were fairly sure that the USE was going to give them imperial city status and get them out of Westphalia. The public reason that the FoJP was putting forth for this was that it would "strengthen the USE's naval position." Frederik suspected that it was because it would give the FoJP another vote in the House of Lords, since the city's political sympathies were strongly in that direction.

He didn't expect any help from Gottorp. Duke Friedrich logically should provide assistance because, after all, the executed serfs had been retrieved from his lands and they had been working on his canal. However, he was a first cousin of Gustav Adolf on his mother's side, and generally more inclined to favor his Swedish relatives than his Danish ones. Since he would classify Frederik as Danish in this instance, even though Gustav Adolf had appointed him to his USE position in Westphalia ... no. Frederik had not been getting much satisfaction from Duke Friedrich, even from the perspective of information gathering.

If the emperor were willing to provide help, there would already have been some military forces at his disposal as provincial governor. That pretty much closed the circle.

CHAPTER 25

Rostock
April 1636

Jürg Behr's wife, née Hedwig von Heimbruch, had taken refuge from *Krystalnacht* in Rostock. In her rented townhouse, she chatted with various visiting noblewomen from Holstein. She didn't exactly love her husband, but she knew her duty. If she'd ever heard "Stand By Your Man," she'd have been in the front row, applauding. Nothing she could do for him would make up for her barrenness, her dereliction of that duty which above all else a wife owed to her husband, but she would certainly give everything else a try.

Behr was in Holstein, in touch with the unhappiest of the nobles, talking about the need for "restoration" and urging action "before it's too late and every natural privilege you possess is revoked by the up-timers and the CoCs." With, he added to himself, the support of the now-unfortunately-conscious but obviously-still-out-of-his-fucking-mind Gustav II Adolf. In February of 1631, before the Ring of Fire, the Swedes had landed in Pomerania. The level of forced contributions they extorted had fallen devastatingly on the Behr properties, which had never truly recovered. On a bar chart, the size of his grudge against the emperor would loom considerably taller than those he held against the newcomers and rebels, but the disgruntlement leaked into his opinions on everything else. The same emperor had made no effort to rein in the second wave of destruction during *Krystalnacht*. Thus, taking a stand against a governor appointed by that same emperor made sense to his way of thinking.

"*Justify* the stand you are taking," he urged them. "Generate some publicity for your cause. It doesn't have to be explicitly political. Appeal to every conservative instinct—not just to the most reactionary. Depict your serfs as lazy, ignorant, drunken; in need of a stern but fatherly hand if they are to be constrained to do all things decently and in order. Argue that an established ruling class is necessary if the world is not to degenerate into improvident chaos.

"Use some the arguments that Luther developed about the responsibility of intermediate lords when he defended the resistance of the electors of Saxony and the other Protestant principalities against Charles V. That should appeal to a lot of pastors, who in turn will preach it to their flocks."

Hedwig von Heimbruch found writers willing to write such pamphlets; printers willing to print them; distributors willing to ensure that they could be found in bookstores all over northern Germany. Including in Lübeck, Hamburg, and Bremen.

In another Rostock townhouse, children in tow, crammed in with one of Gottfried's cousins and his family, Christine von Holstein-Hagen kept up appearances as best she could. That meant attending ladies' parties, at which she chatted with various visiting noblewomen from Holstein.

Christine did not care about the plight of serfs in eastern Holstein. Serfdom was what it was; she had never given it a thought. She did not care about the plans that the nobles of eastern Holstein might be making. She did care about all that she had lost.

Which included an estate called Thedinghausen in *Stift* Verden.

To which Jürg Behr was asserting a claim in the name of his wife.

Because that wife was the sister of *her own father's* mistress. Well, one of his mistresses. The most expensive of them. During her own mother's lifetime! Well, her mother was still alive; she was a tough old bird and might outlast them all. After the *Drostin* Hermeling died so providentially, though, her father had given Thedinghausen to her brother. Who had, at a time when her finances were better, sold it to her.

If anyone had a claim to Thedinghausen, she did.

She'd lost it to the new prince-bishop. Gottfried was suing him in the *Reichskammergericht*.

She wasn't about to lose it to Jürg Behr.

And she was, albeit bastard-born, legitimated and ennobled; a first cousin once removed of the current duke of Holstein-Gottorp, who therefore could not entirely ignore her. She made complaining noises, wrote complaining letters, and distributed copies of those letters widely to anyone who might in her most remote imagination support her (typewriters and carbon paper having made their way from Magdeburg to Rostock and been enthusiastically welcomed by those who churned out the massive correspondence generated by the gentry and bourgeoisie).

Duke Johann of Holstein-Gottorp, still smarting from the loss of his prince-bishopric of Lübeck, for which Gustav Adolf had not given him so much as a provincial governorship as a consolation prize, was rather inclined to lend her a sympathetic ear; his brother Friedrich, the duke-in-office for Gottorp and smarting at being under a Danish governor, not so much so, but he still did not repudiate her requests for money, for compensation, for *something*, out of hand. So she kept writing.

Then she collected it all together, everything she had heard that even tangentially mentioned Jürg Behr and his wife Hedwig von Heimbruch, because it might pertain to the Thedinghausen lawsuit. She sent the cover letter and attachments to her husband, of course; a copy to her brother, who had gotten pretty deeply invested in the lawsuit along with Gottfried. Because that suit was against Frederik of Denmark as successor of the late prince-bishop of *Stift* Verden, she directed a carbon copy to him as an interested party, incidentally including all the informative gossip she had collected about what the nobles of eastern Holstein were planning.

A copy that landed on the desk of a different Hedwig, electress-dowager of Saxony and the governor of Westphalia's regent in Stade.

It had slipped Christine's mind, momentarily, that Frederik of Denmark wore more than one hat. All she had really hoped to get from her paternal cousins was an annuity.

"Christine is still in Rostock," Aunt Hedwig wrote. "She headed there for safety last fall and has told von Hagen that she isn't leaving. It's entirely possible that the Gottorps will make mischief in the *Erzstift* rather than having to provide for her and her family in Holstein."

In his mind, Frederik called a blight and plague down upon the ghost of his late great-uncle.

While he was in Magdeburg for the last session of parliament, he had encountered the fashion fad for zippers. Not succumbed to it, mind you. Observed it.

Along with the accompanying jokes in regard to "keeping it zipped."

Why hadn't Great-Uncle Johann Friedrich managed to keep it zipped? Why didn't men in general manage to keep it zipped? Why did they litter the world so improvidently with offspring who did not fit neatly into a well-planned family tree? Or, more immediately, into an orderly and well-designed strategy of wealth management?

"But Christine also sent ... " Aunt Hedwig concluded her letter. "That's what I need to discuss with you so urgently."

Holstein
April 1636

Godske von Ahelefeldt started gathering his forces. Almost by default, by means of no formal choice, he had become the organizer among the resistance. For so they saw themselves: resisting the expanding tyranny of royal government.

Henning Pogwish gave the speeches. Not in crowds. In parlors; in reception rooms; over dinners; during banquets. Mette Reventlow egged him on.

His older brother, Laurids, would have none of it. Neither would Ditlev von Rathlou; he had married late, had a family of small children, and was staying out. They would keep their mouths shut, though.

Poul Rantzau, in Kiel, Beate's brother, quietly provided links through which they could obtain financing. Nothing came for free.

Quite a few of them, though, saw a dilemma. If they wanted to gather a large number of bodies in case it came to a military clash, they would have to use serfs from their estates. But what rational *Gutsherr* would arm a serf? Otto von Buchwald was increasingly anxious, increasingly nervous. Bendix worried about money, warning that too many of the estates had gone bankrupt in recent years. But they moved around; found sympathizers. Ditlev Reventlow had been driven out of Mecklenburg by *Krystalnacht*; he was currently in Kiel, negotiating for a marriage there with a sister of Hans von Rantzau. Both of those were brought in by Poul. Both, Godske realized, were more articulate than either Otto or himself. Hans produced several pamphlets giving a fairly clear expression of their political goals, which were mainly the defense of their economic status, which was based on *Gutsherrschaft* with its associated *Gesindezwang* and *Anfallzwang*, which could not be maintained without their legal privileges *vis-à-vis* the serfs. Ditlev took those and tied them to the broader need, as he saw it, for the nobility to entrench itself and resist what the emperor was permitting the up-timers and the Committees of Correspondence to do.

Jürg Behr took these and did additional promotion. One could not call it rabble-rousing; the last thing any of them wanted was to rouse the rabble.

But that didn't create an army. Godske realized that they had to have an army. The Mecklenburg nobility, he thought, had fallen so easily mainly—not entirely, but mainly—because so many individual estates tried to defend themselves. Alone. Oh, there had been the big battles, but most were taken down one by one.

They weren't going to get much in the way of cavalry, given that they were hemmed in by the USE on the south, Denmark on the north, and the sea on either side. Nor did he expect anyone come to help them from the western side of the duchy, where the system didn't exist for the most part. So for cavalry, it would be them; the nobles, *Gutsherren*, younger brothers, younger sons, cousins. Not even all of the members of the thirty-five of so families of *equites ordinarii*.

There was no option. The infantry would be overwhelmingly *Insten* and *Gesinde* who would not be "following" their noble lords. They would be driven by their local lords, forced to take part. Some of them, at least, would have to be armed.

They bought weapons in Kiel. Quietly. Kiel was after all directly subject to the duke of Gottorp, who was more favorably inclined toward the Swedes than to the Danes.

Quite a few of the Kiel merchants hoped to do well financially out of this little dispute.

The Holstein nobles believed that the governor of Westphalia would do something.

The question was what. And would he do it in the name of the USE or of Denmark?

Stade
April 1636

Frederik looked at Christine's gossip with frustration. "Hartwig von Schack is actively involved." Which one of them? He could think of three adult males bearing that name, right off the top of his head. Which one of the Rumohrs? Not Asmus, surely—he was from Denmark proper, past fifty, and while no mental giant, still had more common sense. Some connection of old Cai's perhaps? He'd been dead for ten years, but there was a son still alive—and married to a Brockdorff.

Why von der Wisch? Well, Otto's mother, so maybe some of his cousins on that side of the family.

Wensin? Probably one of Pogwisch's in-laws. More Ahlefeldts.

He frowned at the next name. The Brüsehaver family was from Schwerin—*Stift*, he thought. Some of these names must be associates of Behr. There was no reason for them to be involved in this unless someone had a connection by marriage.

Which reminded him. Was his brother Ulrik still bishop of Schwerin? He hadn't heard. If not, who was responsible for the spiritual welfare of the Lutherans of the diocese. Who was acting as *summus episcopus*? He scribbled a note to Rist to send an inquiry.

He moved on to the next paragraph. Ditlev Reventlow, driven out of Mecklenburg; possibly. Hans Rantzau from Kiel; also possible. Detloff von Bülow? Probably not. That family spilled over into Pomerania. Young Barthold Hartwig von Bülow was, he thought, off in Burgundy; he had stayed with Bernhard of Saxe-Weimar. As had young Josias Rantzau from Kiel. Those two were in the *Franche-Comté*, not Holstein. Frederik pulled in his lips, biting them. Wilhelm Wettin's baby brother, now calling himself Grand Duke of the County of Burgundy! How pretentious could the man get?

He focused his mind. Wrote a note to Rist: "For now, find a couple of young clerks or perhaps some students that Schepler knows. Send them up to Altona to hang around in taverns and accidentally drop information that 'it's said' that I'll be bringing a detachment into Holstein, coming in east of Hamburg."

He called Christian Ulrik in. "David Pestel is from Minden and his uncle—one of his relatives—may be on the city council now. He has younger relatives who must know half the law students and clerks in the province. Tell him to scrape together from somewhere three hundred or so young men who are willing, at my expense, to hoist themselves on any rag of a horse they can find and ride, slowly and with as much disorganization as possible, up through the land bridge from Munster and Osnabruck toward Hamburg, trying to resemble dragoons. If they can't ride, tell him to form them into squads of something that might resemble infantry and walk. Tell him to surround them with as many of the Minden city militia as he can roust out so the edge looks vaguely military when observers see them. Militant. I want them to be observably on the move. Go. Use your radio."

Then he returned to the pile on his desk. By the time he sorted through Christine's letter and attachments, he had a list of possibly fourteen more men now involved; only nine of them likely; only five of them certain. All of those belonging to the *equites originarii*, the old untitled nobility of Holstein, convinced that they owed nothing to any king or emperor for no king or emperor had created their status.

But not too proud to hold on tenaciously to the privileges and exemptions once granted to them by a Danish king. His letter to his father was as heavily encrypted as he could make it and did not go through either Rist or the chancery.

Job said, "naked came I out of my mother's womb, and naked shall I return thither: the Lord gave, and the Lord hath taken away; blessed be the name of the Lord." Job 1:21.

What a king once gave, a governor could take away in the name of an emperor.

CHAPTER 26

Minden
April 1636

It occurred to David Pestel that he would be out of radio communication once he left Minden. The network that Christian Ulrik had set up only went from one territorial seat to the others and to the provincial capitals. They had no portable or personal radio units. He sent the governor an urgent message bringing the presence of the four men in Bremen to his attention. He phrased it as a reminder and urged that it would be a good idea for the governor to take them along as guides, as well as witnesses, since they would be able to identify the main offenders on sight.

Then he rode out with the miniature non-regiment he had created *ex nihilo* and decorated around the edges with the Minden city militia. It had been a happy discovery that the Minden armory had more weapons than it had men. Not as many as the regiment had law clerks and students, but anyone who admitted to having ever shot a long gun, even once, was now carrying one, along with a couple of ammunition belts.

The others were carrying belts with extra ammunition and quite a lot of food.

Pestel had enough common sense to put the militia captain in command.

Hinrich Botterbrodt had enough common sense to issue as his first order to his unlikely new command, "Pad your shoulders so you don't all get weeping, bleeding, blisters from those belts."

"Do you suppose we should mention what's going on to someone in Magdeburg?" Thomas Krage asked a little timidly.

"*Nein*," Dirk Waßmann answered. "What's the point? They never pay any attention to what we say anyway."

Stade
April 1636

Frederik gathered an inadequate "domestic" force, mostly out of the villages of *Erzstift* Bremen and *Stift* Verden by way of his status as the episcopal administrator there. He had, maybe, two hundred men on horses, all basically mounted dragoons—not a bit of experienced cavalry. Additionally, there were perhaps three hundred local men who had, over the past years of warfare, gotten some army experience. These were organized into an infantry unit by Erik Stenbock, supplemented by every episcopal game warden who was young enough to march. They brought nothing in the way of common equipment to the muster and he had no common equipment to issue to them.

The *Tech* delivered Pestel's radio message.

Frederik cleared his throat. "A reminder? I do not recall having seen any previous paperwork in regard to these men." But Pestel was correct; as they were there, he should take advantage of their presence.

He moved out to Bremen, leaving a profoundly grateful Rist, who had ridden harder and longer than he ever wished to do again, with Aunt Hedwig. He took Stenbock (naturally), Christian Ulrik, Captain Meyer, and Lütkemann with him.

Bremen
April 1636

Gode, Barent, Hinrich, and Cornelis were somewhat surprised to have a messenger from the governor find them and abruptly end their new jobs. But they found time to tell their new friends good-bye. "The governor summoned us," Bothmann said a little proudly. "He's passing through on his way to some negotiations in Oldenburg."

"Do you suppose we should send someone after him," Peter Schorfmann asked. "To figure out what he's doing?"

"Nah," was Gerrit Bemmeler's answer. "If he isn't even going to bother dealing with the reactionaries in Holstein, what's the point? Oldenburg isn't one of our flashpoints right now."

Oldenburg
April 1636

Frederik's starting point, when he thought about it, was that Anton Günther was an ally, after all. Outside the USE, but an ally. Also a cousin, but then, everyone was a cousin. A cousin not only *in* Oldenburg, but *of* the House of Oldenburg. An ally, but not part of the government in Magdeburg. Not one of those involved in designing Westphalia.

He'd been careful with the provincial budget.

He'd been careful with the allowance from his father.

His new properties weren't bringing in much income yet, but in time they would.

If Anton Günther was willing to take the risk, Frederik could afford a limited number of decent soldiers for a short campaign. Anton Günther might be willing to take the risk. Because. He had built his main residence, Oldenburg *Schloß*, on the foundations of a medieval moated castle. It was inside a set of good, substantial, walls. Not walls that would stand up to modern artillery, the type that the up-timers had used to batter their way past Hamburg, but sufficient to repel anything less.

Given the current demands on his resources, Gustav Adolf would be hard put to bring those huge guns to bear on those walls any time soon. The more cooperative an ally demonstrated himself to be, the less ... what did the up-timers call it? ... the less *moral justification* the emperor could show for invading the county. Not that he had needed any to invade Poland, and the up-timers had gone along with that.

Anton Günther would have his message by now. He would be mulling the same considerations. If he demonstrated a willingness to assist a USE provincial governor in carrying out his duties, would that assist him in keeping his independence? Or if he assisted a USE provincial governor who had been set up to fail by the Swedes in order to embarrass Denmark, would that be a disadvantage in maintaining his independence?

Frederik had to attend a reception and formal banquet, of course.

It wasn't as tedious as it might have been. The count was currently building a town hall and diagrammed the plans and design on the tablecloth.

Frederik was impeccably polite to the count's recently acquired morganatic wife, Elisabeth Margareta, when she took him out to show off the gardens.

"Once upon a time, I was *Freiin* Ungnad zu Sonnegg," she said with some humor, "but Ferdinand II put an end to that when he expelled the Protestants from Austria. The Ungnads aren't 'zu' anything at all, now. Although my brother had hopes that young Ferdinand might be more flexible and forgiving, I feel sure that the Ottomans are currently keeping him much too busy to think about any kind of restitution. So David is over in the Low Countries, trying to bamboozle his way into Fredrik Hendrik's diplomatic service."

Frederik was somewhat surprised by the wry analysis and underlying sense of humor in her conversation. Most people who met her hadn't mentioned them; had described her as "lush." Which might be the word, but he thought that her appearance verged on "overblown, blowzy, and frowzy." There might have been room for one more plume on her hat, if the milliner had made extraordinary efforts.

She was flanked by nurses with two babies, one a toddler and the other still in arms. Plus, unless her figure was extraordinarily lush, another baby-to-be in the not too distant future.

The next morning, as they rode out to see the famous stud—rode sedately, because the count had his toddler son riding in front of him—Frederik duly complimented Anton Günther on his wife. It couldn't hurt to make a compliment. For a man who had abstained for so long, he had clearly plunged with enthusiasm into the pool of marital bliss.

"Don't be mealy-mouthed." Anton Günther drew his horse up and looked forward at the paddocks in front of them. "You've dealt with Christian long enough to know what was going on. I did consider simply keeping her as my mistress; she had already become my mistress. But then—given a world in which the Ring of Fire had happened and who knew what might happen next—I asked myself '*wen kummerts?*' and married her. It's not as if she was a commoner. A noblewoman, even if of lesser rank."

He shifted a bit uncomfortably, aware of Frederik's lack of enthusiasm for Christian IV's morganatic marriage to Kirsten Munk, who was after all also a noblewoman by birth. He cleared his throat. "She was my mother's goddaughter, after all. I could hear my mother's disapproving voice in my ears.

"I was as near to fifty years old as not; what was the point of my advisers' insisting I should hold back and make a marriage that was *ebenbürtig, standesgemäß.* If I hadn't contracted a suitable and proper marriage after having lived nearly a half-century, was I likely to ever do so?

"I'd spent that half-century paying a lot more attention to horses than women; traveled all over Europe choosing stallions to keep improving the breed from its basis in the Frisians. Building on the work that my father had done. He's the one who brought in the Frederiksborgers from Denmark. The first Turkish stallions to breed into it; Andalusians; Neapolitans. Built our strong, plain, Frisians into magnificent war horses. I kept that up—went to all those places; added the best I found from Poland; the Barbary Coast, even.

"The horses are my life. Training them; showing them. Where would a wife fit in? Wanting me to do other things. Elisabeth was already here at the court; she already fit into the life I lead.

"And after all, what if another of those rings came along and moved me and mine to another universe? Christ did not limit himself to one miracle in the New Testament. What would limit God to only one in this day and age? Who would care then, after we were gone to someplace else?"

Frederik rarely smiled; this morning, he did. "The newspapers certainly made the most of your decision. I can't help but ask. Did you promise her marriage in a document signed in your own blood?"

Frederik thought this was innately improbable, but gossip had celebrated a tournament with the circumstances of the count's marriage.

"Pen and ink, I fear, duly drafted by lawyers and produced in multiple copies by the chancery. By the time I made my mind up to do it, she was seven months along with young Anton here—he picked up the toddler, joggled him in his arms, and was rewarded by a delighted laugh. "There was no time to be wasted if I wanted him to be born in wedlock. No time for dramatics. Not that she demanded them from me."

Young Anton was apparently a frequent visitor to the stables. There was a playpen waiting for him. With a rocking horse in it. An older child dashing out from one of the trainers' houses alongside to keep an eye on the little boy.

They paced, up one side and down the other, looking at the famous Oldenburg horses.

"Why don't you keep a stable?" Anton Günther asked abruptly. "A proper one, I mean."

Frederik was riding a serviceable, sturdy bay gelding, strong enough to manage his weight over long stretches, but not, one could say, a horse of distinction. He patted the fellow's neck. "*Böhnchen* here suits me. I have three more like him. Not a matched set for looks—one more bay, but Duxi is a roan and Gauner's a chestnut—but rather for usefulness. I don't have the knowledge to supervise a breeding stable; don't even have the expertise to hire a staff to manage it for me. My time at Sorø wasn't long enough to give me that, nor did it come up during the years I was at various universities. Nor do I want the difficulty of dealing with stallions in a town the size of Münster, either."

The count was clearly appalled. Frederik could see the negotiations washing away like mud in a pouring rain.

He would not say: "I don't care. A horse is a horse as long as it gets me where I need to go."

Instead, he said, "Perhaps on one of the new estates down near Dorsten, once I get them up and running." Then he turned the conversation to his rather wistful wish to see a railroad. "I am almost tempted to make up an excuse to visit the Netherlands and take a look at the one there, but have never had the time."

Then he switched his admiration back to the count's horses. They were beauties: compact and tough, generally; versatile. The Oldenburgers were not just war horses, although that was their greatest fame, along with the dominant coal black color. They were riding horses, happy to carry a saddle; would pull carriages as matched sets; even work the fields if trained to it. As horses went, they were magnificent. And good-tempered, as a general rule, which wasn't something a man could rely on when it came to a ton of horse.

He patted *Böhnchen*'s neck again. If a breeding stable on one of his new estates was what it would take to get the count's cooperation, then a breeding stable there would be.

Another dinner. More gossip, much of it catty and directed at Elisabeth Margareta.

A shrill voice. "Only an imperial title, that *Freiherr* that her father had. It hadn't been in the family more than a century and a half. Originally *Niederadel, ministeriales* from Franconia who moved to Carinthia looking for the main chance. When? Oh, in the twelfth century or so."

The next voice whined. "They say that if Ferdinand II hadn't exiled the Protestants, her brother had his eye on becoming an Imperial Count. They say that he seriously considered staying behind when his parents and sisters fled, thought about converting to Catholicism to keep the family estates and to keep his career on the upswing. Now he's in the Netherlands, since he stayed Calvinist; he'll do whatever it takes to ingratiate himself with Fredrik Hendrik. Pure opportunist, if you ask me."

A pretense of shock. "And the way the mother pimped those girls out, twitching them under the noses of prominent men, when she landed in Ostfriesland as a refugee with nothing but the clothes on her back!"

Frederik listened. Calvinist? Well, Anton Günther was at best a Philippist, probably with crypto-Calvinist tendencies. Gustav Adolf should be glad that the count liked the Low Countries even less than he liked the Swedes, or Oldenburg might already have gone the way of Ostfriesland.

Nor were crypto-Calvinist tendencies anything that Frederik was in a position to complain about publicly, given his suspicions when it came to his own father's private and personal religious convictions.

Much better to keep these negotiations focused on horses. Soldiers and horses. Soldiers mounted on horses.

The negotiations continued to take place in pastures and stables rather than conference rooms and offices.

"I love this county. I love the fug of peat smoke and fat bacon that envelops its villages, because it demonstrates that my subjects are warm and well fed through the worst winter. I love my horses, but I'm happy to export them to other rulers' cavalry forces. I'm happy to share my stallions with my tenants and peasants, to improve the breed generally. Stud fees? Ah, well, not everyone can afford them and it improves the breed. After all, the boys enjoy it and there's always more where that came from."

Finally.

"I can't understand why Gustav Adolf is so determined to take over Oldenburg. Or, at least, some of his military advisers are. Political realities being what they are, I'm willing to stand by Gustav as a loyal ally. I am not willing to bow and grovel as his subject."

Frederik nodded.

Anton Günther quoted:

Maikäfer flieg!
Der Vater ist im Krieg.
Die Mutter ist im Pommerland.
Pommerland ist abgebrannt.
Maikäfer flieg!

" 'Pomerania is burned to the ground.' And still remains so, for all that Gustav Adolf has proclaimed himself as its duke and votes its voice on his own behalf in the House of Lords. If it comes to 'voluntary' subjection or subjection by force, I will, reluctantly, accept the necessity of resistance. Which I request that you make known, personally, to the powers in Magdeburg.

"That's my price for the soldiers you need now. For why will it be worse for my subjects for me to lead them in war than for me to sacrifice them to a ruler who will bleed them dry through forced contributions in order to finance *his* wars?"

The count slammed his hand down on the pommel of his saddle. "My memory is not deficient. Think back to what Gustav Adolf did in Pomerania when he first landed in Germany in 1630; the province still hasn't recovered from the punishment of those forced contributions. He drained it and his appointed officials are doing little to assist the people who are now his subjects. A good part of the reason that Behr is stirring up the Holsteiners now is how Gustav Adolf treated Pomerania."

Another slam of the hand. "If Gustav Adolf tries to take Oldenburg by force, I will resist. If the up-time admiral brings his ironclads, I will still resist, while being grateful that Wilhelmshaven has not yet been dredged into a deepwater port. I will give those of my subjects who prefer not to resist the choice of going into Ostfriesland or the Netherlands without penalty. I will organize those who remain.

"And even though I will eventually be defeated, I will resist considerably more effectively than Brandenburg or Saxony did. For as long as possible, I will bleed the Swede dry and he will regret that he ever decided that as long as he had an army to hand, he might as well use it to conquer a land he had no need to conquer."

That said, he provided Frederik with 500 cavalry. Not trained cavalry units, most of them. Mounted soldiers. Mobile; usable as scouts. And each mounted on a ton or so of horse.

He consented that Frederik should ship his men and horses across by requisitioning the ferries ordinarily used for transporting cattle from Denmark to the Netherlands. Frederik paid for their use but didn't give the captains a choice. He had no compunction about requisitions.

As the strange little fleet pulled out into the Jade Bight, a sailor who had been in Lübeck for quite a while broke out into an English hymn he had learned from the up-timers there. Joined by a couple of dozen others, Frederik embarked to "Jesus, Savior, Pilot Me."

Hamburg
May 1636

Observers saw Pestel's little decoy regiment coming up the land bridge. It passed Verden; at last reports overnighted in Rotenburg. It was clearly headed toward Buxtehude with a probable intention of crossing to Altona west of the city.

Consulted on whether they should do something, the FoJP city council decided it wasn't worthwhile. As one councilman commented, "Nah. If that's all the Danish prince has managed to put together, he's not serious about dealing with those reactionaries in Holstein. Too bad they neither burned witches nor persecuted Jews; if they had, the CoCs would have taken care of them during *Krystalnacht*. Harsh treatment of serfs wasn't on the agenda, though."

The commander of the USE forces in the city kept an eye on it, but nothing in the laws prevented a provincial governor from moving militia forces around within his own territory. He was more surprised that the governor had a regiment at all, as previous reports, combined with Frederik's earlier request for aid, had indicated a startling lack of troops in the province. Maybe the Dorsten business had finally gotten that do-nothing Dane up off his ass.

Both Pestel and the militia captain wished they could have gone east of Hamburg as Frederik's carefully dropped bits of intelligence had been hinting in the taverns, but that would have involved crossing a piece of Brunswick and then a piece of Mecklenburg. Better not.

"Once we get past Altona, though," Captain Botterbrodt said, "I'm going to have us swing around that little northerly projection of Hamburg's territory and go south. That's where we'll find the bastards."

Frederik's hastily sent instructions had omitted to tell Pestel where, or even that, this "regiment" was supposed to stop once it fulfilled its purpose of being conspicuously seen. So he nodded and agreed to the captain's plan.

Holstein
May 1636

Godske von Ahlefeldt didn't have good intelligence, but he thought he definitely knew that Frederik was coming up from Minden with a small regiment. He was also certain that small regiment wouldn't, couldn't, be all that Frederik was bringing into Holstein. Where would he be picking up the rest of his forces? He had to be getting USE military help from Hamburg. That was the only possible explanation.

That determined where they would have to set up, Godske decided. Facing south, toward Hamburg.

Stade
May 1636

Kerstin Brahe gave birth to a son, whom she named Gustav. He was a bit sickly at first, so she had the baptism done quickly by Aunt Hedwig's chaplain. Gustav, of course, was the name of Erik Stenbock's father; it might have nothing to do with complimenting the emperor of the USE. A lot of Swedish nobles were named Gustav.

Denmark
May 1636

Christian IV re-read the last letter he had received from Frederik and waited.

CHAPTER 27

Holstein
May 1636

The Oldenburger captains brought the ferries into Brunsbüttel at high tide, moored, and waited until low tide to offload. The process was not fun, but the captains and sailors were familiar with the waters, loaded and unloaded cattle as their regular occupation, and got the job done. Come in on the high tide; load and unload on the low tide; wait for the high tide to return and go out with it again.

"We'll stand by for two weeks," Captain Claus Harmens said. "If you aren't back by then, you'll have to get yourselves home."

They had better be back within two weeks, he thought. This expedition didn't have so much as a supply wagon or a cook cart. The riders had what they could stuff into their saddle bags; the infantry, what they could carry on their backs. At least grass was not in short supply at this season.

Frederik told Captain Meyer and Anton Günther's officers where they were going and by which route while they were in transit. He'd been all over this landscape as a boy, before he left to study abroad. And to get things organized. He presumed that they would; that was their job and they were all familiar with the kind of terrain that would be under the horses' feet. Next stop, Itzehoe, where Duke Johann

Friedrich had an administrative center for Gottorp. Which was usually managed by Otto von Buchwald, now a ringleader of the opposing forces.

Frederik talked to von Buchwald's deputy at length, persuading him to make some resources available to his officers. In the interest of good relations with Gottorp, he would prefer not to compel the man.

He sent Christian Ulrik and Erik Stenbock to Nicholas Pape, the business manager of the local *Damenstift*, to gather whatever information he might have. They came back saying how luscious Pape's daughter was; they were married men, they said at dinner, but Frederik was unattached and should drop by the Pape household.

"I'm happily married," Christian Ulrik said after his second beer, "but that doesn't mean that I can't look." The two continued with some bawdy raillery while Lütkemann contemplated temptation (*lead us not into*; see also 1 Corinthians 10:13), the evils of fornication (Colossians 3:5 was certainly relevant), and the prohibition upon committing adultery in one's heart (Matthew 5:27-28).

"Take the frown off your face, chaplain," Stenbock said. "I know better than to stray from the matrimonial straight and narrow; Kerstin let me know when we got betrothed that if I ever did, she would proceed to the kitchens, locate the largest cast iron frying pan to be found, take it in a firm two-handed grip, and bash me over the head. And laugh as my body lay on the floor with my brains leaking out. But that does not change that Margaretha Pape is ripe and nubile."

Frederik finally smiled. "No. If I have learned anything from observing young Gustafsson's dilemmas, it's to avoid Margarethas. Even Anton Günther's wife has Margaretha as a middle name. Let this Margaretha marry some ambitious, up-coming young ducal official like Vibeke Kruse's brother. I plan to stay well out of the path of luscious young Lutheran ladies."

At home, Margaretha Pape pouted to her mother that she was sad to have missed seeing Frederik. "The last time the duke was here, I was still playing with dolls, and he patted me on the head. I was impressed."

Frau Pape laughed. "That was ten years ago, at least."

But if Margaretha didn't get to see the duke this time, she got to meet his chaplain. The following day, being surplus to military needs, Lütkemann wandered over to the *Damenstift* "to inspect the church." Men, alas, even clergymen, were men, and thus fallible: he might as well look, even if he dared not touch. It would be a decade before he could afford to marry.

Captain Meyer spent the day in the deputy's office, going over maps with the Oldenburg captains. "From here, we'll basically be following the course of the Stör river until we're east of Neumünster. About thirty miles."

Cornelius Duyts was next to him. In this landscape, a hydraulics engineer was not to be wasted.

"By then," he said, "we'll be close to a hundred fifty feet above sea level. Everything looks flat, but it's not. A mountaineer might laugh, but for the peninsula, it's a pretty good height. You can't call the rise hills, but even a gradual climb will slow things down a bit. It takes a toll on men and horses both.

"There are a lot of large creeks and small rivers, but that's generally true of the whole duchy. It's not as if you have anything heavy, like artillery, that you have to worry about getting across them, or bogged down in the bottoms."

"I only wish we did," one of the Oldenburgers answered. "We're going into this poorly armed."

"I wish," another one said, "that we had a commander with some meaningful military experience."

Meyer glared until he shut up, but a third commented, "I wish we knew exactly where von Ahlefeldt has his people. We're going in blind."

Matthys Irgens, a copyist for Otto von Buchwald's deputy, was the person who had been detailed to bring in the maps that Itzehoe had. He stood there patiently, the model of a minor employee waiting to put maps away when those higher in rank finished using them. As soon as the officers adjourned their meeting, he dashed to his room, changed clothes, took a horse from the stables, and headed out to let the boss know that the enemy was on the way.

Hinrich Bothmann, who didn't have a job assignment that day either and was sitting in the stables gossiping, thought a bit and then followed him all the way to a manor house near Bornhöved.

*　*　*

Godske von Ahlefeldt had pulled together about five thousand people, but most of them were completely untrained serfs from the *Güter.* The most he could do with the majority of them was mass them in front of what trained and mounted men he had, using their bodies to break a charge if Frederik made one.

On royal Danish land. The nobles with whom he worked had been sufficiently selfish not to want their own lands and buildings ruined in a military conflict, fields trampled, livestock inevitably marauded by soldiers, whether a commander tried to exercise discipline or not. Under pressure from the rest, he had led this mass onto domanial land that belonged to the king of Denmark. Now only as a landholder rather than as sovereign, Holstein altogether being within the USE, but still Christian's, still part of Royal Holstein.

Otto von Buchwald was the one who had suggested Bornhöved.

So Ahlefeldt was here. With his forces. With too many young men who were treating it as a picnic expedition. They already had the cooks planning a celebratory banquet for the evening after their great victory-to-be. The villagers had prudently fled, but not quickly enough to take their possessions with them. The cooks were penning up sheep and

266

poultry. Unless the nobles sent back to their estates, the banquet would feature beer rather than wine. Wine cellars were rarely a feature of village houses in Holstein.

He thought wistfully of the wine cellars he had seen in France, back in the days of his grand tour and turned around to ask Buchwald a question when Irgens from Itzehoe came dashing in with, "My Lord, the governor has about eight hundred men with him altogether; three hundred or so militia he scraped together out of the *Stifte* of Bremen and Verden … "

Ahlefeldt motioned him to be quiet. "I knew about those. Where did the rest of them come from, and what is he doing at Itzehoe?"

"He borrowed the other five hundred from Oldenburg. With officers."

Ahlefeldt thanked the clerk. Buchwald told the man to get some food and drink, then hurry back before he was missed.

After Irgens left, profanity poured from Ahlefeldt's mouth. He had expected Frederik to be coming north by land, around Hamburg; combining the few men he had gathered in the *Stifte* with the inadequate reinforcements marching up from Minden and USE troops picked up in Hamburg. He had set up, as best as he might, on that basis. Now he would have to pivot the whole mass to face west. In a hurry or at least as much of a hurry as he could manage with this unwieldy group and no clear chain of command.

No way was he going to try to march out to meet Frederik. It had taken a week to get everybody in one spot. He would have to wait and let Frederik find him.

He worried mildly about the regiment that had been reported as coming north via Altona. If it wasn't with Frederik, where was it and what was it doing now? Other things were more urgent. He dismissed it from his mind, except for sending his stablemaster Peter Harder with a couple of riders down toward Oldesloe to see if they could locate it.

* * *

Captain Botterbrodt asked questions, so the decoy regiment hadn't turned south again. A local had told him, "They're not down that way; not over east, either; decided to fight on somebody else's land rather than destroying their own estates. They've gone up north of Oldesloe and they're waiting for you. They know you're coming."

Botterbrodt looked at Pestel. "What do we do now?"

Pestel shrugged helplessly. "Keep going, I guess."

At Oldesloe, people told them that "the big army" was up north of Segeberg.

They kept going.

"It would help if we knew where the governor is," Botterbrodt said.

At Segeberg, the Danish royal officialdom was seething with frustration. "The king withdrew his troops, of course, once the Swede put Holstein into the USE. He couldn't be perceived as still acting like a sovereign. So it's down to us. A dozen or so rent collectors and tax specialists, a couple of bookkeepers. The shitty locals thought their backsides were safe enough—it's not as if the Swedish officials in Mecklenburg are going to get off their duffs to do anything about it. What's happening to Westphalia is no skin off their noses. Except for having the province's vote in Lords, the whole 'the emperor is the duke of Mecklenburg' thing has been a farce, if you ask me.

"During *Krystalnacht*, the CoCs came, the CoC's left again after they'd accomplished what they wanted, went back into the cities or down into Magdeburg Province, wherever it was that they came from, and there's been a power vacuum at the local level, outside of the cities, ever since. It's not as if the Mecklenburg serfs knew how to run pretty much self-governing villages like they have down south, and nobody's bothered to teach them.

"On up north of here. That's the best we can tell you."

"Best be on our way, then," Botterbrodt said with resignation.

One of the rent collectors came running out after them. "Otto von Buchwald's main estate, Muggesfelde, isn't all that far southeast of Bornhöved. Eight miles, maybe? No more than that. If I was Otto and looking for a place to gather up a big batch of people, that's where I'd head."

"I wish," Pestel muttered, "that we had field radios."

Harder had swung wide to avoid Segeberg and Christian's remaining officials there. When he got to Oldesloe, the news was that yes, soldiers had marched past, but that was a couple of days ago. Which wasn't much for him to take back to Ahlefeldt. And he'd have to swing wide around Segeberg going north again. By the time he could deliver this minimal information, the regiment would have gotten to wherever it was going.

✳   ✳   ✳

"The governor is way outnumbered," Bothman told Duyts when he got back to Itzehoe. By a lot. Five to one, and probably a bit more, from what I could tell. It's not the kind of territory in which a man can be a surreptitious scout. Climb a tree and you have a clear line of sight for miles when the leaves don't interfere."

"You what?"

"Climbed a tree? *Ja.* Even remembered to tether the horse. But most of them are peasants. You've been talking to the governor's officers. You need to tell them"

"You need to tell them yourself," was Duyts's answer.

Captain Meyer called the governor into the meeting.

The Oldenburg officers were highly skeptical of the estimate Bothman made in regard to von Ahlcfeldt's numbers.

"I make mathematical calculations," the boy said, taking no offense. "That's what I do."

Frederik decided to keep Bothmann with him.

So there will be another Battle of Bornhöved, he thought. There had been two already. They were famous in Danish history. The first, in the days of Charlemagne, on the *Sventanapolje,* the Swentine Field, named for the little river, no more than a creek, that rose there and flowed toward the Kiel basin. Its result was that within a few years the border between Denmark and the Holy Roman Empire was set at the Eider River, where it had mostly remained ever since. The second, in the thirteenth century, had been a disaster for the Danes when the Dithmarschers changed sides.

Well, for the purposes of this one, he wasn't, exactly, a Dane.

Perhaps that could be considered a good omen. If he were a superstitious man.

They would go to Bornhöved.

Where Frederik drew up on a slight rise, looking at the disposition in front of him, Meyer by his side.

✳ ✳ ✳

"*Herr* Governor," Hinrich Bothmann said tentatively. "Umm, Your Grace? That is … "

"*Governor* is fine."

"If I may be so bold as to ask, My Lord Governor, how much military experience do you have?"

"After I finished the Latin School there, I attended the *Sorø Akademi* that my father established for the training of young officers. *Academia Sorana,* if you will. For two years. A decade ago." Frederik smiled thinly. "Then I was sent to obtain a higher education more appropriate to a future ecclesiastical bureaucrat. My only military experience came in helping to conduct a retreat."

"More than I. As the son of a pastor in Ribe, they gave me only the education deemed suitable for a future Lutheran pastor. I finished the Latin School at *Sorø* also, but ran away before they could condemn me to the university in Copenhagen. Thus, I have no military training or experience at all. Nonetheless, the quartermaster was talking to one of the local men ... "

According to the local man, there was a good-sized cattle drove coming toward the market in Lübeck by an—um—unsanctioned route that—um—bypassed the royal tolls at Segeberg. "There's a lot of money to be made in Lübeck right now, with so much provisioning needed for the new navy, you understand."

"Might there, possibly, be rustlers in Holstein?" Frederik asked. "*Might*, I emphasize."

"Ah," the man answered, "not rustlers. The profits from such a drove may well be going, however, to the peasants who have been compelled to pasture and stall the cattle at their own expense rather than to the nobles who are the only class with permission to conduct foreign trade in cattle and who force their serfs to raise the cattle the lords then sell to their own profit."

He looked up at the sky. "Perhaps you could think of the operation as more along the line of *smugglers* rather than *rustlers*."

Frederik thought about it. "How many?"

"How many what?"

"Cattle."

The closest that the local man could come was "more than a handful of hundreds."

Presumably that was less than a thousand. It was hard to be sure, since the man's arithmetical computations did not extend to the concept of a thousand.

Frederik's first impulse was to send Bothmann take a look at the herd and make a better -estimate. Then he followed.

Bothmann did whatever magic he did when numbers were involved.

Fredcrik looked at the cattle. Pied, as the Jutland cattle usually were, either black and white or red and white. More of the former; the black ones seemed to be more common these days. Rangy, these fellows, most of them, coming off the winter—and fellows, most of them. Peasants kept the heifers for future milk and breeding. For which a small number of bulls sufficed. Most males turned into steers and ended up in a slaughterhouse.

The horns weren't large, but they pointed up and out. An angry Holstein steer could do a lot of damage; put his head down and slash upward, he could gore the stomach out of a man. Or a horse. A thousand pounds of anything could do a lot of damage.

Bothmann came back with his estimate and they returned to the slight rise.

He looked again at the way Ahlefeldt had disposed his far larger forces. Most of those "foot soldiers" the nobles had gathered would be neither volunteers nor mercenaries, any more than his own troops were. But his were not serfs coerced into being there to defend their own absence of any right to justice, placed where they would take most of the casualties.

It was a pity, in a way. Nonetheless … he could not let eastern Holstein's *equites ordinarii* prevail.

With Christian Ulrik on one side of him and Erik Stenbock on the other, he looked down at the list of instructions that Captain Meyer had drawn up and began to issue orders.

One of the Oldenburg captains mentioned, almost hesitantly, that there was little to be gained in the way of military glory and honor from the governor's plan.

"I don't need glory," Frederik said. "I need a victory." He continued to read from Meyer's list.

Since the orders issuing from the commander's mouth made a fair amount of sense if the only intention was to win, the Oldenburg captains obeyed them and placed their men accordingly, dividing up under the governor's two.—what were they?— nobody had ever said exactly what rank those two noblemen from Westphalia might have. But they were clearly going to be in charge of the flanks.

*   *   *

"Where's Meijer?" There was no role for Cornelis Duyts now. He was at the back of the field with the chaplain and other noncombatants.

"Haven't seen him lately. Nor Jansen."

Gode and Barent had slipped away. They were in enemy territory, among Ahlefeldt's *Gesinde* and *Insten*. Who came from different estates, mostly didn't know one another, sometimes even spoke slightly different dialects, and certainly had no way of telling an *agent provocateur* from some other lord's steward.

"If you see the enemy coming at you, don't freeze and stand still. Don't turn around and try to run backwards, because you'll collide with the *Gutsherren* and their mounted men. Run sideways. If you're standing here—Meijer scratched the turf with a stick—turn this way and run along the Schwentine. If you're on the other side, over here—he scratched again—turn in the other direction. You won't all be able to save yourselves, but more of you will live than if you stand here like sheep for the slaughter."

This was more than anyone else had told them, which was, "Stand here."

"Sheep don't have to be slaughtered like we usually do, cutting their necks," one man said. "I heard someone say it once when I helped take a drove down to Lübeck. They can be hanged. 'Better to be hung for a sheep than for a lamb.' I wondered then what it meant."

Gode stifled his exasperation. "Whatever it meant, when *you* see the enemy coming at you, run sideways."

It was the best idea he and Barent had been able to come up with for saving as many lives as possible out of this mess. They'd gone to Lübeck to protest about the unjust execution of four men, one of them a simple-minded boy. They'd never intended to stir up something that might kill four thousand more.

The two of them had no idea that Frederik had instructed his inadequate supply of mounted men to move to the sides where they could come in on the enemy's flanks.

* * *

Frederik sat on his gelding, now with Meyer on one side of him and Bothmann on the other. And a good half-dozen large men who rode well, mounted on the best of the Oldenburger horses, directly behind him. Meyer intended to keep the governor alive.

"The cowherds know what they are to do?"

Meyer nodded.

"Cowboys," Bothmann said. "I learned about them in Bremen, from the CoC people. That's what the up-timers had: cowboys. That sounds much more exciting than cowherds. 'Yippie, ki, yi, yo, git along little dogies. You know that Wyoming will be your new home.' I wonder if Wyoming was in West Virginia."

Meyer grimaced with annoyance but swallowed his retort. The boy was just nervous.

And who wouldn't be, at his first battle? The good Lord only knew that he had been. Had probably made less sense than that.

Frederik rather hoped that most of the other side's infantry would run fast enough, knowing that a lot of them wouldn't. But without this battle, he would lose all hope of success in governing Westphalia.

He nodded.

Meyer turned and signaled.

From a half-mile away, the cowherds stampeded the drove directly into Ahlefeldt's front line.

Into a scene that soon looked like one of Hieronymus Bosch's visions of hell. He had seen those paintings when he studied in the Low Countries.

CHAPTER 28

Bornhöved
May 1636

When the *Insten* and *Gesinde* in the front line saw the cattle coming, they ran. Probably more efficiently than if they had been facing a cavalry charge. Most farmers had been chased by an angry cow at some time in their lives.

Lars Larsson, a serf from Bendix von Reventlow's Haseldorf, just as somebody or other had told him that he was supposed to do, headed down the banks of the Schwentine. When he saw some cavalry coming toward him, he veered off, opened a gate, and let loose a flock of geese that some resident of Bornhöved, presumably fleeing prudently in the face of an oncoming army, had left behind. Ahlefeldt's cooks had penned them up and announced plans in connection with feeding the fine gentlemen after the battle.

He didn't intend to oppose Frederik's forces who, under Erik Stenbock, were moving in to flank Ahlefeldt's right wing. He had no idea who they were. He vaguely hoped to slow them down as they moved forward, so those horses, monumentally large by the standards of the field ponies he was used to, wouldn't run over so many of his friends and neighbors. Which he accomplished.

The geese were unhappy. Unhappy geese are aggressive geese.

These Oldenburgers were not trained war horses. Those were much too valuable for the count to rent to the governor of Westphalia and risk their eventual purchase price. Anton Günther had included in his calculation of the lease cost that not all the horses would make it back. Nor the men riding them, but that was a price of war. Those he sent were good solid riding horses, under skilled men, but enough of them took exception to the attacking geese that their riders needed both hands to bring the panicking mounts back under control. They were in no position to use weapons. Stenbock ordered them to slow down; then to pull up; not ride in among the enemy one by one. *Hold together as a unit* was his cry.

On the left wing, Frederik's riders under Christian Ulrik arrived as planned and pushed against the mess that stampeding cattle had made of Ahlefeldt's mounted formation, which started to give to the left. But there was no pushback; he couldn't see what was happening on the other side of the field; was afraid that he had a hammer, but no anvil.

But there were geese.

As Christian Ulrik pushed them, Ahlefeldt's mounted troops started to move right, trying to avoid the angry cattle who had not already passed them, skirting fallen bodies so their horses would not lose their footing. When they got to the geese, they had to slow, milling around. Stenbock's riders finally managed to advance as a unit, slowly but with swords out, threading among the fowl.

An unidentifiable officer, from the middle of Ahlefeldt's forces, began yelling orders, a drummer next to him beating them out. The nobles started to reorganize, turn towards the front, where Frederik had—nobody.

Nobody had followed those stampeding cattle.

From the rise, Reineke Meyer spurred his horse, headed down, and ordered the dragoons standing by as a reserve to divide and support the flankers; the game wardens to aim and shoot at any of the enemy horse who managed to make it out of the center and drive toward the rise where the governor was, and the three hundred infantrymen who had marched from the *Stifte* through Bremen, through Oldenburg, and onto those horrible cattle ferries, to follow him.

Quite a few remembered him. Not for himself, so much, but because he had once been a lieutenant under Claus Christian von Bargen, the hero of Minden. Whatever that might mean. But a man had to assume that Meyer knew what he was doing. They followed him. Foot soldiers with pikes, marching against horses.

Frederik would report to Gustav Adolf that Captain Reineke Meyer had distinguished himself on the field of battle.

The nobles of eastern Holstein were stuck; they couldn't go anywhere. Ahlefeldt tried to keep some kind of order; Otto von Buchwald moved to one side, taking stock.

Captain Meyer and his infantry, plus a few standing peasants and cattle, were in front of them; mounted cavalry advancing to the left of them; and a mess of geese and riders to their right. Worse, they were now utterly disorganized, even more cattle mixed up with them, quite a few horses and riders down. Nothing was left that even resembled a coherent unit, despite Ahlefeldt's best efforts. Individually, they turned and ran, now in a disorganized panic, blocked to the east by the swampy turf and wet holes caused by the constant runoff from the mill dam, the only possible way out to the southeast, around Christian Ulrik's incoming riders.

At which point they met Botterbrodt, Pestel, and the decoy regiment that had come up from the south. Of the same school of thought as Bothmann, Botterbrodt, when he heard the noise ahead that signaled the fight was in progress, hefted his substantial fifty-year-old self up a tree, observed the field, and yelled orders. Which, he hoped, he had pushed this collection of academic pen pushers into being able to recognize during the evening drills he had conducted on the march. Not proper military orders. Words that even a law clerk could understand.

If not, his Minden militiamen would position them where they needed to be.

"You who have guns, get your butts into a single line. Next to each other, not behind each other, you idiots!"

After the first evening drill, fortunately unarmed, he had concluded that his first priority was to keep the members of his command from shooting each other by mistake.

"Ammunition line behind them. Sitting down. Keep your stupid heads *down*, ammunition caddies. Not one *inch* higher than you have to be to reach the boxes to your partner."

"Open the ammunition boxes."

"Load the guns."

He looked again at the melee ahead of him, hard to make out at this distance.

"Any rider who comes this way, shoot the horse. They make a bigger target than a man and I don't trust your marksmanship farther than I can *spit*." One thing he knew: a downed horse was a big obstacle on a battlefield; a bunch of them would slow down a retreat a lot and could make an orderly retreat impossible.

Botterbrodt's men, lined up a half mile southeast of the main battle, shot at horses.

Their rate of fire was abysmal. But nobody was shooting back at them, and the riders came one or two at a time, mostly, so the men from Minden, the clerks, and the students managed to hold an astonishingly steady line for nearly a quarter of an hour before Botterbrodt ordered them to get out of the way and let the rest of the bastards try to run. They wouldn't be going far.

His three hundred eighty-four men took seventy-three casualties; only eleven of them fatal on the spot and only sixteen more of them dead later of gangrene and other inevitable results of open wounds in the next few days. Not one of them had shot another. He called it good.

No other unit on the field had it that good.

Three-quarters of the *Stifte* infantry who followed Captain Meyer into that chaos went down, not to rise again until judgment day. The others kept going and had the honor of capturing von Ahlefeldt and von Buchwald, fastening them up with reins cut off dead horses, leading them in fetters—dragging them in fetters, more accurately—in front of the governor.

Frederik considered his next move. "Arrest every adult male of the Holstein *Ritterschaft* who isn't already dead or fled out of Westphalia's jurisdiction," was perhaps an overly comprehensive ruling, but it gave him a place to start.

Stenbock went after Bendix von Ahlefeldt; Christian Ulrik caught up with various Reventlows, Rantzaus, and Pogwisches.

Within the hour, on the main battlefield, amid the cowherds trying to round up the surviving cattle and get the drove moving again, there were local peasants butchering those *Vieh* that had become casualties. Nobody wasted perfectly good *Rindfleisch*. And the horses, as well.

Some of them were peasants who had been on the field and run. Most of those, however, if they came back at all, were identifying corpses. One of them asked Meyer if he knew anyone who could write. There was no way to take all these bodies back to the estates to which they belonged for burial. Someone needed to write down the names of the dead.

"Maybe the chaplain," Meyer said.

But Lütkemann was already on the field, comforting the injured and dying.

"I can do it," Hinrich Bothmann said.

Meyer detailed a squad of captured Holstein nobles to dig a mass grave for their serfs.

How many? How big?

Bothmann provided an estimate.

There was no room in the village of Bornhöved's churchyard for that many bodies. Not even in a mass grave. They weren't talking about a couple of hundred.

Cornelis Duyts arranged the draining of the big pond, almost a small lake, near the village. Captain Meyer insisted that they needed to get this done before the corpses started to decompose and spread illness.

Frederik ordered that his own fallen were to get individual graves in the churchyard. The captured nobles started digging; at this season, darkness did not come early in the evening nor linger long before dawn arrived. Lütkemann performed the rite of Christian burial over and over and over through the night, carefully recording each in his register.

The next morning, Frederik ordered Lütkemann to give a service of thanksgiving.

Exhausted, all the chaplain could think to say was, "What text? God's reaching out his hand? Saving Israel from the Egyptians? Exodus 14:30? 'So the Lord saved Israel that day out of the hand of the Egyptians, and Israel saw the Egyptians dead on the seashore.' It's frequently used." And, he thought wearily, so applicable, given what was still under way at the pond. Most of the dead Egyptians had probably also been poor schmucks who had no choice as to whether to chase after the Israelites or not.

"No," Frederik answered. "Psalm 66. It references that passage in Exodus, but has a broader, more general, application."

So over the stink of the field, to exhausted men, injured men, prisoners, and those who were still inconspicuously harvesting the bounty of dead animals at dawn, Lütkemann complied, reading aloud the third and fourth verses: "Say unto God, How terrible art thou in thy works! through the greatness of thy power shall thine enemies submit themselves unto thee. All the earth shall worship thee, and shall sing unto thee; they shall sing to thy name. *Selah*." And the seventh:

"He ruleth by his power for ever; his eyes behold the nations: let not the rebellious exalt themselves. *Selah*."

With, possibly, the least-prepared sermon he had ever delivered.

After which he climbed the little hill to the St. Jacobi church to pray. The interior was a mess: Ahlefeldt and his staff had been living in it for several days. Coming out, he stood quietly, looking out over in the direction where the Baltic Sea lay, in the direction of Rostock and home. He had been born in Demmin in Pomerania; he hadn't been back since he left for school in 1624 and there was nothing there for him anymore. Poor, afflicted, Pomerania. Rostock, where his parents were living now; the city fathers there had nothing against welcoming comparatively prosperous refugees and his father had been an apothecary and mayor, before the war. He was homesick, missing his family, missing his books. He was so much closer to them this minute than he had been since he left to study abroad—and he would have to go back to Münster in Westphalia, which was far away indeed.

There was more to Psalm 66 than the lines the governor had wanted him to use as the sermon text: "For thou, O God, hast proved us: thou hast tried us, as silver is tried. Thou broughtest us into the net; thou laidst affliction upon our loins. Thou hast caused men to ride over our heads; we went through fire and through water … I will pay thee my vows, Which my lips have uttered, and my mouth hath spoken, when I was in trouble."

Erik Stenbock and Christian Ulrik, realizing that it was only a few miles away, took off a few hours and went sightseeing at the Ahrensbök battlefield. Which, by this time, was just another pasture in Holstein. The peasants had stripped it of anything useful and put it back under grass. A few placid cows, with their calves, were grazing over it. A half-grown shepherd boy was keeping a lazy eye on his flock. Lambs still young enough to race played until they were worn out and then flopped down next to their dams. Somewhat disappointed, they got back to work the next day.

Frederik told the Oldenburg contingent to refill their saddle bags with provisions. "Take some of what's being illegally butchered on the field; it's as much ours as it belongs to the peasants I carefully do not see out there with their skinning knives." And sent them back to Brunsbüttel to catch the cattle ships, safely within the two-week deadline that Claus Harmens had set.

Then he prepared another heavily encrypted letter to Christian IV. Fortunately, there had been no need to summon in the troop transports that the king had placed in reserve off the island of Fehmarn; for purposes of tranquility within the Union of Kalmar, and maintaining Ulrik's amicable relationship with Gustav Adolf, this was probably as well. "I remain, your affectionate and profoundly grateful son, always appreciative of your fatherly love."

Holstein
June 1636

Christian Ulrik located the wives of the noble leaders in their townhouses in Kiel, where they were preparing to celebrate the triumphant return of their menfolk. He intercepted Henning von Pogwisch en route to Schleswig.

Christian IV would take care of Godske von Ahlefeldt's associates around Eckernförde who had supported the others; but not been present in Holstein. They were a Danish problem, out of the jurisdiction of Westphalia, or even the USE.

"There is such a thing as an *investigative hearing*," Frederik said. "I have become familiar with the term reading some of the up-time literature. I am about to hold one."

He set up shop in Segeberg, where he had the bureaucrats who managed the royal domain to assist.

After he had heard all the testimony, he made a distinction among: the lords directly involved in the retrieval of the fugitive serfs; the lord who prosecuted, condemned, and executed the four serfs; the other lords who were present at the arbitrary trial and execution; and the lords who had not been involved in the above actions, but who had subsequently joined in an armed uprising against legitimate imperial authority as represented by the USE governor of the Province of Westphalia. Who had, in other words, committed treason.

At the hearings, Frederik ascertained who the wives of the men in the first category were. Through them, he concluded, the Rantzau and Reventlow lineages clearly had been involved in the original decision to pursue and retrieve, as it was unlikely that such drastic action would have been taken without a consensus among the extended families and lineages. Undoubtedly, that was why so many others had joined in the armed uprising so quickly.

He confiscated not only the estates of Danish-born Bendix von Ahlefeldt, but also that of his wife Beate. *Kohoved. Kuhkopf;* Cow-Head. The irony of the name appealed to him; he directed the building of a memorial to the battle there. "Being related to someone who has seriously offended the ruler" was not, to the best of his knowledge, a crime enshrined in any law code. At least, not precisely in those words. Over the centuries of European history, however, many an *overmighty subject* had experienced its impact.

He was unable to prove anything against Poul Rantzow, the financier in Kiel.

He fully understood the concept of "a speedy trial." That was precisely what every noble in the fourth category who had appeared on the field in opposition to the governor's forces, whether in person or by sending another family member or by sending household personnel or by aiding and abetting, got. A very speedy trial. He imposed economic penalties and revoked economic privileges. Exemptions and monopolies that had accreted to the nobility over centuries fell rapidly by the wayside.

He would rather have liked to behead them all. Traitors deserved the proper penalty for treason. Gustav Adolf's grandfather, in his day, had found beheading to be effective in subduing the unruly nobility of Sweden, but in modern times, what with newspapers, up-timers, and other obstacles cluttering a man's path … and so many of them … He checked with his father, who saw no problem. Those who held their fiefs from the king of Denmark would have to make the best of Norway for the rest of their natural lives.

Those in the first three categories, he would take to Münster.

He would have much preferred not to have peasants out demolishing toll booths, because they would have to be rebuilt. Any son of Christian IV of Denmark had a visceral understanding of the importance of tolls to the government revenue stream. He could deal with the cattle smugglers at his leisure. After all, the nobility had always insisted on receiving precedence as one of their privileges.

Finding people whom he could appoint to the legal and administrative offices of the revised and modified regime of Holstein was not easy. Although it was not a wholly satisfactory solution, Frederik ended up drawing many of them from the ranks of the younger members of the Hamburg patriciate, men in their twenties and early thirties who had studied law for years to prepare themselves to assume increasingly responsible positions in the city and on its council, but whose families had been dispossessed by the events of 1634. Hamburg now had a popularly elected council with a popularly elected, FoJP, mayor. Young men named Moller, Rentzel, Jarre; Lütkens, Schlebusch, and Spreckelsen were unemployed or had not found positions commensurate with the effort they had put into their education. Effectively, he ordered that if a Hamburger applied for a government job in Holstein and displayed a law degree, hire him now and sort them out by competence later.

The FoJP by and large regarded the Hamburg patrician class as retrograde. When compared to the Holstein nobility, its members looked like wild-eyed rebels.

Hard-working wild-eyed rebels, by and large. Lutheran ones, too.

Avoid Calvinists from Bremen, even unemployed patricians with law degrees.

Don't hire Catholics at all. It would be too iffy if they had to deal with Denmark.

Throughout the entire episode, workers had kept right on digging the Eider Canal, which was making surprisingly rapid progress. If nothing else, Frederik's brutal ending of private jurisdiction had largely solved Duke Friedrich's manpower shortage. Landholding peasants, no matter how onerous they found the conditions of their tenures, were largely taking a wait-and-see stance, but *Insten* and *Gesinde*, whose lives held no hope at all for improvement if they stayed where they were, were flocking away, looking for other work.

Jochen Giese and Marcus Langemach, the Kiel financiers who were funding the Eider Canal, over their evening *Dunkles*, jocularly considered having a medal cast for *Hero of Industry* and awarding it to the governor but decided that it would be in poor taste.

Frederik requisitioned sufficient supplies from Segeberg that his now six-hundred-or-so-strong party would not have to forage and headed home by way of the land route, through Altona to Buxtehude, the important prisoners conspicuously in tow. He released the men from the *Erzstifte* with official thanks and bonuses; pensions for the families of those who fell. He stopped in Minden to make a big fuss over Botterbrodt; released the militia with thanks and more bonuses. Looked at the three hundred, more or less, law students and clerks that Pestel had gathered, wondered what to do with them, and took them along to Münster. Chancellor Gießenbier could figure it out.

In the publicity, Andreas Bucholtz presented it as a great victory.

Admiral Simpson, once he collected copies of the reports and finally had time to look at them, summed up the engagement as a "multilateral clusterfuck."

Which Mary reported to Tom when she next wrote. "I said that Frederik of Denmark had at least improvised effectively. Your father said that the governor sat there on a stolid bay gelding named Little Bean, watching the whole time, while Meyer and Botterbrodt improvised."

Hinrich Bothmann hadn't even made it into the reports, much less the peasant who let the geese out.

"It may not have been a thing of beauty from a professional perspective," Tom replied in his next letter, "but Frederik of Denmark did, undoubtedly, manage to win. Meyer and Botterbrodt wouldn't have been on the field and in a position to distinguish themselves without his determination to see the thing through. It makes you wonder how many other men out there could have been great, or come close to it, had the potential for it, but didn't happen to be in the right place at the right time to get noticed and promoted."

Münster
July 1636
Trials.

He brought the worst offenders to Münster because it was the provincial capital. This was not a local issue. A local outbreak, yes. Not a local issue. The entire province should take notice.

Münster had a plenitude of lawyers and, by now, a reasonable number of journalists.

The testimony, finding of guilt, conviction, and sentencing did not take long.

"I would bring to your attention that the governor of the Province of Westphalia has the *right of high justice*," Frederik said. He hoped that the nobility of the *Hochstift* around him were paying attention.

He supervised the executions. Hanging like common criminals; no privilege of nobility as to the form of execution. As the bodies of Buchwald, Pogwisch, and the two Ahlefeldt men were removed from the gibbets, he glanced behind him on the platform. "Schepler, where did you store those iron baskets?"

* * *

"I feel considerable dissatisfaction at the outcome," Frederik wrote in an encrypted letter to his father, "in that the wives, whom I believe, on the basis of information I gathered during the investigative hearings largely prodded their husbands into the actions they took, were not also on the platforms."

They were, however, in Norway.

To Duke Friedrich, in Gottorp, he wrote, "I understand your dismay at the death of Buchwald, who was your steward at Itzehoe and one of your close associates. However, I consider him to have been the most culpable, since it became clear from the testimony that he knew better from the beginning."

SECTION V

When the Going Gets Tough
June 1636-December 1636

CHAPTER 29

Westphalia
June 1636

A ll of which, of course, had been happening in the middle of another national election, for which there had to be determinations of voter eligibility, determinations of candidate eligibility, polling places, poll workers. All amid the vigilant oversight of the CoCs, whose adherents were not to be budged from their conviction that the governor would finagle it to the advantage of the Crown Loyalists if he could.

Westphalia sent a Crown Loyalist majority to the USE House of Commons again.

But not by much.

Münster
July 1636

The continuing controversy over the status of the city of Bremen continued, of course. It was bound to become more prominent now that the election was over, and the up-timer Piazza would become Gustav Adolf's prime minister.

Losing the economic resources of Bremen would not be good for the people of the Province of Westphalia. Depending on how generous the emperor and parliament might be in granting Bremen a hinterland, it could be economically catastrophic for the people of Westphalia. In reply to Chancellor Gießenbier's most earnest representations, with strong endorsements from the provincial treasurer's office, Frederik authorized Rist and Schepler to write a pamphlet on the topic of gerrymandering.

In their spare time.

They turned the task over to David Pestel, who outlined the legal arguments and passed it on to Andreas Bucholtz.

Not that Frederik thought that it would do any good. He didn't actually hold any grudge against the FoJP for wanting to gerrymander an additional vote for themselves in the House of Lords. As a political maneuver, it made perfect sense. If the FoJP could persuade Gustav Adolf to give it imperial city status, they would have one more guaranteed—if, for the time being, Calvinist—vote in the House of Lords (or the Chamber of Princes, left over from the CPE as it had been before a short time 1633; or the Senate, as borrowed from the up-timers). The term people applied to the jury-rigged entity that bore no resemblance to either the old *Reichstag* of the Holy Roman Empire or the House of Lords in the existing English parliament in casual conversation tended to depend entirely on the individual political stance of the observer. Or sheer mental laziness.

That the vote would be Calvinist might be the only thing that would slow down the emperor's inclination to approve their initiative. Frederik scribbled a note directing Rist to see to it that every bureaucrat in the Province of Westphalia paired the words "Bremen" and "Calvinist" at the slightest excuse in any document sent to Magdeburg.

If he were in a position to gerrymander some advantage to himself, he would not hesitate to do so. Manifestly, however, he was not, so there was no point in losing sleep over the matter.

He had nothing against some of the things that the up-timers had brought with them.

One of them was the poetry. There were few benefits to being dragged to Magdeburg every now and then, but the bookstores were surely among them. Some of the poetry was dreary, but some managed to be simultaneously entertaining and clever, perhaps even wise. As in the surprisingly apropos meditations by a poet named Edwin Arlington Robinson upon one Miniver Cheevy, a man born out of his proper time who spent far too much time thinking about his dilemma.

Bremen was a dilemma.

Westphalia could not afford to lose Bremen. Its economy would not survive being squeezed out of access to another major port. Nor was the national FoJP in any mood, apparently, for all of its idealistic rhetoric, to force Hamburg to listen to reason.

Why was the FoJP supporting Bremen's independence?

The vote in the House of Lords.

Frederik kept thinking about it.

Was there anything that would force the FoJP to back off from support for Bremen's independence?

Westphalia had voted close to 45% FoJP.

He was himself an appointed governor, not elected, and therefore not bound to vote with the province's overall majority. Appointed, not hereditary, no matter what the FoJP, even so clever a woman as Rebecca Abrabanel, might believe his ambitions to be.

He'd heard the gossip. Not hearsay gossip. Dirk Waßmann sat right there in the room. He was, after all, a FoJP delegate to parliament. But also a Westphalian. And friends with a man I Minden who had been a schoolmate of Claus Christian von Bargen, who had been Captain Meyer's commanding officer.

According to Waßmann, this was what the leadership in Magdeburg thought: that the emperor would favor their position that Bremen should be added as an imperial city because it would strengthen the USE's naval position. And they wanted Bremen added as an imperial city to ensure an additional FoJP vote in the House of Lords.

Emil Jauch had proven to be a wonderfully competent emissary plenipotentiary in Bremen. When it came to his attention that the young radicals were reading a certain up-time textbook on business management, he had ordered three copies, kept one for himself, sent one to his father, and the third to Frederik.

"Keep your goals firmly in view; but be flexible as to your methods."

Westphalia *could not* afford to lose Bremen. Nearly a million of the emperor's subjects—for whom the emperor had given him the responsibility under God—could not afford to lose Bremen.

The end did justify the means, especially when the end was of critical importance.

Within Frederik's mind, the seed of a wonderful, awful, idea began to sprout.

The next time that parliament met ... which would be in the next few weeks ... well, he would have to see.

Surely, though, nothing else would happen this day.

Christian Ulrik stuck his head through the door. "According to the village council at Ahlen, their sheep are being tormented by werewolves; bitten to death in the night."

Frederik sighed. He didn't have any men to spare. "Talk to the *Schützenbruderschaft* and see if they'd like to go on a hunting trip instead of pointing their guns at targets this year. If the wolves turn into men after they've been shot, I'll deal with it then."

He considered the possibilities. "And if the marauders are men rather than wolves, I'll deal with that, too."

* * *

After considerable meditation, introspection, and searching of his conscience, Joachim Lütkemann submitted his resignation. He felt, he said in his letter, that he needed to return to his original plan of finding a parish to serve in the vicinity of Rostock, where he would be more available to assist his aging parents, than would be the case if he remained in Westphalia.

Frederik was mildly annoyed, since it meant that someone— probably Rist, again; make a note to have him consult Gisenius— would have to locate a replacement. Still, unless one made oneself a lord over serfs, a master over slaves, it was always better not to come to rely on other people. In the natural course of events, they came and went.

"Since you're going," Frederik said, "take a letter from me with you and make a personal call on *Frau* Christine von Holstein-Hagen. I still need a reliable residential caretaker for the *Schloß* at Thedinghausen, and she can't stay crowded in with friends in Rostock indefinitely. She might as well come and live there, if she's so fond of the place. That should take some of the wind out of the sails for her brother and husband with their pesky lawsuit."

After the past months, Lütkemann had been reflecting on the costs of serving a prince, recalling a prior conversation in which Frederik had commented, "And in the same passage He asked, 'what shall a man give in exchange for his soul?' I doubt that any man knows until he has made the exchange." He had been asking himself how much he would be willing to give if he continued as chaplain in this court. Deciding that he didn't want to learn the answer. "Get thee behind me, Satan!"

Which did not keep him from mapping out a route to Rostock that managed to go by way of Itzehoe.

Osnabrück
August 1636

Osnabrück's situation in a valley penned between the Wiehen Hills and the northern tip of the Teutoburg Forest occasionally had some interesting consequences. A young, perhaps two-year-old, brown bear wandered into the suburbs from the *Teutoburger Wald* and took up residence near a kitchen garbage pit belonging to *Schloß* Iburg. A sheltered territory with ample food was nice work for a bear, if he could get it, much easier than foraging for roots in the ground and insects hiding themselves under tree bark.

Two mornings after the bear moved in, the commandant of Osnabrück, in person, came riding pell-mell through the streets of the capital and drew himself up in front of the city hall. In front of the offices where the governor's staff worked—there being no room for anyone except Rist over at the small office in Frederik's residence. He jumped off with the careless competence of a natural athlete and dashed up the steps, banging open the front door before either of the guards could step in front of it, yelling. Down in the market square, two equerries dismounted more sedately, climbed the steps, and followed him.

"If it was a matter of shooting a bear," Gustav Gustaffson communicated with some excitement, "I wouldn't be inviting you. But ... "

Christian Ulrik and Erik Stenbock looked at one another with some resignation. If the kid was excited ...

"It's a fine, upstanding young bear and looks healthy. Do you remember that in Saxony, at Torgau, Elector John George kept a menagerie of bears in the moat?"

"Surely," Kerstin Brahe moaned, "you don't want to add a dry moat with bears to Iburg."

Gustafsson was still rattling on. "Oh. What Kerstin? Not that. It was a dry moat at Torgau, of course ... and when the Swedish army came through, our soldiers ate them."

"What?" Christian Ulrik was not sure what he was hearing.

"Swedish soldiers ate the elector's bears. The ones in the moat at *Schloß* Hartenfels in Torgau. So I was thinking ... "

Erik winced. They had learned through painful experience that when Gustafsson had an idea, the ramifications were frequently ... complex.

"So instead of shooting the bear, I think we should capture it and I can take it over to Torgau and give it to *die Richterin*, since she's in charge of Saxony now, as a kind of apology because the army ate the others. He won't be a *descendant* of the original bears, of course. Perhaps, though, he could be brought to symbolize a new beginning. Over there in Saxony, I mean. And the defeat of everything that went on in Berlin last year; the town uses a bear as a kind of symbol or mascot, you know. Publicity and all that." He beamed.

So they went bear-hunting.

Bente insisted on going along for the ride; she was expecting again and wanted to take advantage of having one infant weaned and in the hands of a reliable nanny while not yet being heavily pregnant with the next.

The easiest way to catch a bear was to bait the bear. Coax it where you wanted it with food, which worked well for hungry bears in the wild. Not so much for a bear who had found a garbage dump of his own.

The kitchen staff had named him Brutus. He didn't have a picky appetite, though he had a clear affection for sweets.

He also, the *Jäger* who were keeping an eye on him said, seemed to be rather clever as bears went. For example, in less than a week, he had noticed that the benevolent bringers of divine bounty, also known as the pot boys from the kitchen, were reluctant to bring that bounty when he was standing right on top of the pit, so now, when he saw the scullery door open and the children come out with baskets of peelings and pits, stems and cores, he would back away some distance until they dumped them out and left again.

The head *Jäger* suggested that they try a large, comfortable cage with large door, a thick layer of straw bedding, and a basket filled with the bearish gentleman's favorite foods. Not, he added, that he was willing to forego having several of his sturdy companions armed with equally sturdy bear spears in the vicinity, just in case. The fellow hadn't been aggressive so far, but with a bear, one never knew. They'd turn on a man in a flash. Though, of course, this chummy boy hadn't been made nervous by the packs of yapping dogs with which men usually hunted a bear. They'd been keeping the castle's hounds kenneled, not wanting to provoke him, what with people around all the time. A hunter only needed dogs if the intent was to kill the bear. Which he understood that it was not.

On the first day, Brutus watched the preparations with considerable interest.

The second day, he paid no attention to the cage and its charms.

"Maybe," Kerstin suggested, "if you stop dumping food into the pit every day, he'll get a little hungry and go see what's in the food basket in the cage."

"And what," the head cook asked, "does the young lady think we'll be doing with the waste if there's no pit for dumping it? It would get pretty ripe in here in no time. It gets pretty ripe out there, but at least it's out there."

This was followed by philosophical meditation on the meaning of life as exemplified by the practice of garbage disposal.

"Couldn't you put something on top of the pit?" Bente asked.

"He'll pull it off, ma'am," the *Jäger* answered.

"Something big. Heavy. Too much even for a bear." Bente looked speculatively at one of the massive ornamental wrought-iron gates through which people entered the inner courtyard at Iburg.

There were no *serious* injuries resulting from taking down the gate. The stable boy's broken arm was straightforward and should heal without problems.

As a result of putting it back *up*, of course …

"I'm pretty sure," the head cook said, "that when they put that thing in place the first time, back when I was a lad, there was a pulley and rope to hold it upright 'til they got the hinge pins in place. Not a bunch of fools trying to push it up when it's twice as tall as any of them."

"And I was thinking, too," Gustafsson rattled on the next morning, "that now that we have the boy … " He patted the wooden bars of the substantial cage with its straw bedding fondly, "now that we have Brutus, I'll take him over to Torgau myself."

Christian Ulrik looked at him warily.

"Why not? I think that Oxenstierna stabled me. He can't have believed that I in particular as Gustav Gustafsson would be needed as a commandant here. He didn't like anyone who might be competition to his influence; he wanted to get me out from the under the king's eye and put me where I'd be invisible. And while the money's good, it's not great.

"The governor can appoint someone to command the Iburg itself in my place, take over the civil administration stuff, and I can get back to the army. I'm so bored here. I'll stop to see the king, well, he's the emperor now, get my colonel's commission reactivated, get a regiment, get back into the thick of things. There's plenty action now in the east; they can find a use for me."

"I think," Kerstin Brahe said, "I think that's a great idea."

"Actually," she said to Erik in bed that night, "I think it's a marvelous idea. Wonderful. Superb."

Christian Ulrik lay in his bed alone, contemplating what the response of his half-brother Ulrik and Princess Kristina might be if Gustafsson resurfaced in the imperial orbit.

Estonia, he suspected. Latvia, Finland. Someplace far, far, away.

If ever a nice, actually fairly smart, if somewhat superficial and silly, boy had been born as "surplus to need," it was Gustafsson. Even more than himself.

He was in bed alone because Bente was having dinner with Margaretha Timmerscheidt.

"You have to make up your own mind. Christian Ulrik did marry me," Bente said, "but that's not why I eloped with him. I'd have gone with him and stayed with him as long as he wanted me, even if no one ever mentioned the word 'marriage.' Are you willing to go trekking with Gustafsson wherever he goes and, in the end, maybe find yourself abandoned hundreds of miles from home in a town that you've never seen before? Not see your father again? Not see the rest of your family again? That's what you'll be risking."

In the end, it was Ernst Wettin, once Duke Ernst of Saxe-Weimar, who got the duty of ceremonially receiving the bear upon its arrival in Saxony.

Quedlinburg
October 1636

Iona Nelson went skipping through the halls singing "Gretchen Richter got a bear, e, i, e, i, o."

"I'm glad I wasn't there when she heard about it," Annalise said to Osanna Merkur.

CHAPTER 30

Münster
September 1636

The duke of Bavaria had been exiled to Italy.

The Ottomans had captured Vienna.

Those things happened far away.

The meeting of the USE parliament was here and now. Frederik put Christian Ulrik in charge of Westphalia as his deputy, got on a considerably better horse than he was accustomed to riding, surrounded himself with a larger entourage, both civilian and military, than he was accustomed to having, and reluctantly made his way to the capital of the USE, where it was possible that things could go very, very, wrong.

Schepler came up with a replacement chaplain while Rist was out of town with the governor. "If you would authorize me to issue an invitation," he said to Christian Ulrik, "I can get this done without having to bother the governor."

"Who are you thinking about?"

"Hermann Jung. He's in Hamburg now, working for Joachim Jungius at the *Gymnasium*. He was born in Holstein; he's about the same age as Rist. He's been thinking about going back to Rostock for graduate work, becoming a Hebraicist. Nice guy, makes friends easily.

Knows Comenius, which can't hurt when it comes to getting along with the up-timers. Also, Jungius, his mentor, is interested in science and has made connections with the technical schools in Magdeburg and Grantville; we certainly need all the help we can get in those fields."

Christian Ulrik considered that unusual list of qualifications for a chaplain. "What's his theological position?"

"Um." Schepler looked doubtful. "Not so sure, but he's a nice guy. Might tend a bit more toward feeling rather than strict doctrine. 'Love your neighbor' and all that. I know he's read Arndt's *True Christianity* several times; he used to carry a copy around with him. He talked about missions—maybe pastoring a Lutheran congregation in the Netherlands and teaching common people, sailors, enough that they could spread the gospel all around the world, everywhere that VOC ships sail, without needing learned theologians."

He looked at the ceiling. "Um. Err. That sort of thing."

He wasn't a man who was normally at a loss for words.

Christian Ulrik opened his mouth, prepared to say, "No."

Andreas Bucholtz sighed. "His father's a farmer in Brokreihe; it can't hurt the governor's public image to bring in a personal chaplain of peasant origins right now. And it might go a ways to soothe ruffled feathers in Holstein to bring in at least one Holsteiner into his personal circle."

"Western Holstein," Christian Ulrik pointed out. "And as peasant farmers go, the family's prosperous."

"It's not as if you'll find peasant boys who made it to the university from eastern Holstein," Bucholtz countered. "That's rather what the battle was about. We can spin it."

"Very well," Christian Ulrik said. "Go ahead and invite him. It can't hurt anything."

When Andreas told his brother, Christoph made a face. "When the cat's away, the mice will play."

Magdeburg
September 1636

"I wish to God that Becky was here too."

Helene Gundelfinger frowned mildly at Ed Piazza's oath. "She is where she is, doing what she must do. Be grateful that I was able to catch the train on such short notice."

"Why in hell are the Crown Loyalists suddenly pushing this so hard right now?"

Helene's frown morphed into a slow, reproachful, gaze.

"All right, I'm sorry. Soap in my mouth and all that."

"Everyone's on edge. How ... " He caught himself. "How on earth did the Commons come to pass it?"

"We weren't paying attention. A little amendment here; a small paragraph there; a sentence altered. It all adds up."

"The parliamentary system we've built sucks, in some ways," commented the prime minister. "Compared to the USA, that is. If it passes Lords, I don't have a veto the way the American president did. There's nowhere near enough support for it to override a veto by a two-thirds majority in either house. If I had one."

"You can try to persuade the emperor to withhold his approval."

"I can. But I suspect that in his heart, he finds it attractive."

"You do?"

"Think of the ways in which he is grooming Prince Ulrik to be, in essence, his successor, even though Kristina will rule. The managing partner, so to speak. Rather like William and Mary in England did ... or will ... or won't. I suppose they've been butterflied out of existence."

Helene reached over to the pot and poured them both more coffee. Annabelle had brewed it fresh, piled a plate high with cookies, and left them to what she called "political stewing."

This issue made for a thick stew. Inheritance laws always did. Inheritance laws with political implications ... All in the name of standardization, of course. Uniformity. Simplification. No more massive confusion for courts, judges, and lawyers, with one little region having primogeniture, one ultimogeniture, one partible inheritance, and more variations, often all within the same province, accompanying by centuries of conflicting precedents and applications. Each province must adopt a uniform inheritance law. No matter how it upended individual families and time-honored customs. Omelettes and eggs. Back in the USA, Maurice Tito had reminded him, Virginia, the parent state of West Virginia, had done in primogeniture and male-only inheritance by statute after the Revolution, which had upset folks at the time.

The idea itself hadn't been so bad.

Until the damned amendment sneaked in.

Yeah, even for the down-timers, the mantra was "rank trumps gender." Witness the regents of Hesse and Tyrol. But not always. That awful von Campe woman from Himmelpforten with her eternal this, that, and the other. One of her main complaints was that she had never been able to take her own causes to court, over there in *Erzstift* Bremen. That her little *Stift* had to have a male provost as a legal representative. That she couldn't make him get off his lazy ass and do anything unless he felt so inclined.

He wondered idly if the same was true for someone as exalted as the abbess of Quedlinburg. Had she voted in person in the *Reichstag*, or had she sat on the sidelines, with a male legal representative casting the vote in her name? He'd never thought to ask. She was high exalted enough that rank probably trumped gender.

Melissa Mailey was on a tear about this! The USA had gotten rid of it in the middle of the nineteenth century; no way was the world going back to it. She hadn't appreciated being reminded that the middle of the nineteenth century was more than two hundred years in the future.

Custom, tradition, long-standing precedent. The idea of male legal representatives for women who owned property outright (nobody wanted to abolish that, even for married women, which was, as Melissa said, at least one way in which the Germans were miles ahead of the contemporary English and their *femme covert* nonsense) was something that—well, the Committees of Correspondence were against it, loudly, but even for a lot of your average FoJP backbenchers, it didn't sound so bad. And the amended bill had passed the Commons. With a squeak, but it had passed.

The FoJP could lobby, but when it came to the Lords, in the final analysis, all Ed could do was watch the likely debacle.

The roll call dropped, one by one.

Frederik sat and waited. If nothing else, one of the charms of being governor of Westphalia was that the roll was called alphabetically by province.

Keep a firm grasp on your goals but be flexible in your methods. Equating that advice to the tried and true "the end justifies the means," he had considered at length what would throw the greatest spoke into the FoJP agitation for Bremen's independence.

The city government of Bremen had its own reasons, but the party at the Magdeburg level wanted another reliable vote.

The vote tied.

Ed waited for the inevitable.

Westphalia voted "nay."

The governor of Westphalia pulled in his thick lips, pinched them between his teeth, and hoped that his gambit might succeed. *Even if it does not,* he thought wryly, *at least Aunt Hedwig and Gerdruth von Campe will love me.*

It would have been counter-productive for him to try to bargain with the FoJP before he had actually cast the vote. He had decided that much even before coming to Magdeburg for this session. For one thing, they wouldn't have believed him.

Once it was done, the bargaining started. If the Fourth of July Party wanted reasonably consistent support of their measures from

Westphalia, then their support of Bremen's becoming an independent imperial city had to die.

"Why?" Ed Piazza asked.

Frederik stood up, motioning. Johann Rist, leaning against the wall, stepped forward and set up an easel.

The governor of Westphalia started to draw with a thick, black, charcoal stick that ensured everyone in the room could see the diagrams.

"Holstein has access to Hamburg. And other ports, such as Kiel, if Hamburg sets out to strangle the province's exports with exorbitant usage fees and burdensome warehousing requirements. Which, I must mention, it is doing. Holstein will have another, once the Eider Canal is functioning. Eventually, if I have to, I can set up export facilities downriver from Hamburg and if you—the federal government, that is—do not blast them out of existence with your ironclads for the pleasure of Bugenhagen and your other members in Hamburg, Holstein's farmers will survive."

He looked pointedly at Albert Bugenhagen; then turned back to the easel, flipping a page over.

"My former *Stifte*, Bremen and Verden, can access the Elbe to the north if Bremen tries to strangle exports. Their farmers will survive."

He flipped another page. "That isn't the case for most of the *Niederstift*. If the Low Countries, now that they have Ostfriesland, close off access to Leer and Emden, the only practical outlet is by way of Bremen.

"For that matter, if Essen and the Low Countries ever close off access to the Rhine, the farmers in the *Oberstift* will be facing the same problem. An *Oberstift* where almost every surviving town is heavily burdened by debt from borrowing to pay off the *Brandschatzungen* levied by passing armies, not just since 1618, but long before that, throughout the Dutch wars. Or, if they could not borrow, are piles of soot and ashes, to which the former residents are only trickling back, needing to rebuild quite literally from the ground up. Where the people cannot afford the wonders of the better looms, the sewing machines, the other possibilities that the new industries offer.

"For that vote by Bremen in the Lords, you would be happy to allow fifty thousand people, not heavily indebted because during the war they were able to shelter behind strong walls, to impose misery on five times that number. Or ten times that many, if ever enough insanity prevails that the USE goes to war with the Low Countries. Or even feuds with Fernando to the point that he closes off access.

"So I gave your FoJP my vote on this. You wanted to remove Bremen from the province to obtain the vote; you got the desired vote from the province itself. You got a better deal, because at the same time, the Crown Loyalists lost a vote—which, I would point out, would not be the case if you merely added Bremen as an imperial city juxtaposed against Westphalia."

Everyone expected more, but Frederik simply sat down. After a few minutes of silence, he said, "I will leave you to your deliberations," arose, and left, followed by Rist with the easel.

There was no immediate decision, of course. The FoJP would not move on this without talking to a lot of other people. Supporters in the states and provinces; from the other imperial cities. Not to mention Becky. And Mike.

"Why is the man so universally loathed?" Ed asked Helene Gundelfinger.

"I'm not sure that he is," she answered. "Loathed, that is. Except by people who only know him by way of their assumptions. And people who get contrariwise to something he's determined to do. As a person, he's more on the order of ... " She paused, "universally not particularly well liked. He does not share his father's charm. Also ... " She hesitated again.

"Also what?"

"He seems to have put together a pretty good working staff. Not full of saints but lacking in obvious sinners."

Ed requested a private meeting.

Frederik obliged.

"If your party persists in supporting imperial city status for Bremen, you can forget entirely about obtaining my support for any measure that arises."

By the end, Ed had a clearer understanding than ever before of why Martin Luther's "*Hier stehe ich; ich kann nicht anders*" had created a revolution in half of Europe a century earlier. He vaguely recalled the kerfluffle over "we shall not be moved" a couple of years earlier and thought that compromise had a lot to be said in its favor.

"And if you wonder why I have done this," Frederik said, "it is much as Anton Günther is determined to protect Oldenburg. A message which the emperor has already received. Understand this, Herr Piazza. To keep Bremen and its port available to the people of the province whose welfare the emperor has entrusted to me under God, I would vote with the party of the devil himself."

CHAPTER 31

Münster
September 1636

It was good to be back. Which was not a sentiment Frederik had ever expected to feel for Münster when he chose it as the capital. Not that it wasn't changing. He'd taken Hinrich Bothmann with him and installed the boy at Imperial Tech while he was in Magdeburg. Now he rather regretfully assigned Christian Ulrik to take over as commandant in Osnabrück. He would miss his half-brother but didn't see any good options.

"And fifthly," he said at the end of a rather long discussion, "you're going to have to put an end to the calendar fight over there for once and for all."

"Calendar fight?"

"Calendar reform. Twenty years or so, the Catholic bishop introduced the new Gregorian calendar; the Lutherans refused to accept it because it was a pope's idea. Still won't use it. Tell them flatly that it's the up-timer calendar, it's been adopted by the whole USE, and they can like it or lump it, but even if they lump it, that *is* the way they will date their official documents from now on." He frowned. "Let them double-date them if they insist, but they will include the modern format."

He stood up, paced across the room, and looked out at the construction site. The new chancery building involved a great amount of excavation and consequently a great amount of mud.

"And no matter what anyone says, old Mayor Modemann's even more ancient mother is *not a witch*. The official position of the government of the United States of Europe is that *there are no witches*. Whether or not there actually are is beside the point." He pulled the window casement open. The air outdoors was as muggy as that inside the room. "Bitches maybe, but no witches. Make it stick. Before Lütkemann left, he said something about the Hebrew word *mekhasheph* in Exodus 22:18 being better translated by another word than 'witch.' I'm sure the world will be a lot better off having 'sorceresses' running around free."

He slammed the casement closed. "And, while you're at it, straighten out the school funding."

Christian Ulrik grinned, nodded, and bowed his way out of the room.

As Frederik prepared for bed that evening, he reflected that he would miss his half-brother greatly. But, perhaps, it was just as well. The commandant's position would be a stepping-stone for him, to higher things. And … he himself had come to be too much at ease in Christian Ulrik's company. He should not have spoken so carelessly today, should not have expressed himself so freely. It was more prudent for a man to keep his own counsel.

As to the vote in Magdeburg, though: Bremen aside, if the Lord himself had been content to see Deborah as a judge in Israel, it seemed unlikely that He would be a stickler about male representation for women in legal matters in the USE.

He recited Luther's evening prayer. Then, in accordance with the great reformer's recommendation, he settled himself to go to sleep at once and be of good cheer.

*   *   *

Otherwise in Westphalia, there was a great deal of furor about a provincial governor's borrowing "foreign troops" to take action against "citizens of the USE." Of course, the furor was not consistent, ranging from reactionary outrage against using foreign troops against lords who were exercising their legitimate prerogatives to CoC reaction against using foreign troops against reactionary lords instead of utilizing proven CoC cadres of domestic origin against reactionary lords.

Not that the CoC had demonstrated any interest in providing assistance to Frederik the preceding spring, but for writers of propaganda pamphlets, that was more or less beside the point.

"It's called *spin*," Johann Rist said. "The people who produce it are called *spin doctors*. You need to hire some publicists, My Lord Governor."

Frederik looked at him. "We have Bucholtz already."

Rist resigned himself to a dearth of publicists. The governor was not inclined to explain his actions, much less his motivations.

Widespread demands for a "coherent" policy approved by the highest levels of government flew from the newspaper editorial columns.

Concerted spin efforts declared, for various reasons, that the writer was in deep opposition to "*ad hoc* reactions" by "unelected individuals."

Nevertheless, under the provincial charter, the *Landtag* convened and voted taxes.

Frederik promoted Reineke Meyer to colonel and assigned him to design and create a Westphalian National Guard with a minimum of three effective regiments and a significant military police component.

Then he sent a general commendation to the tax collection department over at the chancery, complimenting its members on their zealousness.

"It's not, of course," one clerk remarked to another, "as if our own salaries don't depend on our zealousness. I'd have been happier with a bonus than a certificate."

"The bonuses will come once he can afford it," his colleague answered, "so keep on working zealously. The governor's a fair man."

*　*　*

Heinrich Jung arrived, bringing with him a wistful hope for what he might be able to accomplish in his quite unexpected new calling as a private chaplain to the high and mighty.

He arrived, meditating on Psalm 72, with high expectations.

> *Give the king thy judgments, O God, and thy righteousness unto the king's son.*
>
> *He shall judge thy people with righteousness, and thy poor with judgment.*
>
> *The mountains shall bring peace to the people, and the little hills, by righteousness.*
>
> *He shall judge the poor of the people, he shall save the children of the needy, and shall break in pieces the oppressor.*
>
> *They shall fear thee as long as the sun and moon endure, throughout all generations.*
>
> *He shall come down like rain upon the mown grass: as showers that water the earth.*
>
> *In his days shall the righteous flourish; and abundance of peace so long as the moon endureth.*

He arrived dreaming of Johann Arndt's conviction that orthodox doctrine was not enough to make a person a true Christian. That, rather, each person needed Christian experience, to feel repentance, to feel the process of sanctification by the Holy Spirit. To have an intimate fellowship, an almost mystical union with God. Admittedly, by the standards of the Flacians, there was a subjective element in this approach, but still, Luther had included *sola fide* in the three basic principles and faith must work in the heart.

Then he met Frederik of Denmark and remembered that there was more to the psalm.

> *He shall have dominion also from sea to sea, and from the river*
> *unto the ends of the earth.*
> *They that dwell in the wilderness shall bow before him; and his*
> *enemies shall lick the dust.*
> *The kings of Tarshish and of the isles shall bring presents: the*
> *kings of Sheba and Seba shall offer gifts.*
> *Yea, all kings shall fall down before him: all nations shall serve*
> *him.*

It was probably safer to stick with the purely messianic interpretation of Psalm 72, now that he had given the matter somewhat more thought.

Nor had God ever promised an easy life to His prophets.

In the meantime ...

He was to organize the Lutherans of *Hochstift* Münster, beginning with the city, thanks be to God, into superintendencies and consistories on the Ravensberg model, with which he should familiarize himself. He was to investigate the prospects for building a new Lutheran cathedral in the city, see how many parish churches would need to be constructed to meet need, and locate staff for all of those. Compile a list of vendors of church furnishings such as chalices and choir stools. In his spare time, he should check on the status of the Lutherans in Schwerin, which rather concerned the governor.

The government of the city of Bremen was not happy.

The Fourth of July Party in Bremen was not happy.

The Committees of Correspondence in Bremen were utterly frosted by Frederik's action at the parliamentary session.

There were debates. Public speeches. Recriminations in taverns. Spiteful comments at ladies' parties. A few action proposals.

"The question we should be asking ourselves," Tönnies Breiting said, "is this: Is there anything we *can* do about it?"

Emil Jauch was tempted to tell them that they *could* have refrained from inviting Daniel Bartoll as a consultant and adopting his little political gamesmanship as one of their policies quite some time ago. But his assignment was to be diplomatic and soothe ruffled feathers, calm troubled waters. Build bridges between factions, as one of the songs that Knaup's daughters band played went. So he refrained.

＊　＊　＊

Frederik occasionally stood at the window of his office, looking at the baskets, the iron cages, which were once more hanging from the bell tower of St. Lambert's church. Then he went back to work on everything else that needed to be done in the province.

He hired a couple of Schepler's friends who had been in the decoy regiment the summer before and sent them to Grantville to see about acquiring technical personnel. No up-timer evinced the slightest interest in working for the Province of Westphalia, but they came back with a half-dozen recent down-time graduates of the technical college coordinated by a slightly older young man who had been at the University of Jena.

"They're great guys," Schepler said enthusiastically. "No matter how hard a job we set them to doing, they say, '*It's not a problem; it's a challenge.*' and plunge right in."

The governor set them to work planning an alternative radio broadcasting set-up to the one the Jesuits had established right under his nose and had the gall to name Loyola University of the North, which he understood to be some kind of allusion to an up-time institution. Undoubtedly, the Jesuits in Münster conspired with those in Grantville.

His memo was brief. In case his ploy did not succeed in the long run, the one requirement was that the station be located outside of the most extensive possible limits that anyone at all could imagine for an independent imperial city of Bremen but otherwise as close to Bremen as was feasible.

If the parliament should collude with Gustav Adolf and the FoJP and grant the place imperial city status in spite of the best he could do, there was no point in having expended Westphalia's resources only to have the project given away.

Of course, if the parliament should gerrymander an exclave to include the broadcast facility, no matter where it was located, that would simply be beyond his control.

H wouldn't put it past them.

Postscript: he had heard about something called "jamming" radio broadcasts. This had been done by two of the sons of John George of Saxony, so it must not require up-time expertise. Have someone investigate jamming.

Next, write to Anton Günther about the general assumption that once Gustav Adolf cleared up the mess in Poland, he would have an army available—and use it to annex Oldenburg and its wonderful deep-water port into the USE willy-nilly. According to Dirk Waßmann, this was "received wisdom" even within the FoJP leadership, which showed no real inclination to object to such a show of force. There were apparently limits to their belief in the right of self-determination (which they defended so stoutly when it came to an individual's religious affiliation or lack of it). Annexation unquestionably appealed to the emperor, with the prospect that Oldenburg would pass directly into the hands of the Vasa dynasty if the count died without a legitimate heir.

Anton Günther did not care for Christian IV of Denmark, and he had his reasons. He might be more willing to enter into cooperative ventures with the governor of Westphalia. With Frederik wearing that hat.

The letter to Oldenburg drafted and in the Out basket for Rist to put into proper form, Frederik picked up a folder containing a sheaf of reports on Lingen. The Congress of Copenhagen had allotted Lingen to Westphalia. In idle moments, he wondered why the Congress of Copenhagen allotted Lingen to the Province of Westphalia.

What was that rhyme he had seen in the up-time poetry anthology? *He only does it to annoy, because he knows it teases.*

A sneeze causing a temporary mental blackout on Oxenstierna's part was as charitable an explanation as any, perhaps, for if he had done it deliberately … Admittedly, Lingen was on the eastern side of the old land bridge that had connected the southern *Oberstift* and northern *Niederstift* of Münster. A land bridge that was nowhere near as crucial for the Province of Westphalia as it had been for the prince-bishops, since the new geography provide another route.

But Lingen belonged to the United Provinces, having been conquered by Maurice of Nassau-Orange in 1597, reconquered by the Spanish in 1605, and then taken by Swedish forces when the Spanish pulled out in 1632. Probably "taken by Swedish forces" had something to do with it, but that didn't change that Lingen belonged to the Low Countries.

Fortunately, the *Stadhouder* was a practical man. Early on, they had agreed that the Netherlands would re-establish the local administration, Westphalia would not interfere with the local administration, and any questions involving international status would be referred to the USE Department of State.

So far, the USE Department of State had not gotten around to responding, at least according to the most recent information obtainable by the administration of the Province of Westphalia. Frederik sincerely hoped that Gustav Adolf was not intending to provoke a conflict with the Low Countries over it.

That was a longer-range concern. He himself should attempt to put the best construction on everything, as Luther admonished Christians to do in the *Shorter Catechism*. For immediate purposes, a policy of noninterference did not mean a policy of ignoring what was going on in that county, so he started reading the reports.

David Pestel submitted his resignation to the chancellor. He intended to move back to Minden and prepare to run for parliament when Dirk Waßmann retired. Waßmann had been his teacher once upon a time; he hadn't been a young man then.

From the original Westphalian furor about "foreign troops" and "*ad hoc* responses," the debate throughout the USE whirled out of the control of anyone's propagandists and publicists, into increasingly acrimonious arguments over serfdom itself. Arguments over the entire nature of serfdom. Arguments that were caused, to a considerable extent, by the varying historical developments that meant there was no such thing as a unified legal condition that could be labeled "serfdom" within the boundaries of the USE, not only from province to province, but within any given province. This meant, frequently, that remedies proposed by analysts and politicians in one area or region were inapplicable to the situation in another, which resulted in would-be reformers attacking one another's arguments at least as vociferously and extensively, if not quite as fiercely, as they did the positions of the apologists for and proponents of the institution.

For there were apologists and proponents—quite a lot of them, ranging from jurists who were pragmatically appalled by the chaos they saw resulting from a major change in land tenures to Lutheran pastors who saw the governance of a lord over the people on his lands as comparable to the position of authority that a *Hausvater* occupied in relation to his wife, children, and servants.

Almost every paper mill in the land saw a spike in third-quarter profits.

There was a nationwide shortage of copiers; manufacturers found themselves overwhelmed with backorders, and retailers could not keep stock on the shelves.

Generally, outside of the SoTF, there were numerous riots and widespread unrest for which there was no obvious remedy.

Any direct imperial response was constrained by the general prevalence of serfdom in Sweden and Denmark.

* * *

Frederik picked up a folder of reports prepared by Jung pertaining to the administration of the Lutheran parishes in the former county of Ravensberg, now incorporated into the County of Westphalia.

Before he could finish reading them, he had to stop for a meeting with delegations from the City of Lemgo and the multiple counts of the various subsections of Lippe. Resolving this was not a problem. The governor looked at the delegations, tight-lipped. When he did open his mouth, it was to say that the Calvinism of the dukes of Lippe was not to interfere with the Lutheranism of the city of Lemgo and *vice versa*. They were all to stick to the provisions of the Peace of Röhrentrup of 1617, which had granted Lemgo the right to determine its faith independently. He told the delegates that their principals should expect a memo confirming that decision. With an addendum: both parties must practice religious toleration.

He opened the folder of reports on Ravensberg again, but before he could even finish skimming the contents, Gießenbier appeared for a last review of the document by which he would confirm the residential privileges, including synagogue and cemetery, that Count Ernest of Schaumburg and Holstein-Pinneberg had granted to the Ashkenazic Jewish community of Altona in 1611. He approved with the addition of the words "and Sephardic," to make sure that all contingencies were covered, initialed the insertion, and went back to the problems of ecclesiastical administration in Ravensberg.

Three days later, he dropped a memo into his Out box instructing Rist to send a letter to the mayor of Hamburg indicating that the internal affairs of Altona were none of Hamburg's business, as Schaumburg had been incorporated into the Province of Westphalia by the Congress of Copenhagen—add appropriate verbiage.

Three days after that, he met with Gießenbier again, after which he instructed Rist to draft a memo to the current administration of the Province of Brandenburg indicating that, although the county of Ravensberg had fallen to Brandenburg in 1614 by the Treaty of Xanten, the Congress of Copenhagen had placed it in the Province of Westphalia in 1634, which superseded the earlier arrangement. Consequently, Calvinists in Brandenburg had no business mucking about in the affairs of Lutherans in Ravensberg—use appropriate verbiage.

He drafted a memo to the Lutheran pastors of *Grafschaft* Ravensberg indicating that as they had managed their own affairs since the Calvinist elector of Brandenburg became their *Landesherr* in 1614, they didn't need a Lutheran governor to take the job over now. They should consider that there was no guarantee that the next governor of Westphalia would be a quasi-bishop or even Lutheran. *Or even*, his mind informed him sarcastically, *given the peculiar views of the up-timers in these matters and their growing influence over the emperor, male*. The pastors should keep on doing their jobs and not bother the governor of Westphalia with their internal troubles. Specifically, they should reorganize their own superintendency and elect a new superintendent. Sincerely.

He scratched a little itch behind his ear, thinking. *Very* sincerely. The was possibly no one alive who dreamed how *sincerely* he hoped never to hear about the ecclesiastical politics of Ravensberg again.

He reviewed a complaint from the Jesuits that the radio technicians he had employed were converts to an up-time sect called the Church of Jesus Christ of Latter-Day Saints and had come to the Province of Westphalia with the intent of serving as missionaries for that heretical movement while they were being paid to design a radio broadcast system for the governor. The Jesuits in Grantville had confirmed that this heresy was expanding with dangerous rapidity. Moreover, the governor had employed them to design a broadcast system that would compete with the perfectly functional one that the Jesuit Order already had in place. The Jesuits objected on both counts.

He laid down his fountain pen, an up-time innovation that he did appreciate, capped it, turned away from the desk, and paced around the room for a few minutes.

Unexpectedly, the next item was a response to the inquiry he had sent out the previous summer on the problem of who was now ultimately responsible for the administration of Lutheranism in Schwerin. The answer was "not your brother Ulrik, or at least he's done nothing for a couple of years" and "honestly, no one has the vaguest idea."

He prepared a letter to Ulrik, cc: to the emperor and bcc: to the king of Denmark, recommending strongly that for the spiritual good of the Lutherans of Schwerin, *someone* should appoint a full-time ordained clergyman to a new position of General Superintendent in Schwerin under the umbrella of whatever authority that his brother might still possess in regard to the *Stift* and the diocese, no one ever having been elected in his place. As it happened, one Joachim Lütkemann, his own former chaplain, was a man he could recommend strongly as having all the necessary qualifications for the position except a wife. Which Lütkemann was anxious to acquire, having formed, with the approval of her parents, an attachment to one Margaretha Pape of Itzehoe in Holstein which he would be delighted to transform into a betrothal and then a marriage once he had sufficient income.

With an attached memo to Rist: "If this doesn't work, see that Jung follows up."

He drafted a memorandum to Gustav Adolf as duke of Mecklenburg pointing out that something needed to be done about it. Attached a note for Rist advising him to enclose Jung's memorandum explaining the way Ravensberg was currently managing the matter.

He drafted another memo, for Gustav Adolf as emperor of the USE, saying, for the sixth time in two years, that the emperor could not reasonably expect him to establish a Lutheran state church in a province that was approximately forty percent Lutheran, forty percent Catholic, fifteen percent Calvinist, and five percent Mennonites, Jews, and other ecclesiastical minorities (more precise statistics to follow once the census now in progress was completed). Not to mention how many of them, regardless of their official church membership, were in reality either adherents of the FoJP or supporters of the CoCs, and thus probably Socinians. Possibly Arminians, Remonstrants, Anti-Remonstrants, or Hussites; with semi-Pelagians not beyond the realm of possibility.

And noted that Rist should attach a copy of the memo from the Jesuits.

He then scratched out the final two sentences of the draft memo, adding one more note for Rist: "See if you can find some different verbiage to explain the problem this time. Maybe we should refer to the entire religious situation in Westphalia as a *challenge*."

Frederik glanced the seventh letter of complaint he had received about Margaretha Timmerscheidt's non-marital elopement with Gustafsson. This one sent jointly by both of the would-be Lutheran mayors of Osnabrück. The two of them had finally found a common cause beyond loathing of the Catholic former mayor of the city.

A letter from Christian Ulrik said that, at the advice of Aunt Hedwig (she was, after all, his aunt, too), he was calling in a consultant.

Frederik looked at Rist as he meticulously placed the letter in the appropriate box on his desk. "Even her father admits that the girl left voluntarily. Tell them to complain to the pope. Catholic ladies are not my problem."

Rist grinned. "The girl is Lutheran. Alas."

"Curses: foiled again."

CHAPTER 32

Magdeburg
October 1636

Mark Early had not expected his work, way back in the spring of 1633, before the USE, when Grantville was the capital of the New United States, to come back to haunt him. But he'd been on the Special Commission on the Establishment of Freedom of Religion then, and it looked like someone needed something of the sort now.

He hadn't expected to be the first up-timer that almost anyone involved in the administration of the Province of Westphalia had met, either.

But he was. Christian Ulrik displayed him like a prize 4-H pig at the Grantville fairgrounds.

Westphalia was a reality check. When Mark finished—it took him a good six weeks of talking to persuade the residents of *Stadt und Stift* Osnabrück that they were going to have to change their ways whether they wanted to or not—he went back to Magdeburg with a pretty urgent sense that he needed to get across to Ed Piazza, to the whole bunch of the guys who lived in the Grantville to Erfurt/Jena to Magdeburg to Lübeck bubbles, that for a lot of the USE, they still might as well be aliens from Mars.

"Goddam, Suze," he said to his wife. "They're not listening. We knew better than this in the beginning. Remember all the 'hearts and minds' stuff that we did down in Franconia? Still are, for that matter. And over around Fulda? Boots on the ground."

"Yeah."

"Now it's all big picture. Religious toleration? Gustav Adolf passes a law. Witches? Send in the CoCs. Anti-Semitism? Send in the CoCs. Check that one off the bucket list; we're done."

"We're not?"

"Not by a long shot. Not when it isn't all 'big picture' loathing, kind of abstract hatred. Not when armies for both sides rampaged through there back and forth; each one did horrible things; about everybody lost something or someone. That's what I was running into—over at Osnabrück—and the way Rist explained it to me, it's pretty much the same all over the province. A Lutheran mom, 'the Jesuits took away my son's scholarship for their *Collegium* when he was fifteen, so he lost his chance, and now he'll be a landless peasant all his life.' A Catholic father, 'the Swedes confiscated everything our village had in storage for the winter and over thirty people died.' Maybe there's some exaggeration, but basically, they're all telling the truth. Nobody's innocent; no, not one. And if we keep blinkers on, it'll all fester and fester until someday, someplace, there's a Kosovo massacre and *we the true, we the brave, we the pure-hearted* will proclaim that we're 'shocked, shocked, shocked' and claim no responsibility. That unpleasant governor! Those horrible reactionary nobles! Well, what could we have expected?"

"It's not as if there's anything we can do about it."

"One thing we—we up-timers—fucking well could do about it is stop pretending that it's safe to ignore the second-largest province in the USE, population-wise, just because the FoJP has a grudge against Gustav Adolf's having appointed Christian IV's son as the governor. Which, you'll notice, they don't take out on Gustav. They take it out on the administration over there, which ultimately means on the people over there. As long as the navy has its precious access to the sea by way of the Elbe open, we figure that it's all good."

"You *like* Frederik?"

"Only met him once, for about fifteen minutes. He didn't strike me as 'Mr. Cordiality' during that time. I spent a lot more with the half-brother, who does know him well; who definitely doesn't dislike him."

Mark laughed.

"And talking to the half-brother's wife Bente. She's a hoot. Keeps up a lively correspondence with her father, sisters, brothers-in-law, a whole batch of them who are up in the northern part of the province, around Hamburg. They've seen more up-timers; gotten hold of more of the book reprints, know FoJP and CoC people."

"So then, after I finished in Osnabrück, I went up north—actually stayed with Bente's father for a couple of nights. Hellish roads—worse than in the interior of Brunswick. *Frau* Hedwig of the dramatic escape from Saxony was in town; she remembered me, asked to see me, talked for a while. She showed me a cartoon that a FoJP newspaper in Hamburg published. Captioned 'Prince of Westphalia,' of course. Pretty good caricature. The words coming out of his mouth were, 'Never apologize. Never explain.' No idea if either she or the cartoonist connected the saying to Henry Ford. She's working hard.

"Honestly, Suze, we ought to do something. We can't write off close to a million people as hopeless, having neither hearts nor minds that we could persuade—not even if the urban FoJP politicians in Hamburg and Bremen act like they'd be perfectly happy to squeeze the entire place into abysmal rural poverty if that's what it would take to pressure Frederik not to put up a fight when independence for Bremen comes up in parliament. Which it inevitably will, in spite of the governor's bargain with Ed Piazza. Does the FoJP in the rest of the country really still want to push for Bremen's vote in the House of Lords since the governor and Ed struck that agreement?" He shook his head. "I hate politics. The political process is another name for blackmail and extortion."

Susan patted his shoulder. "If we did make … overtures … if you want to call it that. Offered agricultural extension programs through the Grange, for example. Or … what? Do you think that the 'Prince of Westphalia' would welcome them? Welcome a 'hearts and minds' effort. Welcome us?"

Mark shrugged her hand off and paced around the room, his hands clasped behind his back. "I don't think he'd refuse out of hand. Welcome us? No. The last thing anyone would call him is a gung-ho reformer. But I do think he'd use us to buck up the economy if he thought it would help. There might be some possibility for textile manufacturing if they could get it going. There's an awful lot of material reconstruction that still needs to be done. Buildings, of course. Christian Ulrik probably had two dozen reports on his desk that could be summed up, 'the old chapel building that was desecrated nine years ago is so decrepit that the schoolmaster can't use it anymore and has to meet the children in the tavern.' Drainage. Bridges. Even improved fords would be better. Yeah, I think he'd use us."

"But … "

"As we would be using him."

Mark turned around. "I'm putting in for a few weeks of leave."

Erfurt
October 1636

"Steve, it made me sick."

Steven Salatto was at his desk in the SoTF's Erfurt Administrative Center. He'd come out of Franconia in 1635 totally exhausted. Würzburg, the Ram Rebellion. That assignment had stripped him to the bone. He'd welcomed a nice desk job. He and Anita both. Having the older girls back with them and with Diana an active toddler …

But it had been a year. A little over. They'd managed to catch their breath.

Now Mark was here, whirling around his office with passion.

" … because Oxenstierna had a grudge against the king of Denmark and stuck those people with a governor who … "

"Who what?" Steve laid his pen down.

" … who Mike was likely to pick up the grudge against, too. Because of who he was; no matter what he ended up doing, one way or the other. Which has pretty much ended up in the category of trying to make bricks without straw."

Steve heaved a sigh. "I've got three meetings on my agenda this afternoon. Come on over to supper this evening, why don't you? At the house. I'll call Anita; she'll tell the cook. We can hash this over. Get in touch with some of the others, if it seems worthwhile. Johnnie F.'s the only one who might have resources. SoTF Secretary of Agriculture and all that. Almost everyone we worked with during the Ram is piloting a desk in Bamberg now. And needed there. Even in the SoTF, life isn't all hunky-dory. The National Guard presence in Würzburg isn't there to be ornamental. Lowry Eckerlin says they put in a fair amount of time squelching this or squashing that."

"As if everything was just great up-time!"

"There's that."

*　*　*

"The place has some financial potential. It's not going to make anybody a mint, the way mining does. I don't have any idea what kind of industry it might support, with Hamburg out of the economic equation because it's an independent imperial city. Bremen's a fairly decent port for their exports—how long the province can hang onto it though, I wouldn't predict. That's politics. I hate politics. Probably as long as Ed hangs on as prime minister, at least.

"But before the war—not our war, but their war—those prince-bishoprics brought in a nice income for the noblemen who got slotted into them. It wasn't just the *Reichtag* vote that had lords and dukes growling over them like three or four hounds who wanted the same bone. The old lady—Hedwig, Frederik's regent up in the *Erzstift*, told me that in 1600 or so it brought in about a hundred thousand *Thaler* per year over and above expenses for secular administration and the parishes. Which was nice if you could get it, and explains why old Johann Friedrich could build a castle for his mistress if he felt like it. Income's down, now."

"What are they doing with it now? The income?" That was Estelle McIntire. She was still an auditor, now in the less adventurous confines of the Erfurt Administrative Center, but still with a suspicious mind. That sort of went with the job.

"She, *Frau* Hedwig, is pouring most of it back into infrastructure. The way she sees infrastructure, which isn't the same way we would define it. Not with the same priorities. We'd think transportation and manufacturing; maybe law enforcement. She thinks church roofs and chalices, replacing the stuff that was stripped from them during the Edict of Restitution period. A couple of poorhouses, almshouses, here and there; one of her requirements for propping up a collapsing *Stift*, whether male or female, is for it to do charity stuff from now on. She does put a fairly large amount into schools, but those are so connected to the churches that in most of the province, you can't tell them apart. It's only the big towns, and by 'big' I mean between five and ten thousand people, that sometimes have a school that's directly supported by the city council."

"The largest town has ten thousand people?"

"Outside of Hamburg, which isn't in the province; and Bremen, which doesn't want to be. Maybe Münster is bigger, now that all the activities of the provincial capital are there. It's growing, but I doubt that it's hit fifteen thousand. Westphalia's rural, rural, rural, with the

CoCs almost entirely in the towns. They haven't even tried to penetrate the villages; most of them are town boys themselves and have the kind of casual contempt for peasants that you might expect. Rubes and hillbillies. Are there flatland-billies? Ten percent of the population is in the towns, maybe—if you take 'town' down to two or three thousand people. If you're willing to grant that every little burg with a municipal charter that it got from an extinct line of dukes back in the thirteenth century qualifies as a town."

"There's one big economic obstacle that you aren't factoring in." Estelle put her fork down. "Almost every town and village that's still standing over there is heavily burdened with debt. Mostly from borrowing to get the sums that various armies demanded as ransoms in order not to burn the place down. The ones that didn't borrow are the ones that are sodden heaps of soot and ashes, even now, contributing nothing to the tax rolls at all. *Brandschatzungen*. The governor's financial people will have a list of them somewhere. I can guarantee that, practically.

"A lot of those debts even pre-date the Thirty Years War; the Spanish and Dutch were raiding all through there during the Eighty Years War. After the Twelve Years Truce expired in 1621, those raids started up again. The armies are gone. Whether the soldiers were Mansfeld's, Tilly's, or the Crazy Halberstadter's, the debts are legal contracts with the financiers. The interest rates are high enough that even if the towns put the maximum into paying them off, I wouldn't be surprised if some of them will still be at it a century from now. That's going to slow investment a lot, when it comes to local resources. I don't think you want to set up a situation where the whole province will be basically owned by absentee investors out of Grantville and Magdeburg. Or Hamburg and Kiel."

Mark groaned. "I didn't need that."

"You needed to know it. Didn't want to, maybe, but needed to." Estelle was not a woman to tolerate nonsense. She picked up her fork and waved it at him. "What kind of oversight is there? Systematic oversight?"

"None, or not much. They have accountants who meticulously keep track of income and outgo, but there's nobody with the kind of a responsibility that we'd think of as an inspector general. Each of the canons at every cathedral has his own budget; they're jealous of each other and fight over the scraps like the lords and dukes fighting like hounds over the big bones. That's not efficient, but they do sort of know where the money goes because they keep an eye on each other. Systematic it's not."

"How much malice aforethought?"

Mark laughed "Are we using up-time West Virginia as a corruption standard here?"

"There's that."

"It wouldn't be the same as Franconia," Johnnie F. pointed out. "Anyone we could send over there wouldn't have any enforcement authority. It'll all be persuasion. Whether they're talking to your acquaintance Christian Ulrik at close-to-the-top level of the administration or a peasant in a village, it'll still be persuasion. For the peasants, at least, persuasion by people who fall into the category of 'furriners from somewhere else.' I don't see ..."

"They've managed to set up election districts," Mark said. "On their own, without any 'I'm from the federal government and I'm here to help you' input, because the federal government didn't bother to help them. And the census is close to done. If they combined those two sets of information and created agricultural extension districts with elected boards out in the rural areas ... and we sent people in as advisers from an NGO. Not from the SoTF, at least not officially."

Johnnie F.'s head perked up.

"For the peasants, I sort of doubt that any up-timer who showed up would be more 'furrin' than Danes and Swedes. All folks from somewhere else."

"I don't have any up-timers to send. Stretched thin. Gone as far as possible with the people I have available."

"How many down-timers have you trained?"

"Lots. I've got a good-sized cadre in the field now."

Mark smiled.

If he could organize some financing, then ... If he could, he wished he could draft Steve Salatto into organizing the project, or at least showing them how to organize it. Steve was getting a little antsy, sitting at that desk in Erfurt.

There was one big problem with that.

Steve and Anita were Catholic.

The governor of Westphalia, when you came right down to it, wasn't all that fond of Catholics. Was enforcing toleration, presumably because it was the law. Why else? Because sometimes it worked to the advantage of Lutherans? Because he didn't have any other option, given the religious distribution of the population? No way to tell.

The people around Frederik, though? The ones who worked directly for him ? The ones he saw every day or so? Not a Catholic in the lot. Hardly any Calvinists.

Catholics were way out of the man's comfort zone.

Virginia DeMarce

CHAPTER 33

Quedlinburg
November-December 1636

"I don't care. I don't think it's fair." -Annalise Richter huffed, which was about as upset as she ever sounded.

"It's the way it is, Anni," Osanna Merkur protested. "She's boxed in. If the abbess can live with it, then you can live with it."

"But it's especially not fair this year, with the celebration."

The year 1636 was the seven-hundredth anniversary of the founding of *Reichsstift Quedlinburg*, of which Duchess Dorothea Sophia of Saxe-Altenburg was abbess. Or, more technically, since the *Stift* had been converted to a Lutheran institution a century earlier, she was head of it, and the ladies were not nuns but *Stiftsdamen*, who could resign and get married if they ever decided to. Some of them did. But most people still called it the abbey, and called its head the abbess.

"An abbey, but no nuns," Anna Thorold chanted, "No nuns. Not even before the Reformation. No nuns. 'Secular canonesses' is what they were called. They did not belong to any religious order. Unmarried daughters of the higher nobility, gathered together to live a godly and scholarly life. It says so," she pointed to the second page of the pamphlet, "right here."

"Spares," Osanna said. "Don't parrot the party line. They were spares and surpluses, the ones their families couldn't marry off."

"I think they should have let her stay in the House of Lords," Annalise continued, unmoved by the distractions. "She was until the CPE turned into the USE. That was November ... um ... three years ago, now. We covered it in current events. I was a junior in high school, I guess. In Grantville we were the NUS then. I can keep track of when we turned into the SoTF, because it was almost a year before Grandma's husband was killed. It was in April 1634, and then someone assassinated Henry the next March. And I graduated from high school in June, 1635, and came to college here that fall. By then, the abbess wasn't allowed to be in the parliament anymore."

"She can't. *Because Quedlinburg isn't independent anymore.* It's not an Imperial Abbey directly subject to the Holy Roman Emperor. It's a part of one of the USE provinces. We're in Brunswick now. Have you ever heard of what the up-timers call *gerrymandering*? It's as gerrymandered a border as anyone has ever seen, down here where the SoTF, Magdeburg Province, and Brunswick come together."

Annalise jerked her head up. "They deliberately put her somewhere else because she's a woman?"

Osanna threw up her hands in exasperation. "It's not because she's a woman. It's because she's a Crown Loyalist, and they probably didn't want her in one of the Fourth of July Party strongholds. You don't pay enough attention, Annalise. Papa says that was simply smart of them, because ... "

When Osanna started quoting her father, it was clear that Papa always had a lot to say and the content of his discourse relied heavily on CoC pamphlets.

"I don't think they should have taken away her being in Parliament. She's intelligent. I guess they did it to the other women's abbeys too, then? Herford? How many more are there, whose abbesses used to have seats on the clerical bench in the old *Reichstag* before the Ring of Fire?"

"*Ja*, it happened to the other women's *Stifte*, but also to the Lutheran prince-bishops and *Stifte* that had men as their heads: Halberstadt, Bremen, Verden, Paderborn. The bishops and administrators and churches still own their property, like the abbey does here, but they don't run the territories anymore. They're not governments." She jumped up and stamped her foot. "Be reasonable, Annalise. The abbess could always renounce her title and run as a commoner, like Wettin did."

"No, she can't. She'd lose her job. That's what is not fair about it." Annalise brandished a cover sheet for one of the newly printed publicity pamphlets for Mrs. Nelson's winter music program. "It says so right here. Back when nobody was even dreaming about the USE, 700 years ago, the founders of this place put a requirement in their documents that the women who were canonesses here back then and are *Damen* here now have to belong to the German high nobility. *Hochadel.* If she renounces her title to run for the House of Commons, then she can't be abbess anymore. She's been abbess practically forever, since the year after I was born."

"Anni," Osanna asked. "Do you keep track of everything in the world according to how it affects you and your family?"

"Yes. Pretty much. Doesn't everybody?" Annalise folded another pamphlet. "I still don't think it's fair. The abbess is very, very, smart, and there ought to be a way she could still go to Magdeburg and tell the people in the government what they need to hear. So the government ought to fix it. Abolish the abbey's charter and give it a different one, or something."

The argument spilled over from pamphlet-folding time into program-rehearsal time.

"Annalise, dear, that's not how it works," Iona Nelson said patiently. "Didn't your civics class in Grantville explain about the separation of church and state."

"The teacher told us how it worked up-time, and some about how it works now in the SoTF but ran out of semester before he got to explaining how it works in the other provinces. He did say that it's not all the same. I still think ... "

"*Please* stop thinking." Iona threw herself back, slapped her forehead, and said, "*No*, I didn't say that. I can't have said that. I would never tell a student to stop thinking. Of course not! Get a grip on yourself, Iona Nelson!"

"But Mrs. Nelson ... "

"Annalise," she said. "The constitution of the USE does not authorize the government to go out and mess with the charters of these old, established, institutions in the sense of suddenly requiring them to admit commoners as members of the *Stifte*. It lays out conditions for political participation but that kind of enforced social revolution, given that it also has implications for church/state relationships, is not in it. If the USE keeps to the American model of government, it may never be. The Congress of the United States of America did not go around telling the Catholic church that it had to ordain women or ... or ... or ...

"Let me start over again. As of this specific day in the year 1636, the abbess thinks she's pushed the founding documents about as far as they will go by admitting daughters of the lower nobility and commoners to the school and college on an equal basis with those of the higher nobility. She's making changes here that she couldn't make if she resigned. She feels like she has a moral obligation to stay and make them."

"Can't she change the documents?"

"No. Nor can the members of the *Stift* as a whole. They are what they are; not a constitution with a built-in process for amendment if something goes obsolete."

"Now let us say something nice about Saint Mathilda, widow of King Henry the Fowler," Osanna chanted the next afternoon. She had been run through the opening sequence for this year's program once too often this afternoon. "Yea, let's have a big and glorious celebration and all ignore the fact that Saint Mathilda would probably say that the abbess was pushing the envelope by letting 'these commoners'—like me, you will note—into her sacred precincts as anything except scullery maids. Let's all go 'whee' for the great seven hundredth anniversary celebration. I bow to your tomb, most exalted Saint Matilda; that of your husband; that of your son; that of your mass of relatives. This place is full of graves, and I'm glad I'm not superstitious about ghosts." She bowed, pretending to doff a fancy hat. "Pause for applause."

"Osanna," Iona Nelson said in a pained voice. "Please. Just. Stop. It."

Osanna was not in a mood to stop. When they got back to their rooms after the evening rehearsal, she was still on a rant. "I don't see the abbess' precious changes coming fast. Think of this afternoon. Did you see any of the daughters of the high nobility here at the school helping Mrs. Nelson fold pamphlets? No, they were having their afternoon snack in the lounge. Do most of the *Stiftsdamen* pay any attention to the commoner students? No, it's the noble girls."

"It's your turn to be reasonable," Annalise said. "Sabina Lechner is a commoner, but she wasn't folding pamphlets. Bethany Leek is an up-timer, but she was not folding pamphlets. We're both on a kind of program that Mrs. Nelson calls work-study. So is Anna, and there are only so many hours of the day to go around. We can't practice our manners when we're working. Mr. Leek is rich. Sabina's father is a commoner, but he's paying the full tuition in cash, so she is up in the lounge.

"As for the ladies not paying attention to us ..." She thought for a minute. "For one thing, the noble girls are their nieces and cousins, so part of it's natural. The rest of it ... Maybe there's some prejudice. Okay, you're right, sure there's prejudice and a lot of it. But I think it goes back more to those blasted founding documents. They're looking to recruit a next generation for the *Stift*, to keep it going, and the girls from the high nobility are the only ones who can join it. We're not eligible, so why should they care about us except when they're teaching us Greek or Hebrew or whatever they specialize in? Which they can specialize in, because even though women weren't allowed to attend universities before the RoF, these ladies lived here and could learn pretty much anything they wanted.

"If you ask me, it's one more reason that somebody needs to do something about fixing the documents."

Like Miniver Cheevy in that poem they'd studied in English class in Grantville, born outside of his proper time, she thought and thought and thought, and thought about it.

"Mrs. Nelson," Annalise said.

"What?"

"It says here that it used to be that the abbess was subject only to the Holy Roman Emperor for secular things and to the Pope for spiritual things. That has to have been before the Reformation. Who has she been subject to for spiritual things since the Reformation? It can't be the pope, can it?"

"I honestly don't have the slightest idea."

"The pamphlet says that during the Middle Ages, the bishops of Halberstadt were angry because the abbey was exempt from their jurisdiction because women were supposed to be subject to men in spiritual things. Is it subject to the bishop of Halberstadt now? Who *is* the bishop of Halberstadt now? Emperor Gustavus, since he took it over? What province is Halberstadt in?"

"That I know," Osanna said. "Halberstadt is in Magdeburg Province. I *think* the not-a-prince-bishop-any-more is the guy who Emperor Gustavus made the governor of Westphalia Province for the USE. I think that appointment was a consolation prize for not getting to run Bremen and Verden and Halberstadt anymore. I think that whoever held those had to be *Hochadel* too, one of those 'you're either in the higher nobility or you're not eligible' clauses, like for the abbess. I don't think they could promote some pastor named Johann Schmidt to be prince-archbishop of Bremen and then call it a day. Their cathedrals had foundations with 'secular canons' to match the canonesses here. I'm not sure if the bishop of Halberstadt even had to be ordained. I think that he probably hired poverty-stricken university graduates with theology degrees to do the work for him."

"Osanna," Iona suggested. "Please stop thinking and look it up." She suggested that they ask the pastor at St. Servatius when they had time, went up to her room, and poured herself a generous glass of wine.

Virginia DeMarce

CHAPTER 34

Copenhagen
November 1636

To Frederik, archbishop and bishop, governor of Westphalia

My dearly beloved son,

This is to let you know that I have disposed of your half-sister Sophia in marriage, or for future marriage once they reach the Netherlands, to a French Huguenot nobleman who is in the diplomatic service of Bernhard of Saxe-Weimar in Burgundy, thus eliminating the threat that Corfitz Ulfeldt might force a marriage with her now that Leonora is safely in the West Indies.

Your half-brother Waldemar, I have sent to be trained properly as a military officer, either by Fredrik Hendrik in the Netherlands or, failing that placement, by Bernhard.

Ulfeldt made a fool of himself, so is now in exile from the capital, under house arrest. The other families of the rigsraad are displaying signs of resistance to Our handling of the matter, to the extent that sterner measures on Our part may become necessary.

It is Our plan to also end the current betrothals of the three younger countesses of Holstein, your half-sisters. The possibility of Hannibal Sehested may be reconsidered later, as he is also in the West Indies.

The up-time physicians now in this world have confirmed the sad news we learned from their encyclopedias: that the happy marriage of your older brother, Our oldest son, Christian the Chosen Prince, will not be blessed with children. For all the miracles they brought, they have no remedy for this. The crown princess is desolate.

While in this world, since the miracle of 1631, events differ, so that it cannot be certain that your older brother will predecease me, still ... with Ulrik, your younger brother who in that world was dead but for Us in this world is alive again, but having been given over to the Swede and the USE, the order of succession in the kingdom of Denmark should be made clearer than it was a dozen years hence in that other world. If the situation within Our realm remains as it is now, it certainly must by some means be made clearer to the nobles of the rigsraad. However, I am still considering the options, so the time for public discussion has not yet come.

Your faithful father,

Christian

Magdeburg
November-December 1636

The convocation of all the USE governors (as distinct from a meeting of the House of Lords in Parliament, although the personnel were identical) in Magdeburg took place at the most awkward possible time of the year for travel, of course. It was scheduled to deal with all the ongoing furor—he up-timers called it "fall-out" for some inexplicable reason—resulting from the Holstein incident. And what Frederik had been doing since the Holstein incident.

Which was, since the executions in July, nothing discernable. Nothing perceptible. As far as outside observers could tell, the governor of Westphalia had been doing nothing at all during the entire late summer and autumn.

Thus, as the opening ceremonies proceeded, not one of the other governors had the slightest idea what to expect from Westphalia— which did not prevent astonishing amounts of speculation.

They got a position paper that shocked them all—not all for the same reason, of course.

Westphalia recommended that every province of the USE take measures to eliminate pockets of private jurisdiction across the board and ensure that all persons, whether free or serf, were subject only to clear and transparent public laws which were to be administered either by officials paid by and accountable to the government, whether at the level of village, town, city, or province, or, in regions where such entities existed, through such systems as village and municipal courts or juries. Almost as an afterthought, it added a recommendation that in keeping with the elimination of private jurisdiction, forced labor on domain lands imposed by landlords on the children of peasants holding farms, partial farms, or cottages under any form of servile tenure ought to be promptly abolished, and the right of free movement, with reasonable restrictions, such as, perhaps, a year's notice by someone with an existing employment agreement, which need not be a written contract, must be enacted and enforced.

Nobody liked the position paper.

It was obvious why the holders of private jurisdictions didn't care for it. Every province and state of the USE other than the State of Thuringia-Franconia, even Magdeburg and Mecklenburg, still had at least a few pockets of private jurisdiction, whether ecclesiastical, municipal, or associated with noble privileges. Some had many.

The liberals objected to its ignoring almost entirely the economic aspects of serfdom, such as forms of land tenure, because it focused on the jurisdictional aspects.

Debate ensued. At length.

Westphalia responded that the economic aspects of serfdom had not been at issue in the Holstein incident and therefore had not been included in the province's position paper, but the convocation did not have a closed agenda, and any other governor was certainly welcome to introduce for debate a position paper addressing them if the others were inclined to put those complex questions on the table.

"Well," Helene Gundelfinger commented to the abbess of Quedlinburg and Mary Simpson at dinner that evening, "I think that pretty much counts as 'hitting the ball back into the other guy's court' as Ed Piazza would say if he could have made the meeting."

Two days later, Mathias Strigel of Magdeburg Province altered the sporting analogy by picking the ball up and starting to run with it, with Bugenhagen from Hamburg playing as his defense.

After that, it took less than a week for the convocation to adjourn *sine die* with nothing resolved.

Conrad Schepler argued Frederik into going out for a non-mandatory social excursion on their last evening in Magdeburg. "Everyone ought to at least *see* the famous Golden Arches."

The band performing that evening produced the absolute worst excuse for music that had ever passed Frederik's ears. The title of the song was called "Born to Be Wild." Who would want to be wild? Only someone determined to destroy good order.

Frederik did not approve of opposition to divinely established authority no matter who opposed it. Opposition by a lord was as culpable as opposition by a serf. Probably, it was more culpable, because God had entrusted the lord with more responsibilities. As in the case of the *minas*. While Schepler and his friends danced, he stood as far away from the band as he could manage and reflected on Luke 19:12-27. An unprofitable servant remained an unprofitable servant, no matter what his worldly rank.

Thad and Carol Ann Cochran were having an evening out, for a change.

The band was loud enough that they didn't have to whisper.

"Isn't that Prince Frederik?" she asked. "The Danish guy from Westphalia?" She bent her neck a bit so her head pointed to the right and slightly toward the back of the room.

Thad took a look and nodded.

"I wonder what he's thinking, just standing there."

"I know what I'd be thinking if I was him."

"What?"

"I've been trying to follow the news coming out of the convocation. Two dozen people there and no more than a half dozen of them ever going in the same direction at the same time. If I was him, I'd be thinking: *Not my circus; not my monkeys*." Thad took a deep swig of his beer. "He's started something, though. What I'm thinking myself is that when the rest of the governors get back home, they're going to discover from people down at the grass-roots level that they should have come up with some decisions while they were here. And that they're going to have to come up with some decisions pretty damned fast, now, if they don't want the train to leave the station without them."

Thad worked in the USE Department of Transportation. He spent a lot of time thinking about trains.

He said pretty much the same thing to Tom Leek the next time he saw the man.

*   *   *

Everything was packed and ready to go. That was an advantage of having a well-trained and well-treated staff. Profitable servants. In his household, things were, unless faced with immovable obstacles, done when and how they should be done.

Nevertheless, Frederik walked over from the government house to his lodgings to make one last check-up, since he would be leaving Quedlinburg for Münster rather than returning to the USE capital city.

Rist greeted him with, "Another of those pamphlets."

Frederik glanced at it. In no way significantly different from all the others.

"File without response," he said.

The secretary made a note, stuffed the offending pamphlet inside his doublet since the boxes were already packed, bowed himself out, and left the hotel to get into the carriage that would take them to the abbess of Quedlinburg's mandatory, or near-mandatory (Dorothea Sophia of Saxe-Altenburg qualifying as a force of nature) post-conference gathering at her new women's college to see her pet up-time teacher's school music program.

Frederik watched Rist's departing figure with mild annoyance. If he managed to get the University of Rinteln up and running again for the fall term, which seemed likely, he would lose his secretary and have to find a new one.

"Prince of Westphalia."

How utterly absurd.

Let Ulrik have Kalmar and the USE. Sweden, if he got along well enough with Kristina.

King of Denmark.

Virginia DeMarce

CHAPTER 35

Quedlinburg
December 1636

The previous year's program had been such a success that with sponsorship from the abbess and Mary Simpson's National Endowment for the Arts, or whatever it was exactly called, it had been repeated a couple of times, once in the spring, shortly after Easter, in Magdeburg at the DESSSFG, in the presence of Princess Kristina. And hadn't that been a project, transporting the whole school? They'd stayed for three weeks, of course. It wouldn't have been worth the trouble otherwise. They'd taken the students to visit every important site in the USE's capital city, new and old, seen a couple of plays, a musical, and an opera, and eaten from food carts. Overall, the food carts proved to be most popular with the children.

Food carts aside, it was the popularity of the program with many interested adults that meant that there would be a new one this year, again designed by Iona with Annalise's assistance.

The audience for the first performance this year would not be just parents and local citizens. The abbess had been in Magdeburg, a guest of her friend the landgravine-regent of Hesse-Kassel, to see what see could see as to what was happening at the conference of governors and administrators of the provinces and states of the USE. She was gathering up as many of them, and their spouses (if any), their guests (definitely some), and their staff (quite a lot), as she could and transporting them to Quedlinburg for the show. And hosting them, of course, until such time as each of them took a notion to leave.

That was quite a production in itself, but thankfully not Iona's worry.

The attending governors and administrators included the delegation from Westphalia. That particular governor had already, more than once, heard Princess Kristina squeal, "I love it when the girls from Quedlinburg sing" followed by "I love the abbess" and "I love Annalise." He had only escaped being coerced into bringing his future sister-in-law along as one of his guests by saying that he was sure that the program would come to "the DesFig" again next spring. Saying "adults only" hadn't been feasible, since the performers were also, he presumed, children. It was, after all, a school, so they were probably children.

He'd attended school for a long, long, time. His father had demanded that he be carefully educated. He hadn't particularly liked children even when he was one.

✳   ✳   ✳

It *was* Iona's problem that, by popular demand, this year's program was going to be nearly twice as long as the previous one. She decided that she would let the youngest girls go off to the green room and play between their first segment and bringing them back for the one piece after the first intermission and then for the encore. That meant that she had to find mentors for the green room when almost everybody in Quedlinburg was going to be busy with some other duty associated with what was generally termed the *deluge of dignitaries*.

God be praised that Veronica Dreeson had come to the rescue. In response to Annalise's "pretty please," she arrived four days in advance with half the operating staff of the Magdeburg branch of St. Veronica's academy, having successfully evaded several efforts by Princess Kristina to get herself added to the group. Iona would have air-kissed her on both cheeks if she hadn't known that any such gesture would not be welcomed.

They were in the St. Servatius church nave this year rather than in one of the smaller chapels. It had taken quite a lot of time to get the acoustics right. It had also involved sending some men from the abbey stables all around the town with wagons to beg and borrow every chair that a housewife was willing to lend (every one of which then had to be labeled, of course, so they could be returned to the right house). Standing for a church service wasn't something Iona had quite gotten used to and she was certain that standing for a children's chorus performance was a horrible idea likely to lead to unfavorable evaluations of its quality. More than one pastor did or did not have a large attendance at his sermons based on the popular perception of their average length.

Basically, she kept the same format. For the opening "action piece" she picked

Daisy Bell.[22] Yes, it was an old chestnut—for up-timers. For down-timers, she hoped, it would be cute. Most of the "bicycles" were sawhorses with cardboard bicycle cutouts painted in bright colors in front of them, but she had borrowed three up-time bicycles, small ones, from friends in Grantville, and the seamstress had copied 1890s bicycling costumes for the three little girls carefully riding them around the dais.

---

[20]https://www.youtube.com/watch?v=_kd-xg2VZnk Sheet Music Singer "A Bicycle Built For Two".

Then the audience arose to sing "*O Lord, How Shall I Meet You*,"[22] which she had introduced the year before. Presumably, by 1653, Gerhardt and Crueger would write something else.

She came out and introduced the abbess. The abbess welcomed all the guests.

She came out and introduced the head pastor of St. Servatius, who also welcomed all the guests.

She came out again and introduced the theme of the evening as "folk songs and popular songs."

It was pretty hard to go wrong with that theme.

During the welcomes, the little girls had disentangled themselves from the bicycles and fake bicycles, which the stablemen hauled off the dais and stashed away. The little girls came out for a set of three:

Aura Lee,[22] which she simply had to pair, of course, with a large reproduction of a photo of Elvis Presley singing *Love Me Tender*.[22] The boys' Latin School had been kind enough to loan her one of their older students, an aspiring vocalist and instrumentalist, for that one. It had been impossible not to do Elvis: just impossible. Then: *Simple Gifts*,[22] followed by not-exactly-a-folk-song, but irresistible: Ben Mallett's

---

[21]https://www.youtube.com/watch?v=d_up_TRb7GI   Geneva Presbyterian Church, Laguna Hills, CA.

[22]https://www.youtube.com/watch?v=TBDVff2gR5k Concierto de fin de curso. Coro del Conservatorio Profesional de Música Arturo Soria. Madrid, junio 2014.

[23]https://www.youtube.com/watch?v=2lD711_Xh8s   Elvis Presley Love Me Tender (1956) (Official Video).

[24]https://www.youtube.com/watch?v=uLpfWnOFjcc   Rutgers Children's Choir "Simple Gifts". 2012, December 16.

Garden Song.[22] She hummed a bit with the girls as they mimed planting as they sang.

In spite of the stress caused by *El Paso* on first hearing, the western segment had proved to be popular last year, so she had decided to do another one. The girls, aged ten through twelve, came to the front and attacked (that was the best way to put it, she thought) *San Antonio Rose,*[22] which, she thought grumpily, was better sung by men, but you can't have everything. At least a few of the fathers from the town had volunteered to sing along with their daughters, which definitely helped. So did the roll-down illustration provided by Grantville, which this time was the Alamo.

The girls and fathers faded off to the side, and the high school and college girls came forward for *Ghost Riders in the Sky,*[22] which she had, right up to the previous day, considered dropping because the girls had so much trouble getting the rhythm, but it was already listed in the printed program.

---

[25] -https://www.youtube.com/watch?v=R6h-Yb2-_yk The National Children's Choir Ireland 2007 Concert. 3 - Garden Song.

[26]

https://www.youtube.com/watch?v=6l7 rLA9Jm1I Bob Wills & Tommy Duncan, San Antonio Rose with Lyrics 1945.

[27] https://www.youtube.com/watch?v=NcnDlgeUYs4 (Ghost) Riders in the Sky - Sons of the Pioneers.

Then another one that would stretch the audience quite a bit and gave her ever more reason to be thankful for the existence of Osanna Merkur, since she carried the whole thing: *They Call the Wind Mariah.*[22]

Then Annalise came forward to introduce something new this year: up-time German music that they sang in American schools.

Standing backstage, Iona thanked her lucky stars that she was born an Ingli from Pennsylvania rather than, for example, a Baxter from some benighted spot like Mississippi, and a Lutheran rather than a Baptist, because as a Mississippian Baptist, she would have been far less likely to take German as her foreign language in high school and college, much less have landed 350 years in the past in possession of a booklet of popular sing-a-longs ideal for a high school German club—in the view of the teacher, not the students expected to sing them, of course, back in the days when the experience had been inflicted upon her.

The littlest girls came back and sang *O, Tannenbaum.*[22]

The college group performed respectably, if not outstandingly, on *Die Lorelei.*[33]

Annalise was going to solo this year. Not because her voice was anything more than clear and pleasant, but because she was Annalise Richter, the sister of the hero Hans, the sister of the ferocious Gretchen, and because she was graduating this spring; going back to

---

[28]https://www.youtube.com/watch?v=rxHtmmbAftU   Harve Presnell, They Call The Wind Mariah, early version 1965.

[29]https://www.youtube.com/watch?v=j9U1gJy8AvE   "O Tannenbaum" Vienna Boys Choir - Wiener Sängerknaben.

[30]https://www.youtube.com/watch?v=dG1hPUL6vZA Die Lorelei (arr. A. Wiedermann) : Loreley (arr. A. Wiedermann).

Ronnie at Jeff and Gretchen's house in Magdeburg. Quedlinburg would be making a statement when Annalise sang a solo.

Iona had wavered back and forth. Goethe's *Heideröslein* was pretty, he was certainly an important German author, and the melody was Schubert, but it was meant to be sung as a duet by a man to a maiden. Also, the other song went nicely with the mention of evergreens in the first song of the set, so—maybe some other time. For now, it was *Grün ist die Heide*,[33] turn of the twentieth century, pre-World War I utter *Schmalz*, fair maiden, handsome huntsman in his green uniform, soft moss, red roses, irritated mother, and all, by Hermann Löns with a not-too-demanding melody by Karl Blume. And short. In Iona's view, for a soloist with a voice of modest quality, a tentative tenor, for example, or a shaky soprano, short was very, very, good, giving fewer opportunities to crack a note.

That boy from the Latin School was back with his lute.

Almost every head in the audience came up, anxious to get a good look at this young woman and even more to get a sense of the vast changes in their world that her brother and sister had initiated. If possible. Annalise cleared her throat a little nervously and began.

Als ich gestern einsam ging auf der grünen, grünen Heid',
Kam ein junger Jägersmann, trug ein grünes, grünes Kleid.
Ja grün ist die Heide, die Heide ist grün,
Aber rot sind die Rosen, wenn sie da blühn.

---

[31]https://www.youtube.com/watch?v=6_0fz_g-d2M Mein Chor - Männerchor Walsrode - Ja, grün ist die Heide.

In the audience, the governor of Westphalia Province found his hands shaking in his lap.

Wo die grünen Tannen steh'n, ist so weich das grüne Moos,
Und da hat er mich geküßt, und ich saß auf seinem Schoß.
Ja grün ist die Heide, die Heide ist grün,
Aber rot sind die Rosen, wenn sie da blühn.

He pushed his palms together to steady them.

Als ich dann nach Hause kam, hat die Mutter mich gefragt,
wo ich war die ganze Zeit, und ich hab es nicht gesagt.
Ja grün ist die Heide, die Heide ist grün,
aber rot sind die Rosen, wenn sie da blühn.

His teeth started to chatter.

Was die grüne Heide weiß, geht die Mutter gar nichts an,
niemand weiß es außer mir und dem grünen Jägersmann.
Ja grün ist die Heide, die Heide ist grün,
aber rot sind die Rosen, wenn sie da blühn.

Focus on the up-time German, he told himself sternly. There were interesting phonemic differences from down-time German. Focus.

It went all right, Iona told herself. Annalise stayed in key. Now, heaven be praised, after that marathon session, it was the first intermission. With snacks and beverages. *May they return to us fed and happily tipsy*, Iona thought.

It took them a while, but it looked like everybody returned, to be greeted by a song that had spread so fast since the Ring of Fire that she thought every conscious human being in the USE had already learned it. So Sabina Lechner invited them to sing along in unison: *Joyful, Joyful, We Adore Thee.*[33]

That was followed by *Amazing Grace.*[33] She had tried; she honestly had tried. These kids did not swing. They did swing a little more than they had at the beginning of the year, which was what a teacher hoped for.

Then, to show Osanna off and pay some tribute to the musical tastes of the older generation of Grantville's population: *Beautiful Star of Bethlehem.*[33]

Audience participation again; the girls would teach a simple round to the audience. Iona had sternly vetoed,

---

King Louis was the King of France,
before the revolution.

---

[32]https://www.youtube.com/watch?v=eMY3ivdNzwE ODE TO JOY-JOYFUL, JOYFUL, WE ADORE THEE at ROYAL ALBERT HALL,LONDON.

[33]https://www.youtube.com/watch?v=rUHucpaiLJo Amazing Grace- Children Choir Raduga.

[34]https://www.youtube.com/watch?v=QqMXrecqtR4 Loved - Oh Beautiful Star Of Bethlehem.

But Louis got his head cut off,
which spoiled his constitution.

---

which some of the girls who had gotten hold of her well-worn copy of *Rise Up Singing* before class one day suggested. Several of them swore they would sing it to their parents when they went home. Iona wished them well, but the "approved by Ms. Nelson" round was rather Mozart's *Dona Nobis Pacem*,[33] which appeared to be a peaceful interlude much-welcomed by the spectators.

They did Eleanor Farjeon's *Morning Has Broken*,[33] and finished with the Grateful Dead's *Ripple*,[33] which thankfully led into the second intermission. It was a short section for a concert, but the stagehands, otherwise the Quedlinburg Abbey stable hands, needed the time to set up for the next piece.

"If I survive this evening," Iona said to Ronnie in the green room, "I'm taking a vacation. It may last the rest of my life. Why did I ever agree to a longer program?"

"Fund-raising," Ronnie said in a no-nonsense retort. "Remember what Mary Simpson said about fund-raising?"

Iona did.

Even the best intermission came to an end.

---

[35]https://www.youtube.com/watch?v=gKz_aBRhCIk   Chorus Niagara Children's Choir - Dona Nobis Pacem arr. Hal Hopson.

[36]https://www.youtube.com/watch?v=SlmVuVoiOxw Morning has broken (Trad): St Mary's Choir School Reigate 1989 (Charles Thompson).

[37]https://www.youtube.com/watch?v=BMADDgsk7WE   The Grateful Dead's 'Ripple' by The Barton Hills Choir .

She had offered their faithful pianist a chance to show off, and he had grabbed it. From the gospel he had been playing with the year before, he had discovered ragtime, or some version thereof. The opening was a dance by the thirteen-sixteen year old girls to *Bye, Bye, Blackbird*.[33] Then something else lighthearted, another dance, ten-twelve year-olds, with singers: *Hi-Lili, Hi-Lo*.[33] She had divided the high school girls on one side and college girls on the other side of the stage to get an echo effect.

Then this year's next new feature, and she was not sure about it. A Stephen Foster segment, starting with something light:

Camptown Races;[44] then *Ring, Ring, the Banjo*, with instrumental accompaniment[44] on the increasingly popular instrument by their Latin School lutist. Iona harbored a suspicion that his middle-class father was a wealthy middle-class father and an indulgent one as well, given what the man must expend on music lessons and instruments.

The audience rustled with amazement. The abbess herself stood up, along with the other great ladies of the *Stift*. The abbess might have

---

[38]https://www.youtube.com/watch?v=MP_vsfixmVE   Bye Bye Blackbird sing along with lyrics. Standard tune of 1926 Bye Bye Blackbird - words and music: Ray Henderson and Mort Dixon.

[39]https://www.youtube.com/watch?v=Jl7JYUKK6uM   Anne Murray - Hi Lili Hi Lo (With Lyrics). From the CD album "There's A Hippo In My Tub."

[40]https://www.youtube.com/watch?v=yfNUcsTI1ic   Camptown Races - Treasure Valley Children's Chorus.

[41]https://www.youtube.com/watch?v=wC2ATqaULUM A good old Stephen Foster tune from 1851 played in clawhammer style by Rob McCarthy from Australia.

been giving them rather stern looks, but they stood up. Each of them took a stack of paper and started to move up and down the aisles, handing out copies, as if—as if they were servants, and not daughters of the *Hochadel* who received service from such as the parents and burghers gathered at this program.

Iona hit them with *Hard Times*,[44] in English with the German translation that the ladies had distributed, Osanna Merkur soloing again.

Let us pause in life's pleasures and count its many tears,
While we all sup sorrow with the poor;
There's a song that will linger forever in our ears;
Oh, hard times come again no more.

Tis the song, the sigh of the weary,
Hard times, hard times, come again no more;
Many days you have lingered around my cabin door;
Oh hard times come again no more.

Osanna hit it hard, all right, and then she hit it again and still again.

Tis a sigh that is wafted across the troubled wave,
Tis a wail that is heard upon the shore,
Tis a dirge that is murmured around the lowly grave;

---

[42]https://www.youtube.com/watch?v=4zdXr3CnBGs Hard Times Come Again No More (2008 Remaster) · Emmylou Harris.

Oh hard times come again no more.

And, if there was enough applause after that one, after the audience had heard it and read the attached plea for contributions to the anti-plague campaigns, she'd had the combined chorus practice *Country Roads*[44] for an encore. Because she was homesick.

The audience was good for it. They didn't want to go home. The girls were more than half exhausted. Iona cut it off, fund-raising or no fund-raising. There would be more snacks and beverages in the hall.

She sort of wished she'd put *This Land Is Your Land*, with the map, in the program again this year, but she hadn't known all the important officials would be here when she was doing her planning, and the wall map of the USA was long since gone back to Grantville, from where she had borrowed it. It was probably stuck in closed stacks at the state library now—not hanging down in a classroom to teach children about the geography of their country. Because there wasn't any such country and never would be. What could you call it? Future history?

As the singers were presented to the abbess' honored guests afterwards, Annalise looked up, shook the hand of the man currently in front of her, and murmured politely, "It is a pleasure to meet you, Governor," as she did to each of the other dignitaries in the line. Then she stopped abruptly, jarring the girls behind her into tripping over one another's heels. "Governor of Westphalia Province?"

He held his hand steady and produced a courteous if thin-lipped smile. *One could never be too cautious. Especially when confronting a sister of the furious Gretchen Richter.*

---

[43]https://www.youtube.com/watch?v=jBfjAMbFYOo   Contra Costa Children's Chorus perform "Take me Home Country Roads" by John Denver.

"That means you're the bishop of Halberstadt, too."

"I was once elected by the chapter of secular canons as coadjutor to the secular administrator of the prince-bishop of Halberstadt. That meant that when the administrator died, I would have succeeded to his position. If all the chaos hadn't happened."

Annalise blinked. How precise of him. "Can *you* fix it, though?" she asked. "Or find out how to fix it? If Halberstadt is still claiming to be ecclesiastical superiors to the abbey here, can *you* fix the founding documents of Quedlinburg so the abbess doesn't have to be a duchess anymore but can still keep her job? So she can run for the House of Commons and tell the government things that it needs to hear?"

He cleared his throat. *That was unexpected.* "I can, ah, have someone look into it."

"Thank you very much. That's certainly better than nothing."

Annalise proceeded through the rest of the line and wandered back to the green room to find a mug of broth and a bratwurst. It had been a long program and she was hungry.

Virginia DeMarce

SECTION VI

The Tough Get Going
Jan 1637-July 1637

CHAPTER 36

January-February 1637
Quedlinburg

Frederik stayed at Quedlinburg long enough to talk to the abbess about the provisions of the founding documents; more amicably than bishops of Halberstadt had historically spoken to abbesses of Quedlinburg, but that was easy, given that he had never effectively had the Halberstadt office and now wasn't likely ever to have it. They mulled over some options.

She pointed out that although eligibility for the canoness positions required that one be a member of the *Hochadel*, unlike many of the great *Stifte*, Quedlinburg had not been founded by a group of great families back then, 700 years previously, so there would not be so many different lines of descendants to consult in this day and age.

"Its prestige, primacy even among the *Damenstifte*, resulted from its being a direct imperial foundation by Heinrich I of Saxony and his wife, Saint Mathilda. A *Reichsstift*. In 936, to be precise. They had five children. After she was widowed, she headed it until her death in 968, at which time she was succeeded as abbess by her granddaughter; thereafter by a succession of women of the imperial house.

"The Liudolfing Dynasty has long since been replaced on the imperial throne, of course. Henry II died childless in 1024. That was the end of the male line; his elected successor was a Salian. Descendants in the female line … " The abbess smiled wickedly. "Do you need the genealogies of the royal houses of France and England? Or the Habsburgs? Every noble family of Europe, including, of course, your own? And many that are not noble?"

Frederik swallowed. "The elective nature of the imperial office suggests other possibilities."

She concurred.

He suggested bringing the issue up with the duke of Brunswick.

She concurred.

Then she asked why he was interesting himself in the matter (*in light of your recent vote with the FoJP* was the thought running through her head). He referred her to Annalise Richter's expressed concern about how the matter affected the abbess's eligibility to serve in the House of Commons.

The abbess leaned one elbow on the table, propping her chin on the heel of her hand. "Saint Mathilda the Foundress was educated at Herford, of course, which is now in Westphalia. In addition to your tangential claim to have an interest by way of the diocese of Halberstadt, that might give you another reasonable interest, even if it would not be legally tenable."

"My lawyers … ," Frederick responded.

"And mine."

In Brunswick, some weeks later, Loring Schultz looked at the documents that had dropped on his desk, a two-inch thick brief with a three-foot stack, more or less, of attachments, and asked the heavens, *Why, why, why?*

Münster

While the lawyers had been keeping busy, Frederik ordered the building of a proper guberatorial *Residenz*.

"It's amazing," Andreas Bucholtz said. "He's not been interested in publicity, even though he reads widely. He's not been interested in horses, even though he rides well. He's not shown interest in anything you might call *representational*. Even to give the architect a general idea of what he wanted for the exterior, he said that the man should go take a look at Thedinghausen in *Stift* Verden for the building and the *Schloß* where his aunt is residing in Bremervörde for the gardens. The orders are not to design anything larger than that. Nor more highly ornamented on the exterior. Brick and sandstone it shall be, rather than marble. But when it comes to interior decoration … "

Johann Rist nodded. "The townhouse has ceramic tile samples in the vestibule, fabric swatches tacked to the shelves of folders in the office, and shingles with various shades and colors of paint and wood finishes strewn all over the place. Vendt and the maids are going crazy, because he doesn't want anything touched. He says he's getting a sense of how it should all fit together."

Construction started promptly and stayed on schedule to a remarkable extent.

And Frederik had to decide, finally, what to do with Kerstin Brahe and Erik Stenbock. He couldn't keep them more or less directly under his eyes forever, in case they were agents for her brother. He asked himself whether or not, in the final analysis, he trusted them. If he did … he needed a *Statthalter* in Holstein to keep an eye on all the new officials he'd hired there. Not to mention on the multitudinous relatives of unhappy *equites ordinarii*. On financiers in Kiel. On what Johann Friedrich was doing with that canal. Someone to do for him there what Aunt Hedwig was doing in the *Stifte*.

Someone who would get along reasonably well with his father's administrative staff for royal Holstein in Segeberg. Which Erik had done last summer.

He needed someones, in this case, in the plural. He sent them to Holstein.

Bremen

The best thing about Bremen was the bookstores. After duly inspecting what the Lutheran clergy had accomplished in the past two and a half years, with approbation where it was deserved and urges for accelerated effort where approbation was not deserved, sweetened with promises of a subsidy toward the commissioning of an equestrian statue of Gustav Adolf, Frederik had managed to escape, only because he was not officially here yet. Officially, as far as the city officials were concerned, he would arrive tomorrow. He'd come in on foot, with only Lieutenant Meyer, Rist, Jung, and a couple of bodyguards, by way of the Bishop's Needle.

Then he dropped in on old Knaub.

A weary, beaten-down, Knaub.

"I must show you," Knaub said, "what is going on here." They exited the walls and ended up at a damp, cold, barn.

Knaub's daughter and her band devoting an evening to Linda Ronstadt's greatest hits did not bear any recognizable resemblance to the up-time music he had heard at Quedlinburg. Perhaps a couple of them. He rather liked "I Never Will Marry" and "The Sweetest Gift" was quite pretty. Otherwise ... no thank you.

Then, as the waving light that was giving him such a headache focused on one of the back-up musicians ...

"Tell me it isn't so."

Knaub shook his head dolefully. "It is so. A boat came up the river and he hopped off it. He says he doesn't want to join the navy, even if your father will make him an admiral. 'Ships make me so dreadfully seasick,' he said. 'Being at sea even brings on one of my fits, sometimes!' So he was living with Laurits Andersen Hammer and apprenticing in the Copenhagen shipyards last year. 'I thought I'd come south; see the shipping yards in the USE. Starting here. And have some fun!' I regret to have to tell you so, Your Grace, but he has been having a great deal of fun. Expensive fun."

Frederik sighed. Hans Ulrik Gyldenløve. Another half-brother. It wasn't as if he didn't *know* the boy well: he'd been tagged along on his own study tour of France in 1629. Poor Knaub had been stuck, along with his other duties, helping the tutors supervise a fourteen-year-old whose natural liveliness tended to bring on his epileptic seizures.

Hans Ulrik Gyldenløve, sitting in the middle of pounding drums and flashing lights.

"How bad?" he asked.

"Sometimes more than once a week. But he will not stop being part of the band."

What Frederik simply did not need, he thought, was another version of Gustafsson on his hands. *If wishes were horses, then beggars would ride.*

"I have tried," Knaub was saying, "to have Ebbe keep an eye on him; exert a good influence."

And that would have worked how? Knaub's priggish son was the last person to whom Hans Ulrik was likely to pay attention.

But he had to spend the next day conferring with the Bremen's FoJP government. Emil Jauch had paved the way. In so far as anyone could pave the way for civil discourse with lividly furious men.

There were few tactful ways to convey the notion of: *You lost; I won; live with it.*

Frederik was prepared to convey the concept in ways that were not tactful if that became necessary.

While he spent the day in the conference room, several members of his entourage set out to inspect the radio installation being set up a few miles out of the city, beyond any imaginable expansion of a Bremen hinterland had it been the case that the city council had won, seceded from the province, and become an imperial city.

They invited Hans Ulrik, the young Knaubs, and several associated members of the band along, on the theory that musicians were likely to be interested in radio.

"This is fascinating," Hans Ulrik said to the *Techs* from Grantville.

In the end, the expedition had to split up. Half of Frederik's men went back to Bremen with the Knaubs and the band; the other half hunkered down for a long night of Hans Ulrik having fun.

Except ... "We do not drink alcohol," one of the *Techs* said firmly. "The body is the temple of the Holy Spirit and should be cared for accordingly."

This, when Hans Ulrik answered that he could have wine, was met by a firm, "There are no alcoholic beverages on the premises."

But there was so much radio stuff on the premises that Hans Ulrik stayed overnight. The next day. And another night.

"Nobody's going to miss me much," he said cheerfully. "I'm just another bastard. Not that I don't love my father and not that he isn't generous. My mother was the king's mistress between when the queen died and the appearance of Kristin Munk on the scene. My sister died as a young child. Mama is still well and doing well for herself. As I said, the king is generous."

This was far beyond the experience of a gunsmith's son from Suhl who had been transformed into a radio technician in Grantville.

"How does a woman become a king's mistress?" Cunz Hess asked with honest curiosity.

"Oh, she was engaged to a clergyman. They say that my father spotted her at a party, danced with her all night, whisked her away to the palace, and danced her right into his bed."

"And the clergyman?"

"Oh, he didn't suffer." Hans Ulrik grinned. "He married her sister, so he's my uncle-by-marriage, and the king appointed him bishop of Christiania. Oslo, it used to be called, before the king re-named it for himself a few years ago. That's in Norway. He's done well in his duties. Firm on enforcing the moral order; strong in supporting the education of youth. Pretty much everything that a bishop should be."

Hans Ulrik contemplated the nature of the universe for a moment. "Like I said, nobody will ever be able to say of my father that he is not generous-hearted to those who come within his orbit. Overwhelming, sometimes, but generous." He looked down at the object in his hand. "Now what did you say this wire is for?"

Hektor Lobitz picked up a manual. His Grantville foster parents had hurriedly pulled him out of the University of Jena when this Westphalia opportunity came up. He wasn't that much of a tech, which surprisingly enough made it easier for him to teach the basics to people who knew even less. Those being everyone else on the construction crew.

Hans Ulrik went a week without a seizure; then notified Knaub that he'd be staying out at the radio installation for a while.

Knaub breathed a sigh of relief.

Frederik had left town again by then. The issue of possible missionaries for heretical sects having been clandestinely inserted into Westphalia in the guise of radio technicians had slipped his mind.

* * *

Ted Warren was in Magdeburg again this week. Being with the USE Military Medical Department, he came and went. His job was recruitment and coordination with the programs at Leahy Medical Center, the tech college in Grantville, the medical school in Jena, and Magdeburg Memorial Hospital.

Incidentally, because he was LDS, he recruited and coordinated down-time converts. He'd been the one who picked most of the Westphalia radio team.

Now he shook his head at Ben Leek. "You're being short-sighted. Yes, the governor over there has been slow to show any interest in up-time technology ... "

"Slow as molasses," Bill Roberts interrupted. "Slower."

"Look, Bill!" That was Pete Rush.

"Slow, not outright opposed," Ted said. "According to Edgar Frost, there are practical reasons why … "

"He's a do-nothing," Bill persisted.

"Don't shoot yourself in the foot. Nolan Wilson was here in Magdeburg at Imperial Tech for a couple of years; now he's with the forces in Hamburg. I had him get in touch with Hektor Lobitz—you may have met the boy. Willard and Emma Thornton fostered him for the first couple of years after he arrived in Grantville as a refugee; then when Willard and Emma went to Bamberg, Joel and Gigi Carstairs took him in."

Ben frowned. "Don't think I ever met him."

"Hektor got a look at the governor's office in Münster. He required them to stop there and talked to them before he sent them on up to where the installation's going in near Bremen; explained what he wanted. He had no idea of how to get it, but apparently he figured that was why he'd hired them. The guy has reams of pocket folders; one of your own rolodex-style things; In and Out and a lot of other boxes. If he can see a reason for something up-time, he's not going to turn it down just because it is up-time. Aren't you in the business of selling office equipment? His money is as good as any other."

CHAPTER 37

Magdeburg
Spring 1637

T he Quedlinburg school put on its repeat performance of the December show at "The DesFig," to the joy of Princess Kristina, who officially "dragged along" her future brother-in-law.

He sat there, watching Annalise Richter. He had not been able to get her out of his mind. Well, in truth, the first time he saw the girl in Quedlinburg, he had fallen hopelessly in lust. It had never happened to him before, but he could diagnose the condition. He'd observed it often enough when it afflicted other men in his family. She was so pretty. Not spectacularly beautiful. Not a seductress. Just pretty. She stood there, sang in her pleasant little voice, and ornamented the scenery, like an apple tree in blossom in the spring.

This was not in his life plan.

Frederik of Denmark was grimly determined that his biography, when written, should not be a repeat performance of his father's. By the standards of the Danish court, he was practically a teetotaler. By the standards of the seventeenth century in general, he was practically a teetotaler. When he married, there would be no mistresses to confuse his family life, no illegitimate children to clutter up his home and his budget allocations. No Kirsten Munks producing half-royal children.

He watched what he said. He didn't say much. He watched what he wrote even more carefully and wrote less than he said, wary of committing himself on paper. He seldom laughed. His closest associates were his administrative staff.

He had studied theology, because he was destined by his father to become an episcopal administrator. He had studied natural science and Scandinavian history because he found them interesting. He collected books and had the start of an excellent library.

His older brother Christian, the prince-heir of Denmark as ratified by the Council of Nobles, was an empty-headed fool. An amiable enough empty-headed fool. A nitwit who would not have children.

He liked his younger brother Ulrik, and it was all to the good of Denmark that he was affianced to Princess Kristina and destined for the USE, the Union of Kalmar, and Sweden.

He himself had a throne to be grasped, when the time came, in fifteen or twenty years, perhaps.

Annalise Richter was not within the scope of his carefully ordered ambitions.

Annalise Richter, who greeted him cheerfully and, when he encountered her once more at Hesse House at one of the landgravine-regent's receptions, kept talking about the political dilemmas of the abbess of Quedlinburg, blithely oblivious to any personal interest he might have in her.

Which he would never express, because he was not going to duplicate his father's life.

The abbess talked to the landgravine-regent of Hesse-Kassel, who talked to Mary Simpson, who talked to Veronica Dreeson, who talked to Iona Nelson. Then everybody talked to Iona.

They all agreed, at their little *Kaffeeklatsch*, that the musical program that Iona put together at Quedlinburg had been a great success.

Kaffeeklatsch was an oddity in *Amideutsch*, the landgravine remarked. A German word introduced by way of up-time. The conversation meandered on.

Summer was coming. It would be a good thing if Iona could see her way to coming to Magdeburg for the summer. Veronica would love to have her; Jeff and Gretchen's big house only housed her, Nicholas and Thea, and their two toddlers at the moment. She could put together and direct a similar program, but for adult amateur musicians, with songs she considered suitable for both male and female voices. Maybe one public performance and two or three in private venues?

"Is there any market for it?" Iona asked

It wouldn't quite be a commercial venture. Donations requested, of course, for a good cause. The endowment could come up with enough to cover the out-of-pocket expenses. No costumes needed; no expensive props.

Well, yes, of course everyone who was anyone had attended at least one up-time "musical" by now. And Marla. And, perhaps, the orchestra. And … but this was different. They could get a group of volunteer young people together. A mix of up-timers in Magdeburg and down-timers. A chance for them to have fun, get to know one another better, and still learn something new.

"Almost like a bit of community theater," Mary Simpson said.

What Iona could do would be more accessible. Easier to understand, especially with the little introductions, like the girls had spoken at the school programs. It wasn't as if many people could fit into the tavern where Marla and her friends occasionally performed more casually.

"Someone mentioned to me that one wealthy DesFig father said to his wife, 'What those girls from Quedlinburg sang wasn't quite so demanding on the ears, if you know what I mean, as those concerts you've been dragging me to.' That's what we're aiming toward," Mary Simpson said.

Iona agreed.

CHAPTER 38

Magdeburg
May 1637

"I can make this program considerably saucier, I think," Iona Nelson mused. "Quite a bit saucier than a school program, since it will feature singers from the upper secondary level up to, including, and actually more of, a batch of early twenty-somethings. Maybe, for the private performances, I can even make it a little naughty. I'd like a mix of up-timers and down-timers."

"How many of the up-timers do you want to try to involve?" Mary Simpson asked. "There are a lot in Magdeburg, but most of them are desperately busy. Amber Dunn is out of the question. So is Bitsy. There's no one you can call on for help with staging or the choral numbers."

"We don't need a big chorus." Iona put her coffee down. "That's not the effect I'm going for. I'd like to have a few of the up-time guys, but the ones in the military get jerked around so much that I couldn't count on them to start rehearsing on June 15 and still be available on July 15."

"I suppose Sherry Russo from the DesFig can help from backstage and keep a lid on some of the practices. She's expecting, but not until October I think," Mallory Pierpoint said. "I can help with that too, if I can bring the kids along and don't have to pay a sitter. Or Alanna and I can trade off."

The planning session involved coffee, cookies, and rather a lot of women.

"Alanna Reilly nodded. "We can do that. Now, who's available? I declare Heather Rush old enough to be part of this, if someone keeps an eye on her when there are boys around. What is she now? Sixteen, I guess."

Catrina Murphy nodded. "Lisa Roberts is the same age. Not that either one of them will remember much about up-time music. They would have been ten when the Ring of Fire happened. We can probably get all four of the Bartholow kids. Matt and Dave are about the same age as Heather and Lisa, but Tessa and Liz are even younger. I don't think Brenda Straley would let her kids be in this kind of program."

"If you ask any of the teenaged kids from the women at the hospital, you'll have to ask them all," Mallory warned. "They're a tight-knit bunch over there. Craig Hunsaker would be okay, but Lissie is disruptive in a group."

Catrina shook her head. "Betty Jo's sending Craig and Lissie back to Grantville for summer school; she says they're starting to lose their English up here, even though they speak it to them at home. Same for Kaycie and Kara Washaw and Kevin Hunsaker. Tyler Briggs, too, and Allie Fitzgerald. And Lisa Dailey's kids. They're all going down on the train as soon as school here lets out. Marge Washaw is going to take them; after summer school, Cecelia Calafano will bring them back after the librarians' conference in August."

Iona made some more notes. "Okay, scratch those possibilities. Anyone else?"

"Well, Henry Swisher plays the mandolin." Alanna grinned. "He's at Imperial Tech now."

"No," Iona said. "Just no." She had memories of Henry Swisher from her Grantville years. And the mandolin.

"Melody Reardon will be helping Vanessa Clements all summer; also getting ready to head for the normal school in Amberg now that she has finished at Quedlinburg. What about Lisa Hilton?"

"She's starting summer semester at Imperial Tech."

"So it will be the four guys who are at the Department of Transportation, if they're willing and can get the time off. David, Ben, and Joe from the Imperial Tech students. All the others will be too busy, for sure, to come and rehearse as much as this will involve. So, boys and girls together, we can scratch up maybe a dozen up-timers and all the rest will be down-timers who may or may not know anything about up-time music and may or may not like up-time music."

"Like it or not like it, the DesFig girls have been taught to sing at least some of it," Livvie Nielsen said. "But more Marla-style."

"I'll take a dozen of them, then. Ones who aren't totally involved with their delightful patroness' wedding to Duke Ernst, because those won't have time to rehearse with us and will have to be out of town for that for part of June. Let the teachers pick. And there'll be Annalise, of course." Iona closed her notebook.

"I'm not going to do hymns for this," she said at the next committee meeting. "The 1941 *Lutheran Hymnal* has completely escaped into the wild, along with the concordance. They've been reprinted in abundance. Thousands upon thousands of church musicians are studying them, and this program isn't at the *Stift*."

"I thought you were Lutheran yourself."

"I am, and I have my favorite hymns. But I'm not going to ask any audience to sing that arrangement of *Behold a Host Arrayed in White* from a cold start, even if it is supposed to be a seventeenth century Norwegian folk melody."

She started to mutter and make more lists. "I love *Danny Boy*, but Marla and Friends sing it so often that everybody knows it already, and

I don't have anyone, male or female, who can match that girl's voice. So no, Evan Difabri, can't sing it, even if it's his deepest heart's desire. At least not here and this year."

She gave him *Lorena*[44] after sending an emergency plea for succor to Quedlinburg and being rewarded by the arrival of the Latin School student with his banjo.

Scarborough Fair[44] was obvious. But …

"So many of the folk ballads complain about the same stuff," she whined at supper, pushing her fingers through her already-spiky hair. How is a person supposed to pick between *On the Banks of the Ohio*[44] and *Long Black Veil*[44]?"

"Try one in which nobody has killed anybody else," Ronnie Dreeson advised. "*Scarborough Fair* sounds pretty woebegone, but at least nobody's dead."

"That pretty much eliminates *East Virginia*,[44] too. So, *Wagoner's Lad*,[44] with a little bit of class-consciousness and more than a hint of

---

[44]https://www.youtube.com/watch?v=z0cdmHXWYr8 John Hartford - Lorena.

[45]https://www.youtube.com/watch?v=-BakWVXHSug Simon & Garfunkel - Scarborough Fair (Full Version) Lyrics.

[46]https://www.youtube.com/watch?v=7C3r9PnoNTw Banks of the Ohio - Bill Monroe & Doc Watson.

[47]https://www.youtube.com/watch?v=5pYA46dyKh4 Johnny Cash - The Long Black Veil.

[48]https://www.youtube.com/watch?v=uxjQakmwi7o The Stanley Brothers - East Virginia Blues (Live).

women's rights. But using that cuts out *I Never Will Marry*.[55] Maybe I'll do better with more modern ones. Or, oh heck, I'll have them do *The Sweetest Gift*.[55] It's not a love song, but it's good. Or, maybe, *Homeward Bound*,[55] but that would overlap with the railroad segment."

"Weren't there any actual love songs up-time?" Ronnie asked eventually.

"Some, but not many of them were traditional ballads. Somebody's almost always dead in those," Iona admitted.

"Think of some from somewhere else, then."

"One thing you'll need to remember," Mary Simpson warned, "is that for the private performances, there may be quite a bit of overlap in the audience from one to another. Maybe you should have the performers learn some extra songs, and if I signal you on the third night, for example, you could swap out something they sang at the second performance for another piece."

Iona thought she was going to escalate from insomnia to nightmares any time now. But there were some cheerful songs. These, she could swap, if need be. Only two at any given show.

---

[49]https://www.youtube.com/watch?v=_Vuf25juzyI JOAN BAEZ ""Wagoner's Lad.""

[50]https://www.youtube.com/watch?v=xUWcbSWIt94 Linda Ronstadt & Dolly Parton - I Never Will Marry.

[51]https://www.youtube.com/watch?v=wWEQDyrbphE Dolly Parton Linda Ronstadt Emmylou Harris - The Sweetest Gift.

[52]https://www.youtube.com/watch?v=caUIXLxqiPU Homeward Bound | BYU Vocal Point ft. The All-American Boys Chorus.

The Green Leaves of Summer[55]
Lara's Theme[55]
Raspberries, Strawberries,[55] if she could find someone to play bass.

Western segment, same thing. Only two at any given show. And if absolutely necessary, she could switch the theme from High Noon for one of the love songs. She'd never been able to decide whether she liked Tex Ritter or Frankie Laine better. Ritter, probably.

Sweet Betsy from Pike[55]
Red River Valley[55]
Cool Water[55]
Theme from High Noon[55]

---

[53]https://www.youtube.com/watch?v=1BRqA3DSmpc The Green Leaves Of Summer Brothers Four.

[54]https://www.youtube.com/watch?v=FL9IVN9OuUo CONNIE FRANCIS - SOMEWHERE, MY LOVE (LARA'S THEME).

[55]https://www.youtube.com/watch?v=wD3CqdKo35s The Kingston Trio - Raspberries, Strawberries.

[56]https://www.youtube.com/watch?v=gshb3dPl584 Provided to YouTube by The Orchard Enterprises Sweet Betsy from Pike · Burl Ives.

[57]https://www.youtube.com/watch?v=YC1Pu7bscbw The Sons Of The Pioneers: Red River Valley.

[58]https://www.youtube.com/watch?v=amDo-KqUjpA The Sons Of The Pioneers - Cool Water.

[59]https://www.youtube.com/watch?v=5an9OuXKxBw Tex Ritter - The Ballad of High Noon 1952.

"After the intermission," Iona said, I think we should liven things up. How about a salute to the USE Department of Transportation, which has been really cooperative about giving the guys time off?

Wabash Cannonball[66] went on the list because, yes, yes, yes, Joe Straley did have an electric guitar and Melanie Matowski, who was still working on the electricity for the new opera house, had a portable generator that would power it. Then Kevin Norris would lead off on *City of New Orleans,*[66] with Jake Yost on drums, which was enough for railroad songs or otherwise they would take over the whole show. But give them something to which the technology geeks and nerds could aspire. *Leaving on a Jet Plane.*[66]

Then, for people who requested "a new experience in listening," four of the girls (Heather, Lisa, and two from the DesFig, with a preliminary viewing by and permission from their parents) would render *If My Friends Could See Me Now*[66] in genuine cheerleaders' uniforms borrowed from Calvert High School in Grantville. Well, for the private performances. For the public one, it would be skirts and no

---

[60]https://www.youtube.com/watch?v=aZiQ89_s67Q Johnny Cash - """Wabash Cannonball".²"

[61]https://www.youtube.com/watch?v=TvMS_ykiLiQ Arlo Guthrie - City of New Orleans.

[62]https://www.youtube.com/watch?v=zVQAhhlq798 Peter, Paul and Mary - Leaving On A Jet Plane (25th Anniversary Concert).

[63]https://www.youtube.com/watch?v=D4KX0TcZ1e0 If My Friends Could See Me Now - Sweet Charity.

high kicks. That option had been a close tie with *Hey, Look Me Over,*[64] but the choreography was easier. That is, Iona had directed it before.

✳ ✳ ✳

The kids were having fun while they waited for Iona. The boys got into a contest about whether up-time or down-time managed to have the longest songs. The down-timers flourished the many verses of several different hymns. David Leek retaliated by flourishing his acoustic guitar and off the top of his head remembered quite a bit of *American Pie,*[65] which was one of his father's favorites.

The down-timers thought of an even longer hymn. "I don't think you can beat sixteen verses each with eight lines."

"Like the *Little Engine that Could,* I think I can, I think I can; probably don't remember all of it, though." He played a few chords and said a few words. Then Ben Roberts took over and started talking his way through *Alice's Restaurant,*[66] ad-libbing quite a bit of it with reference to various Magdeburg city ordinances, while David strummed.

Dashing down the corridor to the rehearsal room, Iona spotted a man leaning against the doorpost, watching the hijinks as the kids got

---

[64]https://www.youtube.com/watch?v=LNhvqPPDyl0   LUCILLE BALL: Hey Look Me Over from her Broadway Musical WILDCAT! assisted by Steve Lawrence.

[65]https://www.youtube.com/watch?v=uAsV5-Hv-7U   Don McLean- American Pie (with Lyrics).

[66]https://www.youtube.com/watch?v=m57gzA2JCcM   Alice's Restaurant - Original 1967 Recording.

ready. He commented a little ruefully that he was rapidly coming to feel like he belonged in the chairs with their grandparents.

"Kids will do that to you, fast," Iona said. "Every teacher learns it. It seems like one day they're in junior high and the next day they've gotten married and their oldest is beginning to talk; one more and the kid's starting kindergarten, one more and you have the next generation sitting in front of you in the middle school band room."

"I've noticed that children can scarcely wait to talk. Especially my half-sisters. Then they never stop. I've never been one to talk much, myself," the man said. "Being carefully educated to become a bureaucrat will do that to a person."

"Well, at least you got a job as a governor, so the education wasn't wasted." Iona had identified him as one of the group of governors who were at the program the previous December, but beyond that did not know him. The teacher in charge of a children's music program rarely has time to focus on extraneous details and she had been busy that night in December.

✳   ✳   ✳

She'd better calm things down after the cheerleading costumes.

Iona liked Ella Fitzgerald. She just did. So Annalise was going to solo on *Blue Moon.*[66] Her voice had the range, or, more precisely, the melody had a sufficiently limited range that Annalise could sing it. For the rhythm, Iona would drill and drill and drill if that was what it took.

---

[67]https://www.youtube.com/watch?v=dqwSde_eEv4   Ella Fitzgerald - Blue Moon.

Personally, she thought Ella's *Mood Indigo*[66] was even more spectacular, but it wasn't a mood she wanted in this concert.

"I think Annalise has an admirer." She described her encounter at the door at dinner that evening.

"Good Lord in Heaven, Iona!" Mary Simpson exclaimed. "You were talking to *Prince Frederik of Denmark*. The king's son; Prince Ulrik's brother."

"Well, how was I to know? I was perfectly polite to him. He didn't look like a perv or a stalker."

---

[68]https://www.youtube.com/watch?v=jaq9Gx9GT5E   Ella Fitzgerald - Mood Indigo (Verve Records 1957).

CHAPTER 39

Magdeburg
July 1637

The governor who was also, according to Mary Simpson, a prince, didn't haunt the rehearsal room. He ... wandered past the doorway every now and then because he had business to discuss with the landgravine and was at Hesse House in any case.

It was getting close to the first performance. Iona noticed that he was eyeing Annalise again, motioned to the performers to carry on, and slipped out into the hallway.

"Governor," she asked rather abruptly, "Can you sing?"

"No better than the average man. Hymns and such."

"I have an idea. An absolute surprise for the audience. And for the kids, if you're willing. You were at Quedlinburg in December, weren't you?"

"Yes."

"Do you remember the German songs?"

"Indeed." *Did he? Oh, yes, he most certainly did.*

"Could you make time in your schedule to talk to me tomorrow? I don't have the book I need here (here being landgravine Amalie Elizabeth of Hesse-Kassel's largest back parlor), but I'm sure I brought it to Magdeburg with me. I'm staying with Veronica Dreeson, if you know her."

"Not," Frederick said, "personally."

"Well, I'm sure she'll love to meet you. Do you have time? Tomorrow or soon?"

"Tomorrow would be excellent."

"Then let me scribble a note, so the maid will let you in. Come before lunch, or I'll already be over here rehearsing."

"Look," she said the next day. They were having lunch. Veronica, Iona, Annalise, Nicholas and Thea, and a prince. Some of the results of the Ring of Fire were strange, and today was one of them.

"Technically," Frederik was saying, "I'm not a prince. Neither is Ulrik."

"Er," Iona said. "Why? You're the king's son. And, um … "

"Legitimate. Yes. But in Denmark, there is only one prince, and that is the Elected Prince, the Chosen Prince, or Prince-Heir, ratified by the Council. My older brother. Ulrik and I are dukes of Holstein as members of House Oldenburg, but not princes."

"Oh." Iona thought about that for a bit. "But you are who you are. I'm fairly sure that ninety-nine out of every hundred people in Grantville will not give up their belief that the son of a king is a prince. Especially not the son of a Danish king, because almost all of us have to read *Hamlet* in high school. Let's go with 'Governor'; you definitely are that. Now, what I wanted to talk to you about. Look here. Somewhere in Germany, this song is being written this year!"

She showed him *Ännchen von Tharau*.[66] "It's a nineteenth century melody, according to the notes at the bottom of the page, by Silcher. Whoever is writing it this year must be using a different tune, but I

---

[69]https://www.youtube.com/watch?v=I1MCzmDGfec   Ännchen von Tharau - mit Text zum Mitsingen.

386

certainly have no idea what it might be and no way of finding out. A lot of opera singers recorded this, but to be honest it doesn't take an operatic voice, especially if we lower the key. I'm sure that boy could do it."

She paused. "Annalise, what is the name of the boy with the banjo? The lute player. I can't ever remember it."

"Heinrich, I think. The guys call him Heinz. Ummm. *Ja.* Heinrich Sasse. Little Gisela Scharpff in the beginning class is his half-sister, I'm pretty sure. Or maybe his step-sister. He and Osanna Merkur are making googly eyes at one another. The reason he's so dramatically depressed this summer is that she went to visit her parents in Suhl and won't be back for two months, if she comes back at all, because she's finished at Quedlinburg now. And his father is sending him to Weimar next year, to the new academy for church musicians there, so he might be gone already even if she does come back. He's undergoing 'gloom, doom, and agony on me.'[77] Or is that despair? Maybe?"

"Thanks. We can get Heinrich Sasse to copy out the score for you, Governor, and key it down. And practice with you, using his lute, I think. It calls for a down-time instrument. It would be fun to put you into the program as a surprise element. Annalise will be onstage when she finishes *Blue Moon.* You and Heinz can come in from … stage right will do … and that will make a second solo—well, not a solo, a duet, but pretty much the same thing—to calm troubled souls after the cheerleaders."

"It's a love song," he pointed out.

"That's fine." Iona laughed and pointed to Veronica. "She's been making fun of me for having trouble finding love songs in which someone isn't dead. In this one, it's to celebrate a wedding. The young

---

[70] https://www.youtube.com/watch?v=BkzE23pyME4 Gloom Despair And Agony On Me (marriage , money). Hee Haw.

man and woman are getting married, all bright and happy for the future. *Du bist mein Leben, mein Gut, und mein Geld.* 'You are my life, my estate, and my fortune.' The program can use some more- bright and happy."

✳   ✳   ✳

Sensation was a mild word for political and diplomatic reaction to Frederik's appearance. Partly (very small-partly, Heather Rush said impertinently) because he wasn't one of those nobles who were inclined to appear in masques, plays, and similar court entertainments. Nobody could remember an occasion when he had ever done so, at least not since he got out of secondary school and could no longer be coerced by his tutors.

Large-partly, according to Heather, all the excitement was because when he did appear, he sang a love song, if one with a drastically reduced vocal range compared with Iona's sheet music,[77] to Annalise Richter. And repeated it at the three subsequent performances. Including the one open to the public.

O the shock, o the scandal, o the …

"Annalise is a good girl, a *nice* girl," Iona said to Ed Piazza's secretary, who had wandered over just to … ask? "She has spent most of the time while her surroundings were in chaos either in high school in Grantville while also working as assistant manager of St. Veronica's preschools or, since then, at Quedlinburg assisting me and being

---

[71] https://www.youtube.com/watch?v=UAS0gEgk-iU   Hannes Wader - Ännchen von Tharau. VÖ auf dem Album "Hannes Wader singt Volkslieder" 1990. Text: Simon Dach / Johann Gottfried Herder. Musik: Friedrich Silcher.

mentored by the abbess. What if he does fall in love with her? I don't think anyone in the world could do better. No, not even some prince!"

Maybe no one could do better, but the secretary was religious and had mental images of temple columns crashing down around Samson after Delilah got finished with the poor man.

The Danish attaché eyed the eyeing, panicked at the memory of how Christian IV had reacted to his oldest son Christian's infatuation with Anne Lykke a decade earlier (it involved prisons), and panicked again.

First, he tried to throw some distraction into the pot in the form of introducing one Christoffer Gabel from Frederik's permanent staff, more Annalise's age, reasonably good looking, and fun, insofar as an accountant could be said to be fun, to several of the up-time young men involved in the music program, where he could likely meet the infamous Annalise and unloose his charms on her.

Annalise blithely ignored the temptation placed in her path. Not that she disliked Christoffer or deliberately ignored him. She was perfectly polite but didn't particularly notice him.

Of course, it didn't help the attaché's plans that Gabel heard Bethany Leek play the flute and Bethany's father and grandfather realized that Gabel was an accountant with close ties to the governor of the Province of Westphalia, who might possibly have a budget item for the purchase of a large amount of office equipment.

The attaché panicked even more and got hold of his monarch by radio.

And identified to Christian IV who the girl was.

* * *

"It is true," Veronica Richter agreed. "As the Bible says, 'A good man brings good things out of the good stored up in his heart, and an evil man brings evil things out of the evil stored up in his heart. For the mouth speaks what the heart is full of.' Luke, 6:45. But this man doesn't say anything. At all." She pointed at Iona. "His mouth hasn't spoken anything, as far as I know. Except for singing, when you prompt him."

Mary Simpson agreed. "He's taciturn, to say the least."

"Annalise certainly is not in love with him," Veronica continued. "She's never been 'in love' with anyone. She had a passing crush on a young man named Heinrich Schmidt when she was about fourteen, but he never even noticed it and went off to make a career in the army. A successful one, so far, I've heard. She hasn't seen him since. That scarcely qualifies as an outside emotional commitment."

The abbess of Quedlinburg frowned. She had strong views about betrothals and marriages, even though she had successfully evaded both. She had prohibited her clergy from denying absolution to a person who made a genuine and contrite confession. However, if the same parishioner repeated the same sin, there was an escalating series of punishments, which ended with a referral to the consistory.

There were reasons why she and Electress-dowager Hedwig were such good friends. On the important things in life, they were usually in full accord and agreement. Consistently sinning subjects should not be allowed to serve as Lutheran godparents; nor buried in consecrated ground.

She also came down like death in regard to secret engagements and clandestine betrothals. Betrothals should be entered into publicly— with a minimum of three witnesses present.

Fornication and adultery should not be entered into *at all* by those claiming to be Christian men and women!

Her answer was, "Frederik is a reserved man. Enigmatic, almost; it's hard to get any idea of what he's thinking. Though I believe he has become sincerely interested in the puzzle presented by our founding documents."

"Come down to the undertone of all the speculation," Mary Simpson said. "Do you believe that he's thinking of making her his mistress."

"Like Duke Eberhard and Tata?" Amalie Elizabeth emphasized her statement with both hands. "No, not at all. For one thing, not all commoners are created equal. Or, if they are, they don't stay that way. Annalise is in a quite different social position than Tata was. Now. If this war hadn't come along, if there had been no Ring of Fire, if you, *Frau* Dreeson, were still married to a provincial printer in the remoter reaches of the Upper Palatinate, well, Annalise would have been a bit farther up on the middle class ladder than Tata, but not much. Not significantly enough to matter when it came to a relationship. Today, she is the sister of the Lady Protector of Silesia who reports directly to the emperor. Plus, Eberhard was under twenty and an orphaned exile when he plunged into that affair. Frederik is coming up on thirty and holds an important position under Gustav Adolf as well having a very-much-still-alive father."

"He can't be thinking of a morganatic marriage! Surely not! Given the way he is believed to feel about his father's."

Dorothea Sophia of Saxe-Altenburg, abbess of the free worldly imperial *Stift* of Quedlinburg, found that idea to be, ultimately, far more scandalous than a simple affair. Hedwig was right. There had been a disquieting number of *unebenbürtig* marriages lately among the nobility of the German principalities. Even discounting Brunswick, where it was rampant because the family had adopted it deliberately as a strategy to limit fragmentation of the duchy long before the Ring of Fire. Former principalities. As in the case of Georg Aribert von Anhalt-Dessau. Not to mention Georg Aribert's sister Eva and that man Harry Lefferts.

Veronica went back to her original point. "Prince Frederik, Duke Frederik, the governor, whatever his title is, hasn't actually said anything at all."

Mary Simpson agreed. It was not easy to get a read on what the man was thinking.

Amalie Elizabeth wondered, *What puzzle about their founding documents?*

* * *

Frederick was trying to figure out what to do. There would be no Kirsten Munk in his life; no halfway-royal children. If he was to marry, then "morganatic" had to be factored out of the equation. One way or the other.

He held serious talks with Heinrich Jung; more with Peder Winstrup, the recently appointed chaplain to his father's court, and one of the few people there whom he trusted.

He talked considerably more openly with Christian Ulrik and Bente. Summoned Kerstin Brahe and Erik Stenbock to Magdeburg. Asked Joachim Lütkemann to come over from Schwerin.

* * *

"And I met—well, I guess she's his sister-in-law—Frederik makes no secret of his relationship with Christian Ulrik. She's a Danish woman, from Helsingør."

Mary Simpson's mind started to churn, here eyebrows went up as far as they could go, and she exclaimed, "Helsingør? *Elsinore*? Hamlet?"

The abbess nodded. "Yes. Helsingør."

"I want to meet her."

* * *

The landgravine held an evening gathering, an informal group of friends and acquaintances, with amateur performances. Annalise was supposed to reprise the Löns piece from the December program, but Iona suggested that she do something, new, the other song, the one she hadn't managed to fit in at Christmas. Goethe, Schubert, *Heideröslein.*[77] Frederik made it a duet.

Which led to a lot more speculation, public and private. *Nimm dich in ach.*

"Be careful." Heather said. "That's what it means."

"Or it could be, 'Look out!' " Ben Roberts added.

"Another translation that would work would be, 'Watch yourself!' That's actually closer," his sister Lisa protested.

"Be afraid, be very afraid," Joe Staley summed it up.

---

[72]https://www.youtube.com/watch?v=Ham4GlbdjS0 Maite Itoiz & John Kelly - Röslein auf der Heiden 2009.

Virginia DeMarce

CHAPTER 40

Copenhagen, Denmark
July 1637

Even during his first garbled radio exchange with the attaché in Magdeburg, Christian IV immediately grasped the potential benefits of this particular morganatic (as he assumed) marriage. Even if he sacrificed the traditional political potential of the marriage of one of his legitimate sons ... one thing was obvious. The last royal stronghold in Europe that would be toppled and ground to dust by CoC fanatics or rampaging Jacobins would be the one presided over by Gretchen Richter's sister as an honored and valued, happy and contented, daughter-in-law. Or, to look at it a slightly different way, as he put it to the bishop of the diocese of Sjælland, "this could be a splendid thing for Us as we try to survive the current rough and tumble. I have visions of a world as described in Ezekiel 26."

The bishop sipped his wine and nodded solemnly. "I will make with them a covenant of peace, and will cause the evil beasts to cease out of the land: and they shall dwell safely in the wilderness, and sleep in the woods."

The king drank rather more deeply. "I will make them and the places round about my hill a blessing; and I will cause the shower to come down in his season; there shall be showers of blessing."

It didn't quite work out that way. When Frederik came to talk to his father, he put down his one unalterable condition. Not morganatic. No way.

"It's a house rule, after all, for each of the noble families who enforce it upon themselves," he pointed out. "Not a divine law. Not some kind of imperial law. Which, even if it were, would not be binding on the king of Denmark as the king of Denmark, who can simply declare it gone. House of Oldenburg be damned."

Christian looked at his son meditatively.

"Maybe you can't push it through for our claims to Schleswig and Holstein, unless the rest of the House of Oldenburg would agree to abolish *Ebenbürtigkeit* as House Law as well, which the Gottorps won't. But for Denmark, you can. Who knows? If Anton Günther could make his son his heir in Oldenburg itself, I suspect he'd come on board with us in a flash. But the Gottorps won't."

"For Anton Günther's son to become his heir, it would have to be retroactive. And, as you say, the Gottorps will not sign on."

The king stroked his beard. For various reasons that he had not mentioned to his second son (who was, after all, working for Gustav Adolf in the USE), he had been seriously irritated with the Danish high nobility for the past several years and specifically, extremely, irritated with them for the past two.

Frederik had almost certainly noticed, of course, but that was not equivalent to telling him.

Abolish *Ebenbürtigkeit*.

For a moment, Christian reflected ruefully, wondering if it would be possible to make it retroactive, with Anne Cathrine, Leonora, and their siblings *ebenbürtig?* Ruefully, no, probably not. At this point, that would introduce more complications than it was worth.

But he could get in another lick toward controlling the Danish nobility, subordinating them to his will, by abolishing it for them, too, within Denmark and Norway. Henceforth, their scions may go out and marry any bourgeois they please, producing children eligible to inherit. Hah! It wouldn't liquidate them, but it would in time dilute them.

"What does the girl think?" he asked suddenly.

"I have not said anything to her. I needed to know where I stood first."

"What precisely does that mean?"

"I might have ended up a commoner employed by the USE as the administrator of the Province of Westphalia. Or not employed, if you had reacted otherwise and the emperor decided it would be more prudent to cut his losses and protect the Union of Kalmar by firing me. But I didn't think that would be the case."

"You didn't think I would respond as I did to Anne Lykke?" Christian raised his eyebrows.

"She was nearly a decade older than Christian, a deliberate temptress, scheming to advance the interests of a specific Danish noble family. None of those considerations apply. Not to mention the practicality that Annalise resides in the USE and lives under the emperor's direct protection."

"I am a generous father," Christian moaned. "Generous to a fault and foolishly indulgent of my children." He drank the rest of his beer. "A fact of which they are all much too much aware."

He put down the mug ... the one mug, which he had filled once, stood up, and danced crookedly out into the hallway shouting, "The tree of the field shall yield her fruit, and the earth shall yield her increase, and they shall be safe in their land, and shall know that I am the Lord, when I have broken the bands of their yoke, and delivered them out of the hand of those that served themselves of them."

Frederik smiled his usual thin smile and added decorously, "They shall no more be a prey to the heathen, neither shall the beast of the land devour them; but they shall dwell safely, and none shall make them afraid."

Magdeburg
July 1637

Count Anton Günther of Oldenburg signed on to Christian IV's order and proclaimed young Anton Andreas as his heir. The emperor of the USE scowled at that, even more fiercely than he had scowled at the news of the birth of a second son in Oldenburg back in December.

The dukes of Holstein-Gottorp ordered their lawyers to start preparing for an inheritance battle once the current ruler of Denmark, Norway, Schleswig, and Holstein, and miscellaneous islands was no more. Or possibly further in the future, if Christian's eldest son did not predecease him in this world. Or even longer than that, if Ulrik and Kristina asserted claims. When a lineage thought in terms of centuries, it was only prudent to be prepared.

Still, it was done.

"If We are to consent to this marriage," Gustav II Adolf said, "much less expedite it, there will be certain conditions."

"Your Imperial Majesty." Frederik bowed.

"Annalise will retain her USE citizenship," the emperor said. "We can't have the sister of Our Lady Protector of Silesia as a non-citizen, now can We?"

You perfectly well could, Frederik thought, *but it's clear that you aren't going to.* He bowed again.

"Her children will be dual citizens of the USE and Denmark," the emperor continued. He twirled his thumbs around and around for a minute. "At least until they come of age. We don't suppose We can prevent them from choosing then, but We'll deal with that when we come to it, two or more decades from now, We have to presume."

Frederik bowed yet again. "You presume correctly, Your Imperial Majesty. Unless the age of majority changes." *Sweden had declared Gustav to be of age when he was fourteen.*

Gustav slammed a fist on the end table next to his chair. The lamp wobbled precariously.

"Bullshit, Frederik, stop 'Your Imperial Majesty-ing' me," he yelled. "Your mother was my wife's aunt, may she rest in peace. I've known you since you were wearing skirts."

*　*　*

"Annalise," Iona asked. "This whole thing is taking off like it's leaving on a jet plane. Has anybody asked you? What do you want?"

"Me?" A shadow flitted across the girl's face for a moment. "What I want?"

Iona wondered if Veronica and Gretchen had been as successful in sheltering her from the horrors as they thought. Whether the bland and cheerful face she showed to them and to the world was the face she thought that they wanted to see.

"I want to get married and live in peace. To have a home of my own, a family, children, in a place they can grow up happy and safe. That's what I want. It's all I've ever wanted. There's no need for me to try to change the world." A moment of silence. "I would like to have a son I can name after my brother Hans."

Nobody else thought to ask her what she wanted.

*　*　*

"I'm grateful and thankful for your offer, Your Grace. But I see some problems."

Everyone in the room stared at her. It wasn't an intimate moment. "The formal proposal had witnesses coming out its wazootie," as Mary Simpson would later tell John.

Annalise looked at him and said with great earnestness, "I don't think that Gretchen would want me to marry a prince. Or a duke."

It was not possible for any of them to argue with that.

"But," she continued, "I'm the one who would be getting married and not Gretchen, so that doesn't count."

Most of the people in the room breathed a sigh of relief.

"And I'm Catholic," Annalise said.

"But you were at Quedlinburg!" Frederik almost stammered.

"Well, I am Catholic. I've always been Catholic. It was Grandma who decided on Quedlinburg. I was thinking more about Bamberg."

Frederik stumbled again. "My father has, has had for as long as I remember, has had for all of his life as far as I am aware, a deep, deep, fear of Catholic intrusion into Denmark. Of Jesuits recruiting young candidates for the Lutheran clergy and perverting their faith at their schools. Of … " He paused. "He is most sincere in this. Additionally, the bishop of Sjælland, our primate, I suppose you would say, is virulently anti-Catholic. As is his most likely successor, who has written and published a quite vehement defense against Romanism and the papist menace.

"It is … actually … as things stand … illegal for Catholics to inherit property or reside within Denmark and the royal holdings in Schleswig, and Holstein. Not in Holstein anymore, since it is within the USE. Or was, except for Glückstadt. My father granted freedom of religion there, when he founded it. Tax exemption, too. Both were significant considerations because he wanted to make it a major trading center to compete with Hamburg."

"I like almost all the Lutherans I have met, but I am not," Annalise said firmly, "going to convert for their convenience."

Catholic ladies had not been Frederik's problem. He had maintained that throughout his tenure as governor of the Province of Westphalia. It was now apparent that this one *was* his problem.

When Frederik of Denmark, duke of Holstein and governor of Westphalia, got in a mood, it turned out, problems toppled like bowling pins.

"We could have told them so," Christian Ulrik said.

Kerstin Brahe and Erik Stenbock nodded.

Bente Luft giggled. "Nobody asked us."

Joachim Lütkemann, blissfully happy in his significant promotion and recent betrothal, smiled.

Johann Rist ordered another round of beer.

The live band that had come all the way from Bremen played "Another One Bites the Dust." Hans Ulrik stopped by their table during the break but ordered root beer.

The emperor retired to sleep on the problem.

*　*　*

"I perceive the solution." Gustav strode around his desk the next day. "The USE has religious freedom, toleration. I can't say that I'm generally enthusiastic about it. Still, we have it, so the easiest solution would be that you don't take her into Denmark. Keep doing your job in Westphalia. I'll give you a raise."

Frederik quirked an eyebrow. "It wouldn't be hard. So far, you haven't paid me anything."

"What!"

In private, Gustav howled with glee. Christian IV's pre-Ring of Fire maneuvers to obtain Bremen and Verden, not to mention Halberstadt, for Frederik had caused his second legitimate son to grow up with an education that was more German than Danish. This marriage would tie him even more closely to the USE; tug him ever more firmly away from his father's ambitions.

Not that he himself would want to grant Catholics the right to hold property or reside in Sweden, either. Some things were simply unreasonable.

Christian IV declared that if they were to marry at all, they would be married at Roskilde, as Lutherans, and Bishop Resen most certainly would not refuse to perform the ceremony.

Annalise thought a few thoughts about 1 Corinthians 9: *Be careful, however, that the exercise of your rights does not become a stumbling block to the weak.* She could compromise. After all, she had attended chapel at Quedlinburg without complaining about it. She offered that she would be willing to go through a Lutheran ceremony, but not as a Lutheran. If they could have a Catholic ceremony also.

The emperor promptly declared that in that case, they would be married in Magdeburg by Cardinal-Protector Mazzare, who hadn't been asked, but was unlikely to refuse. Or require a year of pre-Cana counseling in this instance.

Annalise looked at Mary Simpson. "How about Tom?" she asked. "He was Heinrich Schmidt's friend, back in Grantville, at the beginning of everything. Gretchen is Episcopalian now; maybe that would make her a little happier. Episcopalians are practically Catholic except that they are something called wasps that no one ever exactly explained to me. Almost every up-timer I met in high school who had anything to say about religion said that. Especially the Baptist minister's son. The clever one. He said it several times."

Mary first gasped with laughter and then looked blank. "Tom has been off on the Eastern Front all this time," she answered. "I'm not even sure that Laud has managed to ordain him yet. They have to go through the laying on of hands. It's a church that does the apostolic succession thing. I can ask John. But maybe we could get it done in time for the wedding. If someone would lend an airplane."

Annalise wrote a letter to Gretchen apologizing for the haste with which everything was being arranged and representing it as a noble self-sacrifice through which she could gently present the ideas of her sister's Good Cause to people who otherwise might not hear them. Or, at least, not hear them in a favorable light.

She referred to how she had the idea of how they could get the abbess back into political life and that Frederik had helped. "Which was nice of him, you must admit."

She hoped that Gretchen would understand.

Annalise was, if nothing else, an incurable optimist.

"What made her think," Gretchen shouted at Jeff, "that I would be delighted to see the abbess of Quedlinburg back in political play? The woman's a Crown Loyalist to the hilt and probably smarter than any other ten of them put together. Amalie Elizabeth excepted. Thank God she's not in Magdeburg Province. Or Saxony."

The news went public even before Gretchen got the letter. There was an instant rise in popularity of the old ballad about *King Cophetua and the Beggar-Maid*.

"I don't mind," Annalise said to Iona. "If you listen to the ballad, the king and the beggar maid lived happily ever after and died in peace at an advanced old age."

Ronnie Dreeson cleared her throat and mentioned David Bartley, stock exchanges, OPM, prudent investments, and Annalise's current net worth. Her granddaughter would not be entering this marriage as a dowry-less beggar-maid. The abbess of Quedlinburg smirked.

Magdeburg's CoC members started to get outraged, some of them yelling about class treason, but Gunther Achterhof weighed in with the opinion that Frederik of Denmark was fundamentally a stone-cold, ruthless, ambitious, SoB who in that other world had transformed Denmark into an actual, legally established, by the grant of his idiotic subjects, absolute monarchy, and the Fourth of July Party was gambling an awful lot on the good sense and basic good intentions of his brother Ulrik. The last thing any sane revolutionary would want was for Ulrik to get himself killed while he was running around the Eastern Front gathering his mandatory stupid military experience and have the emperor and the Danish king slot Frederik in as a substitute fiancé for Kristina.

"Wherefore," he exhorted, "having Frederik tied up in a royally approved marriage he will have a hell of a time getting out of has to be considered a Really Good Idea. Yes, Annalise Richter may get caught in the grinder of Danish royal politics and come out as mincemeat, but balance that against getting Frederik out of the Kristina picture and it's worth it to the movement. Remember the proverb about omelettes and eggs."

One of the women leaning against the wall at the back of the Golden Arches looked at her husband next to her. "The prince is 'stone-cold,' is he? Well, there's that saying. 'It takes one to know one.' "

Gustav II Adolf was a hard man to refuse. In the end, in Magdeburg, they had Mazzare, Tom Simpson, and the Lutheran superintendent of the Magdeburg church officiating jointly with two quickly imported Danish Lutheran bishops. The bishop of Lund was of no particular significance in this instance except as to the office he held. Nobody present missed the implied statement that Scania was an integral part of the Danish crown rather than future pickings for the Swedish crown. The other, the elderly bishop of Sjælland, ever since his appointment by the king two decades earlier, had led the campaign for strict Lutheran orthodoxy within the Danish church, tirelessly combating not only non-existent Catholics (there weren't any left in Denmark and Norway for all practical purposes), but also Calvinists as represented by Dutch immigrants and Philippists and crypto-Calvinists within his own fold.

Theologians short on orthodoxy had fallen to his righteous wrath; professors at the University of Copenhagen who showed the slightest taint of liberal opinions had lost their positions. Right now, Christian IV told him firmly, he was going to officiate jointly with the cardinal-protector of the USE if that was what Gustav Adolf demanded. Whatever else, this marriage was going to stick.

"It might not work," the emperor commented privately to his cousin Erik Haakanson Hand after the ceremony, "not as the up-timers think of a marriage as working, but it will stick. They're as married as they can possibly be here. Once they have the Danish ceremony, they'll be even more married."

"How is Christian handling the no-Catholics-in-Denmark issue?"

"I ordered the Department of State to issue her a diplomatic passport."

"That should do it." Hand stood up and stretched his aching arm. "Neither of them is an up-timer, after all. I rather hope," he added, "that they like one another, once Frederik gets all the first flurry of desperately desired sex over with." He considered the issue briefly. "It's not something I would have expected of the man. Perhaps he's more his father's son than anyone ever thought."

He stretched the arm again, smiling. "I suppose that, upon this auspicious occasion, you will name him 'Prince of Westphalia,' too.'

Gustav Adolf smiled back. "Ah, I think not." His smile faltered a little. "When that time comes that must inevitably come to us all," he looked at his body, "that time of which I am myself now frequently reminded, it would introduce awkwardness." He pushed himself up from the chair. "But neither shall I publicly rule out the possibility. I have no idea where that belief came from. However, while the up-timers and *die Richterin* may be able to push me in many directions where I would not, on my own, be impelled to go. I will not deprive myself of the satisfaction of tweaking their tails, occasionally, in the process."

The Lutheran clergy of Roskilde discovered that once the ceremonies in Magdeburg were over and done and the Danish court had a chance to organize suitable festivities, they were going to host a Catholic choir from St. Mary's in Grantville at the Lutheran wedding ceremony in Denmark. Singing something called *On Eagles' Wings*[77]

---

[73]https://www.youtube.com/watch?v=VW0jDEM1Qxc   "On Eagle's Wings" (Lyrics & Photos) by Michael Joncas.

written by some twentieth-century up-time Catholic somebody. Annalise insisted on the choir. In this, she was an immovable object.

"No priests," her future father-in-law insisted.

Annalise didn't have any objection to that. There weren't any priests in the choir.

"My organist!"

She agreed to that, too.

Denmark had a Lutheran state church—that meant something— and the king was its secular head, which meant even more. Christian had no desire to see a Catholic choir in his favorite cathedral, the burial place of Danish monarchs, but he did want this marriage to stick. So he didn't give the bishop a choice, but then, after the Magdeburg ceremony, the bishop had not expected to have one.

Rehearsing in Grantville, one of the choir members whispered to the alto next to her, "Don't we usually do this one at funerals?"

"Sssshhh."

EPILOGUE

August 1637

"**I** confess that I am distressed by the sequence of events in Magdeburg," Hedwig said to her brother after the Danish wedding. "In truth, though, less so than I would have been if there were even one young woman in the entire *Hochadel* who would be an ideal match for him right now. Keeping the issue of the Ansbach Hohenzollerns to one side, as things stand, any marriage I would have wished to arrange would have had to wait almost as long for its consummation as the match between Ulrik and Kristina."

* * *

"Hah!" Duke Georg of Brunswick exclaimed, looking at Lennart Torstensson.

Torstensson looked back. Both of them were still mired in the apparently unending struggle on the Polish front. Sometimes, it seemed to him as if an eternity had passed since the "glorious victory", as the newspapers still referred to Ahrensbök.

The duke waved one of those offensive newspapers at him.

"*Die Richterin's* sister made off with my future son-in-law, did she? In addition to Gretchen's making off with Saxony and Silesia. With

Gustav's connivance, of course." He paused. "Well, no matter, I suppose. Things have changed so much that it's unlikely he'll be as favorable a match here as he would have been there. My little Sophie's only nine, and by the time I married her off to Frederik in that up-time world, it was clear that his older brother would not have children and he was likely to succeed Christian as king of Denmark.

"Here and now, who knows?"

AFTERWORD

The fictionalization of historical characters is always a challenge. The basis available for a depiction may vary widely, even for the same time period, which is the case here.

There is no comprehensive biography of Frederik, duke of Holstein, who in our timeline became king of Denmark as Frederik III in 1648—not even in Danish. He was a man who spoke little, wrote little, and was not given to explaining himself. As a basis for his writing style in regard to his notes to his private secretary and correspondence with his father as they appear in this book, since he was close to his father, King Christian IV, I have used Carl Frederik Bricka and Julius Albert Fridericia, eds., *Kong Christian den Fjerdes Egenhaendige Breve 1632-1635* (Copenhagen: Rudolph Klein, 1878-1880) and *1636-1640* (Copenhagen: Rudolph Klein, 1882).

For his situation in Denmark, the best introduction in English is Paul Douglas Lockhart, *Denmark 1513-1660: The Rise and Decline of a Renaissance Monarchy* (Oxford: Oxford University Press, 2007). For more detail to the immediate period, by the same author, Paul Douglas Lockhart, *Denmark in the Thirty Years' War, 1618-1648: King Christian and the Decline of the Oldenburg State* (Selinsgrove: Susquehanna University Press, and London: Associated University Presses, 1996).

For some background in regard to his position as a Lutheran prince-bishop and prince-archbishop in Bremen and Verden, the following books are of some use: Robert Robert, ed., *Lutheran Ecclesiastical Culture*

Virginia DeMarce

1550-1675. Brill's Companions to the Christian Tradition, Volume II. (Leiden and Boston: Brill, 2008) and Arnd Reitemeier, *Reformation in Norddeutschland: Gottvertrauen zwischen Fürstenherrschaft und Teufelsfurcht* (Göttingen: Wallstein Verlag, 2017).

For the challenges likely to confront the fictional USE's new policy of religious toleration, there is background in Thomas Max Safley, ed., *A Companion to Multiconfessionalism in the Early Modern World. Brill's Companions to the Christian Tradition Volume 28* (Leiden: Brill, 2011).

There is some background on Lutheran *Damenstifte* (canoness foundations), a concept which most American Lutherans of the twenty-first century find utterly alien, in Hans Otte, ed., *Evangelisches Klosterleben: Studien zur Geschichte der evangelischen Kloster und Stifte in Niedersachsen. Studien zur Kirchengeschichte Niedersachsens Band 46* (V&R Unipress, 2013).

For the activities of the Jesuits in Niedersachsen under the Edict of Restitution, there is unfortunately almost no information in Robert Bireley, *The Jesuits and the Thirty Years War: Kings, Courts, and Confessors* (Cambridge, England: Cambridge University Press, 2003), for it focuses on the highest levels of government rather than the application on policy in practice.

In regard to the underlying circumstances of Frederik's alternate history military campaign in Holstein, see Georg Hanssen, *Die Aufhebung der Leibeigenschaft und die Umgestaltung der gutsherrlichen-bäuerlichen Verhältnisse überhaupt in den Herzogthümern Schleswig und Holstein* (St. Petersburg: Commissionäre der kaiserlichen Akademie der Wissenschaften, 1861). There is also Otto Ulbricht, " 'Angemaßte Leibeigenschaft.' -Supplikationen von schleswigschen Untertanen gegen ihre Gutsherren zu Beginn des 17. Jahrhunderts" (*Demokratische Geschichte: Jahrbuch für Schleswig-Holstein* 6: 1991, pp. 11ff., online at www.beirat-fuer-geschichte.de › pdf). Additionally, see "Leibeigenschaft in Schleswig-Holstein am Beispiel des Gutes Depenau/Kirchspiel

Bornhöved" (online at www.riecken-online.de; also at http://genwiki.genealogy.net/Benutzer:Riecken/Gut_Depenau).

Hedwig, Frederik's aunt, has an extensive section in Ute Essegern, *Fürstinnen am kursächischen Hof: Lebenskonzepte und Lebensläufe zwischen Familie, Hof und Politik in der ersten Hälfte des 17. Jahrhunderts: Hedwig von Dänemark, Sibylla Elisabeth von Wurttemberg und Magdalena Sibylla von Preußen. Schriften zur sächsischen Geschichte und Volkskunde Band 19* (Leipzig: Leipziger Universitätsverlag GMBH, 2007). In English, but far briefer, there is Mara R. Wade, "Widowhood as a Space for Patronage: Hedevig, Princess of Denmark and Electress of Saxony (1581-1641)," in *Renaissance Women as Patrons of Art and Culture* (Renaessanceforum 4, 2008).

For far northwestern Germany generally, see Hans-Eckhard Dannenberg and Heinz-Joachim Schulze, eds., assisted by Michael Ehrhardt and Norbert Fischer, *Geschichte des Landes zwischen Elbe und Weser. Band III: Neuzeit* (Stade: Landschaftsverband der ehemaligen Herzogtumer Bremen und Verden, e. V., 2008). In the general category of "probably more than you ever wanted to know" there are the 642 pages of a superb foray into local history, Armin Schöne, *Die Erzbischöfe von Bremen und ihr Haus und Amt Langwedel: Geistliche und weltliche Herrschaft im Alten Reich, Band 1* (Bremen: Edition Falkenberg, 2016).

For the Calvinism of the city of Bremen, the best currently available is Leo van Santen, *Bremen als Brennpunkt reformierte Irenik: Eine sozialgeschichtliche Darstellung anhand der Biografie des Theologen Ludwig Crocius (1586-1655). Brill's Series in Church History, Volume 69* (Leiden and Boston: Brill, 2016). It was a pity that I could not make any significant room for Crocius in this book without skewing the plot in a theological rather than political direction.

For readers who would like additional bibliography on any topic in this novel, please go to 1632 Tech on Baen's Bar (https://bar.baen.com/index.php?t=thread&frm_id=15&) and request it. I will be delighted to provide.

Made in the USA
Monee, IL
15 January 2021

57745570R00233